UNDRAFTED

PRAISE FOR THE DRAFTED SERIES

DRAFTED

"Drafted hooked me with the first sentence and then it never let go. It is a one-sitting, all-nighter kind of read. From the storyline itself, to the plot twists, to the characters. Tommie Michele has fast become one of my favorite authors." - PARIS KAUFMAN, AUTHOR OF THE **MAGEYE TRILOGY**

UNDRAFTED

"Heart-wrenching, action-packed, and meaningful, Undrafted is an epic conclusion to Tommie Michele's Drafted Duology. The characters who stole our hearts in book one manage to get even better in this installment, and their dynamics with one another even more fascinating. Michele's compelling writing style and perfect pacing kept me hooked from start to finish. The themes of forgiveness and second chances were beautifully conveyed and left my heart warm even after the utterly harrowing climax. The Drafted Duology is, to date, one of the best YA dystopian series I've ever read." - A. M. DAYLIN, AUTHOR OF **WHERE DARKNESS CANNOT FOLLOW**

"After anxiously awaiting the sequel to Drafted for months, Undrafted did not disappoint. If at any point you think you know how the plot is going, I promise a twist is coming. Returning characters, shocking secrets, a journey of healing, and a race to find a mysterious cure...the Drafted Duology is action-packed, beautifully written, and not a story you want to miss." - PARIS KAUFMAN, AUTHOR OF THE **MAGEYE TRILOGY**

SERIES

"The Drafted Duology is an expertly crafted clean, dystopian, refreshing read. Tommie has a talent for constructing real characters who face real struggles while masterfully integrating a corrupt government and a secret plot to unravel. The Drafted Duology is a heart wrenching, fast paced, dystopian novel perfect for those who loved Divergent and Matched."
- NATALIE COLBURN, AUTHOR OF **A CALL FOR BLOOD**

UNDRAFTED

TOMMIE MICHELE

DESCENDANT
PUBLISHING

www.descendantpublishing.com

Descendant Publishing, LLC
PO Box 29
Byron Center, MI 49315

Book Cover by Damonza
Edited By Jeannie Wilson
Map Illustrations by SecondVoltage

ISBN 978-1-965948-02-6 (Hardcover)
ISBN 978-1-965948-01-9 (Paperback)
ISBN 978-1-965948-00-2 (Ebook)

Printed in the United States of America
First Edition November 2024

10 9 8 7 6 5 4 3 2 1

DESCENDANT
PUBLISHING

www.descendantpublishing.com

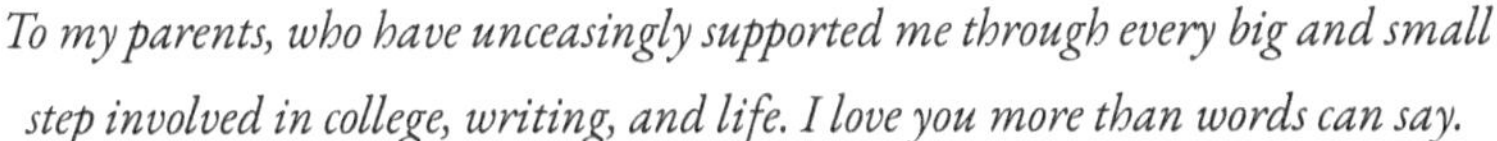

To my parents, who have unceasingly supported me through every big and small step involved in college, writing, and life. I love you more than words can say.

To Jesus Christ, my Lord and Savior, the one true hope, who guided my hand in penning this story and brought it places I never could have imagined.

And to the reader fighting for hope in a world riddled with darkness: this book is for you.

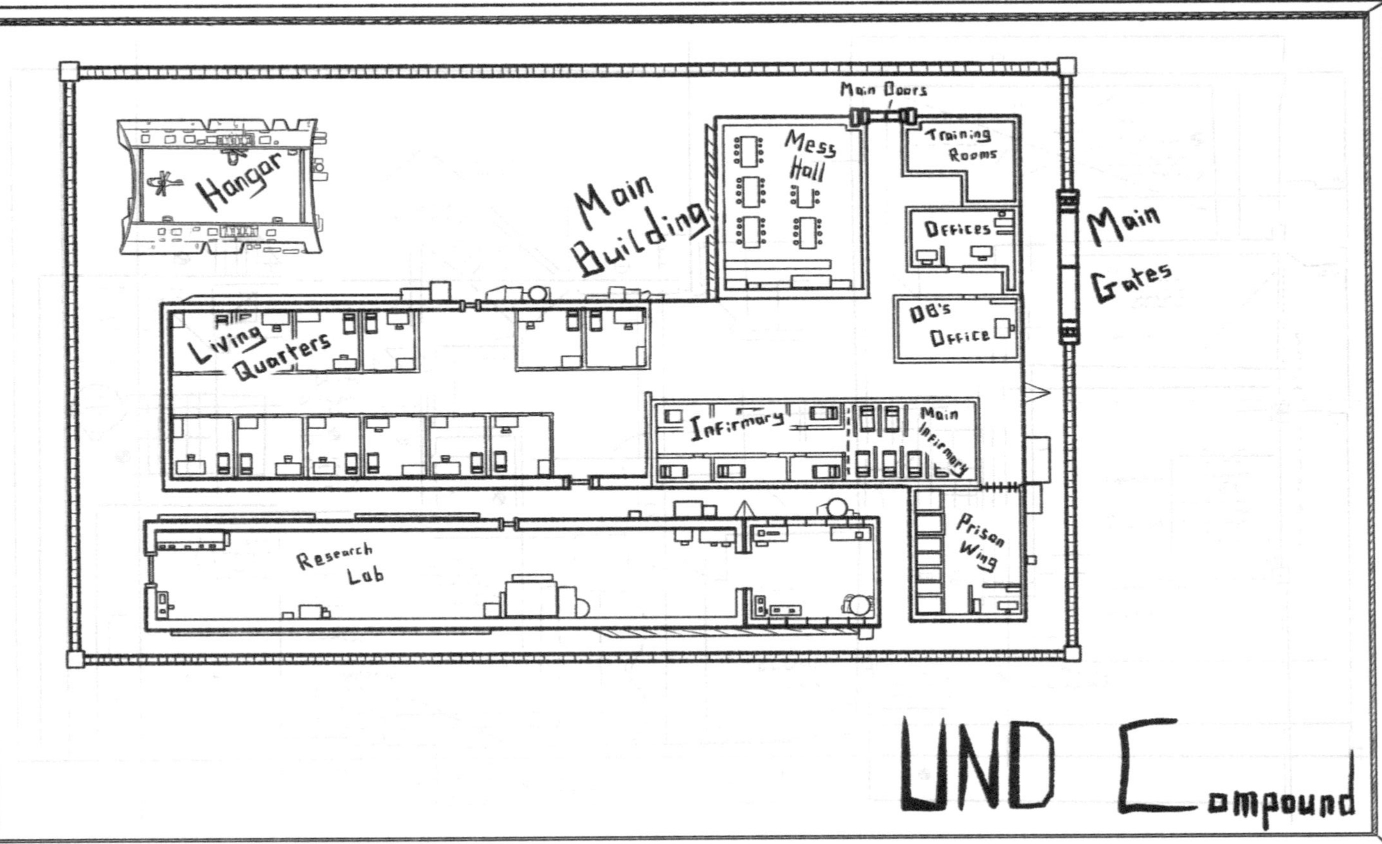

UND Compound
Main Gates
Main Doors
Training Rooms
Offices
DB's Office
Mess Hall
Main Building
Main Infirmary
Infirmary
Prison Wing
Living Quarters
Research Lab
Hangar

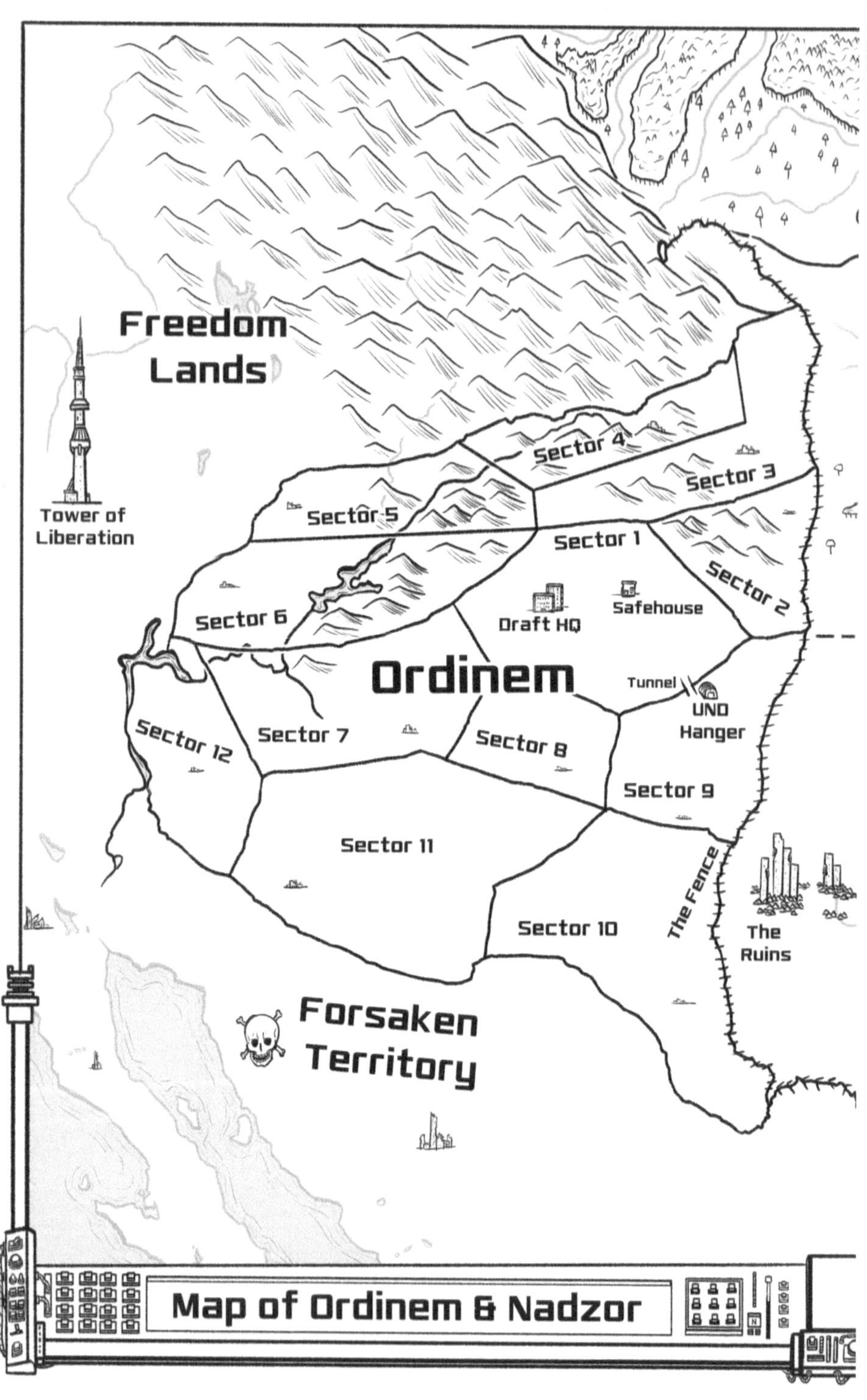

Freedom Lands
Tower of Liberation
Sector 4
Sector 3
Sector 5
Sector 1
Sector 2
Draft HQ
Safehouse
Ordinem
Tunnel
UNO Hanger
Sector 6
Sector 12
Sector 7
Sector 8
Sector 9
Sector 11
The Fence
The Ruins
Sector 10
Forsaken Territory
Map of Ordinem & Nadzor

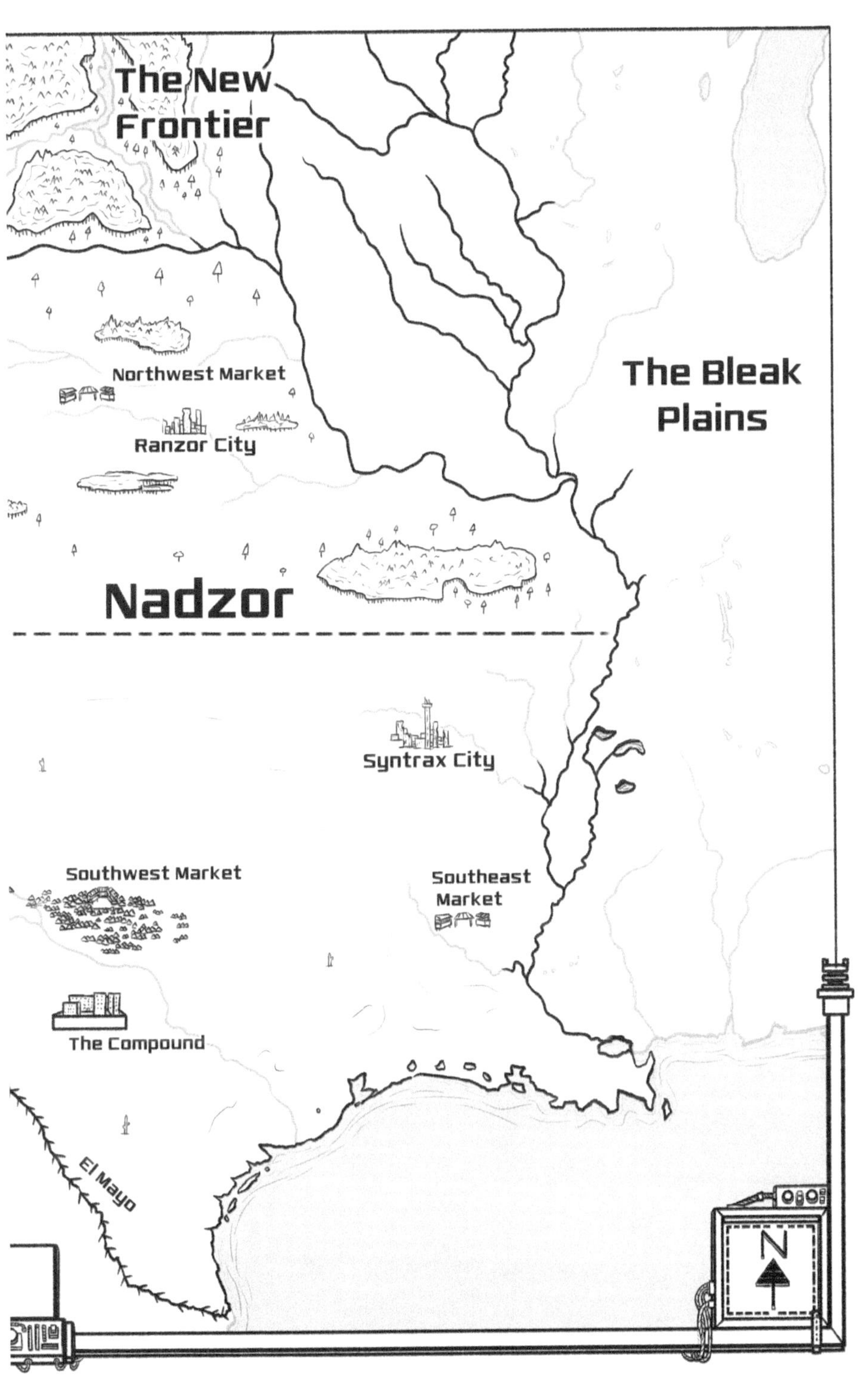

The New Frontier
The Bleak Plains
Northwest Market
Ranzor City
Nadzor
Syntrax City
Southwest Market
Southeast Market
The Compound
El Mayo
N

Chapter One

Reverie Adams

The "suspicious activity" alert blinking on my techpad could mean any number of things.

The last thing I expected was for it to mean Draft kids operating in Nadzor.

Two weeks after our helicopter arrived at the Undrafted compound, I walk the open Nadzor landscape dressed in the same brown as the grainy dust coating everything around me. If Ordinem was a place of concrete buildings and narrow roads, Nadzor is practically a desert. The sun beats down on my shoulders to the rhythm of my footfalls, and I can't take a breath without nearly choking on the dry air. Going on a mission in anything other than my Archer uniform still feels wrong, but I can't afford to be conspicuous in Nadzor. It would lead Holland straight here.

Kazmund Lamar walks next to me, a sheen of sweat coating his dark bronze skin as he matches my stride, one of his for every two of mine. His hair, styled in a flat top, makes him appear a few inches taller than he is, but I stopped being intimidated by his build as soon as Hunter introduced us. Kaz has been Hunter's mission partner and friend for as long as they've both been with the UND—over eleven years, although Hunter hasn't given any indication as to how he ended up in a secret organization as a six-year-old—and I still can't fathom how the two of them get along.

"You think we're actually going to find anything out here?" Kaz asks, breaking the silence.

"Can't tell you." I squint at the ruins in the distance, but we're too far away to make anything out. According to one of the UND's routine recon teams, some of Holland's agents were seen around the northern buildings, but the information is shaky at best. "The report came in a couple hours ago, which is enough time for the Draft kids to have moved on, even if they were here in the first place."

"We've had plenty of reports like these over the past couple of months," Hunter adds, his voice coming out crackly over my earpiece. "It's harder when the market's nearby."

"More people means more reports of 'suspicious activity.'" Kaz makes air quotes with his last words. "So I'll take that as an agreement, then? We think nothing's out here?"

"I never said that."

Kaz's expression shifts into a mischievous grin. "In that case, wanna bet? If we don't find anything, you owe me one of those chicken skewers from that vendor at the market."

Static over the earpiece.

"He's not dumb enough to take that bet, Kaz," I say under my breath.

Almost immediately, Hunter's voice returns. "Deal. And if we find something, you owe me the same."

Kaz winks at me. "Thanks for that. I think the opportunity to spite you really pushed him over the edge."

I roll my shoulders and fix my attention on the ruins ahead.

There used to be a city here, before the Social War. Unlike Ordinem, Nadzor never rebuilt. The people here simply adapted. Further to the east, on the very outskirts of these ruins, a large, open square serves as the setting for this season's market. Around the market square, stretching partway into the ruins and extending in a ring around the square, colorful tents packed closely together house all of the people here for the market and provide a brief respite from the rest of southern Nadzor's flat brown. The area of the ruins we're headed for is close enough to the market to easily explain any people there, but far enough that the UND sends teams to investigate reports regardless. Any potential Draft activity within walking distance of the compound is worth investigating, no matter how improbable it is that Holland is in Nadzor.

Kaz and I veer left, angling away from the busy market area, and the flat dirt under our feet turns gradually to paved road. The buildings here are further apart than in Ordinem, but walking between them through the alleys still feels claustrophobic compared to the rooftop travel that I became so used to as the Archer.

As we progress through the dust-overtaken ruins, Kaz pulls both of his pistols from his belt and shifts his gait just enough to quiet his footfalls against the road. If there's one thing I appreciate about Kaz, it's that he's not nearly as stupid as he can be annoying. Just because he doesn't believe we'll find anything doesn't mean he's going to go in unprepared.

I unclip my new bow from my belt and press the button on the side. The sleek compound unfolds from the grip in my hand and I hold it tight as the tallest of the buildings comes into view. We're nearing the central ruins, and then we'll be through and into the area we're supposed to be scouting.

A flash of shadow to my right makes the hairs on the back of my neck rise, but when I whirl around to face the alley, nothing's there.

Ahead of me, Kaz pauses. "Rev? You see something?"

I study the alley, my eyes roving over every shadow, but there's no hint of movement. "No." I jog to catch up to Kaz. "Nothing."

"I don't see anything, either," Hunter says over our earpieces. He's monitoring a live satellite feed from back at the compound. "Although I can't see too well into the alleys. Just be careful."

Kaz gives an exaggerated salute. "Careful is my middle name."

"No, it's not," I mutter.

"Buzzkill," Kaz grumbles in return, dropping his hand.

Despite the fact that the flash of shadow I thought I saw proves to be nothing, I'm on edge for the rest of the walk through the crumbling city.

It doesn't take long for us to reach our target area. Kaz and I stick together, searching up and down streets for anything out of the ordinary. Hunter chimes in occasionally, reminding us where the borders of our search are, but other than that, nothing breaks the silence. A breeze would be nice, but the air hangs heavy around us as we walk. Even this late in the year, the oppressive sunlight is enough to leave sweat dripping down my face. The weather, Hunter told me when I first got here, is part of the reason the market moves. Northern Nadzor is far more hospitable in the summer months.

"There!" Kaz snaps his arms up, pistols aimed down the road in front of us. "Rev, did you see it? Far in front of us—someone went off to the left."

I reach up and slide an arrow from my quiver, holding it at the ready, but say nothing. I didn't catch any movement, but Kaz doesn't need to add "perfect eyesight" to his list of things to gloat about. "Let's go."

"Kaz, I caught movement, too," Hunter says as the two of us sprint for the end of the road. "I can tell you which alley they went down, but I can't see anything past that."

"Which turn?" I ask, nocking my bow as we run.

"Third on your left. Doesn't look like they've exited the alley yet, unless they went into a building."

Kaz takes the turn just ahead of me and speeds up. "They're here!"

I take a sharp left into the alley. In front of Kaz and me, two girls sprint toward the opposite end of the alleyway, where it intersects with a wider road. *Two girls*—Draft kids.

Kaz fires a warning shot into the air, the *pop* echoing through the alley despite the silencers attached to his pistols. One girl glances over her shoulder at us before the black-haired one next to her grabs her arm and pulls her to keep going.

Somehow, Kaz and I gain on the two of them, and we gain fast. The girl who looked back stumbles, slowing both of them down, and Kaz reaches them first. He launches himself at the black-haired girl and they tumble to the ground as the grunts and yells of a fight fill the alley.

I shift my attention to the second girl and draw my bow as she skids to a stop, spinning around to face us. Her eyes lock on me and she staggers back, tripping over a loose chunk from the wall of the building next to us. She throws her arms up as I approach, and I pause when I catch a glimpse of her face. Tear streaks cut through the layer of Nadzor dust on her face, and she trembles as I draw closer. "Help me," she whimpers, her eyes squeezed shut. "Please."

I look her over, bow still drawn. No weapons, as far as I can tell. Why would Holland send one of her Draft kids to Nadzor without a weapon?

"Why did Holland send you out here?" I ask in a low voice.

"Holland?" The girl cracks her eyes, looking up at me. "Who—who's Holland? Who are you?"

From behind me, Kaz lets out a yell. "Rev! A little help here!"

This girl, it seems, isn't as immediate of a threat as Kaz's opponent seems to be. I shift my aim, loose the arrow so that it sticks into the wall, and stow my bow as I turn to help Kaz. The other girl has him pinned, a serrated dagger in her fist.

I lunge at the girl, leveraging her surprise to pry the blade from her grip, and knock her off Kaz. She grunts as her back strikes the road and I move to bring the knife to her neck before she can regain her bearings.

When I meet her eyes, however, I freeze. The dagger in my hand clatters to the ground.

"Riya?" I whisper.

She snarls and throws me off with strength unproportional to her build. I scramble for my bow, but it skids out of reach as I hit the ground.

"Riya?" Hunter's voice comes in over my earpiece. "Rev, did you just say *Riya?*"

The girl standing over me is undeniably Riya Collins.

And the feral look in her eyes makes me undeniably certain that she intends to kill me.

She steps forward, her serrated dagger back in hand, and I roll out of the way as she strikes, the dagger scraping against the road with a screech. Kaz yells and staggers forward, but I catch sight of the blood streaming down his leg—he's too slow. Riya raises her dagger for another strike and backs me up against the wall.

Before her strike can hit, Riya goes stiff. A tremor runs through her body and she steps back, lowering the knife, her eyes wide.

"Riya!" I push myself to my feet. "It's me!"

She shakes her head, blinks hard, and looks around the alley as if seeing it for the first time. Her eyes drift to the dagger in her hand, then to where Kaz leans against the wall and the other girl cowers across the alley from him, and finally to me. She tosses her dagger down the alley, far out of reach, and stumbles back from us. "I...where—?"

Another tremor cuts her off and the hatred falls back over her face. She glances at the dagger, now far on the other end of the alley, and at the other girl on the ground.

Kaz favors his leg, but still aims his gun well enough. Riya—*not* Riya—snarls at him before taking off in the other direction.

I pick up my bow and start after her, but Kaz calls me back. "Rev! Let her go. You can't chase a Draft kid down by yourself."

In my moment of hesitation, Riya disappears.

"Hunter, where's she going?" I ask, staring down the alley after her.

"Looks like she's headed away from the market. Further northwest. If Holland sent her, I bet they have a pickup point with a helicopter waiting somewhere out there. Kaz is right—you can't take her alone." Hunter pauses. "Rev, did you say that was *Riya*? As in, TJ's sister Riya?"

"Yeah." I let out a slow breath as I turn back to Kaz and the other girl. "Yeah."

"I...never saw her as the type who would work for Holland."

"She's not," I snap, flashes of the night we saved TJ from the Draft sublevels flooding my mind. The way the life drained from his face when he woke up to the news that Holland had Riya. And now Riya is...what? She'd *never* work for Holland voluntarily, and even if Holland somehow convinced her, the look in her eyes today...that wasn't Riya.

Holland can do a lot to a person in such a short time, I think, remembering the flash of TJ's scarred arm that I caught on the helicopter. Some of the scars were about healed, and some were nearly fresh wounds, but I can only imagine how much TJ went through with every single one.

How am I going to tell TJ about this?

"Rev!"

I refocus to find Kaz standing on his good leg, leaning against the wall.

"What about her?" he asks, nodding to the other girl. She still huddles against the wall opposite Kaz, looking between us with wide eyes. "We take her in?"

I meet the girl's terrified gaze and shake my head. "No. She's not a Draft kid."

"How do you—" Hunter starts, but I cut him off.

"She's *not* a Draft kid. Trust me. I've met enough to know."

The implications of that statement hang in the air for a few beats before they truly sink in. This girl *isn't* a Draft kid, but she was running with Riya, likely toward a pickup location for Holland to take them back to Ordinem.

"Holland was going to take her," Kaz says under his breath so that the girl can't hear.

"Why?" Hunter asks. "What use does Anyssa Holland have for a girl who's not even remotely related to the Draft? It's not like she can force new kids into becoming Draft agents—not like the agents she has now."

"Then what did she do to Riya?" I whisper.

At that, the three of us fall silent.

Kaz studies the girl before holstering his guns and pushing off the wall with a wince. He limps toward her and offers his hand. "You alright?"

The girl glances at me, then takes Kaz's hand and lets him help her up. "I—I think so."

"What's your name?"

"Anya," she answers, her voice shaking.

"You're going to be okay, Anya. How old are you?"

"Twelve."

"You know how to get back to your family?"

She nods.

"Good. Go. That other girl isn't coming back."

The girl hesitates, then takes off toward the market.

As soon as she's gone, Kaz limps toward me, grimacing. "I'm fine, by the way. Thanks for checking."

"You got a cut," I say flatly. "Stop being dramatic."

"With a serrated knife! You know what would've happened if she'd gone a little deeper and hit an artery?"

"Well, you're not bleeding out, so I take it you'll be fine," I say.

Kaz mutters something inaudible under his breath and hobbles to my side.

Hunter sighs over our earpieces. "Both of you, just get back here in one piece. And Kaz?"

"Yeah?"

"You owe me a chicken skewer."

Chapter Two

TJ Collins

It's been two weeks since we've moved to the Undrafted compound, and I'm starting to think I've spent more time in the infirmary than anywhere else combined.

I try not to flinch as the red-headed medic in front of me inspects the stitches in my side with gloved hands, shivering as the cold air raises goosebumps on my bare skin. The cushion on the infirmary bed is softer than anything I've slept on in the past three or so months, but it does little to ease the tension in my shoulders as I take in the whitewashed walls, sterile medical equipment, and tiled floors. Unfamiliar medics bustle back and forth—making beds, rummaging through cabinets, coming in and out through the door next to Nora's desk. Other than a man lying on a cot against the opposite wall, it looks like I'm the only patient. This room, despite how many times I've been here since we moved to the compound, brings back far too many memories I'd rather forget.

Across from me, Savi sits on another bed, watching with a distant look in her eyes. Her mind is clearly elsewhere, but I'm still grateful she came with me today. Everyone knows how I hate facing this room alone, and Rev is away on a mission.

"Well," Nora says, straightening up, "your body's been through a lot, but you're recovering well."

"Thanks," I say, tugging my sweatshirt back down to cover the wound in my side. Nothing can fully conceal how weak I've become, but baggy clothes help—and the long sleeves hide my scarred and wounded arm.

"Nora, how long have you been with the Undrafted?" Savi asks, snapping out of whatever thoughts held her attention.

The stocky medic shrugs as she moves to the counter and cabinets along the other wall. "Daniel recruited me soon after starting the program, so...eleven years? I've been on the scientific research team for six and I've run the infirmary for five. I've trained in the medical field my whole life, though—my father was a nurse."

She's just like Riya. The thought enters my head unbidden and I blink hard against the wave of emotion it brings.

Riya came for me, even though she wasn't prepared to go to the Draft compound. Even though I didn't have the decency to say goodbye. Even though she couldn't understand why I forgave the Archer—Rev—after everything she'd done.

She came for me and I *left* her there.

I want to believe that if I'd been fully conscious, able to think straight, I would've figured out some way to save her. I would've traded myself for her and Holland would have accepted and Riya would be safe right now. And maybe, eventually, she would forgive Rev, too.

I pull at the sleeve of my left arm. Would I have done whatever it took? Or would I have turned back and saved myself?

Guilt twists through my stomach at that thought, so I shut it down. There's nothing I can do now except wait. I would do anything to save Riya, but first there has to be an opportunity—a plan.

Nora turns from the cabinet holding something wrapped in white plastic. "TJ, do you mind if I run a few tests?"

"What for?"

"A lot of things, actually. Making sure there aren't any internal injuries I missed when you first arrived, and that the serum you were injected with doesn't have any lasting effects. Maybe find something that could tell us what Holland wanted with you."

I rub my arm, suddenly overwhelmed with the urge to get out of this room. *Tests.* That's a word I'm beginning to hate. I still have trouble handling the feel of metal on my skin. The thought of anyone, even a bubbly, frizzy-haired medic, poking at me with instruments makes me shiver. "I'm fine," I tell her, "and the Undrafted already knows what Holland wanted with me. The cure, whatever that's supposed to mean. There's no need to run any..."

Nora unwraps the package, sliding out a needle the length of my thumb.

My throat seems to constrict, making it hard to breathe. Nora glances up at me when I leave my sentence unfinished. "What's wrong?"

"Nothing," I say, my voice tight as I grip the edge of the bed and avoid meeting Savi's concerned gaze. *She's just taking blood*, I tell myself, *not injecting anything. Not injecting anything. It's not the same.* Still, I struggle to remain still as Nora approaches.

She reaches for my left arm, but I offer the other. Savi doesn't need to see my scars, and I can't stomach the idea of another needle—

I shut down that train of thought, too.

Nora meets my eyes, searching, and her expression softens. "Savi, can you give us a minute?"

I nod when Savi looks to me for an answer.

"Sure," she says. "I'll wait in the hall."

When she's gone, I turn my attention back to Nora. "You didn't have to do that."

"She doesn't know, does she? About what happened to you while you were in the Draft headquarters?"

I wince. "No."

Nora sighs and rolls up my sleeve with a gentle hand. "I figured as much. I knew this probably wouldn't be easy for you, which is why I wanted to give you some time to adjust before taking your blood. Am I right in saying you'd rather she not see you like this?"

I shut my eyes as Nora tightens the tourniquet around my upper arm. She's right, of course—the whole point of the baggy clothing and the long sleeves is to keep the rest of the compound from knowing exactly how broken I've become. I've accepted that my time at the Draft compound changed me, and not for the better, but no one needs to know that. All that would earn me is pity, and pity won't help me find Riya. "Just do it."

"Alright. Ball your fist for me. This'll be quick."

I clench my right fist and feel a pinch near the crook of my elbow. I fight to keep my breathing even, but it quickens anyway. I can't hold back the mental images. Whitewashed walls. Metal clamps. Cold green eyes. Screaming—

"Done." Nora pulls the needle out of my arm and presses a piece of gauze to the spot. I open my eyes to find her holding three tubes filled with my blood.

I shiver, but Nora doesn't mention it as she removes the tourniquet. "Can I go now?"

"Keep this on for half an hour," Nora says, wrapping a stretchy bandage around my arm to keep the patch of gauze in place. "I'm sure this goes without saying, but if you get dizzy or lightheaded, pay me a visit."

I stand, shaky, and raise my brows at Nora.

She sighs. "You can go."

I pull my sleeve back down, covering the bandage, and make my way to the door.

"But, TJ..."

I look over my shoulder, my hand resting on the door handle.

Nora watches me, a debate clearly happening inside her head. "You've been through a lot. More than anybody should. I know you're trying to convince everyone that you're fine, but I also know that haunted look in your eyes."

"What's your point?" I ask, hoarse.

"Don't give up on yourself. Don't let the darkness win." Nora's gaze drills into me, as if she's reading exactly what's going on inside my head. "You're in a battle, TJ. And you're only going to win if you believe you can. If you're willing to fight."

I only have one thing left to fight for, I want to say, but Nora doesn't know about my sister. Instead, I only nod and leave the infirmary to meet Savi.

As soon as I step out of the door, I nearly crash straight into Rev. She steps back, her face flushed.

"I thought you were out on a mission," I say, frowning.

"I was," she agrees, her hand drifting to her folded bow attached to a clip at her waist. Not even the harsh lighting of the UND hallway can cut through the thick layer of Nadzor dust covering her. "We're in the middle of our debriefing right now."

"Then what are you doing out here?" Savi asks.

"I actually came to grab you. Daniel wants you in there for the rest of the debriefing. I'm supposed to catch you up on the way." Rev glances at me. "Actually, I'm glad I found you here. You're..." She exhales slowly, gathering herself. "You need to hear this, too."

She's nervous. That's not good. If *Rev,* of all people, is flustered...well, that doesn't bode well for the rest of us. I'm almost afraid to hear the answer, but I ask anyway. "What happened, Rev?"

Rev hesitates, then the words fall out. "It's about Riya."

Riya. My heart begins to race. "You found her? Is she okay?"

"She's...alive."

Something about the way Rev says the words gives me a nervous chill. *Something's wrong.* "Rev, what happened?"

She fiddles with the edge of her sleeve, although I don't think it's a conscious move. I don't know if I've ever seen her this full of dread.

She's alive. I cling to those words, trying to combat the sinking feeling in my stomach. It can't be worse than that. Whatever's going on *can't* be worse than that. "Rev. What *happened*?"

Next to me, Savi leans forward in anticipation.

"I don't know the details," Rev says. She closes her eyes. "But Riya…Holland's using her."

"For *what*?" My hands begin to shake. "Rev, just tell me what happened!"

"She was in the middle of kidnapping a girl, TJ!" Rev runs a hand through her short hair, opening her eyes to meet mine.

Next to me, Savi looks stunned. I blink, stammering for a few beats before I'm able to get words out. "She—she *what*?"

"I don't know what happened to her, but—well, the mission we were on today was to investigate a report of Draft activity in the northern section of the ruins, and we ran into her." Once Rev starts, the words flow faster. "I didn't recognize her at first, but we fought, and…none of us are sure what happened, or what Holland's done to her, but I saw the look in her eyes." Rev holds my gaze, steady even as my world feels like it's spinning. "The Riya we know wasn't in there."

Only the low buzz of the fluorescent lighting overhead fills the silence that follows Rev's words. I stumble backward as the revelation hits me like a punch to the gut.

After seeing, experiencing, what Holland is capable of, it's not a far stretch to believe she would do *something* to Riya, but…

"No." I shake my head and sink to the floor, my back against the wall. "No. She's still in there. Maybe Holland is controlling her, or manipulating her, but—she's not gone. She can't be…"

Savi watches me with wide eyes, and Rev looks like she has no idea what to say. "I don't know how," she says softly. "I wish I could tell you more. I'm sorry. It seemed like she broke through for a moment, but…"

"She's not gone," I repeat, tears welling in my eyes.

"All I can tell you is what we saw, TJ." Rev closes her eyes, her posture drooping. "Somehow, Holland got in her head. Changed her."

I dig both hands into my hair. "How is this possible? It's been two weeks! That's not enough time to completely change a person, not like you're describing!"

"I don't know, but she did. It wasn't Riya, TJ."

"If Holland really *did* figure out some way to..." A horrifying train of thought strikes me and my head snaps up as I look to Rev, desperate. "What's to stop her from using Riya for other things? What's to stop her from making Riya *kill* for her?"

"We don't know—"

"We don't know anything!"

"TJ—" Savi starts, but I ignore her.

"How are you so calm about all this? This is my little sister we're talking about! Being controlled by Anyssa Holland, the monster who runs the Draft and who tortured me for weeks for information I never had—"

I cut myself off there, breathing hard. Rev stares at me for a moment, then clears her throat. "You never told me what happened," she says softly.

"Because I don't want to relive it!" I snap. "And I'm terrified that Riya is living it right now, because we left her behind!"

"We're going to get her back, TJ! We're *going* to stop the Draft." She crouches down and puts a hand on my shoulder. "Riya's going to be okay."

"You don't know that," I whisper, the energy draining from my posture.

"I know we're doing everything we possibly can." Rev steps back and straightens up, looking to Savi, who's been standing in shock. "Savi, you need to come with me back to Daniel's office. Daniel has a plan for us to investigate what we saw today, and he wants you to be a part of it."

"You're...you're sure?" Savi asks, her voice shaky. "That Riya's..."

"Yeah." Rev hangs her head. "I'm sure. But we're going to do something about it. That's the point of this new mission."

Savi takes a deep breath. "To Daniel's office, then."

Before she leaves, Rev locks eyes with me. "We're *going* to get her back, TJ. I promise. I'd stay here longer, but Daniel—"

"It's alright," I tell her. "Go. Keep me updated."

I sit on the floor of the hallway for a while after Savi and Rev leave, my head sinking into my hands. The way the compound is laid out leaves the infirmary hallway pretty empty most of the time. The infirmary is in the primary of the Undrafted's three buildings, but it's at the dead end of one of the main hallway's turn-offs and it's the only room here besides a storage closet. I'm alone.

I hang my head, my fingers curled in my hair. *Riya.* Under Holland's control, somehow forced to do Holland's bidding against her will. I can only hope she's not going through the same kind of torture I did. That Holland isn't leaving her with the same wounds, physical and deeper, that she left me with. Part of me hopes Rev is right about Riya not being herself—if it's true, then at least I can hope there's something in her future besides an arm covered in needle scars. But if it's true, then *how*? And what does that mean for the rest of the Draft kids?

What does that mean for Eliza?

A pang of guilt twists in my stomach. It's my fault that Holland knows Eliza's relation to Rev, and I have no idea what's come from that—if Eliza is still okay, or if Holland is planning on using her against Rev again. If Rev were to find out that *I'm* the one to blame for anything that happens to her sister...

I have to tell her at some point, but not until I know exactly what I caused.

I use the wall to push myself to my feet. My knees threaten to give out as I walk, but I push through the unsteadiness. *Air.* I need air. And I need to be alone. Truly alone. Outside of this compound.

The UND compound consists of three buildings—the main one, which I'm in now, and a smaller one on either side, disguised together as an abandoned warehouse complex. Anyone who gets close enough to see the pairs of brown-clad guards on patrol and the security cameras everywhere will know differently, but it's inconspicuous enough. The Nadzor government funds the Undrafted, so until Holland showed her presence in the nearby ruins today, we had nothing to worry about.

I flip my hood up and over my head as I exit the main building and step out onto the concrete walkway. Instead of turning left or right to head to another building, I continue forward, toward the main gates set into the chain-link fence around the compound. The sun still peeks over the horizon to my left, casting a glow over the distant ruins far in front. A slight breeze makes me shiver, even under my sweatshirt, but it's nothing compared to the chill I remember from my last night in Ordinem. Then again, more than the weather could've been making me tremble that night after Rev rescued me from the Draft headquarters.

I approach one of the four guards standing at the gates and hold out my arm, pulling my sleeve back to reveal a black wristband as thick as a typical watch. The guard looks me over before pulling out a device that looks like a modified version of what Enforcers sometimes use to scan ID cards. He touches it to my wristband and a light on the corner blinks green.

"TJ Collins. Reason you're leaving?" The guard asks.

"Just need some fresh air."

"Estimated return time?"

I shrug. "Before tomorrow morning."

"Go ahead." The guard steps out from his post to unlock and push open the gate for me, and I set off at a light jog toward the ruins.

In the low light, I can't see the Nadzor landscape well, but other than the ruins and the tents that are here for the winter market, there isn't much to see. The ruins rising to the northwest of the compound remind me of the outer sectors of Ordinem, especially as the sun sets and the buildings turn to shadow. I catch a glimpse of colorful tents further to the right, beginning where the buildings become unrecognizable. Past that, Kaz has told me, is the market square, where traveling vendors from all over Nadzor sell and trade their wares. The people here move from place to place, depending on the markets—southern Nadzor is nearly unlivable in the summer months, which means that although the UND compound is modern enough to offer its near-six-hundred inhabitants comfort, the Nadzor vendors tend to migrate north. Where the markets go, the people follow.

Many of the UND's members are native to Nadzor, marked by sun-tanned bronze skin, dark hair, and—in Kaz's case—an unbelievably poor tolerance for cold. My own pale complexion and light eyes stick out sorely here, and I've already experienced my first sunburn. Southern Nadzor's current winter weather reminds me more of Ordinem's early fall. I can't imagine what it must be like in the summers here. The warm winter, however, feels amazing.

I shove my hands in my hoodie pocket and veer toward the ruins. Flat brown around me turns to buildings crumbled beyond recognition, then to skeletons of buildings, and finally to mostly-intact buildings that loom overhead. Hunter told me he used to frequent this place when he wanted to get away from the compound, and I can understand why. If I can climb to one of the higher floors of a tall building, I can get an amazing view of the sunset. I'm far enough from the northwestern section of buildings to feel safe, and from what Rev said earlier, Holland isn't set up here in Nadzor. She just had Riya running a mission for her.

I shiver despite the mild weather.

A tall building to my left, with only a corner of the roof caved in, seems sturdy enough. Careful not to trip on the cracked cement underfoot, I round the building to find a set of double-doors. Locked.

Well, breaking and entering doesn't count when the building is abandoned. I grunt and shove my shoulder into one of the doors, but receive only a new bruise-to-be and a shower of Nadzor dust for my efforts.

I brace myself to ram the door again, but before my blow strikes, the door swings inward. I stumble as a gloved hand locks onto my arm and jerks me the rest of the way inside. A *thud* sounds from behind me and the light from outside disappears, plunging the room into total blackness. The start of a yell escapes me before another hand clamps over my mouth and stifles my cry. I struggle violently against my attacker and, despite being completely blind, manage to twist away for a moment.

Before I can gain my bearings, a fist strikes my jaw with enough force to make my knees crumple beneath me. Fingers dig into my shoulder. A powerful fist to my temple. My vision explodes with stars.

They don't have any way to find me, I think, panic setting in as my thoughts begin to slur. They won't know anything's wrong until morning. I told them I'd be back in the morning. I fight to make my mouth form words. "Don't—"

That's as far as I get before a punch to my jaw sends me spiraling into unconsciousness.

Chapter Three

Reverie Adams

D aniel Bennett's office is an extension of the man himself: a mismatched combination of old and new. A monitor dominates nearly the entire wall to my right, with filing cabinets along the back of the room and a long desk drowning in miscellaneous papers, binders, and folders against the wall to the left. Above that, Daniel has hung *paintings*, of all things—the kind that I occasionally saw adorning the apartments of the wealthiest of Ordinem. I doubt I'll ever understand why Daniel keeps so many Ordinem mementos when he seems to have no love for the place, but then again, I doubt I'll ever fully understand *Daniel*.

In the center of the room, a polished mahogany desk sits atop a lush carpet like nothing I've seen in Ordinem. Behind that, Daniel himself sits tall, dressed in a dark blue suit that looks like something Ordinem's President might've worn before I was born. His hair, dark brown with hints of gray, is combed back in a way I've only seen in old pictures. And yet, his eyes are bright and alert and his fingers drum on the desk with a carefully channeled energy as he watches me and Savi step into line next to Hunter and Kaz.

Hunter sits on the other side of Kaz, in a wheelchair with both his knees immobilized. Ever since we landed in the UND's helicopter and Hunter began his recovery process, it's like each mission he's forced to stay back takes a little more out of him. Daniel has allowed him to stay on the team for now—like with this morning's mission—because he's a good strategist and because everyone hopes for the best, but Nora hasn't given Hunter a final prognosis on his injuries yet.

Daniel's gaze falls on Savi. "I assume Rev has already filled you in on the details of this morning's mission?"

Savi nods. "I know everything. I think. But, respectfully...why am I here? I'm a hacker—aren't I better in the tech wing?"

"You're here because your team's new mission has a role you'll be perfectly suited for. But we'll get to that," Daniel adds as Kaz, Hunter, and I share a look. New mission? "First, another detail to address. For all intents and purposes, for this mission, the team has a new lead."

All eyes turn to Hunter, who grips the arms of his chair with white knuckles. One of us is replacing him, at least for now.

"What do you mean, a new lead?" Kaz asks. "Hunter's coming back to the team once he's healed. We've been doing fine with him on comms, and there's no reason to—"

Daniel holds up a hand and Kaz falls silent. "Circumstances," Daniel says, "set this mission apart from the others you've run in the last two weeks. Hunter will need to stay back."

"But he's coming back, right?" Kaz looks at Hunter. "I mean, we have Nora, we have all the best technology and teams of people, we—"

"I don't know yet, Kaz." Hunter's posture is rigid. Restrained. "You didn't see the damage Adrian caused before the surgery."

I did. I remember the swelling, the bruising, the way Hunter screamed when Adrian twisted his knee to wake him up in the basement, and wince. Savi, too, looks pointedly away from Hunter's braces at the reference.

"You say something sets this mission apart from the rest," I say, shoving the image out of my mind. "What's this about, Daniel?"

The man leans back in his chair. "You're smart, so you tell me. After this morning's mission, what are your primary conclusions?"

"Holland's found a way to control the kids," Hunter immediately says. "Riya has only been with her for two weeks, which may be enough time to threaten her into cooperation, but an unwilling agent isn't what we saw today. Somehow, Holland...brainwashed her, or something like it."

Daniel nods. "Good. That's the obvious one. And?"

"Holland's sending her agents to Nadzor now," Kaz notes. "That's new."

"Keep going. *Why* is Holland sending agents here?"

"The girl Riya had with her," I say slowly. "Riya was taking her. Back to Holland."

"You're getting closer." Daniel looks between the four of us. "Put that together with the fact that Holland has found a way to control Riya, who she didn't raise as a Draft kid."

Next to me, Savi sucks in a sharp breath. "Holland is taking new Draft kids."

"Bingo." Daniel folds his hands on his desk. "This lines up with what my informants in Ordinem have been able to tell me. Holland has been preparing to take more Draft kids for quite some time, and she began the development of a serum early this year. Based on everything we've gathered, it's safe to assume that this serum is what's happened to Riya. Now that Holland has the serum working, she's gathering more agents."

"Why in Nadzor, though?" Savi asks. "In Ordinem, everyone knows that the government runs the Draft, and the families who had their infants taken from them eleven years ago have almost as much money and power as minor government officials."

The families that didn't speak out, I add in my head. Some Draft parents, like mine, simply disappeared. But Savi raises a good point. All the Ordinem public knows is that the families who contributed to the Draft received unimaginable wealth and that the Draft is a military program for the protection of Ordinem. They believe the kids are being raised to be soldiers in the future, not that Holland is using them right now. So why is Holland coming all the way to Nadzor?

"Silas Johnson's hold on Ordinem's public is shaky, at best," Daniel says. "He's not exactly a celebrated name. Why worsen the situation by taking people's Draft-age kids when Holland could recruit under the radar in Nadzor?"

"That's terrible," Savi whispers, but none of us raise a counterpoint.

"And it means that Holland is close to having what's essentially an army." Daniel's jaw twitches. "As far as we know, Holland's goal is to use the agents to carry out any missions that the Ordinem government needs taken care of quietly, but up until now, she's been limited in her reach. With the ability to recruit more kids without having to raise them from infancy? She could have eyes and hands *everywhere*. Whatever freedom in Ordinem the Enforcers don't quash, her having an unlimited number of kids as spies would destroy."

"So what's our new mission, then?" Kaz asks.

"You three" —he nods to me, Savi, and Kaz— "are going back to Ordinem. I have an agent in the Draft headquarters with information about Holland's serum, but she can't leave the sublevels without suspicion. So, you're going in to collect the files from her."

Savi balks. "Are you *crazy*? We all almost *died* the last time we did that! I wasn't even there! And that was when we knew exactly what we were looking for, and we had a plan, and—"

"Relax, Savi," Daniel tells her, holding out his hand to calm her. "You shouldn't have to be on site. You're there to moderate comms, handle doors and alarms, and communicate back with me in the case of any...adverse events. Other than that, Kaz will be the one reporting back to me."

"So let me get this straight." Kaz folds his arms. "We're going to fly to Ordinem, break into the Draft sublevels, and pick up files from your spy to figure out what's going on with Holland's serum?"

"Exactly. And hopefully, with enough information, Nora and her team of researchers can formulate a cure." Daniel opens a drawer in his desk and produces two white techpads with *UND* engraved on the side. "Each of you will have one of these. Kaz already has one, as he's been on a long-distance mission before. Kaz will communicate with me primarily, but it's good for the two of you to have the option as well. You can unlock them by scanning your credentials." He holds up his hand where his black UND wristband rests. "There's more specific information about how the information exchange will go downloaded on your techpads for you to review when you arrive at the safehouse in Ordinem."

"The Sector 1 Central base?" Kaz asks.

"One and the same."

"*Sweet.*" Kaz grins. "When do we leave?"

"Tomorrow afternoon."

"Tomorrow afternoon?" I ask, my mind spinning. So soon? What am I going to tell TJ? I just gave him the news that his sister is, essentially, Holland's puppet. And now I'm leaving him alone here, when he's just beginning to recover from everything he went through in the Draft headquarters. How is he going to handle that?

Daniel raises a brow. "Do you have some kind of conflict, Rev?"

I hesitate, imagining TJ's reaction when he finds out that I'm going back to Ordinem for an indeterminate amount of time. But I don't have another option. Not if I want to save Eliza and Riya from whatever Holland's planning with that serum.

Maybe this mission will be my opportunity to get Riya back. Maybe I can finally start making up for all of the hurt I've caused TJ.

"No," I say. "This just feels like short notice for such a big mission."

"It is," Daniel agrees. "But we need that information as soon as possible so Nora's team of researchers can get started analyzing it. We either leave tomorrow or have to wait for the next satellite dead zone two weeks from now. And two weeks can make a difference, so you three had better get packing. Oh, and Rev?" he adds as we turn to leave.

I look back at him.

"Congratulations. You know Ordinem best, and you've been in the Draft sublevels before. You'll be taking the team lead for this mission."

25

Chapter Four

TJ Collins

A rhythmic throbbing in my head drags me back from unconsciousness. I groan and shift, trying to ease the headache, but my hands won't move the way I want them to. *Bound*.

My eyes snap open and I struggle to sit upright, the motion making my head pound as my memories come flooding back. The ruins—the locked doors, the gloved hand, the fist to my jaw that knocked me out. That explains the headache.

I manage to maneuver into a sitting position, hands bound behind my back, and finally get a good look at my surroundings. A dusty room—no, an apartment, with a couple broken windows opening out to the night sky. Two doors, one on the wall to my left and one to my right, both closed. Another door directly across from me, darker than the other two, is probably the main entrance into the apartment. This room, which looks to be a living room, is empty except for some ancient furniture pushed up against the wall to my right and the tattered remains of a few cushions and blankets piled in the corner.

I glance over my shoulder at one of the broken windows. Pitch black—it's still night, although I don't know how many hours I've been out. Where *am* I? Who brought me here—and *why*?

A figure steps out from the closed door to my left—my attacker, probably, although he's shorter and less bulky than I imagined. Dressed head-to-toe in black, complete with a black ski mask and gloves, and with...

I take in a sharp breath, my eyes locked on what looks like the hilts of two swords peeking over his shoulders, and swallow hard as he steps forward.

"Who are you?" the stranger asks in a low voice, muffled by the ski mask. His voice is deep, with a little rasp, but it sounds...forced. Like he's trying to disguise it?

"My name is TJ Collins," I say, trying to keep my voice steady. "Where am I? What do you want?"

He reaches over his shoulder and deliberately draws out a curved sword about the length of his arm. The sound it makes as it scrapes against its sheath sends a shiver down my back. If he wanted to kill me, he could've done it while I was unconscious. He wants something from me. And he's going to use those swords to get it.

My attacker steps forward, blade outstretched, and touches the tip to my throat. I flinch and press back against the wall as he crouches down to my level.

"Why were you trying to break into this building?" he asks in a low voice.

Trying to break in. The locked doors—he must've thought I was trying to break into the building, maybe even that I was coming after him. "Look, this is a huge misunderstanding," I say, fighting the urge to look down at the sword against my skin. He increases the pressure on the blade and I press on, my heart pounding. "I wasn't trying to break in. I didn't even know anybody was here! If you let me explain—"

Behind the black-clad swordsman, the apartment's front door swings open, cutting me off. My attacker whips his head toward the entrance, keeping one hand on the sword pressed to my neck and the other hovering next to the hilt of his second sword.

"You know, you should really start locking that door, kid," comes a voice from the front door. "Anybody could just walk..." The curly-haired man in the doorway trails off when the door swings open far enough for him to see us. His eyes widen behind thin-rimmed glasses. "What is going *on* here?"

"I'm in the middle of something," the swordsman growls. "I didn't think you'd be back yet. Just give me a couple minutes—and close that door."

"What do you mean, *in the middle of something?* Who's he?"

"That's what I'm about to find out." The blade on my neck shifts slightly and I wince as I feel a trickle of blood from the cut.

The man closes the door and steps forward. His gaze travels from my bound hands up to the sword at my neck before finally coming to rest on my face. He studies my wide-eyed expression for a few moments before speaking to my attacker. "Let him go."

"Alec—"

"I said *let him go!*" The man throws out one of his hands in a gesture toward me. "Does he look like a threat to you? He's terrified, for goodness' sake!"

"He was trying to break in," the swordsman says in a low voice. "I caught him at the door. We need to figure out where he came from and who sent him. Especially if Holland—"

"Stop." The man—Alec, my attacker called him—shakes his head. "It's the middle of the night. Go get some sleep. You've done enough for today."

I watch the exchange, my mind spinning. *Holland.* What do these two have to do with Holland?

"But—"

"*Go.*" Alec's focus shifts to me. "If he turns out to be a threat, I'll handle it."

The masked attacker hesitates, then sheaths his sword and stands up. I let out a shaky breath and some of the tension drains from my body as he steps back. He's nearly a head shorter than Alec, but that doesn't make him any less intimidating as he huffs out a breath and disappears through the closed door on the right.

Alec sighs and approaches me. "Sorry about him—he can be a little paranoid. You alright?"

"Where am I?" I ask, fighting through the confusion swirling in my head. From the other room, I can hear water running—a shower, or a sink, turning on.

"You're in our apartment." Alec pulls a knife out of his pocket and crouches to my level. I stiffen, but he only reaches for the ropes binding my wrists. "Here. Turn around."

I twist and Alec cuts through the ropes, then pockets the knife. I sit back against the wall and rub my wrists, studying the man. Is Alec trying to help me, or is this some ploy to get me to trust him and his companion? Who *are* they? And what connection do they have to Holland? They can't work for her—if they did, they'd know who I am and I would've been dead hours ago. Maybe.

"My name's Alec," the man says, sitting cross-legged in front of me. "Again, I'm sorry about my friend. I think you have some explaining to do, though. How'd you end up here?"

"I wasn't trying to break in—I really didn't know anybody was here. I was just...looking for a spot to be alone." I raise my hand and gingerly touch my throbbing head. "And then your *friend* knocked me out."

Alec searches my expression, as if looking for a sign that I'm lying. "And that wristband?"

"What?"

"On your arm."

My UND wristband. The blood drains from my face and I lower my arm. "What about it?"

"I'd love to know what a member of the Undrafted is doing breaking into buildings around here. Don't you guys have a nice little compound a couple miles away?"

My mouth moves, but no words come out as I stammer to recover. First his mention of Holland, and now this? "I—how do you—who *are* you?" I finally get out.

Alec chuckles. "Don't worry, kid. I'm not a part of the UND, but I know about them. I'm curious about *you*, though. You're obviously not from Nadzor, so how'd a teenager from Ordinem end up out here with the Undrafted? It must've taken a lot to get you to come all the way out here. Holland?"

My whole body goes stiff. How does he know? *What* does he know? "If you're not with the UND, then how do you know Holland?"

Alec's gaze drops to my clenched fists and his expression softens. "I don't know her. Not anymore, at least. The reason I'm not with the UND...well, that's a story for another time. But it's okay. We're on the same side. I'm from Ordinem, too, you know."

I search his face, looking for anything that'll tell me if I can trust him. *I don't know her. Not anymore, at least.*

Alec watches every shift in my expression, my posture, my hands—I realize they're clenched again—too closely. I use the wall to struggle to my feet, shaking my head. "I—I need to go." Whatever's going on here, if it's important, the UND can handle it. Probably already *has* handled it. But I can't stay here and try to figure it out on my own, especially not with my head pounding the way it is.

I barely make it halfway to standing before my head begins to spin, my vision swimming. I slide back down against the wall, blinking hard to clear the dizziness away.

"Easy," Alec says, reaching toward me as I start to get up again. "When did you get here?"

"Around sunset, I think." I give up and sit back against the wall.

"Then you've been out for a few hours. My friend must've given you a sleeping tablet."

"A *what*?"

Alec shrugs. "Like I said. He's paranoid. He thought you were coming to attack him, so he wanted to make sure you stayed out until he was ready."

That would explain the fogginess in my head, at least, although the idea of a stranger drugging me while I was unconscious doesn't sit well.

"Listen," Alec says, tucking a strand of curly hair behind his glasses. "It's obvious that you have quite a bit of history with Holland, yeah? But I can promise you that you're safe here, despite the misunderstanding. We have some history with Holland, too."

"What do you mean, *history* with Holland?"

Alec stands. "*That* is a very long story. One that I might tell you, if this isn't the last time I see you. For now, just relax for a little while. I think you'll feel up to heading back to your compound once whatever my friend gave you wears off."

I glance at the closed door to my right, which muffles the soft sound of running water. The shower, probably, since it's been going for a while. "Who is he?"

"You'll meet him." Alec smiles. "Just rest. And, again, I'm sorry about the misunderstanding."

I want to ask more questions—particularly about what Alec has to do with Holland—but he turns and disappears into the other room before I can. I let my head rest on my knees and close my eyes. I'm supposed to be back by morning, but Alec's right. A little rest would do me good. And a part of me is too curious about Alec and his friend to leave right away. Alec seems trustworthy enough.

Alec, somehow, has a past with Holland, and so does his companion. But what kind of past would lead them to believe that Holland would send people all the way to Nadzor to come after them?

The Draft.

The way Alec talked about Holland, the way he and his companion are so concerned about Holland coming after them, the way that Alec seemed to *know* that Holland did something to me...they definitely know about the Draft, since Alec knows about the Undrafted. But what if that's the *history* Alec was referencing? And what if Alec knows something that could help save Riya?

Sitting against the wall, head resting on my knees, with no sound except the shower water running in the background, it doesn't take long for exhaustion to catch up to me. Despite my best intentions, my drooping eyelids and throbbing head drag me into sleep.

Chapter Five

Hunter Lane

It's only been a couple hours since I was in Daniel's office for the mission debriefing and the announcement of the Ordinem mission, but the faded light outside the small windows and the sinking feeling in my stomach give the room a more dismal atmosphere. I know what this meeting is about.

Daniel lets me in on the second knock and keeps the silence as I follow him back to his desk. As I push the wheels of my chair, my knuckles flash with purple and red. New bruises, courtesy of the wall in my room. Daniel takes his usual position, hands steepled on the desk, while I roll to a stop in front him. Always so formal. So rigid. Why does that bother me now? It didn't earlier, during the debriefing.

It's because I know what's about to happen.

"Nora talked to me today, while you were with the team," Daniel says. "She wanted me to be the one to tell you."

I take a deep breath. *We all have weaknesses,* Daniel has always taught me. *The key is self-control.* A cold chill of dread washes over my body, but I meet Daniel's eyes regardless. "And?"

"And you'll be able to walk again. On your feet in four weeks, give or take, with support—we're very lucky to have the technology that we do, and a team of researchers as talented as Nora's."

"So why do you sound like you're telling me I'm off the team for good?"

Daniel presses his lips together, which is answer enough. I let out a careful, controlled breath. *Self-control. Don't let Daniel see the cracks.*

Nora warned me after the surgery that this was a possibility. That with the injuries I sustained, I'd be lucky to walk again, let alone go out in the field. But the confirmation of it still feels like a blow to the chest.

"So what now?" I ask, my voice quiet. *You don't have a place in the Undrafted if you don't have a role in the Undrafted.* Even as long as I've been here, I won't be exempt from that rule.

Daniel watches me with those probing eyes. He's known me since I was six years old—practically raised me, here at the UND. Only Daniel, Kaz, and Nora have ever seen this side of me. The side that never moved on from the scared little kid Daniel found all those years ago.

I'm not about to lose another family. I'll do whatever it takes.

"That depends on you," Daniel says, not missing a beat. He's planned this speech, of course. "Your usefulness isn't only in the field, Hunter. You can still be a part of our mission. You'll just have to find a different way to help."

I grit my teeth. If it wasn't for Adrian and that stupid pulse rifle, I wouldn't even *be* in this situation. I can't remember most of that day—from the time Adrian blew out my knees, the rest of TJ's rescue is nothing but a haze of pain—but I remember the important parts. The sick grin on Adrian's face when he put his pulse rifle to my knees and pulled the trigger.

"You have three days to come up with a proposition," Daniel says, standing up. "Until then—"

"I don't need three days." The braces around my knees suddenly feel too tight, too confining.

Daniel raises a brow. "You already know what you want to do?"

"I want to take charge of Adrian's interrogation."

Daniel's eyes flit to my braces, then back to my face. "You sure that's a good idea?"

"Any information he has, I'll get it," I say, my voice low. "I can promise you that."

"I just don't want you to go into something this important with…clouded judgment."

"I can do this."

Daniel rounds the desk, looking me up and down. I meet his level gaze without fidgeting. *Self-control.* This is a test.

Finally, Daniel nods. "Okay. Two conditions. You need to keep an eye on the sister, as well. She likely doesn't know as much as Adrian, but she could be more cooperative."

Or I could play them against each other. "Done," I say. "What else?"

"Don't treat this as a revenge opportunity."

I frown at that.

"I'm serious, Hunter." Daniel pats my shoulder as he makes his way to the door. "I'll take your proposition. Report to me soon."

I leave Daniel's office and head toward the prison wing. I have nothing better to do today, with Kaz preparing to leave for the Ordinem mission tomorrow. I'll talk to Reiko at some point, but for now, I have the chance to interrogate Adrian.

How I'll *enjoy* this. It won't be revenge—but after everything Adrian has done to me and TJ, it feels fitting. And after spending the past couple weeks doing nothing but moderating missions from the compound, the idea of being useful again feels like at least one piece of my life going back to normal.

Not that things will ever be truly normal again, now that I can never return to the field.

What does that mean for the rest of my life? When the UND has fulfilled its purpose—stopping the Draft? The organization will be disbanded. People will go their separate ways, or stay in contact—move back to Ordinem or stay here in Nadzor, or maybe even travel to Olympia. But what will happen to me?

I'll have to figure it out, eventually. I'm no longer the kid Daniel took pity on so long ago. I'm an adult, by legal standards, and a specially-trained field operative. Finding a place for someone like me will be near impossible.

I round a corner, nearly running my right wheel into the wall, and clench my fists. Yes, I *will* enjoy this interrogation.

A *thump* hits the left side of my chair and a girl's voice yelps as she comes around the corner, skipping a step.

I cock a brow as I recognize the face. Reiko.

"Sorry," she mumbles, favoring the foot she stubbed. "I wasn't paying attention."

"I can tell."

Her head snaps up at my voice. "Wait. I recognize you. You're—Adrian..." Her eyes flit to my knees and widen. "Oh. Sorry—I..." She groans, tugging on a piece of her caramel hair. "And I really thought today couldn't get any worse. I'm sorry."

Red rims the girl's eyes and tinges the rest of her face, as if she's been crying.

Well, I'm going to have to befriend her at some point. "You okay?"

"Am I...?" She lets out a nervous laugh, as if the question is preposterous. "Sure. Yeah. Listen, I'm sorry. I'll leave now."

"It's Reiko, right?"

She pauses.

"I'm Hunter." I hold out my hand. "Let's have a real introduction."

Reiko stares back at my hand, tense—like she wants to bolt. "What do you want?"

"What?"

"You know exactly who I am, and yet you're still sitting here talking to me. Why? What do you want?"

Her first assumption, upon me introducing myself, is that I want something from her. The thought sends a twinge of pity through my chest. "I don't want anything. You just...look like you've had a rough day."

Reiko bites her lip, then shakes my outstretched hand. "You could say that."

"What happened?"

"I tried to talk to TJ this morning." She presses her lips together. "You can probably guess how that went."

"Not well?"

She looks at the ground and shakes her head. "No."

"Yeah. TJ's...been through a lot."

"I know."

Reiko looks up at me, and despite her head still being hung, I can see the question in her eyes. "I can tell you want to ask me something. Go ahead."

The slight bit of tension that's drained from her stance comes rushing back at my words and she shakes her head. "It's alright. I'll just go."

"Reiko. Ask your question." This could prove a good opportunity to get some information out of her in return.

Reiko hesitates. "I...this is probably going to sound like a terrible question, coming from me, but...what actually happened that night? During the rescue?"

"Weren't you there?"

"For most of it." Reiko shrinks back a little. "I know a lot of things were—were my fault, but all I know about the rescue is that as soon as I found out the Archer was in the building, I shot Holland and we all escaped. Everything before that—how you broke in, how you found TJ, how Holland had the Archer, how my brother—how *Adrian* was involved...I really don't know much." Her voice quiets. "And nobody else has been willing to talk to me long enough to explain it."

I lean back in my wheelchair, trying to recall the night of the rescue. The first half, up until Adrian shot me, is easy to remember. The rest of it...

Come to think of it, my own memory has its share of holes. I suppose that's what comes with being grounded from missions while everybody else continues on with their lives.

"Tell you what," I say. "Let's make a deal. I'll tell you what happened before you got involved, and you tell me what happened while I was unconscious. Deal?"

"Nobody's filled you in, either?"

I shrug, although the motion feels stiff. "We got TJ out, and that's the part that matters. Everyone else has been too busy to rehash the details with me, and I wasn't about to make TJ relive any of it."

Everyone else has been too busy. With missions. That I'll never be able to go on again.

I ball my fist, imagining Adrian's smug face in front of me.

"You first?" Reiko suggests, shifting on her feet. Nervous—but why?

I take a deep breath, shoving both Adrian's face and my urge to ask questions out of my mind, and explain everything I know—from the moment Savi freed me in the Archer's basement up until Adrian shot me. Everything from there forward is masked by a haze of pain. I remember flashes of being upside-down, TJ holding a pulse rifle, and then...nothing.

"So you don't know anything that happened after TJ found the Archer?" Reiko asks when I finish.

I shake my head. "I wasn't completely unconscious, I don't think, but I was pretty out of it. I don't remember enough to put together what happened."

"Okay. I'm...not totally sure what happened between when you passed out and when I got there, but when I walked in, TJ was on the ground. I think he got shot with a pulse rifle—and Anyssa was about to...well, I'm not exactly sure what she was about to do, but Adrian had Rev and it looked like things were just about over." Her gaze takes on a distant expression and I can imagine the memories of that night playing like a movie through her head, the same way other memories so often play through mine.

"So?" I gently prod when the silence has stretched long enough. "What did you do?"

"I...I shot Anyssa," Reiko says softly, still with that glassy-eyed expression. "Not with a pulse rifle, either. With a pistol. In the leg. And then in the shoulder."

"And that's when she went down," I say, ordering my flashes of memory based on her description. I won't be able to tell if she lies or leaves something out, but her words are the best I have at the moment, and everything makes sense so far.

Reiko nods, the motion stiffer than it should be. "Even with her down," she continues, shaking off whatever came over her, "we had no way out of the sublevels when they went into lockdown, so I convinced Adrian to help us escape. It wasn't easy, and Rev and TJ barely survived a fight with the rest of the Draft agents, but we made it. Somehow."

I would assume that narrowly escaping the Draft would spark a smile, or at least a positive memory, but Reiko's gaze drops, a conflicted expression on her face. "That's not all," I say. It's not a question.

Reiko's head snaps up. "What do you mean?"

The stronger a man's reaction, Daniel once told me, *the stronger his emotions. Pay attention.*

"It's obvious that something's bothering you," I say. "If the escape was really so cut-and-dry, you wouldn't look so..." *Sad? Guilty? Nervous?* I have to be careful how I phrase this—I can't afford to offend her, not when she's already so reluctant to talk.

"Ashamed?" Reiko finishes for me, her gaze drifting down the hallway. A sea of people enter and exit the doors to the mess hall, but most of them head the other direction, toward the living quarters. One of the fluorescent lights overhead flickers. The maintenance crew will have that repaired by tomorrow. "Yeah. You would think, right?"

"You saved everyone's lives," I say. "Most people would consider that a good thing, you know." I don't know why, exactly, I keep pressing the conversation in this direction. Maybe it's because I get the sense that Reiko is something different than I expected—than everybody talks about.

"And that's my problem. I know I saved everyone. I *know* I did the right thing. But..." Reiko shakes her head, her voice fading. "I can't get it out of my head," she says, the words barely more than a whisper. "The look on Anyssa's face after I shot her. The...the *hatred*." Once the words begin, they seem to tumble out of her mouth, as if they've been bottled up too long and now they're eager to be heard. "The moment my bullet went into her shoulder and I saw the blood—I knew my aim was perfect. I *knew* I didn't kill her, but I was still terrified—which is even worse, because I'm pretty sure I *should've* killed her. I'm pretty sure—I'm pretty sure I *wanted* to kill her. But here I am." Reiko hangs her head. "Feeling *guilty* about even shooting her, when I should be feeling guilty for not taking the kill shot and ending all of this. So yeah, shame would be the word."

Silence hangs in the air as I stare at her.

Yes, she *is* different than everybody makes her sound.

"I'm sorry," she says softly. "You—I shouldn't have—"

"Reiko." I wait for her to look up at me. "It's okay. It would be more surprising if you *weren't* feeling conflicted."

She frowns. "I just admitted to feeling *guilty* about shooting Anyssa Holland, and *it's okay* is your response to that?"

"Everybody else is still processing things for themselves. Give them time, Reiko. They'll come around. Eventually."

Reiko just stares at me, searching my face as if she doesn't believe the words. "I'm—gonna go now," she whispers, her voice tight as she turns away from me. Before her back is completely to me, the bright overhead lights catch off of something in her eyes. Tears? Did a single conversation really mean that much to her?

Has everyone else really been treating her so horribly that this conversation seems like a miracle?

I wander the halls aimlessly for a while after Reiko leaves, dodging people as I go. They stay out of my way; it's been years since anybody outside of the few I know personally has tried to strike up a conversation. My bruised knuckles attract a few curious—or concerned—looks as I pass, but nobody dares say anything. I don't know if they hate me, revere me, or fear me, but whatever reputation I've earned myself here, there's no changing it now.

I have Kaz, Nora, and Daniel. That's all I need.

Reiko might be the only person more avoided than me. To some level, I can understand why—from the conversations I had with TJ in the basement, I gathered that the two of them were close, and I know the feeling of betrayal all too well.

Reiko's made mistakes. Mistakes that nearly got TJ killed. But she also turned her back on everything she's ever known to save TJ's life. Knowing what the Draft was, it's likely that Reiko has been psychologically conditioned—or more, considering Riya's current state—by Holland, shaping her into the perfect Draft agent. And still, she betrayed Holland in the end.

Up until now, Reiko was an afterthought in the shadow of Adrian's interrogation. But I suddenly find myself wanting to know more.

Chapter Six

TJ Collins

I squint as I open my eyes, bright white light searing my vision. It feels...familiar. Too familiar. I try to raise a hand to my face, but something sharp digs into my wrist. Metal. *Metal clamps.*

My breathing quickens as my surroundings register in my head. *Whitewashed room. Metal chair. Metal clamps.*

"No," I murmur, bucking against the restraints. I can feel the metal tearing at my wrists and ankles. "No, no, no—"

"Miss me?" The icy voice makes me shiver. Adrian sits in front of me, brandishing a syringe.

"Please," I whimper, sweat beading on my forehead. "I—"

"Too late." Adrian plunges the syringe into my arm. I scream—it doesn't hurt yet, but I know the pain is coming. The edges of the room begin to fade.

Before the room fades completely, I catch a glimpse of my reflection in the one-way glass opposite me—except it's not my face I see.

It's Riya's.

"No!" I scream. I feel a hand on my arm and jerk away, my back colliding with a surface—a wall? "No! No, *no*—"

"Hey! It's okay! It's okay!"

A different voice.

I jolt straight up, gasping for air as my eyes snap open. Yellow light, not white. A wood floor, not a metal chair. And only a few feet away from me, a concerned face I've never seen before.

I lean my head back against the wall, fighting to catch my breath. Sweat plasters my hair to my forehead and my pounding heart sounds in my ears like a drum. The headache I had when I first woke up in Alec's apartment has returned full-force, and the daylight beaming in through the window and illuminating the dust hanging in the air doesn't help. *Just a dream*, I tell myself, and repeat the words until they feel real. *Just a dream. Just a dream.*

Holland still has Riya. What if it's *not* just a dream? What if—

"Are you…" The boy crouched in front of me hesitates, glancing at my shaking hands. "You okay?"

I focus on the face in front of me. Not Alec, although I'm still in Alec's apartment. A mop of messy dark curls hangs to the boy's ears, shadowing the uncertain eyes set into his light brown, freckled face. He crouches with his arm outstretched, a few feet away from me and dressed in all black. My first thought is that this must be Alec's companion with the swords, but…

"You're young," I say, my voice hoarse. He looks to be around Riya's age, although a solemnity haunts his expression and makes him appear older. I can't imagine this timid boy being the stern attacker I met last night.

He sighs and sits cross-legged on the floor. "I thought you'd be out until Alec got back. You were out cold by the time he explained everything to me, and he didn't want to wake you after the night you'd had. I heard you yelling and thought something had happened." He sheepishly tugs on one of his curls, studying a patch of rotting wood floor in the corner. "I'm…really sorry about last night. I get a little paranoid sometimes."

"You *are* the one who knocked me out." I squint at him, trying to figure out how that's possible. I can feel my jaw pulsing, swollen, but the boy doesn't have a single bruise on his knuckles.

He seems to fold in on himself. "Yeah. Sorry."

"I—how old are you?"

"Fourteen."

I stare at him in disbelief.

He fidgets under the scrutiny. "How's your head? Alec told me you might have a slight concussion."

"It's alright, I think." I raise my left hand, my fingers grazing the bruise on my jaw. It throbs, but my vision has cleared up and the grogginess has faded. The daylight brightening the room means I *desperately* need to get back to the UND compound. The guard will have reported my absence by now.

The boy's eyes drift to my raised arm and widen.

I follow his gaze to see the sleeve of my hoodie has slipped enough to reveal a few patches of pale white scar tissue around my wrists—barely healed wounds from the clamps on that metal chair. I let my arm fall back into my lap, tugging the cuff of my sleeve back into place to cover the marks.

The boy flushes and I change the subject, keeping my left arm carefully tucked under the other. "So, who are you? And how did you and Alec end up out here in Nadzor?"

"What makes you think we came from somewhere else?" he asks, tensing.

"Alec told me."

He blinks. "Oh. Then...yeah. We met in Ordinem and we made it out here almost a month ago. It wasn't easy to leave, but you already know that, I guess, since you're here."

"And what about you?"

"What do you mean?"

I gesture at him. "I'd love to know how a fourteen-year-old knocked me out with a single punch, for starters. And what's the deal with you and those swords?"

He shifts uncomfortably. "That's a story I'd rather not tell."

"The swords, or the knockout punch?"

"Both."

"Okay, then. How about a name?"

Even with such an easy question, he hesitates, studying me. The silence stretches for such a long time that I'm almost convinced he isn't going to answer, until he finally speaks. "Max."

"Last name?"

His face reddens. "Don't have one."

The situation almost makes me laugh—first he knocks me out with a single punch, then I wake up to one of his curved swords at my throat, and then he turns out to be a shy fourteen-year-old without a last name—but the look on Max's face gives me pause. Nervousness, a little embarrassment, but also something I recognize far too well. Pain. Alec's words from last night come to mind. *We both have some history with Holland, too.*

"I'm TJ," I tell him, intrigued. "Collins. But then, you already knew that."

He winces at the reminder of his little interrogation. "Yeah. Can I, uh, ask you something?"

"Shoot."

"Collins—were you related to Maya?"

I blink. I haven't heard anyone else say my mother's first name since...well, since the Archer—since Rev...

Max leans in a little, latching onto whatever must've shifted in my expression. "You *were*. You look like her, too, now that I'm thinking about it. How are you related? I know she didn't have any kids, but—"

"How do *you* know her?" I ask, brow furrowed.

"I—through a mutual acquaintance. It doesn't matter. But how are you related? I didn't know she had any family close to my age."

Adrian's voice echoes in my head. *What do you know about your mother's work in the hospital? What did she tell you before she died?*

I can't tell Max who I really am. He and Alec aren't with Holland, to the best of my knowledge, but if they're actively working against the Draft, and my mother played some kind of key role that Holland thought worthy of interrogating me about, telling him I'm the son of Maya Collins might not bode well.

"She was my aunt," I say. "I never saw her much—we didn't live close."

"Oh."

"You sound disappointed," I venture.

"I was...well, I was kinda hoping you might know something about the Archer."

I raise a brow. "Why are you looking for the Archer?"

He shrugs, but the movement looks stiff. "She's just interesting, I guess. She's fighting the Draft. Same as the rest of us. And she's making a difference."

I fight the urge to press him about it more. If I ask too many questions, Max might want to ask one back, and I can't let him know about my connection with Rev, not until I know more about him and Alec.

Thankfully, the apartment's front door opens before Max has the chance to ask any more questions. Alec enters with a napkin-wrapped bundle in his hands, grinning when he sees me and Max. "How are you feeling? I'm assuming Max has introduced himself?"

I nod. "Better, and yeah. Thank you."

"No problem. It was the least we could do. You know, I don't think I ever caught your name."

"I'm TJ," I say, hoping to avoid bringing up my last name again.

Unfortunately, Max has other ideas. "He's related to Maya."

"Huh." Alec studies me and I know he sees the same questions in my eyes as I see in his. Both of us wondering about the other's story.

I need to get out of here.

I stand, the abrupt motion making me dizzy, but the feeling fades. "I need to get back."

"Of course." Alec turns toward the door to my left and looks over his shoulder at me. "But before you leave, you mind if you and I have a conversation?"

I hesitate, glancing at the front door. I really do need to get going if I want to make it back before Daniel gets too worried. Alec already knows far too much about me, for someone I just met last night, but I do owe him one for stopping Max from taking off my head, and his expression leaves no room for argument.

I leave Max in the living room and follow Alec through the door and into a kitchen. Inside, an island takes up most of the room, with a couple of run-down appliances that probably haven't worked in years along the walls. The only thing that looks remotely functional is the sink, the only metal surface not coated in Nadzor dust. A couple of white globes a little larger than my palm sit on the counter, in the direct light from one of the room's two windows.

Alec follows my gaze to the strange globes and laughs. "Those are our lights—we traded for them at one of the markets a while back. They charge during the day with sunlight, and a few of them are enough for us to get by at night. There's not a lot of permanent infrastructure out here, since the people move around so much, so we don't get power. We did manage to rig something up with the water system, though—as long as we keep the water tank full from the well over by the square, we have running water."

Alec's description reminds me of my old apartment, the first one I stayed in with Riya. I suppress the memories and set my mind on Alec instead. "What did you want to talk to me about?"

"Listen, I don't know a lot about you, but I do know you have a past with Holland." He leans his elbows on the kitchen island. "Don't argue—it was written all over your face when I brought it up last night, and you're a teenage kid in the Undrafted. I won't pry. But I do want to encourage you. You're not the only one Holland has hurt." His eyes flick to the door, beyond which Max sits in the living room.

"He knew her too, didn't he?" I ask softly.

"Max's story isn't mine to tell, but yes."

"You never told me how *you* knew her. Or how you know about the Undrafted."

"And I'm not going to—at least, not right now." Alec straightens up. "Anyway. I don't know your situation, or why you were so desperate to get away from the Undrafted's compound that you ended up banging on our door, but you're welcome to come by here if you need anything. I get the sense that all three of us are in similar boats when it comes to Holland, and I know how...*difficult* the UND can be sometimes, so I wanted to put the offer out there."

"Thank you," I say. Knowing that Alec and Max are somehow caught up in all of this, and that they knew my mother, I'm starting to think coming back here sometime might not be a bad idea.

That, and the fact that deep down, Alec's words resonate with me more than any of the hollow assurances I've received from people at the compound in the past couple weeks. *Things are going to be okay. We're going to win this. You're going to be fine.* I nod and smile, but none of them can see through that thin expression. None of them know how different, how hollow, my time at the Draft truly left me.

Maybe I've finally found some people who understand.

On my way out of the apartment, I feel a hand grab my wrist and I immediately stiffen.

Max drops his arm. Now that we're both standing, I can see he's much shorter than I originally thought. The fact that such an unassuming boy could ambush me the way he did still stuns me. "Hey, uh, before you leave, I just...I wanted to apologize," he says, shifting on his feet. "Again. For everything. If there's anything you need, I owe you."

"It's alright," I say, and I mean it. "It was a misunderstanding. To be fair, it really did look like I was trying to break in. You're not the first person I've met with instincts like that."

"Instincts," Max echoes, his dark brown eyes shifting to where his swords rest against the wall. "Yeah."

"Max, really. It's okay." I can't tell if he still feels bad about our encounter or if it's something else bothering him, but the cloud that's come over him doesn't fade until I open the front door.

He shakes off his distant look. "Are you coming back?"

Behind him, Alec leans against the kitchen door frame, also awaiting an answer.

"Maybe." I shrug. Alec and Max seem nice enough, and equally as important, they could have helpful information. "If I can figure out a way to make it work, I don't see why not. The company would be nice."

To my surprise, Max *grins*.

Alec smiles too. "The company would be nice," he agrees. "We'll see you around, then, TJ. Oh, and one more thing?"

I pause in the doorway. "What?"

"Do your best to avoid telling Daniel Bennett about us. We're not against the UND," Alec rushes to assure me. "But like I said, there's a reason we're not with them, either. I get the feeling Daniel wouldn't take too well to finding out we've been...*active* in Nadzor, especially this close to the compound."

Active. What does that mean? Max and Alec are doing more than simply hiding out here? Of course, what else was I expecting with Max wielding those swords? And what kind of issues does Alec have with Daniel?

More questions. More reasons to come back here. I offer Alec a slight smile. "I will."

Chapter Seven

TJ Collins

B y the time I make it back to the compound, the sun is a little under halfway to its zenith. Making the walk in my black hoodie leaves sweat dripping down my back and face, but I can't bring myself to bare my arm to the world. I approach the compound's chain-link fence covered in gritty dust and with my hood pulled over my face to hide as much of the bruising from my fight with Max as I can.

The guard at the gate scans my wristband and the scanner flashes green, but he grabs my arm before I can enter the compound. "I'll have to escort you to Daniel's office."

"What for?"

"You weren't back by your estimated return time of this morning, so Daniel was alerted. He was only a couple hours from sending out a search party for you."

A search party? Since when am I important enough to the Undrafted for a search party?

The guard exchanges words with his companion before towing me into the largest of the UND's three buildings. The air conditioning chills my sweat-covered body, but it's a welcome relief from the desert landscape outside. Ordinem has *never* been this hot in the winter. Imagining a southern Nadzor summer, I can see why the people move so often.

The guard leads me to Daniel's office and enters without knocking. Daniel must be expecting me.

"TJ Collins, sir. He returned a few minutes ago," the guard says.

Daniel, sitting behind his mahogany desk, looks up from his laptop. He studies me, expression unreadable, before addressing the guard. "Thank you. You're dismissed. Close the door behind you."

I'm in trouble now. The sprinkles of gray in his dark hair betray Daniel's age, but they don't make the man any less intimidating. Staying the extra minutes to talk with Max and Alec no longer seems like it was my best idea.

As soon as the door shuts, Daniel fixes his piercing gaze on me. "Hood down. *Now.*"

I sigh and slide the hood back from my head, letting the harsh lighting of the UND compound illuminate my injuries.

I can't tell if Daniel wants to punch me in the face or call Nora. "What *happened* out there?"

"I went on a walk."

"Don't be smart with me," he warns. "You're *hours* past the time you were supposed to return. What did you do?"

"I went a little further than I planned, and I...ran into someone."

He gives me a flat look. "The bruises?"

I shrug, hoping it looks more nonchalant than I feel. The walk back gave me enough time to come up with a cover story for Max and Alec. "I think he meant to rob me or something. And once he realized I didn't have any money, he left me alone."

The electricity of the fluorescent lights overhead buzzes in the silence that follows. I can almost feel myself sweating despite the freezing air.

After what feels like an eternity, Daniel shakes his head. "I don't mean this offensively, but you look *terrible*."

"I haven't seen the damage," I confess, my shoulders relaxing at the fact that Daniel believes my lie.

"You'll have to ask Nora for a mirror. Maybe it'll make you think twice about leaving the compound at night when the market's in town." Daniel lets out a long breath. "TJ, you're not Hunter, or Kaz, or Rev. It's only been two weeks since your rescue, and after what you endured at Anyssa's hand…"

I flinch. "What does this have to do with me taking a walk?"

"The whole point of you staying here is for your *protection*, TJ. I'm sure Hunter has told you about our normal policy—if you don't have a role here, you don't have a place here. You, though, are a special case, because your role is less…*active* than most."

"What is *that* supposed to mean?"

"It means you're not trained, you don't fight, and you're not a scientist, or a hacker, or a doctor. But you *are* valuable to Holland, for some reason, and that means you're an asset." He stands, his hands braced on the edge of his desk. "You're an asset we need to protect. What if it had been a Draft kid attacking you? We already know they're in Nadzor."

"You keep watch near the compound," I counter. "You'd know if they were close by."

"Still. It's not safe."

"You can't keep me locked in this compound," I say, hating the way my voice cracks. I will *not* be locked up again.

Daniel lets silence stretch again as he considers me. I shove my hands into my hoodie pocket and stand up straight, but I can't fight the feeling that his icy blue eyes can see straight through me.

If Daniel knew just how useless I truly am, I wonder how much he'd try to protect me. Holland *doesn't* want me, not anymore. Not after Adrian's torture proved to her that I don't know anything.

Would I even be here right now if Daniel knew?

"No, I won't do that to you," Daniel eventually says, sitting back down and folding his hands on the desk. "You still have the freedom to leave. But you will *not* be going on any more nighttime walks. From now on, you're back before the sun sets, and every time you scan your wristband to leave, I'll be notified—same upon your return. Now go see Nora. You look awful. And after that, you might want to find Rev. She has some updates I think you'll want to hear."

"Thank you," I say, pulling my hood back over my head. "Does she know? That I was back late?"

"I didn't alert the rest of the compound yet. Another hour or so and I would've put together a search party, though." Daniel smiles at me, a knowing grin that sets me on edge—probably because I just lied to him. "You're important, TJ Collins. We just have yet to figure out exactly why."

I keep my head down, my hands in my pockets, and my hood pulled over my face as I make my way down the hall to the infirmary. It's about as busy as usual—a couple of agents attended by medics sit on infirmary beds, having minor injuries treated or long-lasting injuries checked on. Nora sits behind her desk at the back of the room, frowning as she thumbs through a stack of papers. I dodge a fast-moving medic and stand directly in front of her. "Nora?"

She starts, dropping the papers in her hand to the desk. "TJ! Good to see you. What's with the hood?"

I slide my hood back and wince at the face Nora makes. "That bad, huh?"

"You live in a secret compound. How on *Earth* did you manage to get yourself beaten up anyway?"

"It's not as bad as it looks," I promise as she stands and drags me over to a bed. "Just a few bruises."

"Uh, no. This is *not* a few bruises." Nora sits me down and tilts my head side-to-side to inspect the splotches of dark purple. "And don't think I can't tell what that cut on your neck is. I've seen the aftermath of enough blade encounters to know where this comes from. What happened?"

"I went on a walk last night."

Nora folds her arms. "Nope. I need more than that."

"I...ran into a guy. He probably thought I had money or something, and he threatened me with a knife, but after he knocked me out—"

"You were unconscious?" Nora grabs a narrow tool from one of the cabinets along the wall, using her foot to drag her rolling stool with her as she returns to me.

"Not for that long. I was fine after I sat and rested for a little while."

Nora shakes her head and holds up her tool, using it to shine a light in my eyes. I flinch, my eyes watering at the searing brightness.

"Lightheadedness, dizziness, headache, nausea, trouble remembering what happened?"

"A little lightheaded," I admit. "And a killer headache, but it's already starting to get better."

Nora shuts off the light and sets it down next to me before meeting my eyes. "There's more."

"That's all that—"

"TJ, has anybody ever told you you're a terrible liar?"

I glare at her, but the look carries no conviction. I *want* to tell Nora everything, but I can't reveal Max and Alec. "That's everything."

She sighs. "Fine. Don't give me the full story. But did you at least tell me everything relevant to how you got hit?"

I nod, and this time, it isn't a lie. Thankfully, she doesn't ask how my "attacker" knocked me out. A punch shouldn't be strong enough to do that. And yet somehow, Max was able to. And judging by Alec's explanation, that's a very normal occurrence.

"Well," Nora says, rolling her stool back to the cabinets along the wall, "there's not a whole lot I can do about the minor concussion except tell you to take it easy and give you something for the headache. As far as the bruising and the swelling goes, I can give you an ice pack, if you want."

"I'm alright," I say. "I'll be asleep as soon as I get back to my room, I'm sure."

"Suit yourself." She closes the cabinet and hands me a small pill bottle. "These'll help with the headaches. Don't take any more than two at a time, and only take them as needed. And while you're here, do you mind if I check up on your arm and those stitches?"

"Go ahead." It takes effort to get the words out, my throat suddenly dry, as I pull my hoodie over my head and try to ignore the presence of other people in the room. I focus on one of Nora's frizzy orange buns instead of the burning stares of the other medics, or the patchwork of white scars and still-healing wounds on my arm.

Nora inspects the wound in my side first and nods, satisfied. "Good. I'm glad it didn't come open when you got in your fight earlier. That would've added another week or two to your healing. How's your arm?"

"Same as it's always been." I stare at the floor tiles under my dangling feet and grip the edge of the bed with my free hand as Nora puts pressure on different spots of my arm, asking me periodically if anything hurts. Once or twice, I involuntarily flinch, but Nora doesn't press me further when I tell her it feels fine. Of everyone in the compound besides Reiko and Adrian, Nora knows the most about what Holland did to me. And, ironically, it's Nora who pressures me about things the least. If Rev saw my scars, past that glimpse she got on the helicopter, I don't think she'd let me off so easy.

"Everything looks fine," Nora says, leaning back. "Just don't get yourself mugged again, okay? And for the record, I wish you the best of luck trying to explain this to Daniel. He's not going to take 'I got mugged' as an answer."

"Actually, that's pretty much what I told him, and he let it go," I say.

Nora raises a brow. "So you admit that the whole robbery thing is a cover story?"

"I—" I huff out a breath. "Fine. It wasn't a robbery or anything, it was a misunderstanding. The guy who attacked me thought I was somebody else, and he got a little paranoid. Once he realized, though, he felt terrible and helped me out. He let me rest for a little while before I walked back here."

"Do you know who he is?"

"No."

"So let me get this straight. Some stranger attacked you out of the blue, realized it was an accident, and felt bad about it, so he let you hang around to recover with him for a little while?"

"I mean, I wouldn't put it like that, but...kind of, yeah."

Nora sighs and shakes her head. "What *is* it with you and making friends with people who try to kill you?"

"He didn't try to kill me!" I protest.

Nora gives me a flat look.

"Okay, so *maybe* that was a possibility, but when his friend walked in—"

"His friend?"

"Yeah—there's two of them." While I talk, I pull my black hoodie back over my head, getting ready to leave. "His friend is the one who straightened things out."

"You know," Nora says as she helps me to my feet, "sometimes I wonder how you're still alive, especially considering you have no clue how to defend yourself."

"I'm not *completely* clueless. I kept the Archer from skewering me early on," I counter.

"Yeah, only because she didn't *really* want to kill you."

I don't have a response to that, because she's right. If only I knew how to fight—but who's going to teach me? Rev and Kaz are always busy on missions, Reiko isn't an option, and Hunter's dealing with his injuries, not to mention that it's been a while since we've talked. I don't know anybody else who can fight, except...

My eyes widen slightly as a thought strikes me. A crazy thought, but...not outside the realm of possibility. *Max.*

He did say he'd be there if I needed anything, and it would give me a good excuse to go back and talk to him and Alec again. I'd be doing something useful with my time, instead of waiting around for more information about Riya.

I try to convince myself that's the only reason I want to go back, but if I'm being honest, the company of two people who have some understanding of what I've been through doesn't sound bad, either.

That's it. I'll go see Max and Alec tomorrow. And hopefully, I'll be able to find out more about their connection to Holland and their past with the UND.

Chapter Eight

Hunter Lane

I squint as the cell door clangs shut behind me, the dimness of the room leaving me nearly blind after the bright fluorescents of the prison wing's hallway. Getting to Adrian's cell was easy enough. Even the guard instantly recognized me and, after scanning my wristband to prove my credentials, let me in without further questions. Being one of the most feared agents in the UND has its perks.

Where the prison cells in the Draft sublevels are torturously bright, the Undrafted does the opposite. I sit just inside the door for a few moments to let my eyes adjust fully, my hands squeezing the wheels of my chair to an invisible rhythm. After my conversation with Reiko, I stopped by the infirmary to get Nora to wrap my bruised and bloody knuckles.

I don't anticipate those wraps staying clean for very long, but the detour gave me time to think. About the upcoming interrogation. About Reiko.

The small cell, about the size of the bedroom I've had since I was six, is gray and unfurnished, save for a grate in the corner that reeks of sewage and a metal ring driven into the floor in the center of the room. A chain stretches from there to a tall figure sitting straight-backed on the ground, eyes closed. It's just long enough to allow him to stand, if he wanted to.

Adrian cracks an eye at my entry. "Ah. You. It was only a matter of time. Come to kill me, then?"

"If you give me good reason to, I'd be more than happy."

Adrian snickers, opening his eyes fully. "Sure. Shoot the guy who has what you want. See what good that'll do."

"You don't—"

"I don't know what you want?" Adrian gives me a flat look. "I beg to differ. I think your organization's little interrogations over the past couple of weeks have been enough for me to piece together what you're looking for.'

I roll forward, wary. If Adrian catches me off-guard, he might use his chain to try and fight—and trapped in my wheelchair as I am, I would be in trouble. As long as I watch him carefully, I'll be fine. "Don't make this difficult, Adrian."

Adrian chuckles and closes his eyes again. "You're not going to get anything out of me, boy. I don't know if you noticed, but Daniel's lackeys have already tried their hand at it, and they—"

I snatch the front of his ratty shirt with one hand and sock him in the face with my other. I get in three punches before Adrian gets over his shock and reaches for me with his manacled hands. I catch the chain and loop it around his neck, yank it tight as I twist my upper body for a better angle. Adrian's back slams against my right wheel, his hands pinned against his neck by the manacles. I hold him like that until I can hear him wheezing, consider holding him just a little longer—until the sound of his gasps fade completely—then loosen my grip on the chains just enough to let the man breathe. "Why," I hiss in his ear, "is Anyssa Holland sending Draft agents to Nadzor? Why is she taking new kids?"

Adrian hacks and coughs, his face bright red. "There are some people in this world," he rasps, "that you can't break with pain."

My fingers tighten around the chains and I let out a low growl as I twist my hand. A choked wheeze escapes from Adrian. I count. One. Two. Keep holding. Nine. Ten. Adrian begins to struggle, his eyes wide as he realizes that I'm not letting go. Fifteen. Sixteen. Adrian bucks against my chair, but he doesn't have nearly enough leverage from the ground to tip me. I make it to thirty before Adrian's struggles grow weak.

It takes *all of me* not to keep holding on. I let go and shove Adrian away from my chair. He lands on his hands and knees, struggling for air, as I roll back. Now that I get a good look at him, I can see the evidence of past interrogations marring Adrian's face. A half-healed black eye, various lacerations and bruises across all his visible skin, a split and bloodied lip.

Adrian shifts so that he's sitting up, glaring at me. "You're nothing but Daniel's little *puppet*," he spits, the words accompanied by a mouthful of blood.

I shake out the hand I used to punch him and sit back in my chair. The slight smile that crosses my face isn't entirely for show. "The tables have turned for you, haven't they, Adrian?"

"You can't kill me," he hisses. "You need me."

"I need the information you have," I counter. "And you have a sister who might be able to give it to us."

Adrian jerks against his chains. "Don't you *touch* my little sister."

I grin. There's my leverage.

Adrian's expression shifts, a crack in his hard façade as he realizes his mistake. "Ready to talk?" I ask.

Adrian's face falls back into his stony mask. "You want information? Tell me what your organization has done with my sister."

"She's safe." I pause, then add, "For now." If Reiko is going to be my only bargaining chip, I'll leave myself the opportunity to use it down the road.

Adrian bristles. "For now?"

"You want to keep her safe? Start talking."

Adrian's whole body tenses, as if he's ready to tear through his chains and pummel me, but I'm safely out of his range. He balls his fists. "Fine," he spits. "I'll tell you this. Daniel Bennett? The man that runs your life? He isn't the man you think he is."

"I'm looking for information about the Draft, not Daniel," I say, but Adrian's comment unsettles me. *It's a trick. Manipulation.*

"Alright, then here's one for you. Daniel used to work with Anyssa."

"And how could you *possibly* know something like that?"

"I think the better question is, how couldn't you? Hasn't the man practically raised you? You *are* Hunter Lane, right?"

I never told Adrian my name. I sit, stunned. Did I? Maybe he got it while I was unconscious in the basement—TJ or one of the others said something—but...

"I'll give you one more thing," Adrian said, his tone turning dark. "I knew your sister, boy. And whatever you're thinking about me and Reiko, we're not *nearly* as dysfunctional as the two of you."

"You—" I start, then snap my mouth shut. My blood pulses through my veins, urging me, pushing me, to stand up, to *attack*. But I can't. If I let myself lose control now, I don't think I'll be able to stop.

Adrian flashes a grin, although his bloody face and the dark room makes the expression eerie, and I want nothing more than to smash my fist straight through it. But letting him see me snap would be letting him win. And if I do snap, Daniel won't hesitate to take me off Adrian's interrogation—probably exactly what Adrian wants. Why he's goading me.

I force my hands to move, turning my chair to the door. Adrian laughs, almost a cackle, as I leave.

He didn't win this match, but he came close enough to make my hands shake. Or maybe that's the image of my sister burned into my head, reminding me of the things Holland did. The things my sister caused.

Or maybe it's the fact that I'm not sure Adrian was lying about Daniel.

I nearly run over Kaz as I round the next corner. Right outside the mess hall—that checks out.

"Hunter—woah," Kaz says as I wheel around to face him. "I'd hate to see the other guy."

I glance down at myself. Adrian's blood soils the new wraps on my knuckles and some of my shirt.

"What happened?" Kaz presses.

"Adrian."

"Adrian? The-guy-who-shot-you Adrian?"

"One and the same." I draw my lips into a line. "I'm in charge of his interrogation now."

"Ah." Kaz grimaces. "That explains it. Are you...okay?"

"Why wouldn't I be okay?" The words come out sharper than they should, and infuriatingly, Kaz seems to notice.

"Hunter, what did he say to you?"

"It was nothing."

"You're covered in his blood and you look like you're about ready to sock the next person who dares talk to you. It wasn't *nothing*."

I glare at Kaz, but he's not wrong. "He brought up my sister."

Kaz visibly drops whatever remark he had prepared. "Oh."

"Yeah." I wheel past him, but he puts a hand on my shoulder.

"Hunter. Hey."

I grip the wheels, facing the opposite direction. I can see all the way down the hall to the building's main entrance. Past that lies Nadzor, and then Ordinem. Past that lies Holland. Past that lies my traitor of a sister.

Once Kaz is sure he has my attention, he speaks quieter. "Adrian's just trying to make you lose control."

"I'm aware."

Kaz's hand lingers on my shoulder for another moment, and I know he wants to ask the next question—whether Adrian succeeded. But Kaz knows me better than that. He already knows the answer.

I shrug off his hand and his concern as I continue down the hall.

Daniel lets me into his office on the second knock. "Come to report already? You do work fast."

"Not exactly," I say, keeping my expression flat as I roll into the room.

Daniel looks me over as he steps back. I track his gaze as it lingers on my soiled shirt, my bloody knuckles.

Everybody has a tell. It's time to find out if I'm right about Daniel's. He's too smart to give away anything with his eyes, but fidgeting with his suit—straightening the cuffs, more specifically—has proven a consistent one.

"How much of that blood is yours?" His observation finished, Daniel rounds his desk.

"Take a guess."

"Interrogation going that well, then?" He moves to sit.

"Did you work with Anyssa Holland?"

Daniel freezes, his hands braced on the edge of his desk, and a dark look falls over his face. "Ah. Right to the point, then. That's always been one of your best qualities, if not a help to your diplomacy."

"So you *did*." Hunter wanted to jump to his feet, but he couldn't. His pent-up energy had nowhere to go. "Why? Why wouldn't you tell anybody?"

"Hunter, where did you hear this?"

"It doesn't matter."

"Yes, it does." Daniel raised a brow. "Let me guess. Adrian?"

The revelation simmers in my chest, building up heat as I sit in front of Daniel. Daniel has been *keeping this* from me. Daniel, one of the only three people I was convinced I could trust. "Explain, Daniel," I say, my voice low and cold.

"Hunter, you know better than this." Daniel shook his head. "You can't just believe everything you hear, especially from someone like—"

"Explain!"

"*Be silent!*" Daniel slams his hands against the desk, punctuating his command as his voice bellows through the room. He never takes his eyes off me as he sits down. "You are an *agent*, Hunter. There are things above your head. You think I would've worked with the Nadzor government to found the Undrafted if I was on Holland's side?"

He has a fair point there. "Then why wouldn't you—"

"*Silence*. I'll get there. Before I left Ordinem, I was the assistant to Sector 1's Senator. I used to know Silas Johnson, too. When he and Holland started working together, I noticed—and when they tried to bring me in on the Draft and I discovered they planned to kidnap children and use them as soldiers, I didn't want any part of it. I knew it had to stop. So I moved out to Nadzor, the government agreed to help fund me, and the Undrafted was born. It's taken all eleven years to get the UND from what it was then to the full organization it is now."

I hesitate. The story makes sense, but Adrian's words still bother me. *Daniel used to work with Anyssa.* That doesn't line up with what Daniel just told me—he implied that he was never a part of the Draft at all.

"Any more questions?" Daniel asks, his voice smooth.

"No." I give Daniel a respectful nod despite the doubt plaguing me, then roll out the door.

As I turn to shut it behind me, I catch a glimpse of Daniel through the doorway.

A glimpse of Daniel tugging on the cuffs of his suit coat.

Chapter Nine

Reverie Adams

Something about traveling all the way back to Ordinem with Kaz and Savi just doesn't sit right. Since our meeting with Daniel yesterday, with the trip impending, I haven't been able to get it out of my head. Maybe it has to do with the fact that leaving TJ in Nadzor by himself, after all he's already been through, doesn't strike me as a good idea.

Or maybe it has something to do with the fact that Ordinem is the home of the past I've been trying so hard to leave behind.

I fall into line with the crowd of people exiting the mess hall and turn down the hallway leading deeper into the building, past the offices, toward the infirmary, then the living quarters. TJ seems to be...okay, which is the last thing I expected coming to Nadzor. He's mostly himself. But the problem there is *mostly*. He wears baggy and long clothes now, covering up the physical remnants of his time at the Draft, but I remember how frail he was when we first found him. And that glimpse of his arm that I got on the helicopter is burned into my head.

Is TJ really the one you're worried about? a tiny voice in the back of my head whispers. I'm worried about leaving TJ on his own, yes, but there's something that runs deeper.

I'm worried that all the pain and hurt he's accumulated over the past months—much of it my fault—is still inside him. Bottled up somewhere, waiting to explode. I'm worried that I'll return in two weeks to find that it's spilled over, and this whole idea of having fixed things between TJ and me will be nothing but wishful thinking.

I just want to talk to him.

As I pass the side hallway leading to the infirmary, I glance to my left to see the infirmary door swinging open.

TJ lets it shut on its own behind him, making a dull thud. He winces at the noise, one hand on the wall, and doesn't look up until the noise has faded.

My step falters when I see his face. A dark patchwork of bruises mars the entire right side of his face, his eye nearly swollen shut. Despite how he wavers on his feet, a slight smile still rests on his lips. But those *bruises*—where could they possibly have come from?

"What *happened* to you?" I ask, coming to a stop in front of him.

It seems to take TJ a couple seconds to register that I'm talking about his injuries. "I went out for some fresh air last night, after..." He swallows. "After you told me about Riya. Went too far out toward the ruins and some guy attacked me. Didn't steal anything, though. He must've thought I had money or something."

"You went out by yourself? In the middle of the night?"

He shrugs, an infuriating smile tugging at his face. "It was only sunset when I left."

I stare at his injuries. How can he talk like this isn't a big deal? Especially right after I told him about Riya? "What if you'd been attacked by one of Holland's people? She could've killed you, or taken you back—"

He winces and I cut myself off, but it's too late. I've brought the memories back.

When TJ speaks again, his voice is lower. "I'm back and I'm safe—that's what matters. I'll do my best not to get mugged next time, alright?"

I pinch the bridge of my nose. "Next time? You're going *back* out there?"

"I'm sick of people treating me like I'm helpless, Rev!" He runs a hand through his hair, meeting my eyes. "I'm not the same person I was when we first met. For better or for worse, I'll admit that. But I can't just stay cooped up here, terrified of Holland, waiting for everybody else to take down the Draft while I sit and watch. It's no better than being locked up again."

His expression tugs at my heart, the desperation in his eyes reminding me too much of myself—my own drive to save Eliza. "I get it," I tell him. "But…"

I trail off, struggling to find the words to express what I want to say. *I can't watch you get hurt again. I can't watch you take the same path that led me to the Archer. I care. I care so much that it terrifies me, because after everything I've put you through, I don't know if you care the same way.*

"Just be careful," is what I decide on. "Please."

TJ, as always, seems to be able to see right through the words. Thankfully, instead of digging, he simply nods. "I will. Although you act like you won't be here to keep an eye on me." He smiles at that, but the gesture falls when I don't return it.

"That's actually what I wanted to talk to you about," I say. "Savi, Kaz, and I are leaving for Ordinem this afternoon."

"You—you what?"

"We're hoping to figure out what Holland did to Riya. And why," I explain. "I've been trying to find you since the mission briefing yesterday."

"Do you think you'll be able to bring her back?" TJ asks, hope rising in his voice.

"I don't know. But we'll bring *something* back. And it'll help us save Riya. It'll help us save them all."

TJ hesitates. "How long are you going to be gone?"

"Two weeks. We have to leave today if we want to make the satellite dead zone that'll let us in under the government's radar, and the next dead zone is in two weeks."

TJ nods, slowly. "So this...this is our goodbye, then. For the next couple of weeks."

I wish it weren't. "Are you going to be okay without me?" I lace the words with sarcasm, but even so, they're too close to the truth.

"I'll figure it out.'" His gaze drops to the tiles beneath our feet.

I *hate* leaving him like this. When he seems to need support more than ever. If only there were something I could do. "I'll be in Sector 1, you know," I say. "Close to your old apartment."

His head snaps up and he looks at me in disbelief before shaking his head. "Rev, I couldn't ask you to go back there."

"You're not asking. I'm offering. I could bring back a...a photo, or something."

TJ gives a shaky smile, then steps forward and wraps his arms around me. "Thank you," he says softly.

I return the embrace, but there's a tension behind my own movements. A fear that's been festering since I revealed my identity to TJ, since I admitted to myself that I care. It's the same fear that keeps me from admitting to TJ, even now, just how much I care.

What if there are some wrongs I'll never be able to make right?

The helicopter ride to Ordinem takes longer than I remember, likely because I was unconscious for most of the ride the first time. Soon, the dusty brown scenery and dots of colorful tents out the window fade to the bland gray of the outskirts of Ordinem. I can make out the patrolled fence marking the border, snaking north like a dark crack in the landscape, and past that, the crumbling buildings of Ordinem's outer Sectors. Past that, I can make out what looks like...a column of smoke. Fires? Riots? It's only been a couple weeks since we left, but after the chaos I caused as the Archer and Holland's public execution of TJ falling through, I wouldn't be surprised.

Kaz leans closer to the window, his headset bumping against it. "I didn't expect to be back here so soon," he says, his voice crackling through the mic. "I forgot how different the outer Sectors are. You know that thing Hunter and Daniel always say? That if people in Ordinem knew the truth they would all flock to Nadzor?" Kaz tears his gaze from the window and looks at me and Savi across from him. The headset shifts as he moves, leaving a dent in his hair from where it's been resting. "Every time I see Ordinem, I realize just how right they are. These people deserve *better*."

The three of us fall silent and I turn my attention back to the window.

Around sunset, the helicopter approaches a large building that I, upon further glance, recognize as the building where Hunter first led us after we escaped from the Draft. The roof opens—the same way as the hangar works back at the compound—to let the helicopter land inside. From there, Kaz leads us back through the way we first left Sector 1: the tunnel underneath the gate.

When the three of us emerge into the crumbling building with the tunnel's Sector 1 entrance, Kaz holds out a hand to stop me and Savi.

"What's going on?" I ask, pulling my hood over my head.

"Enforcers. They just moved around the corner." Kaz steps back from the entrance and looks at the two of us. "I can try to sneak us to our safehouse, but I'd be surprised if we didn't run into any patrols on the way. Just be ready and stay quiet."

I nod. Next to me, Savi's eyes are wide, but she sets her shoulders and nods as well.

Kaz grins. "Let's do this."

He draws his pistols and sets off, light on his feet. I follow suit, pressing the button to unfold my bow as I enter the alleyway outside the building.

We slip through streets and alleys, circumventing Enforcer patrols as Kaz sees them, but it becomes more difficult the closer we get to the center of Sector 1.

When we round the next corner, first Kaz, then me, then Savi, a yell sounds from the alley we just vacated.

"Is that..." Savi starts.

Kaz glances over his shoulder and our eyes meet. "Run," we say at the same time.

The three of us break into a dead sprint, following Kaz—thankfully, he's the fastest out of us. He ducks in and out of alleyways, leading us steadily toward the center of Sector 1. It doesn't take long for Savi's pace to drag, and I slow to stay with her. "Kaz, how much farther?" I call.

He glances over his shoulder, landing on Savi's struggling gait. "We're almost there!"

"You got this," I say under my breath, running next to Savi. "Almost there."

"Remind me—to never—become—a field—agent," Savi gets out between gasps.

It turns out, "we're almost there" was an exaggeration on Kaz's part. We sprint for at least another half a mile until both me and Kaz are feeling the effects of the exertion. Every time we think it's safe to slow down, one of us catches a glimpse of an Enforcer patrol—or an Enforcer patrol catches a glimpse of us. Finally, Kaz bursts into an apartment building about a mile from the Enforcer headquarters and takes the stairs three at a time.

Savi and I follow him into a room on the second floor and Kaz slams and locks the door behind us. He doubles over, his hands on his knees, smiling wide despite his heavy breathing. "Well, that was fun."

"Fun?" Savi looks like she's about ready to pass out, her face bright red. "I—no." She wavers on her feet, takes a step forward, and loses her balance.

Kaz catches her arm and holds her upright. "Woah, okay. I keep forgetting you've never been out in the field before. Come on."

I can't tell if the deep color on Savi's face is more from exertion or Kaz's attention. He helps her to the black couch in the center of the room and I trail behind, taking in the Undrafted's safehouse. It's laid out the same way as most

Ordinem apartments, with this room being the living room and three doors besides the main—one leading to the kitchen, one to a bedroom, and one to a bathroom, if it's a typical apartment. The furnishing, however, is what sets it apart. A plush couch and a couple of armchairs sit on a square rug, all sharp shades of black and gray, and the musty smell I grew so used to with TJ's old apartment and my basement is nowhere to be found.

Savi collapses onto the couch, sucking in huge gulps of air.

"Put your hands up—behind your head. It'll open up your airways," Kaz coaches. "There you go. Try to take deep breaths, slow your heart rate. You'll be alright in a few minutes. I used to hate running, too." He moves to the windows and pulls a blackout curtain down over each, blocking out the twilight from outside.

"How long has this been here?" I ask. This little apartment is right under Holland's nose.

Kaz shrugs as he takes care of the final window. "Not sure. But you want to hear a fun fact? This is where I stayed the last time I came to Ordinem. Rev, you remember that rescue attempt for Hunter? The guy in the black ski mask?"

"That was *you*?" I ask in disbelief.

"Yep. Soon as we found out Hunter was M.I.A., Daniel flew me here to see if I could figure out what was going on and pull off some sort of rescue."

I snicker. "Some rescue. All you did was give me the leverage I needed to make Hunter talk. As soon as I threatened to come after you, he told me about the UND."

"Hold on, you threatened me?" Kaz holds a hand to his chest, acting offended. "What did I ever do to you?"

"You're annoying," I say dryly, but I can't keep a hint of a smile off of my face.

"Yeah, right. It's not my fault you're boring." Kaz grins at me before heading through one of the doors. "If you ever need any gear," he calls from the other room, "it's all in the kitchen cabinets. We renovated them. And the sink in here works, too."

He returns with two glasses of water, then sits next to Savi and hands her one of them.

I arch a brow. "No water for me?"

"*You* aren't about to pass out, and I only have two hands. "Kaz shakes his head. "Which is horribly unfair, now that I think about it. Imagine how unstoppable I'd be if I could hold four pistols at once."

Savi snorts. "That would be *terrifying*."

"I take it you're feeling a little better, then?" Kaz asks.

Savi nods, and I catch a hint of color on her cheeks. "Yeah. Thanks."

Kaz jumps to his feet and claps twice, like a teacher calling a class to attention. "Okay! Now that we're here, let me give you the tour!"

We start with the bedroom, which, in this case, is more of a *bunkroom*. The only similarity it shares with Ordinem's typical bedrooms is the size. As far as furnishings go, the bunkroom contains two sets of bunk beds with neat iron railings and matching gray bedding—enough to sleep four.

I toss my duffel bag on top of one of the lower bunks—easier for me to get up and fight in an emergency—and Savi follows suit with the bed above mine before we join Kaz in the next room; what would've been the kitchen in TJ's old apartment.

At first glance, the kitchen looks the same, if a little cleaner than TJ's old one. As soon as Kaz opens some of the cabinets and flips a switch, though, I finally understand why this is a UND safehouse.

Instead of empty, dusty shelves, the cabinets are stocked with padded shelves loaded with all the kinds of technology I've come to expect from the Undrafted. One cabinet is full of communication devices and earpieces, another full of gadgets. I spot something that looks like the signal jammer the kids in the Draft headquarters carried, along with the UND's signature darts loaded with a variety of liquids—and one that makes my face light up despite myself.

Kaz glances at me as he opens the last cabinet and smiles when he sees my awe. "Daniel had our people nearby pull some strings to get this stuff here from

Olympia. He thought it might be helpful, and all of it is compatible with your new bow. You brought the folding one, didn't you?"

I trail my fingers over the gadgets, in awe. A ranged sight—an upgraded version of one I've had my eye on for months—professional-looking versions of Savi's arrow variations, and even a sleek black quiver.

"How did you get all of this here?" I ask, barely holding myself back from taking everything to the roof and testing it. "I've been looking at tech like this forever, and I've never been able to get anything into Sector 1." To get just *one* of these would be near impossible, let alone to get all of them.

Kaz shrugs as Savi inspects what look like grapple arrows. "Daniel has friends in high places," he says. "And this is an important enough mission for him to put quite a few resources out."

Quite a few resources. Suddenly, the abundance of expensive technology in front of me seems to be sending a pointed message.

The entire UND is counting on this mission. And as the mission leader, I carry the responsibility of that. Daniel has a clear objective for us, along with the details of when and where to meet his spy, but finding our way into the Enforcer headquarters falls on us. I need to have a clear head.

I need to get my visit to TJ's apartment done as soon as possible.

"Let's get some rest," I say, glancing toward a digital clock on the wall above the door. 8:27 PM. "We'll start planning our infiltration tomorrow."

And tomorrow night, while Kaz and Savi are asleep, I'll pay a visit to the apartment.

Chapter Ten

TJ Collins

The morning after Rev, Hunter, and Savi leave, waking up to Rev's absence leaves me with a hollow feeling—and a little bit of guilt. I still haven't been able to find a way to tell her about the information Holland got out of me—about how I told Holland about Eliza. How I broke under the pressure. I know I should tell her, but I haven't been able to bring myself to sit her down and have that conversation yet.

And now, the knowledge that I lied to her about Max and Alec sits heavy on my mind. Alec specifically asked me to avoid letting Daniel know about him and Max, and after the way Rev reacted when she found out I left the compound at night, I have no idea how she'd handle the rest of the story. Besides, I don't want to worry her as she leaves for Ordinem.

She offered to go back to my family's apartment—to the place where everything started—for *me*.

That thought brings me a slight smile as I stand over my sink and splash water over my face, but it's dampened by the knowledge that Rev isn't going to be *here*. I'm going to miss her.

I wonder if she's going to miss me, or if the trip is going to give her time to think.

What's going to happen when she realizes that I'm not the person she thinks I am? That since my time in the Draft compound, my smile, my endurance, is all a front?

Maybe things will be different by the time she comes back, I tell myself. *Maybe I'll be different by the time she comes back.* Maybe, in the next two weeks, spending time training with Max and Alec can make me stronger.

I scan my wristband with the guard at the gate and set off toward the ruins in the distance. Max told me he owed me one, and now I know what I'm going to ask for. It's time for me to learn how to fight. Or at least how to take a punch.

My jog doesn't last long, with the way that the searing sunlight and pounding rhythm makes my bruised head throb, but it's good to at least know that I can. Even with my black hood pulled low over my face, I have to squint because of the brightness. By the time I reach the first ruins, my breath comes in heavy gasps, but I can't help the satisfaction that comes with having traveled so far. Two weeks ago, I could hardly stand on my own. It's progress.

I navigate through the buildings in various states of disrepair until I reach the better-faring ones near the center. Being back here in broad daylight feels odd, but it's better than leaving at night and having Daniel Bennett on my back.

When I reach the right pair of double doors, I hesitate. Do I knock? Last time Max heard me at the door, I woke up in his apartment with a minor concussion. Not an experience I'm looking to relive.

Then again, maybe if I knock instead of trying to break the door down with my shoulder, he'll recognize me before he comes out fighting.

I lift my fist and rap on the wooden door a few times, then wait. I'm almost convinced Max isn't home when a hand grabs me from behind, whirls me around, and shoves my back into the door. I yelp as the thud sends a sharp pain through my still-healing side and head. *I should've pulled down my hood.* "Max, it's me! It's—"

Max slams his elbow into my throat, cutting me off, before he processes my words. His eyes widen and he slides my hood back, revealing my face, before letting me go. "What are you *doing* here?"

Coughing, I rub my neck. "I guess that could've gone worse."

"You..." Max, wearing his all-black outfit complete with the sheathed swords at his back, steps back and gives me a once-over. "You look *terrible*."

"Wonder why," I say dryly. Rev and Kaz are starting to rub off on me.

Max winces. "Sorry. I just...didn't realize it would bruise that much."

I shrug. "I've had worse."

Max's eyes flick to my left arm, concealed by my hoodie, before he clears his throat. "Seriously, though, what are you doing here?"

"I have a favor to ask you, actually," I say, trying to ignore the way he looked toward my scars. He remembers catching a glimpse of them, then. I was hoping he wouldn't.

Max glances around the deserted alleys, then opens the door to his building and ducks inside, careful not to bump the hilts of his swords on the doorframe. "Come in. I'm sure Alec will be happy to see you."

He leads me up the stairs to the second floor, then down the hall to his and Alec's apartment, stepping over a couple holes in the floor on the way. He opens the door and gestures for me to enter before shutting it behind us. "Alec! I'm back!"

"Did you find what that noise was?" Alec calls from the kitchen area, his voice mingling with the sound of running water.

"Yeah. Come see."

The sound of water fades and Alec emerges from the kitchen. His eyes fall on me and his face brightens. "Hey! Good to see you up and walking. I was still a little worried when you left yesterday—although your face..." He grimaces. "Yikes. You want me to grab you an ice pack or something?"

"It looks worse than it is," I say.

Alec shakes his head, but lets it go. "Not that I'm not happy to see you, but what are you doing back here so soon?"

"I came to ask Max for a favor."

"And," Max says, glancing up at me sheepishly, "I owe him one."

Alec nods. "What do you need?"

"I…" I hesitate, realizing how absurd I'm about to sound. I doubt this is what Max meant when he said he *owed me one*. But I have nothing to lose, and it's worth a shot. "I wanted to ask if you'd teach me how to fight."

Max balks. "You—*what?*"

Alec looks between us, intrigued, but maintains his silence.

Max's eyes dart wildly around—first at Alec, then me, then the rest of the apartment, as if he's searching for help from the ratty cushions piled against the wall. Back to me. "I…you're asking *me?*"

"Who else am I going to ask?"

"Someone at the Undrafted! Someone who's not—who's not me!"

Alec lays a hand on his shoulder and Max snaps his mouth shut, but the look in his eyes makes me take a step back. Panic?

"It's up to you, kid," Alec says softly, "but I think this might be a good idea."

Max whirls around to face him. "Alec, I—I can't—" he stammers, but Alec grips Max's shoulders.

"Hey. Look at me." Alec waits for Max to look up and meet his eyes. "You *can.*"

"I don't want to go back to that," Max whispers.

"This is *different.*" Alec squeezes his shoulders. "*You're* different. And this is a great way to turn some things for good."

What did I say to freak him out? I wonder. All I did was ask him to teach me how to fight, something he's obviously skilled at. "Max, if you don't want to do this, it's alright. Really."

Max turns and looks up at me from under his mop of curls. He tugs on one of them, the motion stiff, before letting out a tense breath. "I'll do it," he says quietly.

"Are you sure? I could just—"

"I'm sure." He sounds like he's trying to convince himself as he echoes the words again. "I'm sure."

Alec dips his head, a proud smile crossing his face.

"So..." Max stuffs his hands in his pockets. "How is this going to work?"

"I didn't think that far," I admit.

"Well, what did you want to learn?"

"There's options?"

Max shrugs. "I know my way around swords, obviously, but you probably don't have any. We could use knives, or do something like Judo, or maybe..."

Alec must notice my dumbstruck expression, because he clears his throat and nudges Max. "I think any hand-to-hand will work, kid."

Max's face reddens. "Right. Yeah. Hand-to-hand."

"How do you *know* all of that?" I ask, incredulous.

"Doesn't matter. We can just start with basic hand-to-hand, then. Right?"

"I—yeah. Right."

"How often can you make it out here?"

Not every day—with Daniel tracking when I leave the compound, that would be suspicious. I'll have to line it up with when I typically take walks. "Every few days, maybe?"

Max inhales deeply, his eyes taking on a distant look. "Okay." He allows a slight smile to tinge his face through whatever else has fallen over him. "Okay, we're doing this."

Max leads me up the staircase to the roof, careful to avoid missing steps and rotting patches of wood as we go higher. He looks preoccupied with something—a little nervous, maybe, but more lost in his head. I wonder if it has to do with whatever freaked him out when I asked him about fighting. After a few minutes of silence, I venture a question. "Is everything okay?"

He starts and nearly trips on the next step. "What?"

"You seem…" I hesitate, searching for a word that won't come across offensive. "Preoccupied."

"I'm fine."

It's far from believable, but his tone stops me from pushing any further. The last thing I need is to give him an excuse to beat me up as a part of his combat lesson.

I blink hard when we emerge onto the roof, the sunlight nearly blinding after the darkness of the building. The lingering effects of my concussion don't help, either.

"Okay," Max says as he turns to face me. "I've never really taught anybody to fight before, but it can't be that hard, right?"

I shrug. "I wouldn't know. I don't think it needs to be anything complicated."

"We'll start simple. You know how to punch?"

"Not really," I admit.

Max holds up one of his hands, palm facing me. "Try."

I swing at him the best I can, my fist slamming into his hand with a loud *smack*, but Max doesn't budge. I step back, trying and failing to keep the awe off my face.

Max laughs softly when he sees my face. "Again. Harder. You can't hurt me, I promise."

I swing harder this time and Max nods when he catches my fist.

"Better. We can work with that." He lets go of my fist and steps back, looking me over. "You don't have a whole lot of weight to throw behind your punches, but I think you'll be able to make up for it with speed and reaction time. Any opponent will probably underestimate you, so that's an automatic advantage."

I let the idea of a retort slip from my mind—I know Max didn't mean the words as an insult. By the way he's studying me, he looks like he's deep in thought. It's the same expression Riya gets when she's analyzing something—Max is just stating things the way he sees them, and he's not wrong.

"Okay," Max starts, snapping out of his contemplation. "I know how we're going to do this. I'm going to teach you the basics, and I'm going to teach you how to think the way I do in a fight. You'll have to get in the habit of using speed as your advantage, although you're a lot taller than me, so we'll have to figure out a way for you to use your height—but I'm getting ahead of myself, aren't I?" he says at my confused look.

"Just a little."

"Right. Okay, your punch. That'll be our focus for today, alright?"

I nod. Sounds simple enough.

"Okay. Umm...let's try that one again. Same as you did before—you had a good angle—but throw your body into it a little more. And untuck your thumb—the way you have it now, that's a surefire way to end up with a broken finger."

I untuck my thumb from my other fingers. "Better?"

"Better. Now swing. Put the rest of your body into it this time, instead of just your arm."

I do as he says, focusing on throwing the rest of my weight behind the punch. Max moves faster than I can process, knocking my fist to the side. The force of my punch carries me forward and makes me stumble, losing my balance. Max gives my shoulder a slight push and I land on my hands and knees on the rough concrete roof.

Max offers me a hand. "Not bad. You had more force that time. Now you just need to learn how to stay in control."

We practice like that for what feels like hours. While he's teaching and demonstrating, focused on the specific task at hand, he seems to shift into a different person. Not the shy, sheepish kid who won't stop apologizing for knocking me out—he's more determined, more confident. The longer the lesson goes on, the more invested he seems to become. He gets increasingly excited when I master certain things, and he grows more determined every time he introduces something new.

We go until both of us are flushed red and out of breath. The next time I land sprawled on the roof, Max offers me his hand. "Let's go downstairs for a few minutes. Grab some water and take a breather."

I groan as I reach up and take his hand. "A breather sounds nice."

Max leads me to the half-crumbled stairwell and we start down toward Alec and Max's apartment on the second floor. We walk in silence at first, but the question of where he came from and how he learned everything he knows at such a young age continues to nag at me. Max's reaction when I first asked him to teach me to fight and Alec's words play back in my head, telling me not to pry, but I can't stop myself from asking the question. "Max, how did you learn to fight like that?"

Even in the dark of the stairwell, I can see his steps become stiff. "Does it matter?"

"I'm just curious. You have to admit, most fourteen-year-olds can't do what you can."

"Yeah, well, most fourteen-year-olds haven't made the mistakes I have, either," he mutters.

"We've all made mistakes," I say. If there's one thing I've learned after everything that's happened with Rev, it's that past mistakes don't define a person. "Besides, whatever happened is in the past now."

"If only," Max says under his breath.

"What do you mean?"

He shakes his head. "You're lucky I still feel bad about knocking you out, you know. I wouldn't be doing this for anybody else."

I can sense that's the end of our conversation, so I keep the silence until we reach Max and Alec's apartment. When I walk in, Alec grins broadly. "How'd the first day go?"

"It went well," I say. "I...have a lot to learn. But Max knows what he's doing."

Alec glances at him, but Max says nothing as he unbuckles the sheaths for his swords from his back. Even while we were training, he kept them on, and he looks unnatural without them.

Max finally looks up and notices the two of us staring at him. "I'll grab some waters for us," he says before retreating to the kitchen.

Alec nods toward the corner of the room where a pile of less-ratty-looking cushions sits on the ground. "It's not really a couch, but I found some cheap cushions at the market this morning. Sit down for a few minutes. You look exhausted."

He doesn't have to do any further persuading to get me to take a seat on the colorful cushions. Alec sinks down next to me, leaning his back against the wall. "Tell me, how did it really go?"

"What?"

"Max is easy to read, once you get to know him. He's in a mood. So what happened?"

"He—it went well. It did!" I protest at the look Alec gives me. "I'll admit, I was a little worried after the way things went when I asked him to teach me, but it went well."

Alec shakes his head. "Nope. Something had to have happened, or else Max would've had more to say than 'I'll grab the waters.' I'm not buying it."

"I mean, I asked him about how he learned to fight on our way back down. That might've put him in a mood."

Alec nods. "Yeah, that checks out. What did he say?"

"He didn't tell me anything. He's been pretty quiet since."

"The training went well, though?"

"It did. I've just never met anyone who can do what he can. I wish I knew more about where he came from."

"I could say the same thing about you," Alec says, leaning forward. "Why do you want to learn how to fight, anyway? And why come here to do it when you have the UND?"

I shrug, hoping it looks more nonchalant than I feel. Alec's directness sets me on edge. "I just wanted to learn how to defend myself, I guess. There's actually not a lot of people at the compound who can teach me. I don't know a lot of people, and the few I do know...well, let's just say that Max seemed like my best option."

Instead of questioning my answer, Alec only nods.

As if he understands, I think. "Alec, what's your story with the Undrafted?"

"It's nothing big," he assures me. "When Max and I came out here, I wanted to join the Undrafted, but Daniel did some...*digging* on the two of us." He speaks slower than normal, choosing his words carefully. "We both have complicated pasts with Anyssa Holland, and when Daniel found that out, he told us to stay away."

I tilt my head. "That doesn't make sense. Pretty much everybody at the UND has a past with Holland. Why would Daniel turn you away?"

Alec's eyes search mine. "Well, everyone else it matters to already knows this, so I guess it couldn't hurt to tell you. Just know that this is all far in the past, okay?"

I nod.

"Daniel turned me away because I used to *work with* Holland." Alec takes a deep breath, letting his eyes drift to a spot of peeling wallpaper opposite us. "I used to work at the Rec Center in Ordinem. I ran the archery department, although I don't use my bow too often nowadays, and that's how I met Max. Before that, though, I worked at something called the Ordinem Crime Center—it's been disbanded since, but when I worked there, I worked with

Holland, and we were...close. She climbed the ranks, made it into some government circles, and brought me with her. I still have some good connections back in Ordinem, although I doubt I'll ever use them. Once Johnson appointed Holland to run the Draft, she tried to bring me into it, and I was on board until I found out her plan to use kids. I backed out just before it was too late and decided to take the job at the Rec Center."

"So what made you move all the way out to Nadzor?"

Alec offers a sad smile. "Max's story isn't as clean as mine."

The sentence carries layers of meaning, but I know that I won't be getting any of them out of Alec. Still, I try. "Is that related to whatever Max's deal with fighting is?"

Alec sighs. "He has a past, kid. Just like you, just like me. He doesn't like being reminded of it. If you really want to know, you'll have to ask him, although don't get your hopes up for an answer anytime soon."

His words stick in my head as Max returns holding glasses of water. *Just like you, just like me.*

The three of us are more similar than I expected, and with that in mind, I want to know Max's story even more.

Chapter Eleven

Hunter Lane

I groan and roll over onto my side, reaching out and slapping my hand on my nightstand in search of my UND techpad—the same kind Daniel gave Rev and Savi to take on the Ordinem mission. The same techpad that's come on so many missions with me in the past. I squint and shield my eyes as the screen lights up. 2:48 AM.

I lie back on the bed, staring at the ceiling. It's been nearly a week since my confrontation with Daniel and my first interrogation with Adrian, but both ordeals stubbornly refuse to leave my mind. The image of Daniel tugging on the cuffs of his coat keeps resurfacing.

Daniel lied. Problem is, I have no way to know what, exactly, he lied about. My best guess is that he's not telling me the full story about his past with Holland—Adrian said they used to *work* together, but Daniel said that he was never a part of the Draft at all.

Are *either* of them telling the full truth?

And Reiko. Somewhere in the back of my mind, our first encounter still lingers. Where Adrian is exactly what I was expecting, Reiko...is less so. She's a real person, with real emotions, and her tense relationship with Adrian reminds me of my own sister. It's cruel irony, really, how similar we are—both of us lacking for family to trust. I can't even trust *Daniel*, the man who practically raised me.

If I had someone like Reiko as a younger sibling, I'd do a much better job of protecting her than my own sister did with me.

I let my head sink back into my pillow and shut my eyes, shifting to make my knees more comfortable. I have a couple hours until lights-on in the compound. Might as well try to get some rest.

It doesn't work.

I jolt up in my bed a little over an hour later, heart pounding and drenched in sweat. Something's wrong—I can't move my legs. Why can't I move my legs? Blood rushing in my ears, I scramble to get out of bed, but it feels like my legs are trapped in an unmoving vice. I land on the wooden floor with a *thud* that makes me wince. Why can't I—?

As I sit on the ground, breathing hard, full consciousness comes flooding back and my eyes catch on the wheelchair a few feet away from me.

Right.

I let my head fall back to rest on the mattress, stifling a scream of frustration, and pound my fist against the floor. Again. And again. I want nothing more than to get up, walk to the training room, and fight until my thoughts are as numb to pain as my knuckles—but that won't be happening. I have nothing to distract me. Flashes of a small, dark space, yells coming from another room, the *bang* of a gunshot, my sister's voice—

I pound the floor again, squeezing my eyes shut. I can't tell if the burning tears springing to my eyes are a result of the frustration or the pain.

My wheelchair is a few feet away—just out of reach. I grunt and scoot to my left, leaning against the bed and pausing every few inches to help move my legs. The pain is getting better, but if I move too far without adjusting, the sideways twist drives spikes of agony through my knees.

I grab the leg of my wheelchair and drag it toward me, but hesitate as I look up at it. The top comes to about my shoulders. Nora helped me learn how to transfer between my wheelchair and things like chairs and couches and beds, but I've never had to transfer from the floor before. It wouldn't be terribly hard if I could use my legs to stabilize me, or even roll to my hands and knees, but Nora strictly charged me to keep all weight off my knees until she says otherwise. She gave me a button to call her—probably for this exact reason, now that I think about it—but I keep it on my nightstand when I'm in my room. The nightstand that seems to mock me from the other end of my bed.

I sag against the side of the bed, rubbing my temples. Not even a month ago, I was on a mission in Ordinem, scheming to break into the Draft sublevels with Rev and Savi. Now I can't even get off the ground on my own.

You'll be lucky if you can climb the stairs. Nora's words play in my mind. Even if I'm able to walk again, things are never going to be the same.

A soft knock at my door pulls me out of my thoughts.

I dig both of my hands through my hair and exhale slowly. There's no good way to explain this. "Door's unlocked," I call. "Come in."

The door eases open to reveal a small figure standing in the doorway. "Hunter?"

I balk. "*Reiko?* Why—what are you doing here?"

"I was walking by and heard noises coming from in here—are you okay?"

At least I'm decent. She must've heard me hit the floor. It *was* loud. Curse these stupid braces.

"I'm fine," I say, my voice grating with the lie. Why couldn't it have been Nora to magically show up outside my door? And Reiko's fully dressed, her hair pulled back into a ponytail like she's getting ready for a session in one of the training rooms. What is she doing walking around the compound at three in the morning?

"You...sure?" Reiko stares at where I sit on the floor. I can't see her clearly, silhouetted as she is by the dim hall light, but I can imagine the expression on her face. Doubtful, with a hint of that tentativeness she always carries.

"I'm fine, Reiko. I just dropped something."

"Why are you on the floor?"

My jaw flexes. "Don't worry about it. Just go back to whatever you were doing out there, alright?"

"You don't need help? You know...getting up? With your knees?"

I draw my lips together, biting back a sharp reply. The truth is, I do need help, and it would be rude of me to wake Nora when Reiko is standing right here. I have to force the next words out. "A little help would be nice."

Reiko nods and crosses the room without another word. Together, we maneuver to keep my weight off my knee braces. Reiko lets me do most of the work on my own, as soon as I have enough leverage to use my arms to lift my body into the seat, but her strength still stuns me. She lifted most of my body weight and made it look like nothing.

I adjust my legs to align my knees—the least painful position to leave them in while sitting—and swallow one of Nora's prescription pills to ease the throbbing that all the sudden motion caused. "Thanks." My voice comes out tight as I snag a sweatshirt from the foot of my bed and throw it on over my t-shirt and sweats. Nadzor may have a warm climate, but Daniel keeps the compound freezing cold, especially at night.

"You're welcome." Reiko holds the door open. "I take it the sweatshirt means you're coming to join me?"

I nod and follow her out the door. This might be the most awkward encounter I've ever had, but rolling around the compound's empty halls is better than spending the next few hours trying fruitlessly to sleep. It's a distraction from the memories that tend to plague me in the dark. Better than nothing.

"What are you doing up this early?" I ask as she walks beside me.

"Couldn't sleep." Reiko glances at me, then returns her gaze to the hall ahead of us. "What were you doing on the floor earlier?"

"I couldn't sleep, either."

"Doesn't answer the question."

"It wasn't supposed to," I snap.

Out of the corner of my eye, Reiko's form seems to shrink. "Sorry. I didn't mean to pry."

I exhale and shut my mouth. Reiko doesn't deserve my frustrations.

We travel in silence for the next few minutes until Reiko's quiet voice breaks through. "Was it the nightmares?"

"What?" My voice comes out too loud for the deserted hallway and I wince.

In the Undrafted's night lighting—strips of dim lights running along the sides of the floors—I can see Reiko's face flush. "I've seen a lot of people have them. TJ had them every so often, back when we were staying in that apartment. He'd freak out when he woke up. I just thought—after everything, maybe..." Reiko trails off and shakes her head. "Never mind. I shouldn't have said anything. Sorry."

"It was," I admit, my voice soft. I don't know why I say the words, but they slip out.

Reiko casts me a surprised look before nodding and returning her focus to walking. "Me too."

"The Draft?"

She hesitates. "Among other things. You?"

"My sister." I'm not sure why I admit that, either.

Reiko offers a slight smile, although it's laced with pain. "You have sibling issues, too, huh?"

And it hits me. I'm opening up to Reiko because something in me recognizes the similarities between us.

Any other time, that realization would make me shut the conversation down. But for some reason, in the dim lighting and the quiet of the hall, talking feels…comfortable.

"Can I…ask you something?" Reiko says quietly.

"Go ahead."

"Don't tell anybody I'm asking about this. Please. I…I know I shouldn't care, but…" She hesitates, looking at me. "What's happening with my brother? I've been worried about him ever since we got here." The glint in her eyes begs me to say something, anything. She has no way of knowing if Adrian is alive, much less what condition he's in, and she was the one to bring him with us to the compound in the first place.

But what can I say? No specifics—nothing about where he's being kept. Can I tell her that I'm in charge of Adrian's interrogation?

Reiko shakes her head at my silence. "I'm sorry. I shouldn't have asked. I just keep imagining all these *terrible* things…but I know better. You can't tell me where he is. Of course you can't. But…" Reiko meets my gaze with wide eyes. "He *is* okay, right?"

She voices the question so quietly, so *timidly*.

My mind flashes to a memory from years ago, when I looked up at my own sister and asked a similar question. *They're going to be okay, right?*

No. I'm going to handle this much better than my sister did all those years ago.

"Adrian's fine," I tell her.

Reiko lets out a slow, relieved breath. "Is he…going to stay that way?"

Is he? That's up to me. And as much as the thought of Adrian's icy expression and cold smirk makes my blood boil, Reiko's presence dulls the anger coursing through me. I find myself nodding. "He'll be okay."

And, seeing the wide-eyed concern on Reiko's face, I discover that I mean the words.

Another idea strikes me then, as I watch Reiko. I need leverage against Adrian, and the girl next to me might be the only person Adrian has ever cared about.

"How would you like to see him sometime?" I ask.

"See him?"

"See him. Not a visit—but you could look in from the outside, to see for yourself that he's okay."

"How? There's no *way* Daniel would—"

"I'm in charge of his interrogation." No going back now.

Reiko pauses for a long moment after that. I can't predict her reaction in the silence, nor can I tell what's running through her head. Her voice is small when she next speaks. "It would be good to see him."

"Then I'll bring you with me next time I go."

She nods, but something's shifted in the way she walks. She keeps her head angled down, slightly away from me.

"Reiko?"

I wait for her to meet my eyes before continuing.

"Your brother's going to be okay. I promise."

It's as if the confirmation lifts a burden off her shoulders. "Thank you," she whispers.

The 5:00 AM lights power on, painting the halls with bright fluorescent white. I roll to a stop, prepared to turn and go back to my room to change into better clothes than sweats.

"Hunter?"

I look over at her, my hands braced on my wheels.

Reiko shifts on her feet, but continues. "Whatever your sister did...she took you for granted. I'd do anything to have a brother like you."

I blink, shocked at the boldness of that statement. A brother like me. The sincerity of her words tugs at my emotions in ways I haven't felt for years, and that one sentence is enough to bring moisture springing to my eyes—tears that aren't the result of anger or frustration.

I offer her a small smile. Anything else, and the dam holding back whatever's come over me might fail.

"You'd make a good little sister yourself."

Chapter Twelve

Reverie Adams

The day after we arrive in Ordinem passes uneventfully. Kaz and I help Savi get her monitoring station set up and Kaz gets me acquainted with the various gadgets and devices the UND has here. I spend most of the day fiddling with my bow and worrying about my plan to visit TJ's apartment tonight.

While I sit in the kitchen with the door cracked, I can hear Savi and Kaz chatting in the main room. Kaz says something that makes Savi laugh in a way I haven't heard since weeks before we left Ordinem. Since she talked to Ethan. I let out a slow breath and set my bow on the counter, propping my elbows up so I can rest my forehead in my hands. Savi and I should visit Ethan while we're here. When we left Ordinem, he was still in a coma—but maybe he's gotten better. Maybe he's up and walking, back to Enforcer training, even. Or maybe he's...

No. I can't go there. Not with the return to TJ's old apartment looming in the near future.

Late that night, once I hear Savi's even breathing above me and Kaz's snoring from the top bunk on the other side, I slip from my bunk and shoulder my empty black backpack before setting off into Sector 1.

The moonlight isn't enough for me to see in the alleys, so I take the rooftops. It feels strange to be running over Ordinem's rooftops against the night sky again, especially dressed in all black instead of my Archer outfit. Knowing where

I'm headed, I can't sort out what's forming the knot in my throat, but I can feel it there, threatening to choke me with every step that takes me closer to the place where all of this started.

Once I get close enough, I take the nearest fire escape down to the ground and enter through the building's front doors. The silence presses in around me as I climb the stairs. On every landing, a small lamp illuminates the same poster hung on the wall.

Protection. Justice. Order. The Draft. Above the words, a picture of rows of Enforcers and Silas Johnson's face rising over it all.

Every so often, I pass doors with the glow of TV lights trickling underneath. When I pause to listen, the quiet sound of news reporters reaches my ears. They talk about unrest among Ordinem citizens, the new security of the Enforcer headquarters, how the Archer and the Thief are taken care of and there's no reason to worry. Silas Johnson's voice comes on occasionally, sounding as out-of-it as ever. He could be on his deathbed, for all I can tell.

Propaganda. After the chaos I'm sure followed the Archer breaking into the Enforcer headquarters, Holland and Johnson putting up more doesn't surprise me. It may have something to do with the fact that she's taking more kids from Nadzor, too. Preparing for...something.

I wonder if any of the parents whose children were taken have spoken up—or if they, like my own outspoken parents, vanished in "mysterious accidents," leaving behind only the families who could be paid off for their silence. Unless Holland has come clean recently, the fact that the Draft revolves around children is still a closely guarded secret, and Holland coming to Nadzor for more Draft kids instead of Ordinem all but confirms that. All the innocent people here know is that the Ordinem government is planning a program to "ensure justice," something that'll be more effective than the Enforcers alone, and that they're keeping the rest under wraps. I'm sure the rumors have spread, but after what happened to families who spoke out—like mine—nobody is bold enough to put their lives on the line by coming forward.

The posters on the wall mock me every flight I climb, making me think of Eliza. Not the three-year-old on the floor of my living room anymore. A young teenager with steel in her wide brown eyes.

And walking in *this* building, thinking about Eliza, brings my mind back to the last time I was here.

I try to shake the feeling off as I kneel in front of the apartment's door with my UND lockpicks. Part of me is glad to be back in Sector 1, feeling the familiar shadows welcome me home. But there's a certain hostility to the shadows now that wasn't there before. Something's off. *I'm* off.

This time, instead of determination, staring at the door to this apartment fills me with nothing but shame.

I hesitate with my gloved hand on the doorknob and briefly wonder if the Enforcers ever cleaned up the blood. Then, I steel myself and step inside.

The apartment is exactly as I remember leaving it, minus the bodies. Even the window across the living room remains shattered, exposed to the alley outside, and torn strips of yellow caution tape flap in the breeze. The carpet, at least, is clear of glass shards, but it looks like whoever Holland sent to clean this place out was on a tight budget. The door to Maya and Oliver's bedroom hangs open, offering a glimpse of a ransacked room beyond. Holland must've sent people to search through their things and make sure no Draft information was left behind. It takes all my strength to tear my gaze from the open doorway and back to the rest of the living room.

The first thing my eyes seek out, almost of their own will, is the blood.

It looks like someone did their best to scrub the stains out, but eventually gave up. Despite my best efforts, tears spring to my eyes as I take in the bloodstain on the wall and the two patches on the floor. That night comes flashing back to me in horrifying, vivid detail—Oliver falling first, then Maya, and Riya's shock, and then TJ...the memory of the way TJ looked at me, those periwinkle eyes so grief-stricken and desperate and hurt beyond repair, is enough to set my entire body trembling. *I did this.*

The words echo in my head, my own voice shouting at me from all directions. *I—I did this.*

I. Did. This.

My legs give out and I drop to my knees, head in my hands, tears streaming down my face. I sob, but no sound comes out. I can't rip my eyes from the scene. The broken window. The bloodstains. The remnants of the worst mistake I've ever made, the mistake that spiraled out of control. So *far* out of control. The remnants of the lives I've broken.

How could TJ *possibly* forgive me after something like this? How can he look at me and see anything other than pure, burning hatred? I come up with the same answer as always—nothing. No explanation for the compassion I saw in his eyes the night I told him about Eliza, no explanation for the total lack of anger he had when I revealed my identity. No explanation for the way he threw his arms around me before I left the compound, telling me *thank you* for offering to bring him a keepsake from here—a keepsake that, by all accounts, should remind him of nothing but the destruction I've brought to his family.

Maybe he hasn't really forgiven me. Maybe he's deluding himself, or maybe he's deluding me. It would make more sense than him just...*forgiving* me, after what I did. It would provide an explanation for the constant struggle I can see going on behind his eyes.

But TJ wouldn't lie to me, not like that. *Would he?*

Kneeling on the floor of this apartment, surrounded by nothing but my past mistakes, one realization makes my throat tighten, squeezing until it's hard to even breathe. *I can't fix this.*

I never could.

The door to the apartment creaks and I snap my head up, scrambling back. Savi stands in the doorway, alone.

She takes in the scene in front of her in silence. Me, half-sprawled on my back, my hair mussed from where my fingers dug in. My flushed face and puffy eyes, the tears still making tracks down my cheeks. I'm frozen in place. I don't know if she's ever seen me cry, let alone...*this.*

"Savi?" I ask weakly. "What are you—what are you doing here?"

"I heard you leave and I thought I knew where you'd go." She steps into the room and lets the door close behind her, looking around. Her gaze finally lands on the bloodstains and her eyes widen.

I move back to my knees, my head hung and shoulders hunched. Fresh tears stream down my face, dripping off the end of my nose and staining my black leggings.

"Oh, Rev," Savi breathes, kneeling next to me and pulling me into an embrace.

I let my head rest on her shoulder, gritting my teeth with the effort it takes to hold back a fresh wave of sobs. After a long while, I sit back on my heels. "I did this," I whisper, unable to tear my watery gaze from the bloodstains. "Savi, I—I *did this.*"

"Rev, look at me." She waits until I shift to face her, away from the blood, and locks eyes with me before continuing in a gentle voice. "You're not the same person who did this."

I shake my head. "I can't fix this." My breath hitches. "I don't know why I ever thought I could. I don't know why I ever thought that TJ could forgive me."

"He *did*, remember?"

I squeeze my eyes shut. There has to be another explanation. One that makes sense.

Savi must see the hesitation on my face, because she keeps going. "TJ forgave you long before you told him who you were, and he still hasn't abandoned you. He's not going to."

"How can TJ possibly have forgiven me," I say, my voice barely audible, "when I can't even forgive myself?"

Savi pulls me back into a hug. "You have to trust him, Rev. He's forgiven you. Just like I have."

I let my head drop on to her shoulder again, trying to make the words sink in, but the reality of this room in front of me is too overwhelming. The reality of the mistakes I have no hope of making up for is too overwhelming.

As is the paralyzing fear that the horrible image of this living room still lingers underneath all of TJ's assurances.

I care about him. I care about him more than I ever thought was possible. And yet, he's the one I've hurt the most. Even if, somehow, he *has* truly forgiven me...

Is there any way for the two of us to get past this? Or is the shadow of this apartment always going to stand between us?

Is it even *possible* for TJ to look at me the way I look at him?

I cling to Savi like a lifeline, my face buried in her shoulder, until the knot in my stomach starts to unravel. The comfort of her presence eases my shaky breaths, and enough strength returns to my muscles for me to stand.

"Thank you, Savi," I say quietly as she helps me to my feet. "I don't know where I'd be without you."

She smiles, her expression tinged with compassion. "Always. Are you ready to head back?"

I so desperately want to say yes—to go back and crumple into my bunk and sleep off the emotion of this night. But I have a promise to keep.

I clear my throat. "Actually, could you...give me a few minutes? I could meet you outside?"

Savi nods. "Of course. Let me know if you need anything."

<hr>

I walk slowly down the apartment's single hallway where I first saw TJ and Riya. The first slightly-open door on my right reveals a bedroom decorated in Ordinem gray, with fluffy pillows and accents of light orange. A medical textbook lies open on the desk. Riya's room, then.

I keep walking. At the end of the hall, the other door is closed. I take a deep breath, my hand on the doorknob, before entering.

TJ's old room is laid out much the same as Riya's—a bed, blue comforter rumpled and unmade, in the corner, with a messy desk next to it and a closed closet to the right. I let my eyes drift over the room, absorbing the details. A couple of hoodies and t-shirts heaped on the floor, a sketch of constellations on his desk. I gently pick up the paper, holding it as if the slightest movement might tear it. TJ's familiar cursive scrawls over the page, labeling some of the stars and the drawings. In a different handwriting, with a colored pen, doodles and mild insults fill some of the empty space—Riya.

Propped against the desk lamp is a photograph of TJ and Riya in a thin black picture frame. TJ has his arm around her, both of them laughing. The picture must be somewhat recent, because Riya looks the same as the last time I saw her, although TJ seems younger. Maybe that's a result of what the past few months have done to him. The joy that lights TJ's face in this picture is a totally foreign sight to me—I've seen him happy, I've seen him joke with Riya, but I've never seen him with this kind of innocent joy in his eyes. I don't know if I ever will.

Looking closely at the picture, one detail catches my eye. It's hard to tell in the dark, but TJ's eyes look...different. As long as I've known him, they've had a tinge of lavender—it's one of the first things I noticed about him. But in this photo, they look pure blue. Maybe the photo is older than it looks, the colors faded, but it's still strange.

I fold TJ's sketch and slip it into the frame behind the picture, then carefully tuck the frame into my backpack.

Kaz, Savi, and I spend the bulk of the next week planning.

All of us have the same video from Daniel on our UND techpads, adding some extra detail to our mission, and we watch it together until we have it practically memorized. Daniel has a spy in the Draft sublevels, although he won't reveal her identity. She can't leave the sublevels without drawing suspicion, so our mission is to get in, get to the meeting spot—a maintenance closet a few hallways down from the entrance—and get out with a flash drive she'll give us. We're to break in the day before we leave for Nadzor, which is a little under a week from now. Early the next morning, we'll meet the helicopter where we were dropped off back in Sector 9, and we'll fly to Nadzor during the satellite dead zone that will allow us to do so unnoticed. It's a great plan, except for the fact that Daniel neglected to give us any help breaking into the sublevels.

While Kaz and I sit in the kitchen and work on drawing up a plan, Savi dives into research at her computer station. She can't do much mission-related, since she's only here to run comms and handle any technological security systems, but she says she has plenty of other Draft research to be working on. The UND's systems are better than anything Savi's had access to before, so she can dig deeper for information.

"You guys!" Savi calls from the living room. "Come here! You're going to want to see this."

Kaz jumps, nearly scrawling a line with his pencil over the blueprints laid out on the kitchen counter. I snicker at him as we enter the living room.

Savi's setup consists of one of the living room's armchairs surrounded by a tangle of cords, three monitors, and an overwhelming amount of electronics I've never seen before. Savi sits in the chair, leaning over the keyboard balanced precariously on her lap and squinting at the monitor in front of her. "Look!" she says, scrolling furiously.

Kaz leans over her shoulder for a better view and I follow suit, barely able to make out the small words on the screen. "What is it?" I ask.

Kaz's gaze darts from monitor to monitor, his eyes wide. He's probably wondering the same thing I am: how does Savi manage all this?

"It took me *forever* to get through to this," Savi says, unaware of Kaz's awe from behind her, "but I think I finally found something about Maya Collins."

I blink as the sentence sinks in. "You *what*?"

"I've been trying to find more about her ever since Holland interrogated TJ," Savi explains as she scrolls. "Since none of us have any idea why, exactly, Holland wanted him, I thought I could try to find the reason, or at least find more about what TJ's parents did for the Draft. And I finally managed to break the firewall on this *trove* of records."

I can't bring myself to ask the next question, but Kaz does. "What did you find?"

Savi leans back from the monitors and grins. "Maya Collins was Holland's lead geneticist. That's why Holland hired her. She did work in the hospital like everybody thought—but her true work was in genetic research. I'm still not sure what that has to do with everything, but it *has* to be related to why Holland wanted TJ so badly."

"Huh." Kaz crosses his arms. "Wonder if it has something to do with how Holland turned TJ's sister into a Draft agent."

"It might," Savi agrees. She opens her mouth to say something else, but Kaz sees something on her screen first.

He lets out a choked noise. "Is that—does that say *Leah Lane*?"

"I don't think I've ever heard you sound so surprised before," Savi says, twisting to look at him. "Yeah, Leah's the one who took Maya's place, after..." She hesitates, glancing at me.

Kaz is too preoccupied to notice the look. He stares at the monitor, his mouth hanging open.

I elbow him. "You want to fill the rest of us in?"

"Leah—that's Hunter's sister."

Leah Lane. Suddenly, I remember the name from the flash drive Savi gave me when I first began looking into Anyssa Holland. She was in a photo with

Holland, the same picture that Alec was in. I still wish I knew how he was involved in everything.

This explains Hunter's infatuation with stopping the Draft and his reluctance to talk about his family life. I'd be angry, too, if my sister worked for Holland.

Kaz shakes his head, slowly coming out of his shock. "We knew she worked for Holland, but we had no idea she was this involved. Especially if genetic research has anything to do with the way the Draft kids seem to be stronger than normal, and however Holland is controlling Riya...Hunter's not going to take this well. Savi, how did you *find* all of this?"

She shrugs, a smile tugging at her lips. "It wasn't too hard with the Undrafted's tech."

"It's *impressive*."

Kaz says the words with a completely serious expression, but Savi's face flushes and she turns back toward her monitors to hide it. "I, uh, actually found something else that'll probably be useful for you guys."

On her monitor, blueprints of a familiar building replace the blocks of text.

"That's a throwback," Kaz says under his breath, his grin fading. "The Draft HQ, right?"

"You've seen these before?" Savi asks. "They were *not* easy to find.'

"It was a *long* time ago." Kaz hesitates. "Hunter might've told you guys this already, but the last time he and I tried something like this, it went *very* poorly."

"Hunter did mention something about trying to break in once," I say, thinking back to when we were planning for TJ's rescue. "What happened?"

"We were trying to rescue one of the Draft kids—if it succeeded, the intel would have been invaluable. But it didn't work." Kaz sets his shoulders, putting a definitive end to the subject. "So, we have six days until the next opening for our helicopter to take us back to Nadzor. Rev and I already have a pretty solid plan for getting into the sublevels, and all we need to do is add you in, Savi. Shouldn't be too hard, since you can do everything remotely."

"Right. About that." Savi twirls a lock of hair around her finger. "I actually can't access the Enforcers' system remotely anymore."

"*What?!*" Kaz and I say at the same time.

"I think they're running everything on a closed server now. Don't worry, I can still access the system," Savi rushes to add when she sees the panicked look on Kaz's face. My expression probably isn't any better.

Kaz tilts his head, confused. "But you just said—"

"I can't access it *remotely*. I have to be on site and find a spot to plug in to their server. Then I'll have full access to everything."

"Are you saying we have to bring you *with* us?" I ask in disbelief. Savi *can't* come with us—she's untrained and the Draft sublevels are probably the worst place to learn how to survive missions like this. She'll be caught right away, or worse.

"I...yeah. Unless you want to go in blind and by yourself."

I pinch the bridge of my nose and Kaz groans. "When were you planning on telling us this?"

"Now?" Savi says with an apologetic grimace. "I didn't know I wouldn't be able to get into the Enforcers' servers until I ran a little experiment this morning."

"Okay." Kaz begins to pace the little living room. "Okay. You know what, we can make this work! It's...not *ideal*, but we'll figure it out. Bringing the techie into the field with us." He gives a nervous half-laugh. "What could *possibly* go wrong with that?"

"Kaz, she can't come *with* us!"

"She has to!" he shoots back. "We can't just walk in there blind. This is going to be dangerous enough without taking away Savi's access to alarms and cameras. It'll be completely impossible without her. And while she's in there, she can download updated blueprints and things that can help us if—when—we have to come back."

"There has to be another way." Even as I say the words, I know Kaz has a point. Without Savi, our chances of getting in, finding something useful, and getting out unscathed become even slimmer than they already are. But after what happened to Riya, the last inexperienced person who set foot in the Draft HQ, I can't bring Savi into that building. I can't risk her life like that. If Holland were to catch her...

Savi stands up. "Rev, I'll be okay."

"I can't justify bringing you in there," I say quietly.

She puts a hand on my shoulder, forcing me to meet her eyes. "It's my choice. And I want to do this." Her voice is calm, confident. *She's already thought this through*, I realize. That's probably why she waited to tell us.

I give her a slight nod and she squeezes my shoulder, then drops her hand and turns to Kaz. "You said you had a plan?"

"We do." Kaz smiles. "And I think I know the perfect way to fit you into it."

I watch in silence as Kaz uses the monitor with the blueprints to walk Savi through our plan, changing the details to include her. Kaz will go out tonight to steal the uniform and ID card of one of Holland's tech personnel, whom Savi will impersonate. She'll go in first, through the front doors of the Enforcer HQ and straight down to the sublevels, where she'll set up in the server room. Once she's connected, she'll unlock the sublevels' alley entrance—the side exit Reiko told us about during the escape, but we couldn't use because of the lockdown—and Kaz and I will sneak inside. We'll make our way down the hall to the maintenance closet Daniel specified, pick up a yellow envelope that Daniel's spy will leave there earlier that day, and get back out the way we came in. Savi will unplug, leave through the front doors, and the three of us will meet back here.

Savi nods slowly as she processes the plan. "Okay. Okay, that makes sense! And once I'm set up in the server room, I can tell anybody who comes looking that I'm there running diagnostics on their system. Chances are, nobody will be able to tell I'm not supposed to be there."

"It's a good plan," I agree, despite how much I wish Savi didn't have to come.

Kaz gives a cocky smile. "Thanks. I try." He looks out the window, where the sky has already grown dark. "Looks like it's time for me to go grab you that uniform. I'll be back in a few hours. And if I'm not, tell Hunter I'm real sorry I never brought him that chicken skewer."

Savi snorts. "Funny. And here, you'll need this." She tosses him a tiny button resembling the ones she made me and TJ a few months back. "If you're in trouble, press it to contact us."

He chuckles. "It's a simple steal. I'll be fine."

"Just in case."

Kaz pockets the button and gives Savi a look that seems to say *happy now?*

"You've got the scanner?" she asks. "To copy the ID?"

"*Yes.* Seriously, Savi, I've got it handled." He takes one of his pistols from his gun belt and twirls it as if to prove his point.

"Just be careful out there."

Kaz rolls his eyes, but once he shoulders his jacket and starts toward the door, he hesitates and looks back at Savi. "Thanks. I will. Promise."

With that, he leaves and shuts the door behind him.

I clear my throat to break the silence between me and Savi. "How would you feel about going on a walk of our own?"

"Where to?"

I take a deep breath. "To see Ethan."

Chapter Thirteen

TJ Collins

I turn on the sink in my bathroom and splash the water on my face before it has a chance to warm up. It's been a week since Rev, Savi, and Kaz left, which means I've had three training sessions with Max. My weak muscles are sore and I can feel every bruise on my body from various kicks and punches, but it's been worth it. It's a distraction from my worries about the team in Ordinem and Riya, and Alec and Max have welcomed me with open arms. I would never wish my experience with Holland on anybody, but it *is* nice to be around people who understand, to some degree or another. Max is starting to remind me of what I always imagined a little brother would be like, although he hasn't quite lost that tentativeness he carries around. Alec seems to treat him like a son, despite the fact that they're not related. Questions about them still burn in the back of my head, but I haven't been able to learn much past what I already know.

I wonder how Rev is going to react to finding out I've found a training partner. She might even know Alec, since he mentioned he used to work at the Rec Center.

The freezing water does nothing to help my racing thoughts, but at least it wakes me up a little, and it feels nice on the now-yellowish bruise spanning the right half of my face.

A sharp rap at my door jolts me out of my thoughts. "Coming!" I call, then towel off my face and pull a shirt over my head.

When I open the door, Hunter cocks an eyebrow. "What's up with your hair?"

"I just got up," I grumble.

"It's almost ten."

"It's—*what?!*" I twist around to look at the digital clock by my bed. Sure enough, the glaring red numbers spell out 9:56. I groan and run a hand through my hair. "I *never* used to sleep in this much."

"Don't beat yourself up about it," Hunter says. "You probably need the rest after the last few months. We all do. Anyway, Nora wanted me to send you to the infirmary."

"What for?"

He shrugs. "Didn't say. Probably a follow-up from that scrape you got yourself into last week."

"Makes sense. Speaking of Nora, how are you holding up?"

"I've..." Hunter pauses. "To be honest, I've been better. But I've been learning that there are plenty of other people in this compound who have it worse than I do. At least I have people to talk to."

I start to ask who he's talking about, but pause when it hits me. "You're talking about Reiko?"

Hunter nods. "I know you two aren't talking, and I know why. But she's trying."

She's trying. For some reason, those words bring forward a darkness in me. "You have no *idea* what happened in the Draft sublevels, Hunter. Because of her. I—" Despite my best efforts, my voice breaks with the images that come flooding back. When I continue, my words come out hoarse. "She sat and watched. For *weeks*. And she—they—" I cut off. *She and Holland; they manipulated me. Into giving up Eliza. Into betraying Rev's trust.* I swallow the words back.

"TJ."

I stuff my hands into my pockets.

"She made mistakes," Hunter says, slowly, as if he himself is trying to understand. "But she regrets them. I don't know if she'll ever forgive herself. You forgave Rev, after everything she did as the Archer—why not give Reiko a chance?"

"That was different," I snap.

"Was it?"

Whatever words I had next get tangled in a knot in my throat. I hold Hunter's gaze for a long while, trying to figure out how to answer—*why* Reiko feels different—but I can't come up with anything. I let out a long breath. "I don't know," I eventually answer, voice quiet. "But Hunter...after the past few months, after everything with Rev, and then the Draft headquarters...I just don't have it in me," I whisper, shaking my head. "Not right now. And I don't know when."

Hunter accepts my answer with a nod. "I get that," he says, his tone surprisingly understanding. "I won't bring it up, then. Tell Nora I said hi when you go. I'm assuming that whatever kind of bedrest she put you on last week, you haven't been following it?"

The corners of my lips twitch up. "Nope."

Hunter chuckles and wheels back from my door. "Good luck. You better hope she doesn't notice."

Unfortunately for me, the first thing Nora asks me is if I've been resting. And unfortunately for me, I'm a terrible liar.

I sit on my usual bed in the infirmary as Nora performs a routine check-up, the rest of the infirmary mildly busy as usual.

She shakes her head as she shines a light in one of my eyes, then moves it to the other. "You can't keep doing this. You know that, right?"

"Doing what?"

"Whatever keeps getting you these bruises!" Nora pokes my side and I wince in pain. She still hasn't told me why she originally called me in here, sidetracked as she is by my fresh bruises from training with Max. Nora leans back and locks eyes with me. "Serious conversation time, TJ. What have you been *doing* this past week?"

"Nothing!"

She snorts. "Sure. Because you got all these bruises out of thin air. Listen, I need to know how this stuff keeps happening! If you don't want people to know how you're spending your time, fine—I'm not going to tell anybody. But I need to know what's going on here. Tell me you didn't expect to walk in here covered in bruises and not have me question that!"

"I...kinda did."

Nora gives me a flat look as I rack my brain trying to come up with an excuse she'll accept. It hasn't been difficult hiding my training with Max from Hunter and everyone else at the compound, but they haven't seen the bruises Max's punches have left underneath my baggy sweatshirts and loose pants.

"TJ. Please. Tell me what's going on." She holds my gaze, her eyes pleading.

She's worried about me, I realize. Genuinely concerned. That, along with the fact that I won't be able to hide this from her forever, makes my decision for me. "You can't tell anyone," I say, lowering my voice. "Especially Daniel."

Nora folds her arms. "Not the words I was hoping to hear, considering I work for him, but okay. I'll keep it between us. Probably."

"Nora!"

She throws her hands in the air. "I have no idea what you're about to say! I can't promise to keep it quiet if you're plotting with someone to undermine the Undrafted or something like that!"

"I'm not," I promise. "This is personal. Mostly."

"Good. I'm all ears."

"Okay." I take a deep breath. "Remember when I told you how I ran into those guys out in the ruins last week?"

"Oh boy," she mumbles. "This'll be good."

"I've been training with them. The guy who knocked me out the first time said he owed me a favor, and I needed to learn how to defend myself, anyway."

"You couldn't have gotten training from someone at the compound?"

"Rev is in Ordinem, Hunter isn't exactly in fighting shape, and I wasn't about to ask Reiko to teach me how to fight. I figured this was as good an option as any." I leave out the fact that learning more about Max and Alec's connection with Holland was a huge part of the reason that I wanted to return. Nora doesn't need to know *everything*.

Slowly, Nora nods, and I can see the wheels turning in her head. "Okay. The bruises make more sense now. But you get yourself into the strangest situations, you know that? I've seen a lot of things during my time at the compound, but this might take the cake. Going from being accidentally attacked by a total stranger to *training* with him."

"Don't tell Daniel," I plead. "He'll *kill* me if he knows I've been meeting with people in the ruins after what happened the first time."

"You have to admit that he has good reason." Nora rolls back on her stool, reaching for her little cart. "You were pretty banged up when you stumbled in here last week. But don't worry," she adds when she sees my expression. "I won't mention this to Daniel."

The tension fades from my shoulders and I stand from the bed. Nora has finished checking all my old and new wounds. "Thank you."

She nods, the buns on her head bobbing as she rummages through her cart. "Of course. To be honest, I'm glad you've got something to do other than sit around the compound and wait. Knowing what I do, I'd assume you of all people want to be doing *something* rather than nothing."

"You know about my sister, then?" I say softly.

Nora straightens up from the cart, a folder in hand, and meets my eyes. "Between what Daniel keeps me updated on and what I've pieced together on my own from seeing you and everybody else, I know as much as you." She looks like she wants to say something else, but hesitates.

"What is it?"

"I—" Nora shakes her head. "It's probably not my place to say this, but I'm going to anyway. Answer me honestly. Is there something you know that Daniel and everybody else doesn't?"

I nearly choke as my knees buckle, dropping me back on the bed. "What do you mean?"

"You know what I mean." Nora sets the folder down on her lap and locks eyes with me. "Out of everybody in this compound, TJ, I know the most about what you went through. I've seen the scars and I've seen the after-effects. They wouldn't put you through all that for weeks for no reason."

I clench my fists until I can feel my fingernails biting into my palms. Adrian's voice rings through my head. *You know exactly what we're looking for—why you're still alive right now. What is the cure?*

"It was nothing," I say, fighting the quiver in my voice. "She was searching for *something*, but she...had the wrong guy."

I nearly convince myself of the words as they come out. *She had the wrong guy.* She *had* to have had the wrong guy. How else can I explain the fact that I know absolutely nothing about what Adrian was interrogating me for? And yet...

What did your mother tell you about her work before she died?

The question that led to the real interrogation had to do with my mother.

I can't fight the feeling that I'm missing the point entirely. That I am who Holland was looking for, that there's something I *should* know, something that could prove dangerous enough to the Draft that Holland would be willing to send her top agent to spy on me, to spend valuable time and resources on trying to torture it out of me, and to kill me when she was convinced I either didn't have what she wanted or would never give it up. The feeling that I'm ten steps behind when I should be a couple steps ahead.

The consequences of everything that happened in the Draft compound, the potential consequences of not having the crucial information that I *should* know, loom over my head, threatening to smother me.

I take a deep breath and muster up the strength to meet Nora's eyes. "You're right," I say softly. "I haven't told anybody all of it. But what I've kept to myself…" I can't fight a slight shiver as the images force their way to the front of my mind. "The parts I've kept to myself don't affect the Undrafted."

Except for the "cure" that Adrian interrogated me about. Except for whatever my mother was involved in, whatever piece of information I should know. Except for—

"Okay." Nora gives me a slight nod. "I was just curious, after I found…well, you'll see."

I furrow my brow as Nora opens the folder on her lap and traces the front page with her finger, squinting at the words. All that, just for her to drop the subject and change her attention to whatever's in that folder? But no, she used this conversation as a transition to tell me about whatever's in the folder, which means that whatever Nora found…

Whatever Nora found could be related to my mother or the Draft.

I swallow hard as her finger settles on a line of text I can't make out from here. "What is it?"

"Don't worry. It's nothing serious and nothing's wrong. I was just doing your bloodwork a couple weeks back and I had some spare time on my hands—a *lot* of spare time. When you first got to the compound, I found traces of something in your blood. I didn't know what it was at first, but it didn't take me too long to figure out it was whatever serum they injected you with back in the Draft headquarters. I'd never seen anything like it before, so I decided to run some more tests to make sure the serum didn't do any permanent damage that I'd missed. One of the tests I ran was a DNA sequence, and I found this."

Nora flips the folder on her lap so it's facing me, pointing out a table with numbers and letters on the top half of the page.

"What does it mean?" I ask. The table and data all look like nonsense to me, and Nora's finger pointing at a specific line does nothing to help my confusion.

"It's your DNA. Fifteenth chromosome, to be exact."

"What about it?"

"It's a mutation. A small one, not harmful at all. I was curious, so I did some research. You know what this particular chromosome controls?"

"No idea. Are you telling me I've had a genetic mutation and never known about it?!"

"Yes—but it's not something you would've noticed easily. Your fifteenth chromosome controls your eye color, TJ." She rummages through her cart's drawers and finds a small handheld mirror. "What color would you say your eyes are?"

"They're blue. They've always been blue."

"Look closer." Nora flips the mirror toward me.

I open my eyes wide, studying my reflection and looking past the yellowish bruises on my face. "Nora, they're *blue*."

"You can't tell me you think those look like plain blue eyes. They're almost purple!"

"They are *not* purple." I lean forward, looking closer at the color. Rev called them periwinkle once—I thought she was exaggerating, but now that I'm actually looking at my eyes in the light, I can see what she meant. Nora is right—there's a tinge of lavender to them. "Okay," I concede, "maybe they're a *little* purple—but they're still blue. It's a natural color, isn't it?"

"You didn't get out much before you met the Archer, did you?"

"Not really. But still, I think I would know if my eye color wasn't natural! If nothing else, my parents would've told me."

Nora shakes her head. "Nope. Whatever blue-purple you have going on there, it's not a natural color. It's a mutation."

"Huh." I sit back, breaking eye contact with my reflection in the mirror. "I have a genetic mutation. Of all the things you could've called me in here for. I certainly wasn't expecting that one. So...are my eyes going to fall out of my head or something like that?"

Nora chuckles, putting her mirror away. "No. It's not going to affect you at all. I just figured I should tell you, since finding a mutation like this is...odd. A mutation this specific doesn't just happen on its own, which is actually why it caught my attention."

"What are you saying here, Nora?"

"I'm not saying anything. It's just...weird. Really weird." Her eyes take on an unfocused glaze for a moment, thinking, before she shakes herself out of it. "Anyway...thank you for telling me about the training. Physically, you're doing fine—just make sure you take it easy, okay?"

"I will," I say, but my mind is still elsewhere. A genetic mutation, one that shouldn't have happened on its own. Coincidence? Or something more?

But what could've *caused* something like this? Nothing plausible comes to mind—nothing implausible, either. The idea that someone or something caused a genetic mutation to change my eye color sounds totally ridiculous to me.

And yet, after all the ridiculous things that have happened to me these past few months, after finding out that somehow, I'm in the middle of all this...

The idea sounds crazy, but a part of me still wonders. What if this isn't a coincidence? And what if the implications are much bigger than just my eye color?

Chapter Fourteen

Hunter Lane

The next time I set foot in the prison wing, a few days after Reiko saw my nightmare, I bring Reiko with me. My word alone is enough for the guard on duty to let her through, although the man's confused gaze follows me all the way down the prison hallway. Reiko walks slower than usual, lost in thought. I let her think, keeping silent as we move down the hall.

"Thank you," Reiko eventually says, even her quiet voice sounding loud in the silence. "For bringing me here."

"You're welcome." I hesitate. "I'm assuming you've guessed by now that there's another reason I brought you along. Since you know I'm in charge of your brother's interrogation."

She glances sideways at me, nervousness flashing in her eyes. "You want to use me against him. I don't blame you—I'd do the same. But I don't think Adrian cares about me as much as you think he does."

"I think you're one of the *only* things that man cares about."

At that, Reiko gives me a sharp look. "He's talked about me?"

"Enough for me to know that you're the only bargaining chip I can use against him. I'd never hurt you, but Adrian doesn't know that, and the only thing he asked me the last time I saw him was if you were safe."

Something like relief crosses Reiko's face, although I'm not sure why. What could make her relieved that Adrian has only talked to me about whether she's safe?

She could be hiding something. I watch her carefully as we approach Adrian's cell. Just because Reiko and I have become closer doesn't mean I've forgotten about her past as a Draft agent. Of course Reiko has secrets, but the relief on her face was far too obvious. What is she nervous for me to find out?"

"So," Reiko says, "I'm here as leverage, then. So you can interrogate him."

"Something along those lines."

"I..." Reiko's expression shifts so I can't pick out any one emotion. Then, she takes a deep breath. "As long as you don't hurt him, I'm...I'm alright with being a part of this. You need answers that only he has to stop the Draft, right? So I'll help."

I nod. "Thank you. And...I'm sorry for not warning you in advance. My first idea really was for you to be able to look in on Adrian."

Reiko stares at me for a moment, expression unreadable, before nodding. "What do you need me to do?"

"Stand by the window until I signal you away. I'll be done in ten minutes." I pause. Reiko might deny it, but the way she looks at that cell door makes it obvious that she wants to actually *visit* Adrian. Unfortunately, if she does, I won't be able to use her as leverage any more—Adrian will know she's safe. But maybe, if I play today's visit strategically enough, I can get what I need. "If this goes well, I might be able to get you an actual visit," I tell her.

Reiko's face lights up. "Really?"

"*Might.* I'll try."

Reiko grins and I find myself smiling back as I flash my wristband at the scanner next to Adrian's cell door. It lets out a soft beep before the lock on the door disengages. I roll inside, leaving Reiko in the hallway.

Adrian, sitting cross-legged on the floor as before, perks up at the sound of my entry. He blinks once, his eyes fixed on the open door, then shoots to his feet as he notices his sister. "Reiko!"

I shut the door behind me, cutting Adrian off. The tiny window perfectly frames Reiko's face, and she does an admirable job of playing her part as the worried sister.

Then again, maybe she's not entirely acting.

Adrian casts me a withering glare as I roll closer, making sure to stay out of the man's reach. The chain stretching from Adrian's manacled wrists and ankles to the hook in the floor rattles as he takes a few steps toward me, but he can't get close enough to do anything.

"What is my sister doing outside that door?" Adrian asks in a low voice.

"Helping me get some better answers."

Adrian clenches his fists, straining against the manacles. "Don't bring Reiko into this. She doesn't know enough to help you. If you hurt her—"

"Sit down." I meet the fire in Adrian's eyes with a stony expression of my own. When Adrian doesn't budge, I wave over my shoulder for Reiko to leave.

Adrian grits his teeth, then lowers himself back to the floor. "What do you want?"

"Simple. I want you to answer my questions honestly." I can't help the rush of excitement in my veins. I have the winning hand—now, it comes down to how I play my cards. "If you want to see your sister again, Adrian, you'll cooperate."

Adrian tilts his head, studying me. Anger still burns in his expression, but a glint of curiosity lights his eyes, as well. "If I give you answers," he finally says, "you let Reiko visit me. And you don't hurt her. That's the *only* deal I'll be willing to agree to."

"You'll tell me everything?"

Adrian hesitates, looking past me at the cell door. "I'll tell you what I can," he says, although it looks like the words pain him. "If you hurt Reiko, though—"

"I can promise Reiko's safety, as long as you give me the answers I need."

Adrian nods. "Ask, then. You may be surprised at how little help I truly am."

This feels *far* too easy. Adrian's track record makes me think he would be much more reluctant to cooperate, and he has no reason to trust me with Reiko's safety, although he doesn't have a choice. Still, Adrian conceding so quickly...was he expecting this? Prepared to make the deal, maybe?

It doesn't matter right now, but it's a detail I keep in mind as I ask my first question. "About a week and a half ago, we saw Riya Collins in Nadzor—she was controlled, somehow, and in the middle of taking a girl about her age to what we presume is a meeting point for their transport back to Ordinem. How did Holland change Riya so quickly, and why is she taking new Draft kids now?"

Adrian appears mildly impressed by the question. "Anyssa's been moving fast, then," he says, almost to himself. Then, to me, "Shortly before you broke into the sublevels to find the Collins boy, Holland's research team completed a prototype of a serum to ensure the Draft agents' *loyalty*, following a defection a little while ago. She didn't want to test it on any of her current agents—twelve to fourteen years of psychological conditioning wasn't something easily replaceable, if the serum didn't work—and while we were still figuring out what to do as far as testing goes, Riya Collins walked into our headquarters. The perfect test subject served up on a silver platter." Adrian shrugs, but the conflict is easy to read on his face. "If she hadn't showed up, Anyssa would've found someone else. Probably from Nadzor, because causing a fuss in Ordinem isn't worth the risk right now. Which leads into your second question."

He's not completely soulless, I think as I study the small shifts in his expression. A downward quirk of his lip, a flash of disdain, a slight hesitation in the rhythm of his words. Adrian, or at least a part of him, knows how *wrong* this is.

I have no idea what to do with that realization, so I focus on Adrian's words. It doesn't matter how much he understands the horror of the Draft—he's picked his side, and he's not in a rush to change.

"You already know," Adrian continues, "that up until this point, Anyssa hasn't been able to recruit new Draft agents. We don't have the capacity, or the time, to raise and condition more agents from infancy, and if we take agents any older, their loyalties are compromised to begin with, not to mention the missed years of training. Now, with the serum, Anyssa has a way to recruit agents that match the age of her current agents while having complete control over them and their loyalties. And she's recruiting from Nadzor because there's no good reason to cause riots in Ordinem right now when she can snag agents from here with no consequences."

The coldness of his words gives me a chill. "How does the serum work?"

"The prototype syncs the agent to a particular handler—in this case, Holland. It alters their emotions and experience to line up with the will of the handler. Riya, for instance, would recognize TJ, but she wouldn't experience TJ as her brother. She would experience TJ as her enemy, which is how Holland wants her to see him. The prototype that Riya has is...faulty. Missing a piece." Adrian shakes his head. "That's the information Holland wanted from the Collins boy, but he evidently didn't have a clue. I can't tell you the effects of that missing piece without seeing Riya under the serum's influence. I can tell you that Anyssa's ultimate goal with the serum is to take *complete*, direct control of the subject's mind—but she can't do that without the piece that Maya Collins kept from her."

I take a moment to let my mind process that information. It lines up perfectly with what we already know—taking what we've seen and putting explanations behind it. I have to fight to keep my shock at bay, considering how much information Adrian is willingly volunteering. "What about a way to reverse the serum?"

He gives a low laugh. "Ah, yes. Anyssa's mysterious *cure*. She's convinced Maya Collins developed it, but died with the information. Hence, TJ's time in the Draft headquarters. So the answer is no. No way to reverse the serum."

"Any other effects?"

Adrian shakes his head. "All of the Draft agents have been raised with…we'll call them *performance enhancers*. Various small implants to increase strength and agility. But those are separate from the serum."

"What if something goes wrong with the prototype? Wouldn't having a brainwashed super-soldier turn against her be a liability for Holland? Especially if she went into testing on Riya knowing that she was missing a piece?"

Adrian *hesitates*. "The prototype—and the serum, when the research teams have figured out how to complete it—has a sort of…kill switch built in. Holland has control over it, and as far as I know, it's only for emergencies."

Kill switch. Those words sicken me. "So, what? Holland can flip a switch and reverse the serum?"

"Don't be dense, boy. I already told you there's no way to reverse the effects. Anyssa can press a button and terminate all of the injected agents within a very close range."

Despite myself, my eyes widen. "*What?*"

"It's called a kill switch for a reason." Adrian's gaze drifts to his shackled hands in his lap. "I don't like it either, to be completely honest with you."

I don't like it either. Is that…regret? It can't be. From Reiko, I can accept it. From Adrian…no. The cold man in front of me is a different story.

"What about Holland's endgame?" I ask instead. "What's she ultimately planning to use the Draft for?"

"Now *that* is a much more complicated question." Adrian sets his shoulders, shaking off whatever emotion had come over him. "Anyssa's ultimate goal, as far as I can guess, is to get more agents, now that we have the capacity, and then integrate them into society as the government's eyes and ears everywhere. To use them as spies that nobody would suspect. And *assassins* that nobody would suspect. But…" Adrian pauses, as if unsure whether to continue.

"Say it."

"I don't know for certain," he starts, carefully, "but I don't think she's working totally alone. I think there are bigger forces at play here than either of us knows."

That is much more information than I expected to get. As Adrian talks, it almost seems like he *wants* to tell me all of this.

Or maybe I'm reading too far into things.

"What do you mean by *bigger forces*?" I ask.

Adrian shifts, his chains scraping against the concrete floor. "The Draft didn't start with Anyssa Holland. And I don't think Anyssa is the only one in charge now, either. She truly hasn't told me much about her life before the Draft, or how she got started, but I know that before she did, she worked as a detective. Crime in Ordinem was much worse fifteen years ago, and Anyssa's husband was killed by a common criminal. Johnson recruited her right after that, telling her that the position was *recently vacated*. She looks at the Draft as an opportunity to ensure order in Ordinem." Adrian presses his lips into a line and I study his expression as he pauses for a breath. He's reluctant, but it's not the reluctance of a man holding back information for secrecy's sake. It's the reluctance of a man giving up his only leverage.

For a horrifying moment, I *sympathize* with him. He's trying to stay alive, and his only guarantee of that is the information the Undrafted needs. The information that he's now given up.

Adrian just gave up all guarantees of his survival to save his sister.

The man looks up at me with a level gaze, but I can see easily through. I could kill him right now, and Adrian knows it.

"My sister?" he says, his eyes narrowed.

"I promised you a visit." I shake my head. "But not today."

His expression hardens and his hands clench into fists. "I know she wants to see me. She'll pretend otherwise, but she *does* care about me, you know."

"I don't think you know her as well as you assume, Adrian."

Mistake. I see it as soon as the corners of Adrian's lips quirk down. I said too much, or revealed it in my tone.

Adrian raises a brow. "Well. You've been using Reiko to bargain with me, but I never had a reason to fear for her safety, did I?"

"I don't know what kind of a brother you think you've been to her," I growl, "but she deserves much better than you."

Adrian stands up, stepping as close to me as the chains allow and towering over me. It takes all I have not to flinch back.

"Whatever Reiko tells you," Adrian says in a low voice, "I've *always* protected her. I had plenty of chances to get out from under Holland's thumb, but I chose to stay. Maybe she does deserve better than me, but I'm what she has, and—"

Adrian cuts himself off with a sharp breath and starts again, biting off the words like a threat. "If you let her get hurt, I won't stop until I tear you limb from limb, boy. We both know I'm not in a position to bargain for myself, but whatever you do with me after this, you *protect* her."

My mind spins. *I had plenty of chances to get out from under Holland's thumb.* What does *that* mean? And *maybe she does deserve better than me.* The latter part—Adrian feels guilty, at least to some level. But *why* would he stay with Holland?

For Reiko. *I've always protected her*, Adrian said. He stayed with the Draft for *Reiko.*

So then is he truly loyal to Holland?

"What do you mean, chances to get out from under Holland's thumb?" I ask slowly.

Adrian's expression darkens, but he closes his mouth.

"You weren't completely on board with the Draft," I press. Is it possible? After the way he talked about the kill switch, and how much information he gave me...

"Stop."

"But between your sister and Holland's power, you couldn't—"

"Stop!" Adrian snaps, his eyes darting toward the window.

I fight to keep Adrian from seeing my shock. Even *he* wasn't fully in support of Holland. "Why'd you keep helping Holland, then?" I ask in a low voice. "How did you get involved?"

"*Those* are questions I'm not going to answer," Adrian bites off, shooting to his feet.

I drift a little closer. "You had doubts," I say, still wrapping my mind around the idea.

I'm so preoccupied, I misjudge how far Adrian's chains reach.

Adrian snatches the front of my shirt and jerks me forward. He doesn't lift me out of the chair, but he leans down and pulls my face close to his own—an awkward enough angle to spark a dull ache in my knees.

"Stop. Asking. Questions," Adrian growls, so close I can feel his breath.

I meet his glare. "Why won't you just admit that you didn't agree with the Draft?"

For a moment, it looks like Adrian is about to throw a punch at me. I brace myself, but the man just drops me and steps back. "If you don't have any more real questions for me, now would be a good time for you to leave."

This time, I can't keep the bewilderment off my face. Adrian just...let me go. I cover my shock quickly, but it still shows. For some reason, though, Adrian doesn't comment.

Slowly, I roll back. Neither of us take our eyes off the other, but something has obviously shifted between us. Adrian realizing I never planned on hurting his sister, me learning that Adrian has doubts about the Draft—there's an understanding between us, however tense, that didn't exist before today.

Finally, I turn my chair and reach for the door.

"Hunter."

I freeze with my hand raised. Did Adrian just use my *name*? I look over my shoulder to see Adrian drilling me with an almost urgent expression.

"You protect my sister," he says in a low voice. "We both know the position I'm in. But whatever you do to me, we both care about her. If I'm right about the Draft being bigger than just Anyssa Holland...things are going to get *much* more dangerous for everyone before this is all over."

I hesitate, then nod.

"Good." Adrian settles back down to the floor, although his posture remains stiff. Probably anticipating any number of fates, now that he has nothing useful to the UND.

"I'm not going to force Reiko to visit you," I say, my voice quiet in the dark cell, "but I'll tell her you're expecting her whenever she's ready."

Adrian's head snaps up at my words, his eyes locking with mine. He picks up on my implication. Reiko can't visit him if he's dead. I don't plan on bringing any more harm to Reiko's brother than necessary.

I give him a slight nod to confirm what I said and, after a beat, Adrian returns the gesture.

With that, I scan my wristband at the door and let myself out of the cell. I never thought I'd have a tentative understanding with *Adrian*, of all people.

But if Adrian has doubts about Holland and the Draft, why wouldn't he just give all of this information to the Undrafted at the first chance he got? Why tell me now, rather than telling Daniel weeks ago?

Reiko answers that question, too, I realize. If protecting her is his top priority, he would've wanted to keep his cards close to his chest. He didn't know where Daniel stood with Reiko or if Reiko was in any kind of danger with the Undrafted. He wouldn't want to reveal anything that could accidentally hurt her. If Daniel's interrogation team had been given more time before I took over, they would've figured out to use Reiko as leverage eventually, but I have something better now.

I have Adrian's tentative trust, and the knowledge that deep down, at least part of Adrian is on our side.

Chapter Fifteen

Reverie Adams

While Kaz is out getting a copy of the ID card, Savi and I trek across the rooftops, much safer and quicker than weaving through the dark alleyways between buildings. By the time we get to Sector 1's hospital, the sun has set completely.

"Are you ready to do this?" I ask her as we stand outside the building.

"I've been wanting to see him ever since we left for Nadzor," Savi says. Her expression softens. "Are *you* ready to do this?"

All I can do is nod. Other than Max and Alec, who I doubt I'll ever see again, Ethan is the last unfinished tie I have to my life as the Archer, to all the horrible mistakes I'm still trying to atone for.

I'm far from ready to face this—but I have to. I missed my chance to apologize to Ethan once. I'm not going to pass it up this time, not when it might be the last chance I have.

That thought makes me hesitate. I can imagine TJ or Savi telling me not to think that way, but between Ethan being in a coma and the risk that taking down Holland is going to entail...there's no guarantee that either of us is going to survive the coming weeks.

We head inside and Savi opens her mouth to check in with the receptionist, but I speak before she can. "We're here to visit a patient. Ethan Anderson?"

The receptionist squints at us from behind wire-framed glasses. She's not the same receptionist we saw directly after Ethan was admitted, but she has the same expression: stoic. Unreadable. She probably has to be, considering the kind of information she has to deliver to people.

"Your name?" the receptionist asks.

"Millie Grant." I haven't used the name since the last time I made a payment on my apartment, nearly two months ago now, but the person I hired to forge my ID did a good enough job to where I've never had a problem. Nothing should have changed since then. Savi gives me a puzzled look, but I ignore her. She can't give her real name—her family is probably looking for her, and Holland is doubtlessly on the lookout as well—and I've had to use my fake name as long as I've been on my own.

The receptionist's fingers fly over her keyboard for a few moments before she meets my eyes. Next to me, Savi tenses. *Bad news*. This is going to be bad news.

I grab Savi's hand and give it a reassuring squeeze.

"I'm sorry to have to tell you this," the receptionist says, "but Ethan Anderson succumbed to his injuries a couple of weeks ago."

Silence.

"No," Savi whispers. "No. No, he's not—he's not gone. He can't be gone."

The noise in my head fades completely save for that single word. *No*. No. Not before we had a chance to talk. Not before I could apologize, fix things, explain. *No*.

I put my arm around her shoulders as she begins to tremble, although I'm shaking as much as she is. *Gone*. Ethan...is gone. I blink back tears as I walk Savi out of the hospital and we start toward our apartment. Thankfully, the walk is short, or else I think we both would've broken down on a random rooftop somewhere. Savi looks like she's in shock, silent tears running down her face.

Gone.

I'm sorry. Ethan will never hear my apology, but I say the words inside my head anyway. I'm sorry I didn't tell you everything sooner. I'm sorry that I couldn't fix this, and that I pushed you away before we could try.

I'm sorry I blamed TJ for this. I haven't forgotten that it was my anger about Ethan's coma that drove TJ to turn himself in, and I certainly haven't forgiven myself for it. I doubt I ever will.

And neither will he, that persistent voice in the back of my head tells me. Despite the way he reacted when I finally told him my identity, I'm starting to believe that underlying suspicion I've had since we got to the UND compound. The fear squeezes my heart, making it hard to breathe as Savi and I stumble into our apartment.

As soon as the door is closed, I pull her into a hug. She collapses into my arms, sobs wracking her body, and we both sink to our knees.

He can't be gone.

I'll never be able to fix things. *I'll never be able to fix things.*

The tears leak from my own eyes at the thought as Savi and I cling to each other. We sit like that, grieving, for a stretch of time that I don't have the presence of mind to keep track of.

Eventually, Savi breaks away and sits back against the living room wall, her eyes puffy and red—I probably look just as terrible. I sit next to Savi and she pulls her knees to her chest, her forehead dropping to rest atop them. "I thought—I thought he was—getting better," she says, her voice barely a whisper.

"Me, too," I say quietly.

Savi crosses her arms over her knees and rests her chin on them, staring blankly at the couch across the room. "The last time I saw him..." She bites her trembling lower lip. "I remember it. I visited, right before we found TJ. If I'd known...how can that have been the last time?"

I shut my eyes, battling another wave of emotion, but I can't stop the barrage of thoughts. I should've apologized. I should've said something, instead of avoiding things like a coward.

Now I'll never truly have a chance to fix things.

On the other side of me, the apartment door swings open. I tense, reaching for my bow clipped to my waist, but it's only Kaz. He steps in with a grin, holding up his new fake ID card, but freezes with his mouth half-open as his eyes land on us.

Savi buries her face in her arms.

I nod for Kaz to come in and he shuts the door before tentatively coming closer. "I—I can go, if—"

"It's alright," I tell him. Maybe Kaz can say something to help Savi. Maybe I'm hoping that whatever he says can ease the emotional turmoil in me, too.

Kaz glances at me before sitting beside Savi. He reaches for her shoulder, but hesitates and pulls his arm back. "Savi, I don't know what's going on, but...how can I help? What do you need?"

She gives a stiff shake of her head, face still hidden in her arms. I can tell from the tension in her shoulders that she's barely holding herself together.

Kaz looks helplessly at me. He has no clue what he just walked in on. His eyes flit to the door leading to the bunkroom, then back to Savi, as if he's deciding between staying or leaving the two of us alone. Then, he shifts a little closer to Savi and settles his hand on her hunched back.

"You don't have to stay here for me," Savi says, her shaky voice muffled by her arms.

"I know." He puts his arm around her shoulders. "You don't have to be strong all the time, Savi. Whatever's going on, I'm here for you."

Kaz's simple gesture seems to be the final straw for her. She curls into Kaz, shaking, and then she begins sobbing.

I've known Savi for years, but I've never seen her cry like this. I've grieved enough times that I know how to numb the emotional pain, at least for now—but Savi is a different story. I don't think I've ever seen her grieve, not like this. It's like everything she's held inside for the past few months, since she found out I was the Archer—leaving her family behind, moving to the Undrafted compound, and now losing Ethan—is bursting out all at once.

Kaz's eyes widen as Savi leans into him, shock crossing his face. Then he pulls her closer, her trembling shoulders tucked under his arm. "I'm here," he says softly, rubbing her opposite arm. "I'm here."

Despite the pain, despite my own hopelessness threatening to overflow, I manage a slight smile. Kaz still looks shocked, although his concern for Savi in the moment overshadows that. He's helping—and as much as I hate to admit it, he's helping more than I can right now.

As Savi's sobs fade and her breathing evens out, she finally raises her head. She looks at Kaz, at his arm around her shoulder, and her face flushes as she pulls away from him. "Sorry. I—sorry. I wasn't trying to—that was..." She wraps her arms around her knees, dropping her head to rest on them. "Sorry."

"Don't be." Kaz's concerned gaze lingers on her for a few beats before he looks at me. "What...what happened?"

"Ethan," I say, my voice coming out as barely a whisper.

Daniel, or Hunter, must've filled Kaz in on Ethan's situation, because it's all the explanation he needs. "He's...?"

I give him a small nod and put my arm around Savi's shoulders.

"I'm so sorry. Both of you."

Savi lets out a long, trembling breath. "I shouldn't have gotten my hopes up," she says quietly.

The silence her statement leaves in its wake settles like a weight over us. *I shouldn't have gotten my hopes up.* Savi's words resonate somewhere deep inside me and I turn my head to the side, hiding the sudden moisture in my eyes.

"Oh, Savi," Kaz whispers.

"Am I really wrong?" She slumps back against the wall, looking more exhausted than I've ever seen her. "I'm starting to think it might be easier to just...stop hoping."

"No," Kaz says, soft but firm. "Hope isn't easy. I know that. And I..." He takes a breath, seeming to steel himself. "I know that pain you're feeling. When you spend so long keeping your head up, *fighting* to keep from giving in to despair, holding on to the hope that things will work out, and then they just...fall apart completely." His voice catches on the last phrase.

"You're speaking from experience," I say, trying to keep him talking. After spending so many years training myself not to feel, not to care, I have no idea how to console Savi. Kaz, on the other hand, seems to know exactly what to do.

Kaz nods, his eyes taking on a far-off look. "It's not easy," he repeats, his voice lowering. "But hope is all we have to hold on to. If we don't have hope, why are we doing any of this? What do we have to live for?"

"And what happens if it's all for nothing?" Savi presses her lips into a line, her chin trembling, fear tainting her green eyes. "What then?"

"It's *never* all for nothing. Nobody said any of this was going to be easy. And..." he swallows hard. "There's no preparing for how hard it truly is. But the Undrafted wouldn't exist if it wasn't for people having hope. And it's better to fight with hope—to *hurt* with hope—than to let go and give in."

"How, Kaz?" she breathes. "How do you do it?"

I lean in slightly toward where the two of them sit shoulder-to-shoulder. This is an answer something within me is desperate to hear.

He inhales deeply. "It's a battle," he finally answers. "Every day. It's a battle I sometimes lose. But I have people all around me who remind me of what we're fighting for—of the kids whose entire lives were stolen by Anyssa Holland. Who remind me of the fact that when everything is finally finished and we see those kids reunited with their families, all that pain will have been worth it. And if I lose hope, then all the sacrifice is for nothing."

Savi closes her eyes, seeming to deflate with the breath she lets out.

Kaz searches her face, some of her pain reflected in his own expression now. "If he were here," Kaz says softly, "I think he would tell you to keep fighting."

Savi nods and the tension slowly drains from her shoulders. Her breathing evens out and she slumps deeper against the wall, her eyes still closed. The pain on her face fades into peace. The exhaustion must've gotten the better of her.

"I'll take care of all the report stuff," Kaz whispers so he doesn't wake Savi. "Daniel and I have been talking—Hunter got some important information out of Adrian, but nothing you and Savi need to worry about tonight. I'll tell him about this so you and Savi don't have to rehash it, if you're okay with that."

I nod. "Thanks, Kaz. And...thank you for being here. What you said...it really helped. For both of us."

"Let me know if there's anything either of you need."

As the three of us sit there, against the wall, thinking, Kaz's words play back through my head. *It's a battle.* He's right. Savi, me, TJ—we're all fighting for the same thing. We're fighting to find hope.

And Ethan would want us to keep fighting.

Chapter Sixteen

TJ Collins

A few days after my chat with Nora, as I make my way to Max and Alec's apartment for our sixth training session, there isn't much I can do to hide the dark circles under my eyes.

My periwinkle eyes.

Even days later, I haven't been able to stop my mind from spinning in circles. The mutation I have isn't natural, so how did it get there? Someone must've *done* something to me. But going through such effort to change my genes, just for my eye color? Why would anybody do that? And why would my mother have allowed it?

Unless she was a part of it. I wouldn't be particularly surprised, after finding out she was involved in the Draft all my life. But I can't make myself believe it. It would be so...so *wrong*. My mother may have been in deep with the Draft, but believing that she experimented with the genetics of her own son? I can't. I *can't.*

But the worry remains stubbornly lodged in my mind as I approach the ruins. She did give me vaccinations a few months before she died—at least, she called them vaccinations. She never gave Riya the shots. I don't know what to believe any more.

What if? What if my mother *did* alter my genes?

When I reach the apartment, Alec greets me at the door and tells me Max is out on an errand, but he'll be back for our training session soon enough. In the meantime, the two of us can talk. We sit on the cushions against the living room wall, facing each other. This is the first time we've had an opportunity to sit down and talk, just the two of us, since I started training.

"Seems like training's been going well," Alec says, smiling. "Having you here has been great for Max, you know. He's been happier since you've been around."

"Training has been great for me, too," I tell him. I hesitate, then add, "In more ways than one."

"I'm glad." Alec leans back against the wall, facing the opposite side of the room. "Max hasn't been able to pry your backstory out of you yet, as far as I know."

"He hasn't."

Alec shakes his head disapprovingly, although there's no resentment in his expression. "I was really hoping he'd be able to by now. I really am curious about you, kid. You already know all of the important parts about me, but I know next to nothing about you other than that you came from Ordinem and you have had some pretty bad experiences with Holland."

"Is this you asking me to tell you the story?"

"If you're willing, I really would like to hear it." Alec pulls up one knee and rests his arm across it as he meets my eyes. "You've only known me for a week and a half, so I'd understand if you don't want to. But I know how nice it can be to have someone listen."

I run a hand through my hair, sitting back against the wall next to Alec. He's not wrong. It would be nice to have someone listen without asking questions. To be able to talk freely without worrying about the pity in Rev's eyes or the prying questions about my time in the Draft sublevels.

I also *want* to talk to Alec. So, I let the words go. "I had a...a *run-in* with the Archer a few months back. That's when I found out about the Draft, and how I ended up on my own. I was just trying to keep myself and my sister alive, and long story short, we weren't registered in Ordinem, so we couldn't get any rations. So I—well, you lived in Sector 1, right? Remember that thief who stole from rations warehouses?"

"That was *you*?" A bemused smile plays across Alec's face, but after a moment, the implications dawn on him and his expression turns serious. "That was you. The thief Holland caught."

"Yeah," I say softly. "But she...interrogated me first." I don't give the details and Alec doesn't press.

"How did you get out?" he asks. "I left Ordinem with Max soon after you were first caught."

"The Archer saved me." A slight smile twitches my lips, although Alec frowns at the words.

He watches me with a strange expression, shifting to face me fully again.

"What?" I ask, fidgeting under the scrutiny.

"Nothing. I'm just...curious about something. You, as the Thief, knew the Archer?"

I hesitate, but nod.

"And you had a day life, too, I'm assuming?"

"I did. Why?"

"Did you know someone named Rev? Reverie Adams?"

Despite my efforts, my muscles seize and I go stiff. *Rev.* Does Alec know? *How?*

Alec's eyes go wide and he freezes—this might be the first time I've seen the man truly surprised.

"Why?" I ask, trying and failing miserably to keep a straight face. "Did you know her or something?"

"She was the Archer, wasn't she?" he asks, suddenly quiet.

"I—"

"She *was*!" Alec drags a hand down his face. "Everything makes so much more sense now. I can't *believe* I didn't put it together earlier. At least now I know why she left so abruptly, and why she was so interested in—"

He cuts himself off, seeming to remember my presence. *This was a mistake*, I think, my heart racing. Now Alec knows about Rev, which means that Max will soon. Rev is going to *kill* me when she finds out I accidentally gave her identity to two strangers.

My mind is whirling so fast that I hardly notice when Alec puts his hand on my shoulder. "It's alright," he says when he sees the panicked look on my face. "I had my suspicions already. Rev was the best archer I'd ever met at the Rec Center, and I figured there weren't too many people in Sector 1 who could shoot like the Archer. I really already knew—all you did was confirm what I was already thinking." Alec chuckles softly. "You know, Max has always wanted to meet the Archer. He's figured out that her mission is to fight against the Draft. Imagine how surprised he'll be to find out—"

"Don't tell him," I say, desperation edging my voice.

"Why not?"

"She'll kill me. Not literally," I add when his look shifts to concern. "But I think she'd rather tell Max herself, especially if they used to know each other."

Alec pauses, then nods. "How is she?" he asks softly. "There seemed to be…a lot going on when she left."

"There was," I say. "but she's okay. I'd say this is the best she's been in a long time. She's always had something to be fighting for, but now she has people who are fighting with her."

"Good." Alec exhales, appearing to deflate slightly. "Ever since I started thinking she was the Archer, I've been worried about her. She always carries so much on her shoulders. Don't let it crush her, alright?"

"I'll do my best," I say, although deep down I know that my best probably isn't enough. Rev is the strong one between the two of us.

The front door to the apartment opens and Max enters, ending our conversation.

Today, it seems I'm not the only one who's distracted. As we spar, Max doesn't fight as hard as he normally does and I actually manage to pin him to the concrete, my knee digging into his back where his sword sheaths usually rest. Right now, they're lying on the ground a few feet behind him.

"Nice," Max grunts.

I let him go and he rolls over onto his back. "You seem distracted," I say, offering him a hand.

He takes it and lets me help him to his feet. "What makes you say that?"

"I'd never be able to pin you on a normal day. And don't try to deny it," I add when he opens his mouth to protest. "We both know I'm right."

"You seem pretty distracted, too. Those dark circles are more obvious than usual."

"Don't change the subject," I say, fighting the flashbacks to my latest nightmare. More than theories about that genetic mutation kept me awake. The longer I stay at the UND, the less frequent the bad nights become, but they still happen. I keep my mind focused on the present in an attempt to distract myself from dwelling on the memories. "What's going on with you today?"

"Nothing. I'm just a little tired, that's all."

"You're a terrible liar."

Max glares at me.

I shrug. "What? It's true."

Max shakes his head. "Fine. You're right, something's up. But you don't need to worry about it."

"If you, of all people, are worried, I should *definitely* be worried. Does it have to do with Holland?"

The way Max tenses and checks over his shoulder makes me even more certain. I take his hint and lower my voice. "Max, if it involves Holland, you have to tell me what's going on."

"I don't, actually. Trust me, however you're connected with Holland, this is over your head. This...it's more personal. That's all you need to know."

That sounds almost exactly like what I told Nora when she asked me about Max for the first time. I wasn't entirely lying, and I can tell there's an element of truth in Max's words now. Whatever's going on with him and Holland, it *is* personal. "You're not the only one with something personal against Holland, you know. Whatever's happening, I want to know. And I probably want to be a part of it."

"TJ, Holland wrecked my entire life." Max turns away from me and crouches, grabbing his sword sheath off the ground. I get the feeling that picking up his swords isn't the only reason he turns away. "If it wasn't for her, I'd be living a happy, normal life right now. Maybe I'd have siblings. I'd definitely have parents, and a home. At the very least, I'd have a *chance* at being happy." His tone takes on a dark quality that, coming from such a young face, sends a shiver rippling across my body. "But Holland took that away from me. Just like she's broken so many other families."

As he finishes buckling his sheath around his body and straightens up, I wonder what Holland did to him. Maybe he has a similar story to Rev—maybe Holland took someone close to him, or was responsible for the death of his family. When he turns to face me, I catch a glimpse of something familiar in his eyes—the same thing I see every time I look in the mirror. It's in this moment, with that look, that I'm absolutely certain of what I already suspected.

Max is hurting, too.

Before I can change my mind, I slide up the left sleeve of my sweatshirt to my elbow.

I can't bring myself to look at the mottled skin underneath, so I watch Max's reaction instead of looking at the scars. The constant reminders of just how broken I truly am.

Max's gaze travels up my arm, from where my wrist was torn up by my thrashing against the clamps to where Adrian's needles pierced again and again. Finally, his eyes widen and flick between my face and the scars.

"You saw these," I begin softly, "when we first met. A glimpse of them, anyways." I tug the sleeve back down, covering the patchy and pale skin.

Max's focus lingers on my covered arm before returning to my face, his expression brimming with questions. "Holland—this was her? But—how? When?"

"You're not the only one who has something personal against Holland," I repeat. My voice is low this time and I can feel the blackness creeping in on the edges of my vision. The same blackness that nearly led me to pull the trigger on Adrian back in the Draft sublevels.

Max stares at my arm in silence.

I roll my shoulders back and stuff my hands into my pockets, suddenly self-conscious. Other than Nora, Max is the only one who's truly seen what's under my sleeve. Rev—and possibly Hunter—saw the wounds on the helicopter ride from Ordinem, but that was different. That wasn't *voluntary*.

"She broke you, too," Max finally whispers, his eyes wide.

I hesitate, then offer him a slight nod. Something between the two of us seems to click: a mutual understanding.

Something about Max is so disarming—I've told him more in the couple weeks that I've known him than I've told Nora in over a month. And for some reason, I don't find myself regretting the choice. Maybe it's because this is something we share.

Max *actually* understands. And from his expression, I can tell he's thinking the same about me.

He tugs on one of his curls, studying me from under his tangled hair. He opens his mouth and closes it a few times, as if struggling to get his words out. Then, finally, he manages. "TJ, I—we need to talk."

"We're talking right now," I say, in hopes to lighten what's come over him.

It only seems to agitate him more. He chews his lower lip and shifts on his feet, looking more scared than anything else.

"Max? What's wrong?"

He meets my eyes. I don't know if I've ever seen him nervous like this. "I—"

A scream pierces the air from the alley below.

Max snaps to attention, drawing one of his swords in the blink of an eye, conversation forgotten. It's like somebody flipped a switch in his head. He rushes to the edge of the roof, peeks his head over, and pulls back. "Go get Alec!" he barks at me.

"What's going—"

"*Go!* Tell him to head north from the doors!"

"Max, what are you going to—"

Before I can finish my question, Max sheaths his sword and leaps off the side of the building.

Chapter Seventeen

Hunter Lane

A few days after my conversation with Adrian, I find Reiko sitting outside on an eastward-facing bench along the wall of the compound's tech wing. Through the chain-link fence, I can see the sun just barely cresting the dusty horizon, and to my left, I can make out the colorful tents surrounding the market square and the edges of the ruins rising next to them. The people will be in town for another six to eight weeks before moving elsewhere, and then the tents will slowly dwindle until the next horde of vendors arrives.

I wheel forward along the concrete path, putting myself next to Reiko. "Watching the sunrise?"

She starts, but relaxes when she sees me. "Yeah. It's nice, watching what's going on outside. It's so...*different* from Ordinem. I like to try to see the market sometimes, even though I know there's no way I can see anything from this far away."

"The market is probably my favorite thing about Nadzor," I tell her, nodding over my shoulder to where I know the tents are set up. "Kaz and I go, sometimes. The guards at the gate don't care, so long as you have your wristband with you to scan when you come back."

Kaz. I wonder how the Ordinem mission is going. The team is supposed to return tomorrow morning, and after how long they've been gone, I'm starting to miss Kaz's energy.

"You've *been*?" Reiko asks, her face lighting up. "What's it like?"

I smile. "Chaotic. It's worth it for the skewers, though, when the vendor's in town. Kaz owes me one off a bet, actually."

Reiko twists to look in the direction of the market. Past the compound, the very edge of the collection of colorful tents is visible in the distance.

"You want to go?" I ask.

"What?"

"Do you want to go?"

"Really? We can?"

"Why not? You don't have a wristband, but I do, and the entire security team knows me. I can get you out and back in."

A grin spreads across her face. "I'd love to."

A little under an hour later, Reiko and I weave our way through colorful tents bustling with people. My wheelchair is meant for the smooth tile floors of the compound, not the heaps of dust obscuring the ground underfoot, but Reiko doesn't complain as she pushes my chair. I remember what Adrian told me before, about the Draft kids' performance enhancers. Is this why Reiko always seems to have more endurance, more strength, than someone of her build should?

The clustered tents open up into the expansive market square, an area easily the size of the UND compound's main building, with a cobbled stone floor and wooden carts set up as stands. People yell and barter, small coins and other miscellaneous items change hands, and the smell of various sizzling meats and spices mingles with the odor of packed-together bodies and sweat.

Reiko's pace slows as she looks around with wide eyes. "Woah," she breathes.

I smile. "Just wait until you taste the food. Last time I checked, the cart with the skewers is in the back."

The crowd jostles us as Reiko navigates us through, and a knee collides with my wheelchair more than once in the packed space. When the cart comes into view, Reiko stops.

"Reiko? What happened?" I twist to look at her over my shoulder as the crowd continues to flow around us.

Her eyes are wide, fixed on something to our left, toward the ruins. It takes me a minute to follow her gaze and find what she's looking at.

Three young teenagers, around Reiko's age—one girl and two boys.

"I know them," she whispers, her voice barely audible over the ruckus of the market square. "I—I know two of them."

"Draft kids," I realize.

Reiko nods, never taking her eyes from the trio. "But I don't know the third."

I squint, trying to make out the details. One of the boys has a firm grip on the other's arm, and the other looks...scared. Terrified. I remember what we discovered right before Kaz, Rev, and Savi left for Ordinem.

"They're taking another Draft kid," I say under my breath.

Reiko looks sharply at me. "*What?*"

"Holland's discovered a way to...control kids against their will. It's what she's doing with Riya. Now that she can, she's taking more."

Reiko stares at the trio, now headed for the ruins, for a long moment. "I have to help them," she says quietly.

"Reiko—"

"I can't just watch them force somebody else into the Draft!" She lets go of the handles on my chair, backing away with an apologetic look. "And I can't bring you. I won't let you get hurt because of me. Just meet me at the stand we talked about."

And before I can get another word in, she darts off through the crowd.

I curse and shove my wheels, forcing my way through the mass of people after her. It's an agonizingly slow process, but I keep sight of Reiko's caramel ponytail. At least the crowd slows her, too.

I break free from the main crowd soon after her and race between colorful tents toward the ruins. Reiko sprints ahead of me, halfway between me and the trio in the distance. One of the Draft agents—the girl—looks over her shoulder and spots both of us.

Reiko only speeds up.

The girl says something to the other two, and the boys split off, breaking into a run and disappearing into the ruins. The girl, a curly redhead, turns and runs toward Reiko.

Reiko slows, but doesn't stop her approach. I push the wheels as fast as I can possibly go, finally drawing close as the girl reaches Reiko. I tense, expecting a fight as the two girls collide, but the redhead wraps her arms around Reiko instead.

They knew each other, I realize, finally catching up.

The redhead pulls back, holding Reiko at arm's length. "I never thought I'd see you again!"

Reiko smiles, but there's a tension to the expression. "Good to see you too, Amber."

The girl, Amber, gives Reiko a once-over. "Where have you *been* all this time? Everyone's talking about you, you know. They say you're a traitor. Even Anyssa. But I think there has to be more to the story, because you're—well, you're *Reiko*. You're the last person who would ever betray us." She grins. "I bet you're undercover again, aren't you!"

Reiko deflects the girl's speculation. "What are you doing in Nadzor?"

"You don't know? We're—" Amber's focus locks on me, ten paces behind Reiko. "Behind you!"

She moves before I can blink. Reiko whirls around, her eyes widening when she sees that I've followed her. Amber's behind me before I have a chance to try evading her, not that I would be able to with my chair, especially considering the uneven, sandy ground underneath us. I raise my hands, prepared to defend myself, but an arm hooks around my throat. I pry at Amber's grip, but her arm doesn't budge. *Performance enhancers.*

The barrel of a gun presses into my temple. "Hands down," Amber orders.

"Amber, wait!" Reiko's eyes dart between the two of us, frantic.

"Hands down," Amber repeats to me, tightening her arm around my throat.

I hesitate, then comply. She's a Draft agent. Even if I were at my full strength, I wouldn't have a chance at breaking her grip.

"Amber!" Reiko steps forward. "Let him go."

"You know him?"

"I do. Let him go."

Instead, the gun digs painfully into the side of my head, making me wince. "If you know him, that's an even better reason to shoot him," she says in a low voice. "You're undercover. Him knowing all of this would blow everything for you. I can make it look like—"

"I'm not undercover!" Reiko takes another step. "I left, Amber."

The elbow around my throat tightens, making it difficult to breathe. I grit my teeth and focus on relaxing my racing heart. Panic is only going to make this worse.

"Are you telling me that everyone's right about you?" the girl behind me hisses. "You really betrayed us?"

"There's more to the world than those sublevels," Reiko says, raising her hands slightly. "There are good *people* in this world. I met some of them. And now I'm *done* killing for Anyssa Holland."

A loud *click* next to my head. The gun's safety. I clench my fists.

"You can come back," Amber eventually says. "I can get rid of *him*. Make it look like an accident. Make it look like we took you, if you don't want the people you're with here to come looking. If you tell Anyssa you went undercover, tell her the things you've learned, renew your loyalty, I'm sure she would welcome you back."

Reiko looks as if the words are a physical blow. Her breathing quickens, her eyes flicking back and forth between me and Amber. "Anyssa would never take me back," she says quietly.

My heart pounds as I watch the debate going on behind her eyes. "Reiko—"

"Quiet." Amber's grip tightens, closing off my airway enough to keep me from talking. "We could convince her. Please, Reiko. You know what's right. And you know where Adrian is—if you help Anyssa find him, things could go back to normal. You could be the hero."

Reiko chews her lower lip, tears springing to her eyes, and I can guess exactly what's going on in her head. After being all but shunned with the Undrafted, the idea of returning to a place where she's celebrated, somewhere she has friends...it has to be tempting.

She's going to go back. The words hit me with a sudden burst of horror. She's going to betray me for Holland. Just like my sister. This is going to be my sister all over again—

"Okay," Reiko says, her voice barely audible. She draws within arm's reach, pointedly looking everywhere but at me, and holds out her hand. "I'll do it. Give me the gun."

I can't see the girl's face behind me, but I can hear the smile in her voice as she hands the pistol to Reiko. "I knew you hadn't truly changed. Now let's get this over with."

Reiko steps back, standing to my side and aiming the pistol at me with both shaking hands. Amber doesn't move, holding me still—she must be incredibly confident in Reiko's aim.

"Reiko, please," I gasp. *It's my sister all over again*. I'm paralyzed. Shaking in a way I haven't since I was six years old. Right when I started to trust her. Right when I started to think of her as the sister I never had.

"I'm sorry," she whispers.

A deafening *bang* as the gun fires. I cringe, waiting for the searing pain, waiting for anything, but the only change is a scream from behind me and the release of the choking pressure around my neck. I suck in breaths of dusty Nadzor air, nearly doubled over in my chair. I'm not dead. *I'm not dead.*

I whip my head around to find Reiko with her pistol still raised, her entire body trembling. Behind me, the redhead is on one knee, gripping her leg and scowling up at Reiko.

I'm not dead. My hands tremble just as much as Reiko's, despite my efforts to calm my body. The elbow around my neck is gone, but it's still just as difficult to breathe.

"I'm sorry," Reiko says again.

"You're really going to kill me?" Amber snarls. "After all the years we were friends? You're going to shoot me, just like that?"

"No." Reiko shakes her head. "Just—just go. Get out of here."

"You really are a traitor," the girl hisses, struggling to her feet. "You're *dead* to us."

"Go," Reiko whispers, her bottom lip trembling as her eyes turn glassy. "Please."

Amber limps toward the ruins, casting Reiko one last withering look as she disappears.

Reiko re-engages the safety and drops the gun, shaking so violently it's a wonder she's still standing, and stumbles back a step. "I'm sorry," she says, a tremor in her voice. "I'm sorry."

I can't tell if she's talking to me or if she's in shock. I can't seem to pull *myself* out of shock, still breathing heavily. The terror of Reiko's near betrayal is only just beginning to fade.

"Are you—did she hurt you?" She gets the words out between short, shallow breaths, digging her hands into her hair and messing up her sleek ponytail. "Hunter, I—that was never supposed to—I'm sorry—"

"Breathe."

Her gaze snaps toward me, eyes wild with confusion and fear. "What?"

"*Breathe*, Reiko. It's alright." My voice comes out calm, despite the raging emotions making my own breathing difficult.

She stands there for a few moments, taking deep breaths and staring at me like I've said something crazy. "That was never supposed to happen," she says quietly, shaking her head. "I never thought—I never thought it would go like that. We were friends. I never thought I'd see her again—that she'd look at me like I..." Reiko buries her head in her hands. "I'm tired of everyone looking at me like a traitor," she says in a small voice. "Even if they're always right."

"Reiko. Hey." I wheel closer to her. "Look at me."

She barely lifts her tear-streaked face.

"You're *not* a traitor. You just saved my life. You had the chance to go back, but you didn't."

The words don't feel adequate for the choice Reiko just made, but they're all I can come up with through the overwhelming relief and the still-fading terror.

Reiko gives a slight smile through the emotion.

"You know what sounds good right now?" I ask.

"What?"

I nod toward the market. "A chicken skewer."

She snorts a laugh and swipes the tears from her eyes as she bends to pick up the pistol. "Yeah. Yeah, it does."

As we make our way back to the market square, the fear and horror finally drains from my body, replaced by sheer relief. Relief that I don't have to experience the betrayal of another sister.

On the way back to the compound, I hold four chicken skewers wrapped in a thin cloth napkin as Reiko pushes my chair over the dust-covered path.

I twist to hand Reiko one of the skewers. "Here."

She grins and takes it. "Thanks." A hesitant pause. The events of the day still hang heavily over both of our heads. "Hunter? Can I ask you something?"

"You don't have to ask every time you have a question for me, you know," I say with a slight smile. "Of course."

"What's your story?"

I tense, my smile fading. "What do you mean?"

"How'd you end up with the Undrafted? And why does everybody give you this...this special treatment?"

I keep my eyes fixed straight ahead at the compound in the distance. For a few moments, the only sound is the soft shifting of the sand-covered path under my wheels.

"Hunter?" Reiko asks.

I clear my throat, fully intending to tell her that I'm fine and my past can stay a secret, but the words that slip out surprise even me. "I was only six," I say quietly.

Reiko's intense curiosity radiates from behind me, but I don't turn and look. Once the words start, they keep coming. Daniel and Kaz are the only two who know my full story, although Nora knows more details than most. Reiko, apparently, will be next.

"My sister." I swallow hard. "She worked for Holland. I'm not sure for how long, and I'm not sure what, exactly, she did. But she started having doubts, once Holland took the kids. Holland found out and...it didn't go over well."

"What did she do?" Reiko whispers.

I grip the skewers in my hand so tightly I can feel the juice leaking through the napkins and onto my fingers. "She wanted to teach my sister a lesson about loyalty. And so, one night, I woke up to the sound of pounding on our door. My mother hid me in my closet—told me to stay silent, no matter what I heard."

I close my eyes, battling the memories. A dark, tight space. Screams. Gunshots. Tears streaming down my face as I shake, silently screaming, in the blackness.

"Holland killed both of my parents," I say softly. "My sister was there. I heard everything. But Holland never came looking for me. I don't think she knew about me, or else she would've. I don't know how long I stayed trapped in that closet—days, maybe, until Daniel came to investigate. Someone from Ordinem told him that Holland had been here, and so he came to see what had happened. That's where he found me."

Silence hangs in the air as Reiko processes my words. I glance over my shoulder. What is she thinking? Is she going to pity me?

"I—I had no idea," she says, meeting my eyes. "That Anyssa—I'm so sorry, Hunter."

"It wasn't your fault." His expression hardens. *It was my sister's.* "After all that, my sister chose to stay with Holland. The coward."

"What was her name?"

"Leah. Leah Lane."

Reiko sucks in a sharp breath. "*She's* your sister?"

"You know her?"

"She worked with us. A lot. I don't know exactly what she does, but I know she's really involved. And I think she's the one who took over for Maya Collins." Reiko's pace slows as she pushes my chair. "I can't believe Anyssa did that to your family," she says, lowering her voice.

Why is this affecting her so much? It's a sad story—but Reiko almost seems to be taking it personally. "Reiko. It wasn't your fault. You didn't know, and there's nothing you could've done. You were what, three at the time?"

"I just..." She shakes her head. "Every time I hear another horrible story about the things Anyssa has done, it feels like a punch to the gut. I looked up to her. I almost *idolized* her, until I met TJ. To think this whole time, she's been...well, herself..." Reiko trails off and our conversation lapses into silence for the rest of the walk.

I steal a look at her as we approach the compound. Lost in thought, pondering my words. It makes sense that hearing stories about Holland would affect a Draft kid so much—but there's something more to Reiko's tone, her posture. A certain nervousness.

She's hiding something. But what? It's related to this story—to my sister, or to Holland, or to the Draft.

One thing I do know, from the way Reiko talked about my sister, is that Leah Lane is no longer simply a bitter figure of my memory. She has a part to play in all of this.

And I'm going to find out what it is.

Chapter Eighteen

Reverie Adams

The day before we're supposed to meet at the Sector 9 warehouse to fly back to the compound, Savi, Kaz, and I prepare for our infiltration. Kaz let Savi and I rest for the days after we received the news about Ethan, taking care of all of the communication with Daniel in the meantime. He eventually filled us in on the information Hunter got out of Adrian: that Holland is developing a serum to control the Draft kids, that Riya has the prototype of that serum in her blood, and that the serum has a missing piece, which explains the moment I saw her break through. That Riya is serving as Holland's *test subject*, since the kids that are already loyal to her are too valuable to sacrifice if anything goes wrong. That there may be bigger forces than Holland at play here. Kaz also filled Daniel in on everything that's happened here in Ordinem, which isn't much aside from our plan and the news about Ethan.

Kaz, Savi and I stand in an alley across from the Enforcer headquarters, in the shadow the afternoon sun casts past the massive building. In order for Savi to successfully pose as tech support, we have to pull this off during normal working hours, which means broad daylight.

Savi takes a deep breath and adjusts the backpack hanging on her shoulder, staring up at the building with wide eyes. "It's much bigger than the blueprints."

A reconstruction team looks to be making good progress on the wall I destroyed a month ago, although they're not even close to being done yet.

Other than that, only small things seem to have changed. New security cameras installed on the walls of surrounding buildings, more Enforcers guarding the area.

Kaz grins at Savi. "You ready to become a field agent?"

"This will be the first and last time you ever catch me out in the *field*," Savi says, but I can see right through her attempt at a humorous tone.

"You'll do great, Savi," I tell her.

"Yeah," Kaz adds. "Just remember we're all counting on you. No pressure or anything like that."

He's nervous, I realize, watching the way he shifts on his feet. Nervous for the mission? Or nervous for Savi?

She glares at him. "Not helpful."

He raises his hands. "Sorry! Seriously, I'm sure you'll do great. You have the easy part—all you have to do is get to the server room and unlock the side door for us, and then guide us to the drop point. You won't even have to talk to anybody!"

She gives him a dry look, but it fades into focus—and nerves—when she looks back at the Enforcer compound glinting in the sunlight. "Okay. Okay, I can do this."

"Whenever you're ready," I say. "Kaz and I will wait here until you give us the all-clear."

"Your earpieces are on?"

We both nod.

Savi lets out a breath and her knuckles, gripping the strap of her backpack, turn white. "Okay. Here we go, then. Wish me luck."

With that, she raises her chin, straightens the button-up shirt of her IT uniform and adjusts her matching blue cap, and sets off toward the main entrance of the Enforcer headquarters.

Kaz looks like he's on the verge of running in after her, but he restrains himself. When Savi disappears through the door, Kaz's eyes linger there for a few beats before he turns back toward me.

"You're worried about her," I note, reaching up and flicking a tiny switch on my earpiece. The UND's tech comes with a mute button. Useful, for the conversation I anticipate.

Kaz mutes his own earpiece. "Aren't you?"

"Savi's been my best friend for as long as I can remember. Of course I'm worried about her, but her part of this mission is the least risky. You've known her for all of one month and you seem to be more worried than I am."

"Really? What gave you that impression?"

I give him a flat look. "You were just about to go in after her. It was *killing* you to send her in there alone, wasn't it?"

Kaz shrugs, but it's not convincing. "She's inexperienced."

"That's not an answer. And I saw the way you were with her that night when we got back from the hospital. You care for her, don't you?"

"I..." He trails off, clearly scrambling for words. I've backed him into a corner and he knows it. Finally, he sighs and gives me a slight nod. "I do."

"That's something we have in common," I tell him. "I'm not going to pretend that I have the power to keep her safe, but I'm going to do absolutely everything I can. And if you hurt her, Kaz, I *will* come for you."

He stands there with his mouth half-open, probably trying to decide how to respond. Eventually, he lets out a long breath. "I won't," he says, voice soft but firm. A rare moment of seriousness. "I would never. And considering the fact that her best friend is a crazy bow-and-arrow-wielding vigilante, I think I'd end up crippled for life."

"You would," I say with a completely straight face.

Kaz does a good job at hiding it, but I can tell at least a part of him believes me. His next words come out tentatively. "You...won't tell her, right?"

"Tell her what?" I ask, feigning innocence.

He glares at me. "You know what. Rev, if you—"

"I won't mention anything," I assure him. "Although I would love to know how you were planning on finishing that sentence."

He shakes his head and looks back at the Enforcer compound, no longer bothering to disguise the worry on his face. "She's been in there for a while."

"She'll be fine, Kaz. Focus on the mission."

As if on cue, Savi's voice comes through our earpieces. The sound is much clearer than I remember from our old comms, thanks to the UND's better technology. "I'm in," she says, sounding breathless. "Into the servers, into everything."

Kaz glances at me, his hand hovering next to his ear. "Please tell me you were on mute."

"I almost wish we weren't. *That* would've been a fun conversation to watch."

He lets out a relieved breath and flicks the tiny switch on his earpiece. "Are you safe?"

"I wouldn't be talking to you right now if I wasn't safe, Kaz."

"Right. Where are you?"

"I found a little nook in the server room to set up. You two ready for me to unlock the door?"

"We're ready," I say. "Anything we should know about going in?"

"You won't have more than fifteen minutes," Savi says. "I ran into an Enforcer on the way here. He checked my ID card and said they weren't expecting tech support for another 15 minutes—which means that by the time the new tech person gets here, we need to be gone."

"Fifteen minutes?" Kaz looks at me in disbelief. "We're supposed to get into the Draft sublevels, take the flash drive from the drop point, and get out in *fifteen minutes*?"

I shrug. "We've beaten worse odds."

"True, but..." Kaz shakes his head. "Alright. Let's just get in there."

"Door's unlocked," Savi says as the two of us duck our heads and slip out of the alley toward the side of the building. "Through the side door, down the stairs, and turn right to get to the main hallway. I'll guide you from there."

"Gotcha." Kaz pulls up in front of the door, which he opens for me with a cocky smile. "Ladies first."

I tighten my grip on my bow and slip into the stairwell. It's dim up here, but I can see fluorescent white lighting at the bottom. Kaz follows me silently down the stairs and we pause when we reach the end.

"You've got two Enforcers on the other side of that door," Savi says. "They're about twenty feet away, coming your direction."

"Perfect," Kaz whispers. Bright light leaks through the crack under the closed door, highlighting his grin as he looks at me. "Your aim had better be as good as they say."

I don't reply as I nock an arrow—one of the three taser arrows I brought, courtesy of the UND's tech cabinets at our base. "Open the door."

Kaz complies and I step out into the hallway, releasing my first arrow before the Enforcers have time to process that I'm not supposed to be here. He goes stiff as the taser arrow lodges itself in a crack between two plates of his suit, then falls in a heap on the ground. I have another arrow nocked, drawn, and loosed before his companion can even aim his pulse rifle.

Kaz nods. "Nice."

Savi directs us to a nearby storage closet and together, we drag the two Enforcers into it.

"Ten minutes," Savi says. "Your route to the drop point is clear, as long as you move fast. Take your first right, your third left, and then the third door down. I don't see anybody nearby, so Daniel's spy must've already dropped the flash drive."

"Copy that." Kaz sets off at a jog in the direction Savi described, and I follow suit. True to Savi's word, the hallways are clear. Kaz and I make it to the maintenance closet without running into anyone, and Savi clears us to go in as soon as we reach the door.

Inside, the closet is as well-lit like the rest of the sublevel, revealing mops, buckets, and bins, all the same white that Holland favors in the Draft sublevels. A quick glance around, though, reveals a problem.

"Where's the drive?" Kaz asks under his breath.

"It's supposed to be in a yellow envelope," Savi tells us. "It's not there?"

"I don't see anything," I say.

Kaz and I share a look, then begin to tear the closet apart.

"How much time?" Kaz asks, pushing past a stack of buckets to search a table at the back.

"You need to be out of that room in five minutes!" The sound of intense typing comes over our earpieces. "Oh. Oh, no."

"Savi, what's wrong?" I ask, grunting as I shift a large bin to the side.

"You have someone coming your way. Walking fast, headed straight toward the room you're in. It doesn't look like an Enforcer—you need to get out of there. You have maybe thirty seconds."

"We need to find the envelope!" I hiss.

"You don't have time!"

"We—"

The door slams open before I can finish my sentence.

A heavy-breathing woman with frizzy blonde curls stands, wide-eyed, in the doorway. Kaz whips out both of his pistols and I draw my bow, but the woman raises her hands. "Wait! I'm—I'm sorry I'm late. You don't have much time."

In one of her raised hands, she clutches a yellow envelope, but that detail only catches half my attention. I *recognize* her.

And so does Kaz. His jaw hangs open, but he doesn't lower his guns. "You're Leah Lane," he breathes.

The woman nods and, searching her face, I see the resemblance to Hunter. They have the same cobalt-blue eyes and sharp jaw. "I don't know who you are," she says, her voice shaking, "but you can put down the weapons. Please. I'm just here to deliver this."

Kaz tightens his grip on his pistols and nods for me to take the envelope. I collapse my bow and snatch the envelope. "What's in it?"

"It's some of my own notes about the serum and a flash drive," Leah explains. "With a video file that Holland found among Maya Collins's things. It's a message from Maya to—I can't remember his name, but it's to her son. It's about the serum, I think, or the cure, or—would you *please* put the guns down? I'm not going to hurt you!"

Kaz scowls and lowers his pistols, but keeps them in hand.

"Listen, I'm really sorry I'm late. You two need to get out of here. I heard rumors of your friend in the server room, which means the Draft agents are going to be searching—"

Kaz steps forward. "Where is she? Our friend in the server room? What happened?"

"She's okay!" Leah flinches back from Kaz's looming figure. "At least, as far as I know. I haven't heard anything. But the Draft agents are going to be looking for you, and there are Enforcers going to check on her, and if they catch me with you—you *need* to go."

"She's right, Kaz!" Savi's voice comes over our earpieces. "I see the Enforcers—I still have a few minutes, but you two need to get moving. *Now.*"

Leah's eyes dart between the two of us and she steps back toward the door. "Good luck," she says. "I hope that flash drive gives you what you need."

Then, she's gone, set off down the hall.

"I can't believe Hunter's *sister* is Daniel's spy," Kaz whispers. "And we were never supposed to meet her in person—which means—"

"Daniel was never going to tell you," I finish for him.

"Figure it out later!" Savi's voice is tense. "We're running out of time here. You're going to need to take a different route to get back to the exit—there are Enforcers in your way. Get out of that room, take a right, and *run.*"

"Let's go!" I pocket the envelope and duck out of the room, Kaz right on my heels. Savi directs us in a massive loop, taking us deeper into the Draft headquarters.

"Savi, how are we doing on time?" Kaz asks, breathless.

"Uh, not good." She sucks in a sharp breath. "Not good at all. I'm going to have to unplug."

"*Now?*" I ask, glancing nervously around the hallway. "Won't that leave us running blind?"

"You're not too far from where you came in! Just take your next right and a left at the end of that hall—it'll take you right back to the stairwell."

"How do I get to you?" Kaz's voice takes on a little of Savi's panic.

"I'll be okay! As long as I—oh, no. I gotta go!"

"Savi—!"

A *click* over our earpieces signals Savi's system going dark.

Kaz stops in the middle of the hallway and meets my eyes. "I'm going to find her."

"Kaz, she's smart! She'll be okay! You don't know where—"

"I'm going to find her!" His breathing comes labored and his dark eyes are wider than I've ever seen them. "Keep your earpiece in. I don't know why she had to go dark, but you and I can stay in contact. I'll be smart, but we can't just leave her on her own, and I think I remember how to get to the server room from the blueprints."

I hesitate, but there's nothing I can say to stop him, so I nod. "Go. Keep your earpiece on. I'll find the exit. If *any* alarms go off—"

"I'll get out right away," he promises. "Get to the exit. I'll meet you."

With that, he takes off in the opposite direction. I follow Savi's instructions, hoping I don't run into any Enforcers, and I seem to be having good enough luck as I barrel down the hall. One of the rooms catches my eye through the tiny window set into the door as I go past—expansive, with tables full of technology I don't recognize lining the room. Leah Lane stands inside, her back partially to me, holding up something connected to the computers. The device looks like a headband, wire-thin, with two flat circular nodes where the band would rest on a person's temples.

I don't have time to speculate as I make the final turn. Before I make it to the stairwell door, a figure stops me in my tracks.

A girl with long, raven-black hair stands before me, brandishing a pulse rifle. I suck in a sharp breath when I meet her eyes.

"Riya," I breathe. "Riya, it's me. You know me."

Riya stares back at me, her brown eyes void of recognition.

"Rev?" Kaz calls, the pitch of his voice rising. "I heard that! I'm coming to help—I'll be right—"

A high-pitched ringing noise cuts through our earpieces, ending our communication. The same ringing that we heard last time we were in the sublevels—some kind of signal jammer that the Draft kids carry. I'm on my own.

"Riya," I say again. "Please. It's—"

Before I can finish my sentence, Riya pulls the trigger.

Chapter Nineteen

TJ Collins

I stare at the empty air on the roof where Max was only moments ago, my jaw hanging open.

He just *jumped*.

I stumble backward, then tear down the stairwell. "Alec!" I yell as soon as I reach the right floor. "*Alec!*"

"TJ!" Alec sticks his head out the door. "What's wrong?" He searches the hallway behind me and his eyes go wide. "Where's Max?"

"He—jumped—there was—a scream—" I get out between breaths.

Alec grabs my shoulders as I skid to a stop in front of him. "Slow down. There was a scream. Max jumped? To go help?"

I nod. "He—told me to—to come get you."

"Alright. Stay here. I'm going to go check things out."

"Stay *here*?" I shake my head. "I'm coming with you."

"Fine. Just try to keep up, and whatever happens, do *not* get involved." Alec whirls on me, drilling me with a serious look. "You hear me?"

I give him a sharp nod and he takes off down the hallway, slinging his longbow over his shoulder as he sprints.

"Do you know what's going on?" I yell, pounding after him as he starts down the stairs two at a time.

"Long story!" he calls over his shoulder. "Max can tell you later!"

By the time we burst out of the ruined building and into the sunlight, I'm too winded to question Alec further. It's all I can do to keep up as he sprints down the alleyway Max jumped into and takes a sharp right turn.

At the end of the new alley, Max and two other boys stand in what looks like a stalemate. Max stands with his feet apart, both of his swords drawn and gripped in white-knuckled fists. Across from him, one boy holds a short blade to a younger boy's throat. *Draft kids*—or at least, one of them is. The younger boy looks terrified, and I remember what Rev told me about Holland taking new Draft kids. This must be one of them. None of the three seem to notice me and Alec standing in the mouth of the alley.

"Let him go," Max says in a low voice, taking a step toward the other two.

The young boy winces as the other's grip on him tightens. "I know who you are," the other boy snarls at Max. "*Traitor*. You aren't the first I've seen today."

Max visibly flinches at the words. "I don't want to hurt you," he says, nearly pleading. "Let the kid go."

"Or you'll do what?" The other boy laughs. "You've already proven that you don't have the strength to be a part of change, Max. Stay out of what's above your head. Or maybe Amber will show up and take you to Anyssa—let her give you the punishment you deserve."

Max's swords tremble as he takes a defiant step forward, but he freezes when the other boy presses his blade closer, sending a trickle of blood down the young boy's neck. He whimpers, looking at Max with desperate, pleading eyes.

"Alec," I hiss, twisting to look at him. "We have to help—"

Nothing but empty air. I whirl around, searching for him, but Alec is gone. *Where?*

I focus back on Max, my heart racing. He needs help, and if the Draft kid has a friend coming, he needs help *now*.

Before I can think through my plan, I'm moving. There's no way I can fight the boy, but I don't have to—all I need to do is separate him from the younger boy so Max can make his move.

I reach the Draft kid and grab the arm holding the knife, jerking it away from the young boy and shoving him away. The boy stumbles toward Max, who doesn't miss a beat before pulling him out of reach and guiding him to a spot a little way down the alley.

An arm slams me against the wall, elbow digging into my back. I grit my teeth and twist my body to the side, trying to escape his grasp, but the boy doesn't budge. His hand snatches my wrist and wrenches my arm up behind my back before he grabs the collar of my shirt and spins us to face away from the wall. I fight his grip, but he releases my collar and holds a blade to my throat instead. "You're going to pay for that," he hisses in my ear as I meet Max's eyes.

Max still holds his swords, standing protectively in front of the terrified boy. He grits his teeth, looking like he's barely holding himself back. "Let him go. He has nothing to do with this."

"He's here, isn't he?" the boy holding me counters.

"He's here by *accident*. There's no reason to—"

The Draft kid lays more pressure on my arm and I cry out, dropping to one knee. *He's going to break my arm,* I think, clenching my teeth against the pain as my fingertips brush my shoulder blade. *Or worse.*

Max cringes at my cry of pain, his fighting stance weakening. "What do you want?"

"I want that boy," the Draft kid growls. "And I want you to stop *meddling* with our business here. It's getting annoying."

Max's eyes dart between me and the trembling boy behind him. I can almost see his mind racing, the panic setting in as he realizes the impossible decision he's looking at—give up an innocent kid or risk my life.

Impossible decision. Suddenly, in Max's place, I see myself, watching helplessly as Holland holds a pistol to Reiko's head. Watching Holland ask me who Rev's sister is for the final time. Hearing the name slip from my mouth. *Eliza.*

The pressure on my arm releases as the boy behind me cries out. I scramble away, cradling my aching arm and stumbling to my feet next to Max, who steps in front of me with his swords. He's watching the other end of the alleyway with wide eyes, and my expression morphs to match his as I follow his gaze.

Alec is back, and he's holding a polished wooden bow in his outstretched hand.

The Draft kid grits his teeth as he uses the wall of the alley to stand, but when he tries to take a step toward Alec, he winces.

Alec's arrow protrudes from the side of the boy's ankle, the tip embedded in the wall next to him. I gape at the sight—not only did Alec manage to hit a target that small from the mouth of the alleyway, but he hit it in such a way that the tip lodged between two stones on the other side. If he'd been even an inch to the right or left, the arrow wouldn't have stuck to the wall and the Draft kid would probably still be able to fight. It looks like a one-in-a-million shot, and Alec made it under *pressure*.

He's as good as Rev, I think in disbelief. *Maybe better.* "How—?"

Max doesn't let me finish the question. He sheaths one of his swords and shoves me toward Alec. "Go!" he yells, then crouches next to the younger boy and says something I can't make out.

Alec ushers me out of the alley, Max following with the boy in tow. Max takes the lead and after a few minutes of running, he bursts through the doors of his crumbling building, holding them open for the rest of us. He lingers at the door as Alec and I take the stairs, and a *thud* echoes in the huge space as Max bars the doors.

We all sprint up the stairs to the third floor, then down the hall. Alec holds the apartment door for me, then for Max and the boy. He slams the door behind us, locks it, and finally turns to face the three shocked faces staring at him.

Max, surprisingly, looks just as stunned as me, and the younger boy wavers on his feet like he's on the verge of fainting.

Alec sighs, leans his bow against the wall, and kneels in front of the boy. "You alright, kid?" he asks, putting a gentle hand on his shoulder.

The wide-eyed boy just stares at him, mouth hanging slightly open. I can't tell if he's terrified or in shock. Probably both.

"Come sit down. Catch your breath." Alec guides him to the cushions along the wall.

The boy sits hard, his panicked eyes flicking back and forth between me, Max, and Alec. "What—what's going to happen to me? Please—I—"

"It's okay. You're safe here. I promise," Alec says, crouching in front of him. "Water?"

The boy hesitates, then gives a slight nod.

Alec disappears into the kitchen and the sound of running water filters through the doorway.

"What...just *happened*?" Max asks under his breath, his eyes fixed on the boy.

"I was going to ask you the same thing." I keep my voice low enough that we can't be overheard.

"I knew Alec could shoot, but..." Max shakes his head slowly. "Not like that. *That* was..."

"It was incredible."

"It was...yeah. Incredible." His eyes float to the kitchen doorway, where Alec returns with a glass of water and sits in front of the boy.

"You don't think so?" I ask.

"I never thought I'd see Alec shoot anyone," Max says softly. "And I never wanted to be the one to put him in a position where he had to."

I put a hand on his shoulder, hoping the gesture is more comforting than I feel. Seeing Alec, of all people, put an arrow in someone *was* disconcerting. I didn't even know he could shoot.

Max stiffens at the touch and stares at my hand on his shoulder, a wave of conflicting emotions washing over his face, before the tension in his shoulders fades. We stand there together, watching Alec's quiet conversation with the boy, until Alec finally stands back up.

"I need to take care of some things with these two," he tells the boy, inclining his head toward me and Max. "We'll just be in the other room. Let me know if you need anything, and try to rest, alright?"

"Thank you," he says hoarsely.

Alec smiles and nods. "You're welcome."

With that, he gestures Max and me into the other room. This one looks like it's meant to be a bedroom, with worn and dirty carpet, bare of furniture except for two makeshift bedrolls and cushions along one wall to match the ones in the living room.

As soon as the door shuts behind us, Alec lets out a breath and sinks down on the cushions, looking up at me. "We owe you an explanation, don't we?"

"Alec, I don't think—" Max starts to protest, but Alec holds up his hand.

"No more putting it off, kid. After what just happened, TJ deserves to know what we got him caught up in. If you don't tell him, I will." Alec pats the cushions next to him, shifting his focus back to me. "You might want to sit down. This is a bit of a long story."

Chapter Twenty

Reverie Adams

The pulse blast from Riya's rifle sends me crashing into the wall of a hallway behind me. The force of the blow rips my bow from my fingers, and a swift kick from Riya sends it skidding away from me as the envelope in my hand falls to the ground. Normally, I'd reach for an arrow to defend myself, but...

This is *Riya*. TJ's little sister. I can't imagine pulling any sort of weapon on her.

"Riya!" I inch back as she steps closer, but with the wall at my back, I have nowhere to go. My heels slide over the tile floor as I scramble away. "Riya, it's me! You know me!"

"I don't know you," she snarls.

I get to my feet and manage to grab an arrow, but I know as soon as I have my fingers around the shaft that I won't be able to use it. The look in Riya's eyes is identical to how it was the last time I saw her—empty, except of hatred.

Of all the ways I imagined this mission going wrong, ending up in a fight with a brainwashed Riya wasn't one of them.

Riya moves faster than I can process. She slams me back against the wall, one hand tightening around my throat as her other scrabbles for the arrows peeking up from over my shoulder. Her grip is stronger than should be possible and I gasp for air as I pry at her hand, but the attempt is futile. "Riya," I choke out, a final attempt at getting her to recognize me.

She only glares at me with that empty expression, holding her ground. The edges of my vision blur.

Then the pressure releases. I double over, coughing, as Riya staggers back.

She's conscious, unharmed, and the hallway is empty except for the two of us. Riya presses both hands to her temples, her face scrunching in pain as she drops to her knees. One of her hands clutches a sedative arrow from my quiver.

I watch, wide-eyed, as Riya gives a strangled cry of pain and rocks on her knees. Her cries abruptly cut off with a sharp gasp. Her head snaps up, her eyes locking on mine.

"Rev?" she breathes, terror flooding her face.

My mouth works, but I can't get any words out as I rub my aching throat.

Riya's eyes drift to the bruises, to the sedative arrow in her hand, back to me, and she seems to come to a decision. "I don't know how," she says, her words rushed, "and I don't have much time—but the serum...it doesn't completely *work*. Sometimes I can break through—"

A groan of pain and she squeezes her eyes shut again, her whole body tensing up until it passes.

"I can't—fight it—much longer," she gasps, "but take me—with you. *Please.*"

With a shaking hand, Riya lifts the sedative arrow. Her whole body trembles, every last drop of her effort going into the motion. Then, she locks eyes with me.

She plunges the sedative arrow straight into her chest.

"Riya!" I rasp, crawling toward her.

"TJ," Riya murmurs, lying back on the floor. "The serum, or the cure. Holland wants...wants TJ."

"Riya!" I grab her shoulder. "What do you mean, Holland wants TJ?"

"And Holland...knows...Eliza..."

The sedative takes its hold.

Footsteps pound down the hallway and I whirl around to see Kaz, panting as he approaches. "Rev! Are you okay?"

I get to my feet, one hand braced on the wall. "Fine," I say, my voice hoarse.

Kaz stoops to grab the envelope and my bow as he slows. "What happened? Our comms went dark—"

"The Draft kids."

Kaz hands me my bow and steps toward Riya. "Why do I recognize her?"

"That's Riya Collins."

"TJ's sister—the one we saw in Nadzor, right?"

I nod, watching Riya's relaxed features. "She's not completely under Holland's control, Kaz. She...*woke up*. And she knocked herself out—to stop herself from hurting me, I think."

"Wonderful. Someone's going to find her soon, so we need to get out of here."

"We can't just leave her here!"

"Why not? She's a Draft kid, Rev! We have no idea what would happen if we took her with us!"

"She's not completely Holland's!" I crouch and slip my arms under Riya's back. "We're bringing her, Kaz."

He studies me as I stand, hefting Riya's body with me, before sighing. "Here. Let me take her. We need to move fast, and you're still recovering."

"Thank you."

He gives a sharp nod as I take the envelope and let him carry Riya. "She has the serum in her blood. Hopefully Nora can use that. Now let's go."

I hold the stairwell door for Kaz and we tear up the stairs two at a time. Remarkably, Riya doesn't seem to slow Kaz down at all. With their different personalities, I tend to forget that he and Hunter have been through the same training. Either he's in incredible shape or I'm slower and more winded than usual after my fight with Riya. Probably both.

"Did you get Savi out?" I ask as we climb.

"No—I had no idea where she was once she unplugged and I had to come save you." In the dark, I can make out the shake of his head. "I hope she's safe," he says quietly.

I shove the door at the top open and hold it for Kaz, then let it shut on its own and take off after him. We run as hard as we can back to the UND's apartment base. By the time we reach it, I can hardly breathe. Kaz has to stand by the door, his hands full with Riya, and wait while I fumble with the doorknob.

"I don't think I've ever seen you out of breath," he notes.

"I've never been strangled by a Draft kid before." I finally manage to open the door.

Once we're inside, Kaz takes a deep breath, slowing to a walk as he climbs the stairs. By the time we reach the second floor, I've nearly regained my breath, but I can tell the effects of Riya's attack won't be going away soon.

The door to our apartment is locked when I try the handle, so I knock. "Savi?" I call. *Please let her be here,* I think, my pulse quickening.

The lock disengages with a metallic *clunk* and the door slowly swings open to reveal Savi, holding a pistol with a trembling, white-knuckled grip.

I raise my hands on instinct, but Savi's already dropped the pistol. She scrambles to where I stand and wraps her arms around me, nearly knocking me over.

I laugh and hug her back. "You know you're not supposed to just drop a loaded gun on the ground, right?"

"It wasn't loaded," she says, her voice muffled against my shirt. "I was so worried—Kaz!"

Savi pulls away from me and frantically looks around the room. As soon as her eyes settle on Kaz setting Riya down on the couch, she rushes over and throws her arms around him.

Kaz's eyes go wide and as he meets my eyes over Savi's shoulder, I have to stifle a laugh. He looks utterly stunned.

I give him a nod of encouragement and he gently wraps his broad arms around Savi, a tentative smile stretching across his face. "I'm glad you're safe," he says softly.

She pulls back and clears her throat, her face bright red. "Sorry—I—that was—"

"Don't be sorry." Kaz looks steadily at her, the same slight grin on his face.

Savi blushes harder and looks away, but her smile fades as soon as her eyes settle on Riya. "Riya—what happened? You got her back? Is she..." Savi trails off, looking at me and Kaz.

"Well, she tried to kill Rev, so there's that," Kaz says.

Savi kneels next to Riya's unconscious form, brushing a strand of raven-black hair out of her face.

Kaz steps back, giving the two of them space, and ends up next to me. He watches Savi uncertainly as she looks at Riya, different emotions flashing across her face.

"You think she'll be okay?" Savi asks quietly, "when she wakes up?"

I rub my bruised throat. "I don't know, Savi. But she's still in there." I explain how, for just a moment, Riya broke through whatever hold Holland had on her.

"I can't believe..." Savi shakes her head, standing up. "I can't believe *anybody* would do this, even Holland. It's just so...it's so *wrong*." Her expression hardens as she turns to face us, locking eyes with me. "And now it's personal."

She moves to stand next to me and Kaz, all of us looking at Riya in silence. Even without seeing her face, I can feel the tense anger radiating from her. Now, with that rage, Savi is finally experiencing what I've been lost in for the past eleven—nearly twelve—years.

"Now it's personal." Kaz puts his hand on her shoulder and Savi bows her head.

"We're going to get her, Savi," I say softly, resting my own hand on her other shoulder. The glimpse of TJ's wounds I caught on the helicopter, the perpetual fear on Max's face back in Ordinem, Ethan's death, and now whatever's going on with Riya—all of it, and my sister's face, flash through my mind in an instant. My hand tightens on Savi's shoulder. "We're going to get her before she can hurt anybody else."

———

None of us sleep well through the night.

Kaz takes first watch, staying up to keep an eye on Riya. Even with Kaz awake in the living room, my mind races too fast for me to sleep, and I can tell from Savi's uneven breathing that she's experiencing a similar problem.

"Can't sleep?" I ask.

Savi's mattress creaks as she shifts above me. "You neither, huh? How could you tell?"

"Your breathing."

She snorts a laugh.

"What?" I ask. "Was that funny?"

"No, it's just...you do know that most people don't just *know* if someone's awake, right?"

I smile. "Sometimes I forget that not everybody lives like me."

"So, why are you still awake?"

"Just can't sleep. Still not used to sleeping through the night, maybe." It's only a half-truth, but in the darkness, it's enough. "You?"

"I can't. Not knowing Riya's out there." Savi goes quiet.

"How are you doing?" I ask softly.

"I could be better." She lets out a laugh, but I can hear the barely-contained emotion behind it. "First Ethan, and now Riya, not to mention the hundred other things going on right now...it's—it's a lot to handle. But I know..." Her voice breaks and she continues in a whisper. "I know I'm not the only one. And to be honest, I think knowing that I'm not alone is the only thing keeping me going."

"You're not alone," I tell her firmly.

Her mattress creaks again. "I miss my family, Rev," Savi finally says, barely audible. "I know we're fighting for a cause, and I believe it now more than ever—but I still miss my life. I miss not having to worry every day about whether my friends would live or die. Does that make me a terrible person? Knowing we're out here fighting to save lives, but still laying awake at night missing what I used to have?"

"Missing a time where we all weren't fighting for our lives doesn't make you a terrible person, Savi. Neither does missing your family. I know they miss you, too. This fight won't last forever, and as soon as it's done, things will go back to the way they were. The good things, at least."

"You make it sound so simple," she whispers. "How do you do it all, Rev? How do you keep it together?"

"I don't." I stare up at the boards of Savi's bed. "You just get really good at pretending, after a while."

We lay in silence for a time after that, but I can tell that Savi is still awake. She needs more from me. She needs to know she's not the only one for whom this fight is personal.

"The first time I heard about the Draft," I start quietly, "I was five years old."

Savi lets the statement hang for a few beats. "You never did tell me why you became the Archer," she whispers.

"I know." I take a deep breath. Being in this dark room, unable to see Savi's face, makes it easier to continue. "I have a sister. Eliza. She's fourteen now, and she's...Holland took her. Eleven years ago, when she started the Draft."

Savi processes that in silence.

"Remember when I ran off in the Draft sublevels?" I ask her. "When I turned off my earpiece and did my own thing? I was looking for her. Eleven years, and still, I haven't gotten my sister back. But I know that we're going to."

"It's like what Kaz said." Savi's voice comes out soft. "About fighting for hope."

"He was right." I stare up at the underside of her bunk, wishing I could see her face, to see if I'm helping. "We're fighting right alongside you, Savi. You're not alone."

Kaz's knock comes at the door before Savi gets the chance to respond. I sit up as he sticks his head in the doorway, dim light from the living room silhouetting his figure. "Rev. Your watch. And I don't think the first sedative should last much longer, so there's another one on the kitchen counter for you in case you need it."

I take a deep breath, swing my legs over the side of the bed and head into the living room.

It isn't long before Riya begins to stir.

I sit on one of the plush chairs facing the couch, watching her shallow breathing. The dim light of the single lit lamp reflects off of her sleek black hair, although it's messy and tangled from the events of the day. She lays on the floor next to the couch, her hands bound to one of the couch legs. It's an awkward position, but the couch is the heaviest thing we could come up with, and none of us understand the strength of the Draft kids yet.

I hold the sedative dart in my hand as Riya groans, then struggles to sit up, her hands behind her.

"Which Riya am I talking to?" I ask softly, casting a glance at the closed door to the bunkroom. The plan was to keep her sedated until we reach the compound in about twelve hours, but if Riya is herself for now, it won't hurt to talk to her first.

She sits up straight and lets out a breath, her head sinking back against the couch. "It's me," she whispers. "I don't know how long. Seeing familiar things helps me fight the serum, I think."

I study her, trying to figure out if she's telling the truth.

Riya notices my expression. "TJ loves the stars," she says. "Our mom taught us the constellations together." She closes her eyes, seeming to deflate. "Did I hurt anyone?"

"No."

She breathes a sigh of relief and finally takes in the room around her. "Where are we? Where's TJ? Does he—does he know? About me? The serum?"

I tell her the basics: how we found refuge with Hunter's organization in Nadzor, how we saw her a couple weeks ago in the ruins, how we know Holland is taking new kids. "We're leaving to head back to the compound in the morning," I finish. "The researchers there are some of the best there are. They'll be able to find a fix for the serum."

Riya shakes her head. "Rev...I don't know the details, but I've overheard some stuff. The serum has a missing piece—I'm assuming that's why they tested it on me instead of risking the Draft agents, and it's why I keep...*flipping*. In and out. Holland is convinced TJ has it, but I don't know anything else."

"What about the other thing you said? The cure?"

"All I know is that Holland thinks it exists, but nobody knows where, or how." Riya shifts, wincing. "It's the only way to counteract the serum. Holland thought TJ knew about that, too. It's why she kept him alive so long." Her voice turns hoarse. "How is he?"

"He's recovering," I promise.

"Keep him safe." She meets my eyes. I've never seen so much fear and pleading in hers. "Promise me you'll keep him safe. I'm not sure exactly what, but Holland found something new. She wants him again. *Badly*."

"I'll do everything—"

"*Promise me*." She pins me to the spot with her eyes. "Do *not* let Holland have my brother, Rev. If she gets TJ, it's game over, and we lose."

"I promise."

Riya nods and her eyes slide closed again.

"Riya? You mentioned someone else. Back in the sublevels."

"Eliza? Your sister, right?"

I hesitate on instinct, but there's no use hiding it anymore. "Yeah. Is she...?"

"She's okay. Holland knows she's your sister, but she'll be fine as long as she stays loyal." Riya pauses. "They're people, you know. The Draft kids. They have personalities. Souls. Holland made me stay with them, train with them, and...I got to know some of them, Rev. They're not brainless."

Another beat of silence as my unspoken question hangs in the air. *What about Eliza?*

"I got to know your sister," Riya says softly.

My heart beats wildly, my hands shaking. "And?"

"She reminds me of you." A slight smile touches Riya's lips. "You'll love her, when you get to meet her. When all this is over."

I want to ask her another question, to ask her a million questions, but her whole body goes stiff and she lets out a strangled groan.

"Riya? What's wrong?" I stand, sedative dart clutched in my hand.

She jerks against her bonds, then doubles over, gritting her teeth. "It's—taking control," she chokes out.

"Can you fight it?"

She shakes her head violently as another wave of anguish wracks her body. "Sed—sedative. Before I—hurt you—"

I only hesitate for a moment before using the sedative dart. The tension drains from Riya's form as her pain melts into sleep. I sit back on the floor across from her.

TJ is going to be *devastated* to see her like this. Imagining his reaction to seeing the effects of Holland's serum on his sister, along with the news about Ethan, makes my stomach turn. It's my fault TJ turned himself in to Holland in the first place, which means it's my fault Holland had Riya, no matter how indirectly. How is TJ going to look at me after seeing Riya in her current state?

Even after all the progress I've made, after all the apologies and assurances that I've been forgiven, the shadows of my past are still chasing me. And it's starting to look like eventually, they'll catch up.

Chapter Twenty-One

TJ Collins

Alec waits for me and Max to sit down before he leans back against the wall, looking between the two of us. His eyes settle on Max first. "You okay?"

Of all the questions Alec could have asked, this one catches me off-guard. Max isn't physically injured and he seemed fine while Alec was talking to the boy earlier. What is Alec seeing that I'm not?

"I'm fine."

"You're not convincing. I know that wasn't easy for you to watch."

"It...wasn't," Max admits, his gaze dropping to the floor. "But you had to do it. I'm alright, Alec."

Alec nods at him before turning his focus to me. "And you, I assume, have some questions."

"That's an understatement," I say. My eyes flit to Max, but he seems too preoccupied to notice. Before everything went crazy, Max was about to tell me something important. Now, with the high emotion of the moment I showed him my scars fading, I wonder if he's still planning on telling me.

"I'm sorry you got dragged into everything before you knew why, but I'm hoping to fix that now." Alec spares a concerned look for Max, who still looks deep in thought. "You already know that Max and I moved out here because of conflict with Anyssa Holland. But that's only part of the reason. Holland has her agents in Nadzor now, and she's..."

"She's taking more kids," Max says in a low voice, finally tuning in to the conversation.

I pause. *That's* what they've been so reluctant to tell me?

Alec must take note of my lack of surprise, because he tilts his head. "You knew that, though, didn't you?"

No point in lying. I nod.

"Right." Alec folds his arms, leaning back against the wall. "I keep forgetting you're with the Undrafted. Daniel keeps up on these things, too. But that's why Max and I stayed out here after Daniel turned us down. We thought we could make a difference—like for the boy we saved today."

"Makes sense," I say. "Although I still don't understand why Daniel turned you down. You're the last person I would expect to be with Holland."

Alec presses his lips together, seeming to debate with himself, before coming to an apparent decision. "Anyssa and I were...more than friends."

I blink. "Oh."

"It was before the Draft was created." A distant look glazes his eyes. "We were young. Different people back then, both of us." He shakes off the memories. "But anyways. As far as I know, that's why Daniel refused to let me join the Undrafted. And I suppose I can't totally blame him for that."

I run my hand through my hair, Alec's revelation about his and Max's mission bringing Riya to mind. The hundreds of images I've conjured up based on Rev's description—Riya, a mindless soldier being controlled by Holland—flash through my head in one painful burst and I have to fight back a wave of emotion. I battle back the images with another question. "Why is Holland taking more kids now?"

"Because now she has a way to control them," Max says, his gaze fixed on the frayed edge of Alec's cushion. "Ever since she raised the first fifty or so and began expanding, she's been developing a serum to control new agents." His voice drops. "And to ensure the loyalty of old ones—keep them from turning on her. She can get more agents, equally as loyal, without having to take the time and resources to raise them from infancy like she did with the first. And then she can integrate them *everywhere* in Ordinem."

Max, sitting cross-legged, balances his elbows on his knees and buries his forehead in his hands.

All of the details hit me at the same time. "Max," I start, slowly. Tentatively. Max is fourteen. He can fight. *She broke you too*, he said, up on the roof—he has something deeply personal against Holland. And now he knows details about the Draft that he shouldn't. I'm almost afraid to ask the question, because I think I already know the answer. "How do you know all this?"

His fingers curl into his hair, his shoulders hunched.

Alec stands with a reassuring hand on my shoulder. "I'm going to go check on our guest out there," Alec says, glancing at Max. "I'll be back in a minute."

With that, he leaves.

"Max?" I ask when the boy doesn't budge.

"I was going to tell you," he whispers. "When you showed me your arm. On the roof today. But then the fight happened and—" He lets out a shaky breath, seeming to fold even further into himself. "You probably put it together by now, after everything that just happened."

The pieces click together with this final confirmation. "You were a Draft kid," I breathe.

He looks up, meeting my eyes. "I'm sorry. I should've told you a long time ago, but the first time I saw those scars—and I knew that was Holland—I thought you'd hate me for it. TJ, please—" His voice breaks with a desperate hitch in his breath. "*Please* don't hate me. I don't think—I don't think I'd be able to live with myself, knowing—"

"Max."

He grits his teeth and closes his eyes, his face twisting in a way that makes it look like he's in pain. The expression brings me back to my own struggle months ago, right after Ethan slipped into a coma, when I was convinced the Archer hated me. I'm not going to let Max believe the same.

"Max, look at me."

His jaw is clenched so hard, I can see it trembling. I wait for him to open his eyes and look at me, then continue. "I don't hate you. I would *never* hate you."

Max blinks. His mouth works, struggling to form words, before sound finally comes out. "But—you—Holland—"

"Holland gave me my scars, not you." I close my eyes and take a deep breath, fighting off the memories. "I'm not going to hate you for your past, Max."

"You don't know what I've done," he whispers, tearing up as his shoulders sink.

"I know what you're doing right now." I lean forward, forcing him to look up at me.

Max gives a weak half-laugh. "Dragging you into all this stuff you never wanted to be involved in? Yeah. *Awesome.*"

"Putting your life on the line to help those kids."

Max chews on his lower lip but stays silent.

I nod toward the door. "That boy out there? He'd be in Holland's hands right now if it wasn't for you."

"Alec saved him, not me."

"You're the one who noticed something wrong in the first place. And that doesn't change the fact that you left everything in Ordinem behind to come out here and make a difference."

"I wish I could do more," he murmurs.

"You're doing what you can. No matter what your past is, Max, I know the person you are now."

Max bites his lip and shakes his head, looking to the side. "You should stay far away from me," he says softly. "Far away from this battle we're in, far away from Holland."

He swallows hard, his voice dropping to below a whisper. "I already dragged you into all this, and after I watched Alec shoot someone—because of *me*—I can't...I—" He squeezes his eyes shut, visibly fighting his tears. "I already have too much blood on my hands, TJ. I can't add yours to that list."

I grip Max's shoulders, but he won't turn his face to meet my eyes. "I'm not leaving," I tell him. "If something happens to me fighting Holland, it won't be your fault. It's my choice to stay, Max, and I want to fight Holland as much as the two of you do." I hesitate. "My sister is one of the new kids she took, you know."

His lip quivers the same way Riya's always did when she was on the verge of tears, but he still refuses to look up at me.

"I'll never hate you, Max," I say softly. "No matter what you've done."

With those words, Max finally cracks. He buries his face between his hands, shoulders hunched and trembling as a silent sob escapes him.

He's still just a kid. As I watch his façade finally crumble, the words have never felt so true. He's carrying a constant weight on his shoulders—the bloody burden of his past.

Anger bubbles within me as I watch the effects of what Holland has put the boy in front of me through. Of what Holland is *currently* putting my sister through. I'd love nothing more than to be marching through the Draft sublevels, a pulse rifle in hand, to hunt Holland down for everything she's done.

As soon as the thought strikes me, it flees. Who am I kidding? I can't even stomach the thought of returning to Ordinem. Holland broke me four weeks ago—I'm not the strong one who's going to stride in with guns blazing and bring justice.

I wrap my arms around Max's shaking form. At least I can do something for him.

He goes stiff for a few beats, his expression frozen in shock, before he accepts the hug and buries his face in my hoodie.

In another world, Max could've been my brother. The relationship we've built in only a couple weeks, the scars we have in common, the way he reminds me of Riya, the way he trusts me—

You don't deserve this, a voice in the back of my mind whispers. *You don't deserve his trust. Not after how you betrayed Rev.*

How can I sit here, persuading Max to trust me, when I still haven't told Rev about Eliza?

I manage to banish the thought before it takes over, but it still leaves a bitter aftertaste. How much longer can I go without telling her?

But how *can* I tell her? How can I tell Rev that I betrayed her sister to Holland? That whatever Holland might do with that information is my fault?

"Thank you," Max says, his soft voice muffled by my sweatshirt.

I give him a reassuring nod as he pulls away, swiping at red eyes. He takes a shaky breath, offering me a weak smile. In that look, I can tell that whatever wall Max has been hiding behind is now gone. The way that he's always acted with me—how he's been so reluctant to tell me anything related to himself—makes sense now.

"Can I..." Max clears his throat. "Is it alright if I...ask you about something? Now that you know how I'm connected?"

"Of course."

"You said you were related to Maya Collins, right?"

My mother's name makes my muscles tense, but I force myself to relax as I nod.

"I'm assuming you know she was involved in the Draft?"

"Yeah. I didn't find out until the Archer went after her, but I know now."

Max tilts his head. "See, that's what doesn't make sense. You're related to Maya, who worked for Holland, but for some reason, Holland did..." He glances at my arm. "Whatever caused those scars. And the Archer—you said she saved your life, right? Why would she go from targeting your aunt to saving you?"

He has an incredible memory, I think, remembering what I told him about Maya being my aunt during our first meeting. I let out a slow breath and meet his eyes. "You want to hear the whole story?"

His eyes light up. "Everything?"

"Everything."

The door to the room opens and Alec walks in, closing it gently behind him.

He pauses when he turns to face us. "Should I...leave for a minute?"

"No, it's fine." I gesture to the cushion next to me. "You'll want to hear this, too."

As soon as Alec sits down, I tell them everything. I tell them that Maya is actually my mother, that Riya and I were kept secluded from the world, and then I start from the night I met Rev. I tell them about how I became the infamous Thief, how the Archer and I grew closer, how I found out my parents were involved in the Draft.

As soon as I mention Reiko, Max's eyes widen. "Wait. I knew her. She's—"

"A Draft kid, I know. "Holland sent her to spy on me and Riya, and she did her job. In the end, she and Holland staged something to get me to turn myself in."

"And that's when everything happened," Max says quietly, glancing at my arm.

"Yeah." I take a deep breath. Do I tell them the details? "I'll...spare you the specifics, but for some reason, Holland...thought I had information that I didn't. Something about a cure. Apparently, my mother knew something about it and Holland thought she planted the information in my mind, but I turned out to be just as clueless as everybody else. And..." I trail off, unable to find a way to tell them about what Adrian did to me. Instead, I roll up the sleeve of my sweatshirt enough for patches of scar tissue to be visible. Alec's eyes go wide and Max, despite having already seen my arm, still looks a little stunned.

"She...she tortured you for it?" Alec whispers.

I wince. "Yeah. A couple weeks, I think, and then she realized I didn't have what she wanted and tried to kill me. I made it out, but she still has my sister."

"How'd you get out?" Max asks, a hint of awe in his voice.

"The Archer."

Max nods. It's all the explanation he seems to need.

"How *did* you two know my mother?" I ask, now that I'm finally able to speak freely about it.

Alec looks to Max. "You want to answer that one?"

"Yeah." Max tugs on one of his curls. "I didn't know her very well, but I saw her around a few times, and I heard her name every so often. She was a scientist. A geneticist, I think?"

"Huh. What did she..." I hesitate, almost afraid to ask the question. "What did she do?"

"She was working on the serum. The one Holland's using now. It's been in development since..."

He trails off, looking down.

"Since what, Max?" I ask.

"Since I..." He swallows hard. "I messed up."

Alec leans forward, a flash of intrigue in his eyes. This must be a story he hasn't heard yet.

"I was almost thirteen when Holland sent me out on my first big mission," Max says quietly. "A few months before I escaped. I'd already done plenty of terrible things for Holland, but this...I didn't know what she'd eventually ask me to do. She told me it was just a reconnaissance mission, at first. Befriending another kid so that I could get close enough to keep an eye on the parents—one of them worked for Holland and she was beginning to doubt their loyalty. I spent long enough around them..." Max looks to the side so I can't see his face. "They were the closest thing I had to a family. When Holland confirmed her suspicions, she asked me—she *ordered* me—to kill the father, but I—I couldn't. And when I refused..."

Max grimaces and hangs his head. "When I wouldn't do it, Holland made me watch as she—as she..." He bites his lip and closes his eyes.

Alec puts his arm around Max's shoulder and Max leans into him, a tear leaking down his face. "It's my fault," he whispers. "The whole family. Including the two innocents, even the kid. Holland...it was because of me."

Alec rubs Max's shoulder. "You're not the one who did it, Max. That was Holland."

"She only did it because of me." He shakes his head hard, like he's trying to rid himself of the memories. "I don't think I'll ever stop seeing the look on their faces—the betrayal, when they realized...and then when Holland..."

Max leans his head on Alec's shoulder, his face twisted. "Like I said," he says, so quietly I can barely hear, "I have too much blood on my hands."

"Oh, kid," Alec says gently, pulling Max into a full embrace. Even Alec's eyes are watering as he meets my gaze over Max's shoulder.

There's nothing I can possibly say to comfort Max. I know the guilt of betrayal all too well, and Max has had to deal with way more than me. I can't even begin to imagine what he's going through right now, let alone try to help him through it.

And yet, Alec and Max...they live with a purpose. With strength, and determination, even through their hurt.

Maybe it's possible for me to do the same.

Chapter Twenty-Two

Hunter Lane

For the next day after my visit to the market with Reiko, things between us stay...relatively normal. For some reason, that isn't what I anticipated. But Reiko, contrary to what I expected, doesn't seem to look at me any differently after hearing about Leah, and neither of us brings up the altercation with Reiko's old friend. If anything, I feel closer to her now than ever before. Both of us have issues with our older siblings—having that shared wound forges a bond between us.

And both of us have a bit of hope for our older siblings—even if Reiko mentioning that she knew my sister as a Draft agent makes me want nothing more than to find Leah and swing a few well-deserved punches.

I, at least, can be here for Reiko. The more we talk, the more I see her as a younger sister, and the more frustrating the rest of the UND's treatment of her becomes.

Today, as we make our way through the halls toward the prison wing, people take notice. They make an admirable effort to hide their stares and whispers—my reputation is enough to scare them out of outright bullying—but I notice regardless as we dodge people on their way to and from the mess hall, the living quarters, and the training rooms.

Reiko's eyes catch on a woman watching us from the other side of the hall. Tall, deep bronze skin, sharp features. From Nadzor, if I had to guess—and the fact that I don't recognize her means she's newer to the Undrafted. The *audacity* she has, outright staring like she is. A tremor runs through my hands, itching for a fight.

I turn my attention to Reiko instead, nudging her over the arm of my chair. "If I didn't know better, I'd say you're dreading this."

She casts one last look at the woman before we round the corner, putting her out of sight. "It's not that. It's all the people. They're whispering about you. Spending time with the traitor."

"And?"

"You don't care?"

I shrug. "I have better things to care about than what the rest of the people here think of me. They've been looking for an excuse to whisper about me for years."

Reiko doesn't quite raise her head, but I catch a sliver of a smile on her face. The tension in my muscles eases and we make it into the prison wing without trouble.

Reiko's steps drag as we approach Adrian's cell.

"Are you sure you want to do this?" I ask. "You don't have to visit him, you know. All I promised him was that I'd let you, if you were up for it."

Reiko shakes her head. "No, I'm ready. It's just...this is the first time we've talked since I convinced him to come up with me, and it's really my fault he's here at all. I don't know how he's going to react to seeing me. And..."

"And what?" I ask when she doesn't continue.

She stares at the cell door. "Maybe I sound crazy, but I don't know what side he's on anymore. Ours, or Holland's." She takes a shaky breath. "I'm just...nervous. That's it."

From the way Reiko avoids my eyes, I get the feeling her nervousness has to do with something more than her brother. I can't tell what, though.

Her words bring to mind my last conversation with Adrian, making me hesitate to open the door as I scan my wristband. Adrian *does* have doubts.

So what side *is* he truly on, now that he's no longer under Holland's power? Now that all his cards are on the table?

The lock disengages with a whir and I push the door open to reveal the dim cell inside.

I roll in first and Reiko follows, letting the door shut gently behind her.

"Adrian?" Reiko says, her whisper echoing in the room.

Adrian's head snaps up at her voice, and he stares at her from his cross-legged position in the center of the room as if he doesn't believe she's real.

Then, his face breaks into a disbelieving smile—the first genuine one I've seen from the man. "You seem to be faring better than me, I see."

Reiko glances at me and I shake my head. "They didn't hurt him."

"Not badly, anyways. Although this one"—he juts his chin at me—"wanted to." Adrian continues to watch Reiko. More emotion washes over his face in these few moments than I've seen from him as long as he's been here.

I catch a flash of bright red skin as the manacles around his wrists shift. Blood? The edges of the metal must be rubbing his skin raw.

"I missed you," Adrian says, the tiniest catch in his voice.

Reiko hesitates, her eyes flicking back and forth between him and me. Finally, she comes to a decision and sits directly in front of him, matching his cross-legged position.

Adrian's shoulders sink in obvious relief. "How are you?" he asks.

"I've been...worried about you," Reiko admits. "And...it hasn't been easy, being here where everybody knows my past. But it's good to be fighting for a cause." She looks up at him, steel in her expression. "It's good to be fighting against the Draft."

To my surprise, Adrian only gives her a nod at that. "You've learned a lot about Anyssa, I assume. The parts she didn't let you see as a...Draft agent."

Reiko's posture droops. "I have," she says softly.

I lean forward as I watch the conversation. I can't fight the feeling that I'm missing an important detail or piece of context, but I don't interrupt.

"Now you know why I stayed, then," Adrian says, his head dipping slightly. "I had to protect you. Working for Anyssa was the only way I could see."

"Why didn't you tell me how—how *horrible* she was?!" Reiko digs one of her hands through her hair.

Her sudden outburst reminds me of my conversation with her on the way back from the market. She took hearing about Holland's cruelty so *personally*, and now she's doing it again. It makes sense for a former Draft agent to be affected by Holland's actions—but to react so strongly?

What am I missing?

"Reiko, I couldn't," Adrian says. "Do you know how much *danger* we would've been in if Holland had found out I put my loyalty to you above my loyalty to her?"

"You could've at least *told me*, Adrian! You could've done something other than let me *idolize* her!"

Adrian shakes his head. "I had to keep you safe." His voice comes out gentler than I've ever heard it. "And she wouldn't have hesitated to have either of us killed if she doubted our loyalties. It was better to let you believe in her than to make you doubt her and force you to cover it up."

"But...it's *us*." Reiko's face twists with emotion as she meets her brother's eyes. "She wouldn't have hurt *us*."

Adrian hesitates. Shifts in his chains. Looks down, to the side. His voice scrapes as he answers. "I wish I could tell you that was true."

"But Adrian, we're her—" Reiko cuts herself off there, looking at me.

What has she not told me?

Adrian doesn't seem to notice, lost in whatever memory Reiko's words brought to the surface. He's still looking away when he continues. "You think that would stop her?" He gives a hollow laugh. "No. Being her children offers us no protection."

I freeze.

Reiko's eyes, still fixed on me, go round.

Her children.

"Adrian," Reiko whispers.

The man finally looks up, dragging his hands down his tired face. The exhaustion fades, though, when he registers me rolling toward him. "He didn't know," Adrian says, inching away from me. Fear—the first true fear I've seen from him—flashes over his face as I snatch the collar of his shirt and jerk him face-to-face with me.

"Holland," I say, my voice low, "is your *mother?!*"

Out of the corner of my eye, I can see Reiko stumbling away from me.

Adrian grimaces as I twist his collar, anger simmering under my skin. "She couldn't tell you," he grunts. "Don't be angry at her."

"This whole time," I growl. "The two of you were Holland's *kids.*"

"That doesn't mean we're—"

"Was it all faked, then? Your *doubts*?" I hiss, quiet enough that Reiko can't hear. "I thought maybe, just *maybe*, you had a little bit of good in you, Adrian."

Adrian raises his hands slightly in defense. "If you don't believe me, believe Reiko. I'll admit, when we first escaped the Draft, I wasn't sure where I stood. But Reiko always knew. She's on your side."

I very nearly deck the man right then and there.

Holland's son.

But I look over my shoulder and see Reiko standing with her back to the wall, looking terrified. Desperation floods her expression—a silent plea for me to not hurt Adrian.

Holland's daughter.

But...does this really change anything? The encounter with Reiko's past friend flashes through my head. If I'd known about this then, I wouldn't have been any less confident that Reiko had truly switched sides. I would've still believed her.

No. Reiko's loyalties did change.

But the same question I've been asking remains. *Have Adrian's?*

I hold him for another tense moment before shoving him away, sending him sprawling on the concrete with a rattle of chains. Then I turn to Reiko.

"Hey!" Adrian shoots to his feet, but I'm already out of his range. He lets out a frustrated yell, jerking at the end of his chains. "Don't blame her! Hunter, stay away from her!"

"I'm sorry," Reiko says, shifting on her feet as I approach. "I wanted to tell you, but Adrian—I was worried, if you knew—I didn't know what might happen to him—"

I hold out my hand and she falls silent. "Look me in the eyes and tell me whose side you're on, Reiko."

She swallows hard and meets my gaze unflinchingly. "Yours. I switched sides the minute I left."

"And I believe you." I give her a nod.

Reiko lets out a breath, relief washing over her face. "Thank you."

I turn back to Adrian, who stands at the end of his chains, breathing hard. "And you," I say. "Whose side are you on, Adrian?"

Adrian looks at me through his matted sandy curls, his eyes narrow. He stands taller than me, but after everything I've seen from him—his care for Reiko, the way his demeanor shifted when he talked about Holland—he doesn't scare me like he used to. He's nothing more than a desperate man in a desperate situation, and if anything, I can sympathize with him.

I almost think he's not going to respond when his quiet words fill the cell. "Reiko's."

The single word is heavy with meaning, reinforced by Adrian's steady gaze. He doesn't know where his loyalties lie, except with Reiko.

For now, that's answer enough.

Chapter Twenty-Three

Reverie Adams

As soon as our helicopter lands in the Undrafted compound's hangar, the place becomes a blur of chaos.

We didn't have any sort of sendoff when we left for Ordinem because of the short notice of the mission and Daniel's tendency to keep his cards close to his chest. Word must have gotten around in the couple short weeks we were gone if the crowd in the hangar is anything to go by. Savi rubs her bleary eyes as the door opens and people rush to help us down. Kaz, the dark circles under his eyes as pronounced as my own, nearly stumbles as he carries Riya's unconscious body out.

Nora is the first to shove her way forward through the crowd, recognizable for her bright orange hair and stocky build. She checks Riya's pulse, shares some words with Kaz that I can't hear over the clamor, and takes Riya from him before running off toward the infirmary.

Kaz approaches me and Savi, brushing off the people vying for his attention. They press in around the three of us, shouting questions about the mission.

"We need to get to Daniel!" Kaz yells, putting one arm around Savi and the other around me. I'm too exhausted to protest as he guides us through the crowd and around the Undrafted's second helicopter, forcing the people to make way for us to get into the main compound. I catch a glimpse of raven hair that looks like TJ's over some of the heads, but Kaz and the crowd don't give me time to shove through and see. I'll have to find him again after the debrief.

When we're about halfway to the main doors, the crowd parts to reveal Daniel making his way toward us. He gives a nod before turning back to the doors and leading us inside. The people part easily, almost reverently, before him as he leads us into the main compound, then down the hall to his office.

As soon as the door shuts behind us, blocking out the noise of the crowd, I can hear Savi's sigh of relief. Three chairs sit in a line facing Daniel's desk.

Daniel stands behind his desk before turning to face us. "Sit. You three look exhausted."

Savi collapses into the nearest chair without further prompting and I follow her lead. Kaz gives Daniel an appreciative nod before sitting on the other side of Savi.

"I know it's been a long couple of weeks," Daniel says, sitting in his own chair, "so I'll keep this as brief as I can. Kaz has kept me updated along the way, but I need to know what's happened in the past twenty-four hours."

Kaz nods and starts at the beginning, with our plan and Savi going into the Draft headquarters first. I hand Daniel the envelope Leah gave me—the fact that we met Daniel's contact doesn't faze him as much as I expect, unless he's just doing a good job at hiding it—and explain about Riya. Savi, too, was able to download some blueprints while she was connected to the Enforcers' system, and I describe the room I passed on my way out, with Leah working on some kind of device. Other than that, Kaz hits all the major points.

I fight a shudder at the memory of how Riya tried to kill me. The look in her eyes will be burned into my mind for a long time, along with her pained cries when she managed to fight the serum. The idea that Holland can do that to *anybody* with her serum is horrifying. The only consolation is that she won't use it on the rest of the Draft kids—on Eliza—until she finds her missing piece.

"I'll get this drive to Nora," Daniel says. "Hopefully, she and her research team will be able to formulate a cure from the information here, combined with whatever she can figure out based on Riya."

I remember Leah's words to me back in the sublevels. *It's a message from Maya to—I can't remember his name, but it's to her son.* "Actually..." I trail off. Is Daniel even going to consider this request? "Can TJ take a look? When you're done with it? Leah said it had a message from Maya to TJ, and he deserves to see whatever it is."

Daniel nods. "Of course. I'll give it to him myself, as soon as I download the info and get it to Nora. And speaking of TJ, you're free to tell him everything. He deserves to know, particularly about his sister. And I haven't told him about Ethan yet—I figured he would take it better coming from you." Daniel shakes his head. "My condolences about your friend, Savi and Rev. I admire you both for executing your mission regardless."

Savi's gaze drops to her lap and Kaz casts her a concerned look.

The two of them invite me to come to the mess hall with them once Daniel dismisses us—none of us have eaten since yesterday—but I set off in search of TJ instead. I see him from a distance, near the living quarters, in the sitting area at the end of the hall. He sits on the edge of a small couch with his elbows on his knees and his head in his hands.

I hesitate as I draw toward the end of the hall. What is everything I'm about to tell him going to do to our relationship? How long is it going to take him to remember that Riya's situation is my fault, and to react accordingly?

He must hear my deep breath, because he shoots to his feet, his eyes locking on me. "You're okay!" he says, sounding relieved. "I couldn't find you in the chaos at the hangar, so I tried the infirmary, but Nora told me I couldn't go in—Rev, what's *happening?* Is everybody okay? And Riya—?"

"Riya's alive," I tell him. "But...remember what I told you the first time I saw her out in the ruins? About whatever Holland did to her?"

I can practically see the excitement drain from him. "No," he whispers. "She's not gone. She can't be gone." He snaps his head up, drilling me with an urgent look. "I have to see her. Rev, you have to get me in to *see her*—"

He starts for the hall, but I grab his arm and pull him back. "Nora won't let you in, not until the sedative wears off and she's stabilized."

TJ stares longingly down the hallway, but doesn't fight my grip. "What happened? How is she here? Are you sure she's—she's—"

"She goes back and forth," I tell him. "When we were in the sublevels..." I rub my neck where Riya's grip left bruises.

TJ follows the motion and his eyes go wide as soon as he sees the marks. "Riya...that was *Riya*?" he breathes.

"She tried to kill me." I break the news as gently as I can.

TJ stands frozen. I nudge him toward the couch, the nearest seat, worried he'll collapse. His knees buckle, dropping him hard onto the cushion.

"She's not gone," I say, hoping to ease the pain on his face. "Once we got her, and she woke up, she was herself. For a little while. I think seeing you will help her."

TJ stares at the wall on the other side of the room with an empty expression. "How did Holland do it?" he asks quietly. His eyes brim with moisture, but underneath his voice, I can hear barely-contained rage.

"Nora is going to try to figure out the specifics of Holland's serum. We got a flash drive and some notes from Daniel's spy in the Draft that should help her." I pause. "The flash drive...was from Maya."

TJ exhales slowly and his head sinks back into his hands. "Of course it was," he murmurs.

"It was for you. Daniel's going to bring it to you as soon as he's downloaded the info and shared it with Nora. And..." I sit down next to him. "That's not all."

"Please tell me you have good news," he says softly.

"I wish I did." I take a deep breath. "While we were there, Savi and I visited Ethan, and...they told us he wasn't there anymore. Before we got to Ordinem, he..." I trail off, closing my eyes against a wave of emotion.

TJ processes in silence, his head still buried in his hands, and he eventually begins to tremble.

I lay my hand on his shoulder. "This isn't your fault," I say. "You know that, right?"

"Sure." His voice comes out hollow.

"TJ, I mean that."

"That's the thing." TJ sits up, looking somewhere in the distance with teary eyes. "It *is* my fault, Rev. I'm the one who got Ethan involved, and now he's—he's gone, because of me. And Riya—Riya came into the Draft sublevels for *me*, and I didn't even—"

His voice cracks and he takes a breath to steady himself. "I didn't even say goodbye," he whispers. "To either of them."

I wrap my arm around his shoulders as he hunches over. "We all make mistakes, TJ. We all have fights. But that doesn't change the fact that this is *not* your fault."

TJ grits his teeth, his face twisting. He looks like he wants to say something, but can't bring himself to. We settle into silence, thinking. Grieving. Supporting each other, silently.

I'm the first to shatter the silence. "I have something for you."

"What?"

"I promised I'd go to your apartment, remember?" From my pocket, I produce the carefully-folded picture of TJ and Riya, along with TJ's sketch of the constellations.

He blinks, stunned, before taking the pieces in shaking hands. "I remember drawing this," he whispers, tracing his finger over some of his cursive. His attention shifts to Riya's doodles in colored pen. "Riya snuck in when I wasn't paying attention and started writing all over it. And the photo…" He looks up at me, eyes bright with tears. "Thank you."

"You're welcome." The look on TJ's face makes the overwhelming pain of that night more than worth it.

His gaze lingers on the pictures for a few long moments before he carefully folds them and slips them in his pocket. "There's…something I should probably tell you," he says. "You know how you used to work at the Rec Center?"

I nod, confused, as memories of Max and Alec and days of target practice flash through my head. TJ never had anything to do with the Rec Center.

"Well…I might've met Alec."

"You—*what*?" I pull my arm away from his shoulder and lean back, twisting to face him.

"And—" TJ hesitates, obviously nervous, before the words come tumbling out. "He knows you're the Archer."

"*What?*" The revelation circles in my head. *Alec knows my identity.* "TJ, how on *Earth* did you meet Alec, and how—what *happened* while I was gone?! How does he know who I am? What else does he know?"

"I didn't know you used to know him!" TJ protests. "We met by accident. It's a long story that I'll tell you sometime—and he was really nice, and I figured out that he used to be connected to Holland somehow—and then he asked me about you!"

"So then tell him I'm *not the Archer*!" I rub my forehead as I stand, my mind scrambling for answers. How did Alec end up in Nadzor? What's going to happen now that he knows my identity? What does he think of me now?

"Rev, what's so terrible about him knowing?"

"He—" I let out a breath and begin to pace. "He's one of the few people who cared about me. I just…don't know what he's going to think of me, knowing…everything." I pause, facing TJ. "How'd he react?" I ask. "When he found out?"

"He already suspected, I think," TJ says. "And he made it sound like you two had a lot to catch up on. I think he really wants to see you. I'm going back to his place in a couple days for a training session—you should come with me."

"Training?" I ask, raising a brow.

"I told you I'd do my best not to get mugged again." The corners of his lips twitch up. "And I had to do *something* while you were gone."

I give a faint smile, but it's overshadowed by my worry about seeing Alec again. "Are you sure he wants to see me, after...?"

"Rev, of course he wants to see you. The first thing he asked me when he figured things out was how you were doing. He's worried about you."

"That *does* sound like Alec."

"He worries a lot," TJ agrees. "So you'll come with me?"

"I'll come with you."

He smiles slightly. "You know, that went a lot better than I expected."

"Telling me about Alec?"

He nods. "Something told me you wouldn't be thrilled with him knowing your identity. I got worried."

"After everything we've been through?" I shake my head. "It's going to take a lot more than an identity reveal for you to get rid of me, TJ."

He smiles at that, but behind his expression, I can tell my words strike something deep within him. "Yeah," he says, but his eyes take on a far-off look. He quickly pulls himself out of his thoughts. "You eaten yet? Since you got back?"

I shake my head. "I wanted to talk to you first."

TJ runs a hand through his hair, his other fiddling with the strings on his hoodie. As his sleeve slips down, I catch a glimpse of scars circling his left wrist, but I don't mention it as he meets my eyes. "Want to grab breakfast, then? Well—brunch?"

The corners of my lips turn up. "Of course. And TJ? We're going to stop her."

His hand falls from his hair as he turns toward the hall, away from me.

"We're *going* to stop her," I repeat. "For Ethan, and for our sisters. Before she can hurt anybody else."

"Yeah." TJ takes a deep breath, and I can tell in that gesture he doesn't fully believe the words. "Before she can hurt anybody else."

Chapter Twenty-Four

TJ Collins

Despite Nora telling me not to visit Riya until further notice, my self-control wears thin by the time night comes around and the compound's lights dim. I find myself standing outside the infirmary door a little past two in the morning, knocking continuously until a bleary-eyed Nora answers. It was a gamble, hoping to find her here this late, but it paid off.

The dim light of the infirmary behind her makes the shadows under her eyes more pronounced. "TJ? What are you doing here?"

"I have to see her," I say, trying to keep my voice even. I'm not leaving here until I do.

Nora sighs and pulls half her hair over her shoulder, then gathers the other side on top of her head and twists it into a bun. "I already told you, she's supposed to be in isolation until after I've run some tests."

"I'm assuming you stayed up all night to run those tests?"

She presses her lips into a line as she twists the rest of her hair into a second bun. "Daniel *specifically* told me—"

"Daniel wouldn't approve of me training outside the compound, and you've kept that secret for me," I point out. "Please, Nora. It's my little sister. I have to see her."

She studies me from behind a few stray curls that didn't make it into her buns. I hold my breath as she considers, hoping she'll listen. If not, I have a long day of hallway waiting ahead of me.

Nora leans out the doorway, checks down the dimmed hall in both directions, then steps back and opens her door a little wider. "Come in. You're not going to tell *anybody* about this, you hear me?"

I grin and step inside. "Of course. Thank you."

Only a single lamp, sitting on Nora's desk, lights the room. Looking at her face, I realize that my comment about her staying up all night might actually be warranted. I glance around the rest of the room. Aside from one in the back corner, the row of beds is empty and neatly made, with the privacy curtains tied back. In the shadows of the opposite corner, I can make out a bed with a rumpled blanket and pillow that don't match the rest of the infirmary.

I twist to face Nora again. "You slept here, didn't you?"

She shrugs. "I had a late night."

"What kind of tests were you running on my sister?"

"It wasn't all Riya," Nora admits, flipping one of the folders on her desk closed. I crane my neck and catch a glimpse of the tables Nora showed me a week ago, when she told me about my mutation.

I frown. "You're looking into that genetics thing, aren't you?"

"I just can't figure it out!" Nora huffs out a breath. "I thought Riya might have the same mutation as you, but she doesn't. Which isn't *huge*, but it supports my theory that someone messed with your genetics."

Genetics. A thought suddenly strikes me. "My mother was a geneticist," I say quietly, looking up at Nora.

She just stares at me, neither of us wanting to state the obvious implication.

My own mother manipulated my DNA.

Nora puts a hand on my shoulder. "But that's not why you're here, and unless I make some radical discovery about how or why your genes were manipulated, it doesn't affect anything. Let's go see your sister, yeah?"

I perk up. "Where is she?"

"I..." Nora hesitates. "Well, it'll be easier to just show you. With all the staff we keep here during normal hours, you didn't think the infirmary was only this one room, did you?"

As she guides me to the door behind her desk, I keep my mouth shut. I *did* think this was Nora's only room.

She opens the door to reveal a hallway and flips a switch on the wall, flooding the space with white fluorescent light. I wince at the brightness and by the time my eyes adjust, we've already reached another door halfway down the hall. Nora pauses before opening it, turning to me. "Before you go in...just know that it looks worse than it is."

"What's that supposed to mean?"

She fishes in her pocket for a key and unlocks the door. It swings inward to reveal another dark room, about the same size as my bathroom. I draw my brow. "Where is..."

My gaze drifts to the right and I step forward, eyes wide. The entire wall looks to be made of glass, with a larger room on the other side. Aside from a single hospital bed in the center, the room is unfurnished. The bed is less of a bed and more of a reclined chair, with armrests and footrests, along with a heart rate monitor and other medical devices on a stand next to it. And on top of that hospital bed, my little sister sits with her eyes wide open.

"This is why I said it would be easier to show you," Nora says softly. "We have to keep her in an isolation room for now. She's a flight risk—and a fight risk—plus, this one-way glass lets us observe her, just in case. I know she's your little sister, but...be careful in there, alright?"

I nod, my eyes fixed on Riya.

Nora opens a door next to the glass wall and Riya's gaze flits toward the motion. "Who's there?" she calls, tensing up.

Something's wrong. I can't pinpoint what it is, but something in her voice gives me pause as I walk into the room.

Riya sits straight up, her eyes tracking my every movement, fingers gripping the armrests. Thin bonds, not unlike the nylon ropes Rev uses for her grapple arrows, secure Riya's wrists to the armrests. I bristle at the sight, but I can't blame Nora after seeing the bruises Riya left on Rev's neck.

Something's wrong, the voice in the back of my head repeats as I meet Riya's eyes. "Riya?" I ask, taking another step.

She narrows her eyes. "How do you know my name?"

I freeze mid-step, my breath catching in my throat. *It's just the shock,* I tell myself. *It's just a side effect. She'll recognize me.* "Riya, it's me. It's TJ. Your brother."

"TJ Collins," she sneers. "I know about you. Maya's son, the one that Anyssa can't *wait* to get her hands on."

Her words make me hesitate. Doesn't Holland want to kill me? *Unless something's changed.* My heart races at the thought. "Riya, I'm your *brother.*"

She scoffs. "I don't have a brother."

Her eyes dart to the one-way glass behind me. I twist and look over my shoulder to see what caught her attention—maybe Nora—

A crash from Riya's direction makes me whip my head back around, but I'm too late. The tall stand with the heart rate monitor on top lies on the floor, the screen shattered, and I recover from the surprise just in time to see Riya snap the set of bonds on her second wrist, as easily as if they were made of paper. She leaps out of the bed, snarling, flying toward me with fingers outstretched like claws.

I yelp and my instincts from sparring with Max kick in, allowing me to narrowly escape Riya's attack. She barrels past, just missing me, and switches direction. "Riya!" I yell, ducking out of her way again. "Please! I'm not here to hurt you!"

A low, guttural sound comes from her throat and she throws herself at me before I've recovered from my last dodge. The shift in direction throws me off-balance and I barely manage to throw myself to the side in time, landing sprawled on the floor. I scramble back as Riya's slight form looms over me, my shoes slipping over the polished tile, but I run into the glass wall behind me before I can make it to my feet.

Riya, her expression twisted, balls one of her fists in the front of my shirt and jerks me to my feet. I pry at her grip, but her fingers don't budge as she slams me back against the glass. The air rushes from my lungs at the impact and I gasp as she pulls me forward, then slams me against the wall again, harder this time.

In her other hand, the light reflects off a glint of something sharp. A shard of glass from the shattered heart rate monitor.

"Riya," I force out, fighting to pry her hands open. She's *never* had this kind of a grip—why is she so much stronger than me? Have I really declined that much?

She holds me tight against the wall, bringing the point of the glass shard to hover under my chin. I raise my hands in surrender, palms open, hoping it'll get her to ease up.

The door to my right bursts open and Nora rushes in, but stops short a few steps in. Riya's head whips toward her. "Stay back! Or I'll hurt him!"

Nora goes still, watching us with wide eyes.

"You're going to take me out of here," Riya hisses, turning her attention back to me. "And you're going to give Holland what she wants."

"I don't have anything Holland wants!" I protest, my breathing becoming quicker, shallower. I've said those words before. In a whitewashed room with icy green eyes—

"Liar." The glass presses against my skin.

I wince. "Riya, *please.*" I lock eyes with her, begging her to remember, but all I can see in her expression is anger. Anger, confusion, hatred—nothing close to recognition.

She shifts the shard so that it's pressing into the sleeve of my left arm. "You have five seconds before this becomes *significantly* more painful. How do we get out of here?"

Riya's face blurs as moisture obscures my vision and my hands shake. Desperation floods my body, making my voice tremble. "Remember me, Riya. *Please!*"

The pressure on my arm increases and I squeeze my eyes shut, preparing for the slit I know is coming.

Instead, there's a clattering sound. The glass shard dropping to the floor. My eyes snap open as Riya releases me, stumbling back.

"Fight it, Riya," I breathe. "*Fight.*"

Her knees buckle and she drops to the ground in a heap, her head buried in her hands. "It hurts," she groans, then, louder, "TJ, it *hurts!*"

I stand, trembling, against the wall as she rocks back and forth on her knees. "Nora, what's happening to her?!"

"She's fighting the serum." Nora lets out a relieved breath as she moves to stand next to me, kicking the glass shard far away from Riya. "You're lucky. She isn't able to do this often, but if what Rev told me about her last encounter is anything to go by, seeing familiar faces helps her come to."

"So she's...herself? Now?"

Nora nods. "I don't know how long it'll last, but you have at least a few minutes with her. I'll step out, if you want me to—but I'll be back in *exactly* two minutes to knock her out. We need to move her to a more secure room for when the serum takes control again."

Riya lets out a cry of pain and I drop to my knees next to her, nodding at Nora. She steps out, closing the door behind her.

She sucks in huge gasps of air, holding her head. "It's getting worse," she gets out through gritted teeth. "It's worse every time—TJ—"

"I'm here." I wrap my arm around her hunched shoulders and she curls into me, the pain ripping soft cries from her throat.

After almost half a minute, the pain appears to fade and Riya sits up, immediately looking me over. "Did I hurt you?" she asks hoarsely, looking back at the chair. "What—how did I get down here?"

I rub my arm where the glass shard pressed against my scars. "No. I'm alright. I'm glad you came to when you did, though."

Riya throws her arms around me, nearly knocking me flat on my back. "I missed you, you idiot," she says, her face buried in my shoulder. "I woke up, and you'd turned yourself in, and I—"

"I'm sorry," I tell her, rubbing her back. "I should've told you I was leaving. I knew you'd convince me to stay, though."

"I'm so glad you're not dead." She pulls back, her eyes wide. "I don't know how much longer I'm going to be able to fight it, TJ. It gets harder every time—seeing your face was the only reason I was able to pull through again, and I don't—I don't know if I'll be able to next time."

Nora reenters the room, brandishing a syringe. Instead of fear, something like relief crosses Riya's face at the sight.

"Hey." I grip both of her shoulders until she meets my eyes. "I'm going to get you out of this. I swear to you, Riya, this is *not* going to be the last time we talk. Okay?"

She nods, tears brimming in her eyes. "Don't let Holland win," she whispers.

"We won't." I pull her into a tight hug as Nora approaches and injects the sedative. "I love you. I'll talk to you soon."

I hold her until her body goes slack, the sedative kicking in.

After helping Nora move Riya to a different room—one with stronger bonds so she won't be able to snap them again—I sit on one of the main infirmary beds, my back leaning against the wall. The room is still deserted, although it'll be bustling when the compound wakes up in a couple hours. Nora sits across from me, both of us still processing.

"I can't believe her strength," Nora says, shaking her head.

"All the Draft kids have it." Bitterness gives my voice a sharp edge. "*Performance enhancers*. It's sick."

"Not that." Nora glances toward the door behind her desk. "I'm talking about fighting through the serum. She was in a *lot* of pain, but she still managed to break through. If anyone's going to pull through this, it's her. And TJ...there's something else you should know."

"That doesn't sound good."

"Holland built a kill switch into the serum."

I inhale sharply. "What does that mean?" I whisper.

"The way Hunter explained it to me, it means that there's a button somewhere out there—and if it's pressed within a very close range..."

She doesn't have to finish the sentence for me to put it together. *Riya would die.*

I'm almost afraid to ask my next question, but I have to know the answer. "Can you bring her back?"

Nora presses her lips into a line. "I don't know," she says softly.

I close my eyes and let the back of my head hit the wall. She can't be gone. She *can't* be gone. One of my trembling hands reaches up, my fingers digging into my scalp. *She can't be gone.*

"I'm working on it," Nora says, resting her hand on my knee. "I'm doing everything I can to find something to counteract what Holland did to her. Hopefully, the tests I ran overnight and the information Rev and Kaz brought will give us some answers when I review it. I can't promise you any results, but I *can* promise that I'll do everything—*everything*—in my power to bring your sister back."

I nod, but my eyes still well with moisture as I stand. "Thank you." My voice scrapes as it comes out.

Nora takes in my haggard appearance, my sunken shoulders, before stepping forward and pulling me into a hug. "I can't imagine what you're going through right now," she says quietly. "I won't rest until I find a way to help your sister. And if there's anything I can do to help *you*, tell me."

I bite my lip, forcing a fresh wave of emotion into submission until it becomes numb. "Thank you for letting me see her," I whisper. "Thank you for everything."

"She's not gone yet." Nora holds my shoulders at arms' length, locking eyes with me. "Don't lose hope, TJ. Promise me that."

I nod, but even Nora can see how uncertain the motion is.

Her grip on my shoulders tightens. "*Promise me.*"

"I promise," I say hoarsely. The words are enough to convince Nora, but I can't fool myself. My *hope* has been steadily draining ever since I first met the Archer, ever since I first discovered how much of a lie I'd been living, how cruel the world could truly be. And now, with Riya, I can feel the last dregs of it slipping away.

But deep down, I fear that more pain, worse pain, is coming for me before all this is over. And the thought of what yet another loss might do to my already broken self...

That thought *terrifies* me.

How much more can I take before the pain breaks me completely?

On my way back to my room, Daniel Bennett himself intercepts me.

Of all the times. Why is he out in the halls right at lights-on? I try in vain to comb my fingers through my tangled hair and straighten out my rumpled hoodie.

Daniel grins when he sees me, but it doesn't do much to put me at ease. What does he want? Does he know about Max and Alec? My technically-not-allowed visit to Riya?

"TJ. Just the man I was looking for."

I muster up a weak smile in response.

Daniel's face shifts to concern as he takes in my appearance. "You're up early. Is everything okay?"

"Fine. I just didn't sleep well." Not a lie, and it seems enough of an explanation to satisfy him.

"Rev told you about the mission and the flash drive, I presume?"

So *that's* what this is about. My heart races, torn between relief and nervousness. "The flash drive from—from my mother."

Daniel nods. "I wanted to deliver it to you myself. I've already downloaded the contents for Nora, and hopefully they'll help her with her research. But this rightfully belongs to you." He produces a plastic bag from the inner pocket of his coat and drops it in my hand.

"Thank you," I say, my throat dry. Something from my mother. For me. I don't know how I'm supposed to feel about that.

"Of course," Daniel replies, a sympathetic smile crossing his face. "TJ, I know the past weeks—the past *months*—have been difficult. And having your sister here, with Holland's serum running through her blood…" He shakes his head. "I can't imagine. I brought you this in person to give me an opportunity to talk to you."

I swallow. The leader of the Undrafted, making a special trip to talk to *me*? Why? I'm not important, not to him.

He only grips my shoulder, meeting my eyes with compassion. "If you need anything, don't hesitate to ask. I'm always available for you. Alright?"

I nod, confused. Is…is that all? Did Daniel Bennett himself seek me out just to tell me that?

I'm not quite sure what to make of it, but the thought that he cares sends a pulse of warmth through my chest.

As I pocket the flash drive, though, the warmth fades. *From my mother.* That thought makes my palms sweat as I finish the walk back to my room. I'll watch it, but not today. After seeing Riya, I don't know how much more emotional turmoil I can handle.

I spend the rest of the day in my room. Nobody comes knocking, so I assume Nora has made up some kind of excuse for me. I do my best to doze off through the day, physically and emotionally exhausted, but sleep becomes a lost cause. Every time I close my eyes, I see Riya's face.

When I wake the next morning, Rev meets me outside the UND gate with her Archer uniform on. The guard doesn't question it—people go out on covert missions all the time, and the Archer tends to merit a little extra respect.

"Why the suit?" I ask her.

"You said Alec has a friend. It's just in case." She looks me over and her face shifts to concern. "What happened?"

"What?"

"What. Happened?"

I rub the back of my neck. "That obvious?"

"Your dark circles have never been worse, and..." A pause. She steps closer. "You've been crying." It's not a question.

I pull my hood over my head, trying to shadow my eyes. "I went to see Riya." I look to the side.

"She didn't recognize you?"

"She attacked me, and then she came to. I've never seen her in that much pain." I exhale, forcing down a lump of emotion.

Rev grimaces. "I'm sorry, TJ."

"It's not your fault she's like this." My expression hardens, fire burning in my chest, and I look to the horizon, where I know Ordinem is. "It's Holland's."

Chapter Twenty-Five

Reverie Adams

It doesn't take too long for us to reach the ruins. As the shadows of the buildings loom over us, I feel my muscles tensing, ready for a fight. I pull my hood lower over my face and periodically check over my shoulder as TJ walks in front of me. Too many shadows hide the alleyways, too many places for a potential attacker to be watching.

Somewhere in these ruins, Alec is waiting. How is he going to react to seeing me, knowing I'm the Archer? TJ's words should be reassuring, but my heart pounds with fear instead of anticipation. I can't see any way Alec would want to see me. I can, however, see him being angry. Angry that I used what he taught me to become the monster I was.

I jog to catch up to TJ, the anticipation making me restless. "TJ? How far—"

Something jerks me back, the strap of my quiver pulling against my chest and nearly throwing me off-balance. A short cry escapes my throat as my back strikes the brick wall of a building. I manage to keep my grip on my bow, but when I catch the flash of light on metal, I know I won't be able to use it.

A sword. No, *two* swords—crossed at my neck. I won't be going anywhere.

TJ whirls around, his eyes going wide.

I grit my teeth and study the figure at the other end of the curved swords. He's shorter than me—significantly so—and a black ski mask covers his head.

"Wait!" TJ yells, running toward us.

I shake my head slightly and drill him with a look, trying to get him to turn back, but he ignores me. He probably can't see my expression under my hood, anyway.

The figure in black glances over his shoulder, notices TJ, and hesitates. I can only see his eyes, but as his focus returns to me, I catch a glimpse of surprise in them. He seems to truly take in my outfit for the first time and his swords falter at my neck. "You're—you're the Archer."

I don't know how someone from Nadzor knows the Archer, or why it gives him pause, but I take advantage of his momentary distraction. I kick at the side of his knee and he drops with a yelp, one of his swords clattering to the ground as he clutches his injury. Twisting the hilt of the other sword to weaken his grip, I plant my foot on his shoulder and throw all my weight behind the shove. He lands flat on his back with a grunt as I rip the other sword from his hand. I level it at him as he props himself up on his elbows, letting the point hover just underneath his chin.

"Wait—wait!" TJ steps to the side of the figure in black, holding his hands up. "Both of you, hold on! I can explain!"

I narrow my eyes and nod toward the swordsman. "You know him?"

TJ hesitates, but nods, glancing between me and the figure in black. "Put the sword down. He's a friend."

I look down the sword and meet my attacker's eyes. He stares up at me, tense, breathing hard. Slowly, I lower the weapon.

He inches away from me, favoring his injured knee. TJ reaches down and helps him to his feet, looping his arm around his shoulders. "You hurt?"

"I'm fine," the boy in black says under his breath. His short stature, and now his voice, are enough to determine that he's certainly younger than me. Despite his words, he limps as TJ walks with him to retrieve his swords. I reluctantly hand over the one I'm holding and the boy casts a glare at me as he takes it, sliding it into a sheath on his back.

I give TJ a sideways look. "You have a *lot* of explaining to do, you know that?"

He answers with an apologetic smile. "To be fair, that's not how I expected this to go."

I walk behind TJ and to his right, the boy in between us, as we head for a building that's in good shape compared to the rest of the ruins. The boy keeps the mask over his face, so I keep my hood pulled low. He glances over his shoulder at me as TJ helps him walk. *My kick must've done a number on his knee,* I think, watching his uneven walk. I hit it from the side—that would be enough to do some damage, which *was* my intention at the time.

We enter the building and I tense as the door shuts behind us, plunging the room into darkness. We pause and a *thunk* signifies a bar falling into place, securing the entrance.

"This way. Third floor." TJ's voice echoes in the space. As my eyes adjust to the dim light, I can make out the two of them approaching a stairwell that looks like it might collapse at any moment.

The boy stifles a cry as he hops up the stairs, leaning heavily on TJ. I sigh and take his other arm, helping to support him up the two flights. He glances at me in surprise, but grunts and accepts my help.

TJ opens one of the doors in the hall and heads inside, the kid hobbling at his side. I linger in the hall, steeling myself. Alec is on the other side of that door. And he knows everything.

I take a deep breath and step inside, closing the door gently behind me. To my right, TJ kneels next to the boy, rolling up his pant leg to take a look at his injured knee. After a few moments, Alec emerges from a door along the same wall—the kitchen, by the glimpse I catch over his shoulder.

He opens his mouth to say something to TJ and the masked boy, but freezes as soon as he sees me. I shift on my feet, unable to meet his eyes. Alec grins and crosses the room to me in a few lanky strides.

I open my mouth to start explaining, to apologize, to say *something*, but Alec just throws his arms around me and pulls me into a tight hug. "*Man,* how I've missed you, Rev," he says in my ear. "Are you okay?"

"I—I don't understand," I whisper. "Don't you know everything?"

"I do. I had my suspicions from the start, especially after everything Max told me and after you left—but all that changes *nothing*. You're like a daughter to me, Rev. You always have been." He pulls back, holding my shoulders at arm's length. "I'll *never* stop caring about you. I'll admit, it took some processing on my end when I figured everything out, but that still holds true."

Through the emotion swirling in my chest, another word sticks out. "Max—have you seen him since I left? Is he okay?"

A crease appears between Alec's brows, then he takes a step back and laughs. "Nobody told you?"

"Told me what?"

Alec looks back toward TJ and the boy, who's watching our exchange intently. "You can lose the mask, kid," Alec calls to him.

"Are you sure that's—"

"Perfectly safe. Promise."

The boy hesitates, then pulls the ski mask up and over his head.

My jaw drops at the sight of the familiar tanned skin and dark mop of curls. "*Max?*"

"How—how do you know me? How do you know *Alec*?"

I slide my hood back from my face.

Max and I stare at each other for a few beats, both of us too shocked to say anything. Next to me, Alec looks like he's barely holding back a burst of laughter.

"You're..." Max shakes his head and blinks hard, as if trying to make sure he's not seeing things. "You—hey, easy!" he yelps as TJ puts pressure on his knee.

TJ winces and pulls back. "Sorry. I've never been as good at this stuff as my sister. Just...try to hold still. I might be able to figure out what's wrong."

Max grimaces and looks back at me. "You're...you're the Archer," he says, his voice coming out quieter.

"Yeah." I sit cross-legged next to him, collapsing my bow and hooking it to my belt. "And you're...running around in a black ski mask? With swords?"

He stares at the wall across from him, looking distant, so I close my mouth and let him process.

TJ steals a few questioning glances at us as he wraps Max's knee and elevates it on a stack of cushions, but neither of us offer him an explanation. As he finishes, Alec nudges him. "Let's give these two a minute."

TJ looks up at me, a brow raised, and I give him a slight nod. He and Alec disappear into the kitchen.

Max continues to stare into the distance, his good knee pulled up to his chest and his arms crossed atop it.

"Sorry about your knee," I say, mostly to break the silence.

His eyes flit to me, then back. "It's alright. I would've done the same. It'll be back to normal in a couple weeks."

"A couple weeks? That seems..."

"Short? Yeah. I heal faster than most."

The conversation lapses back into silence. Max's shoulders hunch and he rests his chin on his knee.

"Hey." I nudge him with my shoulder. "What is it?"

He lets out an empty laugh. "I've been dying to meet the Archer ever since I figured out what she—*you*—were doing. Come to find out, the Archer met me first." He purses his lips and his gaze drops to the floor. "At least it explains everything. Why you cared so much about me back in Ordinem. You knew I was a Draft kid—you were looking for information."

"So *that's* what this is about."

Max shrugs. "I don't know what else I was expecting back then. I should've been suspicious when you were so interested in my life, but—"

"Max."

"What?" He turns his head, still resting on his knee. "Am I wrong?"

"Of course you're wrong! Just because I'm the Archer doesn't mean our relationship wasn't real!"

"Rev, I'm not stupid. I knew you wanted something from me when we first met, but I was so desperate for a friend…" He sighs and returns to looking at the far wall. "I don't blame you. I would've done the same, in your position. It's just not easy finding out that one of the only people you thought cared about you was actually just out for information."

"I wasn't…" I trail off before I can complete my protest. Max has a perfectly valid argument, and I'm not going to lie to him any longer. But…something changed between when I was only out for information and when I left Ordinem. I truly did grow to care about him.

His jaw flexes. "See? I knew it."

"You're right," I admit. "The first few times I talked to you, it was for information. As soon as I knew you'd escaped from the Draft, I obviously wanted to know more. But Max, that's *not* all there was to it, especially as we got closer. You remember that day the Enforcers came to do identity checks?"

He gives a slight nod, looking at me out of the corner of his eye.

"That was before I knew you were a part of the Draft, and before I'd even *considered* how useful you might be. I was in danger that day, too—but I would've done absolutely everything I could've to protect you from the Enforcers." I take a deep breath. "I made some mistakes, and I'm so sorry for the times I manipulated you for information. But don't let yourself believe the lie that I never cared about you, because that's far from the truth. If you don't believe me, ask Alec—he can tell you how many times we talked, trying to figure out some way to take that weight off your shoulders."

Max takes a moment to process that, then finally meets my eyes. His voice comes out so soft, it's nearly a whisper. "You promise? That it was real?"

"Promise."

He leans back against the wall, relief overtaking his expression. I open my mouth to ask him about the swords, but before I can, a crash sounds from the kitchen where TJ and Alec are.

I jump to my feet, unclipping my bow from its place at my hip and reaching for an arrow, and Max follows suit, although he favors his injured leg.

TJ and Alec burst out, slam the door, and Alec yells one word over his shoulder as he holds the rattling door closed. "*Run!*"

TJ snags my arm and pulls me to the apartment's front door. Max doesn't hesitate to follow, seeming to forget about his pain, and we make it through the door before a yell and a loud, splintering *crack* announces the failing of the kitchen door. Alec skids out the front door as the rest of us are almost to the stairs. "Draft kids!"

Max's eyes go wide and I pass him by, TJ still holding my arm. "We have a place!" TJ calls back to them. "If we can make it to the compound, we'll be safe!"

Alec, sprinting toward us, nods as the Draft kids pour out from the doorway—no faces I recognize. He seems to understand, although I have no idea how he'd know about the UND. TJ, probably—but I don't have time to ask him about it as we tear down the stairs, Alec and Max right on our heels.

We emerge into the dark, open first floor and TJ grunts as he hefts the bar on the doors, struggling to lift it. I join him and together we manage to dislodge it just as the Draft kids reach the bottom of the stairs.

Max unsheathes both his swords, standing between us and the Draft kids while TJ shoves the doors open. I draw my bow and take aim with my first taser arrow as soon as the blinding light floods the room.

"Let's go!" TJ shouts, standing just inside the doors as the Draft kids rush to engage Max.

It doesn't take more encouragement than that. I launch as many taser and sedative arrows as I have in my quiver, incapacitating the nearest handful of agents and giving Max a chance to make a break for the door.

TJ is the first out, with me and Alec right behind. Max's hand, wrapped around his sword hilt, digs into my back as he shoves me the final few steps over the threshold.

But he doesn't follow.

He meets my eyes from the other side of the doorway and time seems to freeze as we come to the same realization. We can't outrun them, not with Holland's performance enhancers.

"Make this worth it," Max says, the words filled with both resignation and courage.

"Max, *no!*" Alec screams from just behind me, but Max slams the doors and the *thunk* of the bar falling into place sounds just before Alec's shoulder rams into the wood.

Max might be a good fighter, but he won't be able to beat ten Draft kids.

He just sacrificed himself to buy us time.

Alec lets out a frustrated yell and bangs his fist against the door, but there's no way to help Max now. The first floor of this building has no windows or other exits.

"We have to go!" I snatch Alec's wrist and drag him away from the door.

TJ stares, wide-eyed, at the doors, but doesn't fight me when I push him to start running toward the compound. He must have come to the same conclusion as me.

"We have to help him," Alec says, even as we pick up speed with the building at our backs. "We can't just—"

"There's no way for us to help him now!" The words burn as I say them. "He knew exactly what he was doing, Alec. We would've never been able to outrun them, and Max is the best fighter of all of us. He knew our only chance was for him to hold them off."

Alec grits his teeth and, looking up at him, I can see the glint of tears behind his glasses. He doesn't protest, though.

"What were they there for?" I ask between breaths as the ground underfoot turns to the grainy sand of Nadzor. "Max?"

"Me," TJ says, his head lowering as he runs just ahead. "They were there for me."

Chapter Twenty-Six

Hunter Lane

For the first time I can remember, as I roll into the mess hall, I'm not the one who draws the most stares.

The usual low buzz of conversation has swelled into a noise that sounds more like thunder than anything else—people convening to speculate about the mission, especially after seeing Riya pulled from the helicopter unconscious. Kaz's debriefing should be finished by now, which means this will be the place to find him. And sure enough, following the way people's heads are turned leads my eyes straight to the flat top of Kaz's hair, peeking out from behind a group of people on the far side of the mess hall. At least Kaz had the sense to sit away from the main crowd.

He sits with his feet propped up on the chair next to him, his plate balanced on his lap, and shovels a forkful of salad in his mouth. He doesn't seem to hear my approach.

"Kaz, sitting alone? That's something you don't see every day."

Kaz starts and whips his head around, grinning when he sees me. "I wasn't *alone*."

"Really? Because those empty chairs say otherwise. I'm surprised nobody's tried to take those spots, actually." I nod toward the rest of the room. "Seems like you're just as famous as me now."

Kaz groans. "A few have asked, but Savi managed to small talk them until they went away."

"Oh?" I say, raising a brow. "Savi's with you?"

"She just left." Kaz glares at me. "You're the worst, you know that? We were both just hungry, and Rev had somewhere else to be."

"I'm kidding, I'm kidding." A slight smile tinges my face as I adjust one of the chairs to make room for myself to roll in. For all the jokes he throws at other people, Kaz never fails to be gullible. "So? How was the mission?"

The light in Kaz's expression fades and he sets his fork back on his plate. "It was...a lot. I'm guessing you know we brought back Riya?"

"That's all anybody's been able to talk about."

Kaz shakes his head. "It was rough. Remember when we saw her out by the ruins?"

I nod.

"Well...she's not better. She attacked Rev and probably would've killed her, if she hadn't broken through the serum in time."

From there, Kaz explains the mission from the beginning, starting with the planning and the information Savi discovered about Maya Collins, talking about the folder with the notes and the flash drive, and ending with the escape from the sublevels.

He speaks much more carefully than usual around two subjects; the first of these is Savi, but I expected that. I probably knew about Kaz's interest in her before Kaz himself figured it out. The other, however, makes my palms clammy.

"You said you found a name," I start, nearly afraid to voice the question. "The scientist for Holland who stepped up to take Maya's place. But you never mentioned who."

Kaz winces.

That reaction is all I need to confirm my suspicions. I exhale slowly, propping my elbow on the table and letting my forehead rest on my hand. "It's her, isn't it?"

"Yeah. It's her."

The conversation lapses into silence, with nothing but the chatter of the mess's other occupants in the background. *It's her.* Of *course* it's Leah. Of *course* Leah is the one to take over in Maya Collins' absence, the one working on a way to control those kids with a serum.

"But there's something else," Kaz says, pulling me out of my mental spiral. "Hunter, she's Daniel's spy. She's the one who got us the information."

I blink, struggling to wrap my mind around the revelation. "What?"

"It was supposed to be a simple drop-off—we were never supposed to run into her," Kaz explains. "But she was late and we ran into each other."

"But you were never supposed to know her identity," I say slowly.

Kaz taps his fork against his hand, nodding.

I take a moment to let the implications sink in. My sister...spying for Daniel? But also, leading the research department, leading development on the serum, still working for Holland after what she caused that *monster* to do to our family. What am I supposed to make of that?

I'm not sure, so I snatch the first emotion I can think of to drown out the confusion. Anger. My voice turns dark. "I can't believe she's *leading* development on the serum."

"Hunter, she's *spying* for Daniel! This is what you've been hoping for—that she's not really Holland's!"

My fist comes down on the table hard enough to make Kaz's plate rattle, drawing several curious pairs of eyes, and he flinches. Those were the wrong words, and he knows it.

"What I've been *hoping* for," I say in a low voice, "is that maybe, after watching Holland shoot both of our parents, Leah would get out of the Draft." *Come find me. Make things right.* I squash the thoughts. "But I shouldn't have been hoping. I knew the kind of person she was the moment she made her choice."

My fist, still on the table, trembles. Kaz's eyes flit from that to my face and he takes a deep breath, steeling himself. "It's *always* okay to hope. Especially for your own sister."

I hold his gaze, my knuckles itching with the urge to *fight* over those words. Instead, I roll back from the table, turning toward the exit and putting my back to him. "It wasn't hope, Kaz. It was denial. There's a difference." I should've known from the moment Leah betrayed our family that she'd never leave the Draft. Yes, she gave Daniel information—but that doesn't mean she was fully willing. Daniel has bribery, blackmail, and a plethora of other options at his disposal. The truth is that Leah chose to stay with Holland all these years, letting her little brother fend for himself.

She chose to be a part of making the serum.

But what if she has *changed?* a stubborn voice in the back of my head presses. *What if she's truly against Holland?*

"Hunter." Behind me, Kaz's chair scrapes along the floor as he leaps to his feet. "*Hunter.*"

"What do you want me to say, Kaz?" I snap, spinning to face him. "It's my sister's fault that Holland destroyed our family, and she still stayed with Holland. I don't know how Daniel got that information from her, but Leah *chose* Holland all those years ago."

"But—"

"Kaz, she's *leading* their research department!" Heads turn our way at my outburst, so I restrain my voice. "*She's* the one behind whatever's happening to Riya and the rest of them!"

"I'm not justifying what she's doing," Kaz says, stepping toward me. "I'm telling you that it's not wrong to hope, Hunter. Especially considering what we just found out."

How can he say *that?* Kaz knows everything—other than Daniel and Nora, and now Reiko, Kaz is the only one who does. And yet here he stands, looking me in the eye with that sincerity of his, telling me I should hold out *hope* for the sister who left me for dead.

As I turn back toward the exit, Kaz bites his lip—a signal that he's holding back. Eventually, though, instead of pressing further, Kaz steps up behind me and rests his hand on my shoulder. "Let me know if you need anything."

Without looking at him, I nod.

Kaz's grip tightens. "We're getting close, Hunter. I can feel it. We're *going* to win this."

I press my lips into a determined line. Kaz is right. We're going to win this war. Regardless of whether my sister is allied with the opposing side.

"And maybe," he continues quietly, "once all this is over, and you can talk to her again, she'll have changed. And you'll be able to reconcile."

With that, his hand slips from my shoulder and he lets me continue into the hall. I thought about finding Reiko and bringing some food to Adrian today, but now I have a more pressing destination in mind. I let my familiar rage burn, fueling and strengthening me as I settle into the rhythm of pushing my wheels. One other detail from Kaz's explanation sticks in my mind.

Kaz was never supposed to discover the identity of Daniel's spy.

Daniel's been *keeping this* from me.

I burst into Daniel's office without knocking. If I'm going to get in trouble for something today, it's not going to be showing up unannounced.

The man has the gall to *smile* as I slam the door closed behind me.

"My sister," I say, narrowing my eyes. "When were you planning on telling me?"

Daniel stiffens, but his motions are smooth as he closes his laptop and leans back in his chair. "Hunter, you need to understand—"

"My sister is *spying* for us. Why wouldn't you tell me something like that?"

"I wanted to." Daniel's steely blue eyes fill with some mix of sympathy and sincerity, but it does nothing to douse my frustration. "I truly did. But can you look me in the eyes and tell me your drive is just as strong as it was yesterday?"

I open my mouth to answer, but hesitate. Kaz's words about hope, my own doubts about my sister, flood my mind. *What if?* What if, maybe, she's on our side?

"Exactly," Daniel says.

I *hate* how well he knows me.

"Hunter, I know this feels like a betrayal to you," he continues, leaning forward with his elbows on his desk. "And I, more than anybody else, know how that affects you in particular. But I *needed* you as a field agent. You're one of the best we have, and now that we're so close, I couldn't risk clouding your judgment."

As frustrating as it is, he has a point. If I were in his position, I can't say I wouldn't have made a similar decision. "How long?" I ask, some of my rage draining.

"Recent. Since Maya was killed and Leah moved up in the ranks. I saw an opportunity there and I took it."

I scan for any of his tells, but no fingers reach up to tug his coat sleeves. He's telling the truth, and it makes sense. I let out a long breath, digging a hand through my hair. When did I become so *paranoid?* Daniel has always been the person I can trust. Tough, yes, and often closed-off, but trustworthy. And he cares about me. The concern on his face makes him look like he's aged years since our last conversation.

Kaz's words still floating through my mind, I muster up the courage to voice my traitorous thoughts. "Whose side is she on?"

"*That* is a rather complex question." Daniel tilts his head, considering. "I'm not sure, to be completely honest. She gave us information, but she's still making a significant amount of progress for Holland."

I nod. If I press the issue further, all I do is prove Daniel's right. "I'm not a field agent anymore," I say instead. "And *nothing* will take away my drive to stop the Draft. So you can stop sheltering me."

I expect him to rebuke me for being so bold, but instead, he offers a slight smile. "Noted."

My mind spins as I leave Daniel's office, though. His explanation makes sense, and it's a good policy to eliminate personal motivations whenever possible, but...

This isn't the first time he's kept something from me. Adrian's words from the first interrogation come to mind. *Daniel used to work with Anyssa.* And Daniel's brief explanation of his story, saying that he was never a part of the Draft at all, that he never worked with Anyssa—the brief explanation that included at least one lie, based on the tell I caught on my way out.

Maybe it's paranoia, or maybe it's instinct, but something still feels off.

Chapter Twenty-Seven

Reverie Adams

A few days pass from when TJ took me to see Max and Alec, when the Draft kids came for TJ. Daniel didn't seem thrilled about welcoming Alec to the Undrafted, and he didn't give Alec credentials, but TJ managed to convince him to let Alec stay.

There's nothing I can do except overthink—about why Holland suddenly seems to want TJ again, about Max and whether he's okay, about *TJ*. The whole compound is in a state of *waiting*. Daniel has Nora and her research department working through the files on the serum and the cure, but no real action can be taken until we know more about the serum and how it works. The point of taking down the Draft is to save the kids. If we don't want to risk their lives, we can't do anything until we understand how the serum affects them and how to combat it.

On the flip side of that, though, the pressure builds with every passing day. If we don't find the cure, our only chance at saving the rest of the Draft kids is to get to them before Holland finds her "missing piece," completes her serum, and injects them with it.

The fact that we have nothing to do but *wait* is killing me.

One night, I awake to a loud *thud*. I shoot straight up in bed and scan my room, but nothing seems to be out of the ordinary. Outside, from somewhere in the hall, the sound of heavy footsteps and a door squeaking closed reaches my ears.

I throw on a jacket over my baggy shirt and leggings before easing my door open, careful not to make any noise as I peek out. Kaz and Hunter have rooms just across the hall, and Savi's and TJ's rooms are on the other side of mine. I reach for my bow, which sits folded on a table by the door, and bring it with me as I step into the hall.

The fluorescent lights are dimmed for the night, but the strips of light running along the base of the walls give enough light to see. My thumb hovers over the button on my collapsed bow, ready to activate it at a moment's notice as I search the hallway, but...

I pause. Only one figure populates the hallway. He's huddled against the wall with knees pulled up to his chest, his head resting on them. Over the quiet buzz of the night lighting, I can hear his jagged breaths from here.

"TJ?" I whisper, setting my bow back down before stepping into the hall and letting my door shut behind me.

No response.

As I move closer, I can make out his white-knuckled fists, his violent trembling. Another nightmare, although if he's out here in the hallway, he has to be awake. I crouch in front of him and gently grip his shoulder. "TJ?"

He jerks at my touch and his head snaps up, his eyes wide open. *Terrified*.

"It's okay," I say. "It's just me."

He slumps back against the wall, dragging a trembling hand down his face. "Sorry," he rasps. "I woke you up, didn't I?"

"It's alright. You look..."

"Terrible, I know." He tips his head back against the wall. The dim lighting reflects the tear stains on his face and makes the hollow shadows around his eyes more pronounced than usual.

I settle against the wall next to him. "Another nightmare?"

"I thought I was getting better," he says, his voice less than a whisper under his ragged breathing. "I thought I'd figured out how to be strong. And then..." He shivers and wraps his arms around himself, curling into his oversized black hoodie. "And then this week happened. I've been to see Riya every single day, Rev, but I haven't been able to talk to her once. She's getting worse—Nora says it's been days since she broke through the serum. And—and *Max*. It's killing me."

"When's the last time you slept through the night?"

He looks to the side, away from me. "I don't think you want to know that answer."

We sit in silence after that until TJ's shaking eases and he gets to his feet, leaning on the wall for support.

I frown as I follow his lead. "Where are you going?"

"The roof."

"The—why?"

"It..." He trails off, seeming to debate with himself. "It helps, on the bad nights. Sometimes I sleep out there."

I want to press him further, but instead I walk with him. As we climb the stairs, I'm almost convinced his knees will give out and send him tumbling back down, but he manages to keep a shaky balance. He drops to his seat on the edge of the roof, letting his legs dangle, and stares out at the stars on the horizon. I settle next to him and wait for him to speak first.

"My parents," he eventually starts, "had these cheesy little nicknames for me and Riya, you know."

I glance at him out of the corner of my eye. That wasn't the way I was expecting this to start. The mention of his parents brings back the knot in my stomach and all the what-ifs that live inside. *What if he hasn't truly forgiven you? What if things will never get better between—*

I silence the thoughts and focus on TJ's voice, although the unrest lingers.

"My mom taught us about the constellations," he says, voice quiet. "When Riya used to be scared of the dark, she took the two of us to the window to see the stars. She told Riya and me that I was the Big Dipper, and she was the Little Dipper—and that no matter what, nothing could separate us. Even the dark."

"That's why you come up here," I say. "On the bad nights. To look at the stars."

He nods.

"She's not gone, TJ."

He looks down and to the side, hiding his face.

"TJ." I lay my hand over his. "She's *not* gone."

"I don't know if I can handle another loss, Rev," he says, his voice cracking. "I don't know what it would do to me, if Riya—after everything else..." He takes a long, shaky breath and finally meets my eyes. His fill with tears of desperation, and with the hopelessness I recognize so well. "How do you do it? How do you keep going?"

I shake my head. "You don't want me as an example."

"Rev, it's tearing me apart!" He runs both of his hands through his hair, grimacing. "I've been trying to hold on. I really have. But it's getting more and more difficult, and convincing myself that things are going to get better is starting to feel more like lying to myself than anything else. How do you stay so—so strong?"

"You don't have to be strong all the time, you know," I say softly, remembering Kaz's words to Savi back in Ordinem, after we found out about Ethan.

"Yes, I do." He shuts his eyes, his face twisting. "Because if I don't, everyone's going to rush to shelter me. They already look at me as delicate—easy to break. If anybody knew how broken I truly was, any chance I have of helping my sister, and of helping stop the Draft, would go out the window. They'd just put me away somewhere until things are over, and that would be even worse."

I nod. Being unable to do anything but watch is the worst in any given situation. But...

"You can't carry all of this on your own," I say. "No matter how much you want to convince yourself otherwise, that much is true. I know from experience."

"Do you really think we still have a chance?" TJ whispers.

"Hope is a battle," I respond softly, Kaz's words from Ordinem returning to me in full. "Every day. Some days, it's harder to find. But it's always there."

"I'm starting to worry that I'm losing that battle," he confides, pulling his knees up against his chest. "I don't know what to do, Rev."

"You're doing everything you can," I say, squeezing his hand. "You have to lean on the people around you. You have to trust them. To let them help."

TJ glances up at me out of the corner of his eye. "You sound like you're speaking from experience."

"I am." I lock eyes with him, unwilling to let him give up. "You have to hold on, TJ."

"To what?" His voice cracks at the words.

"To the people around you. To hope."

He lets out a breath and lays back on the rooftop, closing his eyes. His face twists with pain and a silent tear runs down his cheek. "I'm trying," he whispers.

We sit in silence after that, the light of the moon reflecting off the tear-streaked pain on TJ's face. I don't know what to do except sit here and hope my presence is a help to him. I can hear my own heartbeat in the quiet, blending with TJ's stifled cries. I would do anything to ease the anguish on his face, but I'm powerless right now.

You'll never be able to help him, the traitorous voice in my head whispers. I watch as eventually, his exhaustion begins to claim him, the raggedness fading from his breathing and then tension from his shoulders. *Maybe it would be better for me to leave.*

I get to my feet and turn toward the stairwell, careful to avoid making noise in case TJ is asleep. Before I can take a step, however, I hear TJ's hoarse whisper.

"Stay. Please," he says, voice slurred with exhaustion and his eyes still closed. He's not fully awake.

"Are you sure?" I ask, tentative.

"Help...keep the nightmare...away," he mumbles, voice thick.

I settle down next to him, laying on my back, and he laces his fingers in mine. I glance down in surprise, then at TJ's face. His breathing is deep, even, and his expression relaxed. It's been so long since I've seen him at peace, I'd almost forgotten what it looked like.

I shift so that I'm looking straight up at the stars.

TJ isn't the only one fighting for hope. But Kaz's words earlier and this moment are making it easier to believe it's possible for us to win.

Chapter Twenty-Eight

TJ Collins

Nora lets me into the infirmary before I even have a chance to knock. She smiles when she sees my raised hand and I lower it sheepishly. "You were expecting me?"

"You've been in here every morning about five minutes after lights-on. Yes, I've learned to be expecting you by now. Come on."

She steps back so I can join her in the infirmary's main room. "How is she?" I ask as soon as the door closes.

"Same as usual. She hasn't been herself since the last time you saw her. About to be sedated today, though." Nora moves behind her desk and rifles through one of her cabinets.

"Sedated?"

Nora produces a syringe and shuts the cabinet. "I have to run some tests, but she won't hold still long enough for me to do anything. I'm nervous she'll break that chair again, to be totally honest."

I rub my neck, flashes of Riya's near-feral expression making my skin prickle.

Nora sighs. "Sorry. I didn't mean to bring that up—I haven't been thinking straight recently. How are *you* doing?"

"Same as the last time you asked. And the time before that. I'm fine." I force a smile, although I know it can't possibly be convincing. Nora frowns and I stuff my hands in my pockets. "Really. I just need to see Riya."

"TJ, you need to deal with what's going on. You need to process."

I shake my head, clenching my fists inside my hoodie pocket. "What I *need* is for my little sister to be okay."

The way my voice cracks as I say the words is embarrassing. As Nora studies me from behind her round-rimmed glasses, I'm convinced she can see right through my weak façade. Straight to the nights I've spent on the floor of my room, slowly crumbling from the inside out.

Instead of pressing me further, thankfully, Nora nods toward the door behind her desk. "Come on. You can come in while I put her out, if you want, although I don't know if you really want to watch."

"Thank you."

I follow her down the hall to Riya's room, keeping my eyes far away from the syringe in Nora's grasp. It's much smaller than the ones Adrian had, but just the thought of a syringe is enough to make my hands shake.

Nora opens the door into the observation room, identical to the old one. Behind the one-way glass, Riya straightens up and looks toward the entrance as soon as Nora unlocks the second door.

"I'm not letting you run tests on me," Riya growls, her eyes fixed on Nora as the medic makes her way into the room. "You tried that before. It won't work."

Nora raises her hands halfway, causing Riya's attention to shift to her syringe. Riya narrows her eyes, tracking every movement. "And I'm definitely not about to let you stick me with whatever's in that."

Moisture springs to my eyes and I take a shaky breath, fighting it back.

She's *so much* like herself. Watching the way she's reacting, all I can see is my little sister. Full of fight and too smart to trust. Her resilience, her *fire*—that's all her, not the serum. Riya's still *herself*—she just believes she's on the other side. She believes I'm her enemy.

That almost makes it hurt more to watch her like this. Especially knowing that Riya is in there somewhere, that it's getting harder and more painful for her to break through.

Nora looks over her shoulder, but when she doesn't see me, she continues forward. "Take it easy, Riya. I have to run some tests, and unfortunately, I have to do them whether you want me to or not—so if you won't cooperate, I'm going to have to knock you out."

Riya snarls at her, but as Nora draws closer, the bonds on the chair hold. Riya begins to fight, keeping Nora from a clear shot at her arm, so Nora grimaces and jabs the needle with the sedative into her thigh. Riya's expression immediately shifts, a flash of pain crossing her face—a small enough detail that I doubt Nora notices, but it's obvious to me. I've seen her make that exact face countless times. I wince and finally give in to the urge to look away.

"I'm sorry," Nora says, so softly that the microphones in the room barely pick up the words for me to hear. I'm not sure if she's talking to me or to Riya—probably both.

I can't bring myself to look back up until the sounds of Riya's struggling have faded completely. Even then, it takes Nora re-entering the observation room to finally get me to move.

I muster up my confidence and enter Riya's room.

I may have visited Riya daily, but this is the first time I've been past the observation room since the attack—I haven't been able to stomach the kind of reaction Riya would likely have to me. The suspicion, the *hatred*. I know it's not her, not really, but seeing her like that...it hurts.

Riya's head rests slightly to the side, her breathing deep and even now that she's out. I hear the sound of Nora gently shutting the door behind me, leaving the two of us alone. I kneel next to the chair-bed and unbuckle the restraint on her wrist. I gently take her limp hand and bring it up against my forehead, closing my eyes.

Sitting like this, eyes closed, the dull hum of the air conditioning and medical machines the only sound, I can imagine that nothing's wrong. I can pretend, just for a moment, that everything's okay. Riya's okay. *I'm* okay.

And then the moment flees and the tears begin to flow. Somewhere in the back of my mind, I'm aware of Nora watching me from behind the one-way glass, but I can't hold back the emotions that have been building for the past week. Being in here, actually seeing Riya, finally tips me over the edge.

"I'm going to get her," I whisper, gripping Riya's hand tighter. "I'm going to get you back. I'll do whatever it takes, Riya. I'll do anything." My voice cracks. "*Anything.*"

I press her hand to my cheek, feeling my face twist. "I don't know if you can hear me, but I miss you. It was always you and me against the world. Without you...without you, I'm barely holding it together. I need my Little Dipper back." A shaky breath escapes my lips. "I don't know the next time I'll be able to talk to you like this, but if you can hear me, no matter what, know this: I love you, Riya. You have to fight. *Please*, fight your way back, because I—" My breath hitches and the knot in the bottom of my stomach seems to tighten. "I can't lose you, too."

A soft knock sounds on the door and Nora's gentle voice follows a moment later. "TJ?"

I glance up, not bothering trying to straighten up my appearance. Nora has seen me in worse states than this.

"I need to talk to you," she says. "Whenever you're done, I'll be in the main room, alright?"

I nod. "I'll be right there."

As Nora shuts the door behind her, I stand up next to Riya's chair. I gently buckle the restraint back around her wrist before leaning down and planting a kiss on the top of her head. "I love you, Riya. No matter what Holland does, I'll always love you."

I linger for another minute, watching her peaceful sleep, before leaving to meet Nora in the infirmary.

When I arrive, Nora sits behind her desk, files and papers scattered all around her.

"What happened?" I ask. "Something about Riya?"

"Sort of." Her eyes travel over all the papers in front of her. Behind me, a couple of the UND's other medics begin trickling in, adjusting the beds and disappearing through the door behind Nora's desk. "Between what those files from Leah said and what I can gather from Riya, I've learned that the serum functions almost like a virus, but it's not targeting her cells like a virus should. There *is* an anomaly in her muscle tissue and bone structure, but I'll have to do some more tests to figure out exactly what that is—but back to my point." She adjusts her round glasses, collecting her thoughts. "TJ, did your mother ever give you any...injections? Vaccinations? Within the last year?"

I shrug. "Sure. Some vaccinations. What does this have to do with Riya?"

"I'm just curious about something. Do you know what the vaccinations were for?"

"A bunch of different things. My mother never really went into specifics."

She lets out a soft hum as she returns her focus to her papers.

"Seriously, Nora. What's this about?"

She gives me a strange look. "Daniel gave you that flash drive, didn't he?"

"A few days ago," I admit. "I...haven't been able to bring myself to watch it yet."

"I don't want to pressure you," Nora says, "but I think you should. I know you think you're not important to all this, TJ, but you're wrong. And that flash drive proves it."

I hesitate, thinking of the Draft kids who showed up at Max and Alec's place. Looking for me.

Is it possible? Does Holland want me—*again*?

Nora sighs and props her elbows atop the messy papers on her desk, letting her forehead rest in her hands and digging her fingers into her loosely bound curls. Already, her buns have turned frizzy. "If there's a way to protect your sister, I'm going to find it. I promise you, TJ, I'm doing everything I possibly can." She looks up at me and for the first time, I notice how dark the circles under her eyes have become. She looks *exhausted*. "Those notes from Leah are helpful, and Hunter's recovery is coming easier now, so I'll have more time—"

"Nora."

She presses her lips together.

"Thank you," I say softly.

Nora hesitates, then nods. "I'll tell you when I find anything. And you watch that drive."

The bag with my mother's flash drive weighs heavily in my pocket as I leave the infirmary. I haven't taken it out since the day Daniel gave it to me. A large part of me has been too scared of what I might find.

This flash drive came from my mother—my mother, who was involved with Holland. My mother, who was involved in the creation of the serum, who manipulated my genes for some reason. My mother, who might've left me something on this drive that could save my little sister. If it weren't for that, I'm not sure I would ever look at whatever's on here.

But after Nora's words, I can't stall any longer. It's time to see what this flash drive contains, and I don't want to do it alone.

Chapter Twenty-Nine

TJ Collins

I find Rev in one of the UND's training rooms, practicing with moving targets projected onto a wall that looks to be made of some kind of foam. She releases three arrows in quick succession, all of them striking their intended targets, before the projected targets move again.

"Rev?" I say, leaning against the doorframe.

Her next arrow strikes the target, quivering as it embeds itself in the wall. She turns to face me and smiles. "Hey. What's up?"

"That's a lot of arrows." I nod toward the target wall, which is littered with arrow shafts. "How long have you been in here?"

"Since lights-on. Maybe a little after. These are all from the past fifteen minutes, though."

My mouth hangs slightly open. Rev's arrows cover nearly the entire wall, and it's a large wall, at that. "Fifteen minutes?"

She shrugs and reaches up to put the arrow in her hand back into her quiver. "I'm a fast shooter. Give me a few minutes to clean this up and I'll meet you outside?"

"I'll help."

Between the two of us, it doesn't take long to pull all the arrows out of the target wall.

"Do you have anywhere to be after this?" I ask, bracing my foot against the wall to pull out a particularly stubborn arrow.

"Not that I know of. Daniel's finally giving me a break, although sitting in the compound and waiting is almost worse than being away."

"Good." The arrow pulls free and I stumble back, handing it to Rev. "Remember that drive you brought back from Ordinem?"

She takes the arrow, seeming to move a little slower than before I brought up the drive. "Daniel gave it to you, then. Did you open it?"

I pull the flash drive out of my pocket and hold it out to her. "I was going to ask if you'd open it with me."

Her eyes flick to me in surprise. "You want me to open it with you?"

"I don't want to do it alone, and you're probably the only person I trust enough with something like this. Something from my mother."

Rev stares at the flash drive for a long moment before handing it back to me. "Of course."

Her tone, along with the way she immediately walks into the hallway, tells me there's something she's not saying. It probably has to do with the fact that this is from my mother—anything to remind her of how we first met can't be easy for her. And, now that I'm thinking about it, remembering that night puts a sour taste in my own mouth.

"You have a techpad?" Rev asks as we leave her training room.

"A techpad?"

"I'll take that as a no." Rev raises a brow and looks at me out of the corner of her eye. "How were you planning on seeing whatever's on that flash drive without any technology?"

"I didn't plan that far ahead," I admit.

She smiles at that, but it doesn't reach her eyes. Although I can already guess what's bothering her, I still ask. "What is it?"

"Nothing. Why?"

"Your whole mood shifted as soon as I brought up the flash drive."

She grimaces. "It brings back…unpleasant memories."

"You don't have to do this with me, you know."

"I know."

Rev's room is the exact same as mine—a single bed with gray blankets in one corner and a nightstand, a simple desk and office chair, and a dark gray armchair and end table in the corner nearest the door. She grabs a thin device with a black screen from the desk and rolls the office chair next to the armchair, then sits and nods for me to take the armchair.

I hand her the flash drive as I sit and she plugs it into a near-invisible port. A couple minutes later, she opens the contents of the drive to reveal a single file. A video file. Labeled *for_ TJ.MOV*. The rest of the notes must've been in the papers Leah included with the folder.

Rev's finger hovers over the file. "You ready?"

I stare at the video's thumbnail, my heartbeat growing louder in my ears. Within the tiny picture on the screen, I can make out my mother's raven hair and sharp features. *She left me…a video.* I'm about to see her face, hear *her* voice.

I swallow hard and nod, not trusting myself to speak past the lump in my throat.

Rev taps the screen.

The image expands to show my mother sitting at the desk in her room, with light streaming through the window in the background. The pictures hung on the wall behind her match how I remember my parents' room right before I left, and my mother looks exactly the same. This is recent, then.

In the video, she glances around, then leans toward the camera. "I don't have much time, but I needed to record this as soon as I could. Just in case something…happens." She presses her lips together, her eyes watering. "TJ, I hope you never have to see this. I hope you're never in a position where you have to know what I'm about to tell you, and if you're watching this, that means…it means I'm no longer there to tell you in person. And in that case, I'd like to start off with telling you that I'm so sorry, because whatever happened to bring you to this place was likely my fault."

I can sense Rev stiffen in the office chair next to me. *I should've known this would be hard for her.* Why didn't I think about that before I asked her to do this? Her finger taps on the arm of the chair and I put my hand over hers, hoping to reassure her. She relaxes, just a little, but still refuses to meet my eyes. The tension is almost tangible.

"If things happened the way I guessed they would," my mother continues on screen, "you likely already know about the Draft. And my involvement. And if you don't..." She sighs. "Well, I suppose it can't hurt to explain it."

Rev and I watch in silence as she explains everything we already know. That the Draft's purpose isn't to raise future soldiers or Enforcers like everyone believes, or to protect Ordinem from the surrounding dangers, but that Holland is using the kids *now*. That Holland ultimately wants to have kid spies in every corner of Ordinem, cementing the government's control over the people. That my parents weren't only close friends with Holland—that they worked for her. And what we most recently found out—that my mother wasn't just a nurse. She was Holland's lead genetic researcher and she had just started working on the serum when she filmed this.

Every so often, she looks over her shoulder, as if making sure nobody can hear her, and she pauses to catch her breath after finishing the basics. "The rest of it..." Her eyes take on a glazed expression. "There's too much to say here. To be honest, I'm glad. I don't *want* to tell you the details. I know you're already going to look at me differently from now on, and for you to know everything...I don't think I'd be able to bear that."

She looks away from the camera, the water in her eyes nearly spilling over. My body feels numb. This is the woman who raised children to be soldiers. Who was a part of researching a way to *brainwash* them. Who did something to her own son's genetics, and who kept her children from the world—who kept the biggest part of her life secret from her children. But she seems so...

So much like my mother. The woman I knew.

"All of that, you probably already knew, or maybe you guessed it. But what I'm about to tell you…" She glances over her shoulder one last time, as if making sure nobody can hear her, and her voice takes on an urgent tone. "Nobody else knows the rest, not even Anyssa. Keeping this secret has been dangerous from the start, and now it's more so than ever. And so, I'm recording this video. Because I don't want this information to die with me—just in case."

She takes a deep breath. "The serum has a back door. I built it in as soon as I fully understood what Anyssa wanted to do with it. I wanted to get out of the Draft by then, but it was far too late to do so without endangering you and Riya, so I did what I could. I made a cure possible, and I hid the final piece of the serum somewhere Anyssa would never find it. I'm the only one who knows this, although I believe Anyssa has her suspicions about the cure, at the very least."

My mind spins as my mother pauses to catch her breath. Two thoughts war for my attention.

This is *not* the woman I imagined, after finding out everything about the Draft. The woman on this screen had doubts—regrets. She wasn't *supporting* Holland—she wanted out.

And the missing piece of the serum. And the cure. The word usually comes with flashes of Adrian's face, a haze of pain, memories of agony, but now it comes with a tiny spark of hope.

My *mother* made the cure. If I can figure it out from whatever she tells me in this video…

I can save Riya.

On the screen, my mother continues. "I can't say everything here, just in case someone other than you is the one to find this, but if I'm…if I'm *gone* before I can see this cure through…" She hesitates, searching for the right words. "There's a way to find the cure. A key, of sorts. It's not written down or recorded anywhere—no files or anything else to find. That would've been too dangerous. But I couldn't let the cure die with me—that would've been irresponsible."

Her eyes lock directly on the camera with an intensity that freezes me in place, rooting to my seat. "*You* are the key, TJ. The missing piece. And the cure. You're the key to everything. I hope to one day be able to explain this to you, and I wish I could give you more here, but I can't—just in case this falls into the wrong hands. I can only hope that by now, you know enough to understand what I'm talking about."

You are the key. But what does that *mean*?

A man's voice, barely audible in the background, calls for my mother and she jumps, then looks back at the camera. "I have to go now, TJ. I wish I could give you more than this, but I can't risk it. If I'm not here..." Her eyes water. "Figure out the cure, if you can—if you need it, which I'm sure you will. Be safe. Don't let Anyssa have her missing piece. And protect your sister." She gives a sad smile and I want nothing more than to reach out and touch the screen, to reach out and touch her face. The face of my mother, not a monster. *Don't go*, I silently plead, but the video continues without mercy.

"I'm sorry, TJ," she says, voice soft. "For all I've done, and for not being here to have this conversation in person. I love you."

The video stops, freezing my mother's face in place. Teary eyes, stricken expression, laced with just a tinge of hope.

Hope for what? For me? To find the cure, to finish her work and undermine Holland once and for all? If that's the case, I've already failed. If there had been anything useful buried in my head, Adrian's torture would've brought that out. Either whatever my mother is talking about didn't work, or I'm missing something very, very important.

"You okay?" Rev asks quietly, her eyes still fixed on the screen.

"That..." I clear my throat and rub my eyes. "I don't know what I expected, but that wasn't it."

"Yeah."

We stare at the video's last frame in silence, both of us lost in thought.

My mother made the cure. My mother hid the missing piece of the serum. But instead of information I can use, information I can act on, I get a cryptic message telling me *I'm* the key.

"I think it might've been a good thing she didn't say anything specific," Rev eventually says. "Since Holland found this first."

"It makes sense. I just...I feel like I'm missing something, Rev. Something *major*. This, on top of what Adrian was trying to get from me..." I clench my fist, moving my hand from Rev's. "Everyone seems to know something I don't. Everyone seems to think I'm the key to finding the cure, but I'm just as clueless as the rest of us. If Holland saw this drive before us, it makes sense that she's coming after me again. Now that, apparently, I'm her *missing piece*. Even though nothing's changed since Adrian..." I trail off and Rev watches me, a tentative look on her face.

"You never talk about what Adrian wanted to know," she says softly. "It was related? To all this?"

I meet her eyes, overcome with the sudden urge to run. *Change the subject. Hide. Hide.*

Instead, I give her a slight nod. It's time to tell her about this.

It's time to tell her everything, a small voice in the back of my head persists. *It's time to tell her how you've betrayed her trust. How Holland found out Eliza is her sister.*

I swallow hard, shoving down the thoughts. One thing at a time. "Holland wanted to know about the cure, and she thought I had the answers—because my mother was her lead geneticist. So she had Adrian..." I force the words out through the lump in my throat, my voice coming out strained. "*Interrogate* me."

I look the other way as I roll up my left sleeve, baring my scars to Rev for the first time.

She reaches for my arm—slowly, as if waiting for my permission—and although it takes all of me not to pull away, I let her.

"I saw some of this on the helicopter," Rev whispers, turning my arm over and tracing a particularly rough patch of pale scar tissue. "But...*TJ*."

"It's bad. I know. You, Max, and Alec are the only ones who've really seen."

"What caused all this?" Her gentle fingers drift to my wrist, where my struggling against the clamps tore the skin over and over. "These are self-explanatory, but...the rest of it?"

I look away from the scars, focusing on the opposite arm of the chair. "They had some kind of—some kind of serum." Getting the words out takes as much physical energy as I can muster. "It didn't do any physical damage, but it...made me feel pain."

I take deep breaths, trying to calm my racing heart. *Breathe. Breathe. You're safe. Breathe.*

"I—" I clear my throat, but my voice still trembles. "I couldn't do anything to stop it. Couldn't sleep, or pass out from the pain—they laced it with adrenaline—could barely even *move*—"

Breathe. Rev encloses my shaking hand in hers and my mind latches on to the contact. *Safe. You're safe.*

"They wanted to know about the cure," I say, my voice dropping below a whisper. "Probably to destroy it. And they—tortured me until they realized I was useless. That's when Holland—talked to me herself. She put a gun to Reiko's head and asked me..."

"About the cure?" Rev offers when I don't continue.

I bite the inside of my cheek and shake my head. *Tell her.*

You can't tell her. It feels like barely any time has passed since that night in the basement, when we talked without masks for the first time, when we truly resolved things between us. How can I possibly tell her the one thing that might ruin that?

Her deep brown eyes search mine, tinged with concern. "TJ?"

How can I *not* tell her?

In her expression, her reassuring hand on mine, her solid presence by my side, I find the strength I've been so desperately needing. I don't want to tell her—but I have to. It's her sister, and it was my mistake. I can't keep it a secret any longer.

"TJ, you don't have to—"

"She asked me about your sister," I finally whisper.

Rev nods. "She knew about Eliza. We know that."

"She knows about Eliza *now*." I hang my head, breaking our eye contact. "Because of me. I told her everything."

Rev goes still. I'm too nervous to look up and see her expression—to see the betrayal on her face.

"I'm sorry," I say, although I know that's not nearly enough. "Holland knew you had a personal motivation—she threatened Reiko and started asking me questions, and she asked me for a name, and—" I bury my free hand in my hair, my fingernails digging into my scalp. "That's how she knew to use Eliza against you. It's my fault."

Rev moves her hand from mine, leaving nothing but cold and empty air in its wake. A bitter chill cuts through my heart and tears spring to my eyes.

"I'm so sorry," I whisper, balling my fists against my watering eyes. *Nice going, TJ. You ruined it. Again.* And then, another thought, one that drowns out everything else in my head.

When am I going to stop breaking everything I touch?

Rev's silence is sharper than any retort she could possibly give me. The emptiness is like a sword plunged through my chest, making it ache. *Another loss. I can't take another loss. I can't...I can't...*

"Say something," I plead softly, still unable to bring myself to look up at her. "Be angry, yell at me—just *please* say something. I don't...I don't want to lose you, too, but..."

I can feel Rev lean closer to me and I tense, expecting to finally take the brunt of her anger—something that, once, would've been my worst nightmare. Still *is* one of my worst nightmares.

Instead, I feel her arm slide around my hunched shoulders, her strong presence returning to my side.

I look up at her, my brow furrowed, struggling for words. A soft, confused "what?" is all I can manage.

"That was *not* your fault, TJ."

"But—"

"*No.*" Her face betrays the fact that what I said shook her. But…it's not full of anger. It's…understanding? Sympathy?

I look back down, shaking my head. "You're supposed to be angry," I say, my voice cracking.

"I'm not. It's not your fault, what Holland did to you. How she manipulated you."

"How she broke me," I say quietly.

Rev pulls me closer, rubbing my shoulder. "You," she says, voice soft but firm, "are not *broken*. You're still TJ Collins. You're the same person I met four months ago. You're the same person who changed me from who I used to be. You're *healing*. There's a difference."

"I'm starting to wonder if I'll ever truly heal."

It's a confession I've hesitated to even make to myself. Rev's hand pauses on my shoulder. My words hang in the air for a long moment before she finally responds. "I…know what you mean." She takes a deep, slow breath. "But if there's hope for me, TJ, there's hope for you. I think eventually, when all this is over, we can both heal. And in the meantime, I'm not going to blame you for something that wasn't your fault."

As Rev gently rubs my hunched shoulders, the tension begins to drain from my body as the guilt I've been carrying since the Draft compound finally eases.

"Thank you," I say after a few minutes have passed.

"For what?"

"For having hope."

She just nods, continuing to rub my shoulders.

I can only hope that one day, I'll have the same amount of faith in my ability to heal as Rev seems to.

Chapter Thirty

Hunter Lane

After nearly a full month without walking, being on my feet again feels strange, but supportive braces and a crutch from Nora to lean on makes it doable. I shoulder through people on my way out of the mess hall, ignoring the strange looks I get for the tray of food awkwardly balanced in my free hand, and head toward the prison wing.

I can't shake my questions about Daniel's past, and I only know one person who may be able to help me answer them.

I balance my crutch under my arm and scan my wristband to unlock Adrian's door, then shuffle inside, trying not to tip the tray as I wedge my foot against the door to keep it from shutting.

Adrian barely lifts his head and his voice is so hoarse, it's barely audible when he speaks. "What are you doing here?"

He's weak, is the first thought that hits me when I look him over. It's only been a week since Reiko and I last saw him, but I was too preoccupied with the conversation at hand to notice Adrian's condition. His skin sinks below his cheekbones—Daniel's been keeping him alive, but evidently not by much—and blood smears his hands from the manacles digging into his wrists. His blonde curls are overgrown, matted, and hang just past his eyebrows. His posture, once so rigid and straight, sags as if there's a weight on his shoulders.

"I want to talk."

Adrian sighs. "I've already told you all I..." He trails off as he looks up to see the tray in my hands.

Painstakingly slow, I maneuver to sit in front of him, resting my crutch and the tray across my outstretched legs. Being able to sit like this again is incredible.

"So Daniel *didn't* send you to kill me," he says, warily eyeing me.

"Daniel didn't send me at all." I hand him the tray, which he takes with a clank of chains.

He studies me, disbelieving, before taking a tentative sip of water. He closes his eyes at the first taste and gulps down half the glass before wiping his mouth, taking a breath, and clearing his throat. "Why all this?"

"Because I'm no longer convinced we're enemies." I pause. "And because I want something."

"Ah. There it is." Still, a little life returns to the man. "So?"

"You told me, the first time we talked, that Daniel used to work with your mother."

Adrian twitches at my words, although he does an admirable job of hiding it.

"I want to know if you were telling the truth," I say. *Maybe my suspicions are unfounded. Maybe Adrian was lying to catch me off-guard. Maybe—*

My hope sinks when he nods. "I was."

"What else do you know?"

"Truthfully, not much." Adrian takes another swig of water. "Daniel left Ordinem around the same time Anyssa was put in charge. I know they worked together before that, and Anyssa makes it sound like they worked for the Draft—part of the reason I think there are bigger forces at play than Anyssa. But I don't think Daniel left Ordinem...*willingly*. It seemed like something happened."

"So once Anyssa was put in charge, Daniel left Ordinem for a reason we don't know."

"That's what I've gathered." Adrian tears a piece off a roll on his tray. "But I'm not sure. All that truly matters is that Anyssa is dangerous."

"So you admit you want to stop her," I say.

Adrian takes his time chewing his bread, considering. "I want to protect my sister," he says carefully. "That's all. Right now, the way to do that is by working with you."

That's more of an answer than I anticipated, and I can tell it's all I'll be getting, so I move to another question. One that's been in the back of my mind since I first interrogated Adrian, and one that's more pressing after Kaz told me the details of the Ordinem mission. "You said you knew my sister," I start, leaving the unspoken question hanging in the air.

Adrian nods, studying my expression. "You want to hear about her, I assume?"

I hesitate. "Do I?"

"She doesn't know if you're alive," he says, swallowing another chunk of bread. "And after what Anyssa did to your family, she's terrified of her. She's trying to survive. And, on the off chance that you *are* alive, she's trying to keep Anyssa from coming after you like she did your parents."

His explanation is blunt, painful, and hopeful to me all at once. A reminder of the past. A reminder of what Leah caused. A reminder of the reason I'm here with the Undrafted, fighting against the Draft. But also...put together with the fact that she's spying for Daniel...

I'm less sure about my sister than I've been since the day Anyssa shot my parents. But I'm sure of one thing.

At the very least, the spark of hope I gave up on so long ago is back. Maybe there's a chance for her.

"Adrian?"

He looks up from under his matted hair, one brow cocked.

"Your wrists," I say.

Adrian gives his manacles a half-hearted shake. "What about them?"

"You should probably get them treated. They could get infected."

He glares at me. "I don't know what kind of sick joke you're—"

"I'll take you to Nora. Our medic. She'll be willing to do me a favor."

His hands freeze, the last chunk of bread held halfway to his mouth. "You mean…"

I pull a slender key out of my pocket. Daniel gave it to me thinking it might be helpful for interrogation purposes, but it's finding a different use now. I wave for Adrian to move toward me and, after eyeing me warily for another moment, he does. I unlock the manacles around his wrists and ankles and lean back, letting him climb to his feet. He shakes out his hands, looks at me with narrowed eyes.

I only stand, crutch under my arm, and nod toward the door. "Let's go."

"People aren't going to have a problem with me just…walking around?"

I pause. He has a point.

Adrian sighs. "We need to make it believable, don't we?"

"Probably a good idea."

"Go ahead." He gestures at his face and closes his eyes. "Punch me. I know you want to. If I look beat-up and you wear that face you always put on for interrogations, we'll be fine."

I only hesitate a moment before taking a swing.

Chapter Thirty-One

Reverie Adams

The day after I watched Maya's flash drive with TJ, the two of us sit with Kaz in the mess hall for lunch. Hunter left a few minutes ago with a tray of food, but he didn't provide an explanation. He likely went to eat by himself, or possibly to find Reiko. We eat mostly in silence, all three of us apparently preoccupied.

The video of Maya Collins circles through my mind constantly, but the thing that weighs on me even more is the conversation that followed.

I knew from the moment I first talked to TJ after his rescue that something was weighing on him, and I caught a glimpse of his scarred arm on the helicopter before he covered it up, but imagining what he must've been through...

Why didn't he tell me earlier?

I understand why he kept the details about what Adrian put him through to himself, and why the flash drive is what brought him to finally tell me, but...*Eliza?*

It wasn't his fault. Everything I said to him during that conversation was true. I can't possibly be angry with him, not after seeing the extent of what Holland put him through. If I'd been continuously tortured like that, then watched Holland put a gun to *TJ's* head, I would've done the same. There was no reasonable way for him to have kept Eliza's identity a secret, and even if he'd managed it, Holland would've figured things out eventually.

My first reaction wasn't anger, but...something I still struggle to define, even after having it stewing inside of me for the past couple days. Confusion, disappointment, fear—some mix of these. I haven't been able to shake whatever the feeling is.

Why didn't TJ tell me?

He was scared. That much was obvious. But why? What would make him so nervous that he would keep this secret for so long?

He's scared of me. Still, after everything. He's scared of the Archer who killed his parents. And I can't possibly fault him for that.

I force myself to take a deep breath, closing my eyes and focusing on the cool silverware in my hand. *TJ forgave you long before you told him who you were, and he still hasn't abandoned you.* Savi's words, from back in Ordinem. *He's not going to.*

But I can't ignore his reaction. He was *scared* to tell me. Scared of how I would react.

Is this how it's always going to be? Will that memory of what I did, the constant fear of who I used to be, always haunt him when he thinks of me? Always taint our relationship, no matter how hard we try?

Is there even hope for the two of us?

A figure busts into the mess hall, red-faced and breathing hard, snapping me out of my thoughts. Savi.

Kaz jumps to his feet, turning some heads from the nearby tables, but he ignores them. Savi picks her way between tables, mumbling apologies as she brushes past people, and makes it to us.

"What's wrong?" Kaz asks as soon as she's in earshot.

She leans in, dropping her voice so the adjacent tables can't hear. "You all need to come outside. *Now.* There's—there's a Draft agent, right outside the gates—I caught it on the monitoring station in the tech room. And Daniel thinks if you go now, you can catch her."

Kaz and I share a look before taking off for the door, just slow enough to avoid drawing attention from everyone else in the room. Savi and TJ follow and all four of us break into a run when we emerge into the hall.

A Draft agent, right outside.

I wonder briefly if it's Eliza. And if I'll have the strength to fight if it *is*.

Kaz bursts through the main doors first and I press the button to unfold my bow as I follow, although I don't have my quiver on me. Holding the weapon still offers some small sense of security.

I briefly consider telling TJ and Savi to go back inside, but according to Savi, it's *one* Draft kid. Kaz excels at hand-to-hand. He can handle a single Draft kid.

As soon as we draw close to the gate, I spot a glint of red hair in the near distance.

"She's running!" Kaz calls, motioning urgently for the guards at the gate to open it as we approach. "We can't let her get back to Holland—if she tells Holland where our compound is, we're in trouble!"

Kaz and I speed up the moment we're past the gates, our feet pounding against the dusty Nadzor ground as we sprint toward the girl. She looks to be about halfway between us and the ruins. TJ and Savi lag behind, but do an admirable job keeping up. And somehow, all four of us gain on the girl—quickly.

"She's not running very fast," I say to Kaz under my breath.

"She's facing the other way. I don't think she knows we're coming."

"Maybe." But that doesn't seem like a mistake a highly-trained operative would make.

Either way, Kaz catches her first, leaping at her from behind. The girl barely starts to turn before the two tumble to the ground. She gets in a couple punches before Kaz hauls her to her feet, arms pinned behind her back.

Savi and TJ pull up behind me and Kaz cracks a grin. "Easy."

The girl spits to the side, glaring at the rest of us, but says nothing.

The walk back to the compound takes an agonizingly long time, especially with all of us checking over our shoulders to make sure we're not being followed by any Draft agents out to rescue their friend. But none show.

Kaz marches triumphantly in front of our group, leading us toward Daniel's office. TJ lingers behind, absently playing with one of the strings on his hoodie. His sleeve slips down, revealing some of the scars around his wrist, but he doesn't seem to notice.

"Something's bothering you," I say quietly, falling into step with him and Savi.

He glances at me. "How can you tell?"

"Because something's bothering me, too."

Savi nods. "This was…"

"Too easy?" I supply.

She and TJ both nod, and our gazes drift toward the redheaded Draft kid. She doesn't even put up a fight as she walks with Kaz. Did she…did she *want* to get captured?

"Kaz, wait up," I call, jogging to catch up with him.

The girl casts a look over her shoulder. Meets my eyes. And her expression shifts.

She wrenches herself free of Kaz's grip with a burst of strength and takes off down the hallway before any of us can blink. But she doesn't head for the exit. She heads deeper into the compound, toward the living quarters and the…

And the infirmary.

As she turns a corner ahead, I catch a flash of red in her palm.

TJ lets out a terrified yell and barrels down the hall after her. "She's going for Riya!"

She's going for Riya. My eyes widen as I break into a sprint, barely gaining on TJ's adrenaline-fueled run. The red thing in her hand.

The kill switch.

As soon as I sprint past Daniel's office, the door opens. I cast a quick glance over my shoulder to see Alec emerging and Savi running straight into him, but I don't stick around to see what happens. We have to catch the girl before she can use the kill switch.

If she hasn't used it already. Hunter said it was meant for extremely close range, but what does that mean?

I burst into the infirmary right after TJ to see the girl knocking Nora aside as if she weighs nothing. Out of the few patients in here, I recognize two faces. Hunter and...*Adrian?*

Both of them shoot to their feet at the chaos, and yells come from some of the other medics, but the girl shoves through the door behind Nora's desk with TJ on her heels. I vault over the desk and follow. Sounds of pursuit come from behind me—Nora, Hunter, and Adrian, from their voices—but I don't have time to turn and see.

The girl slows slightly to scan the placards on the doors and TJ nearly manages to catch her. He has his hand outstretched, his fingers wrapped around her arm—

She grins. Grabs the front of TJ's sweatshirt and slams his back against the wall, then shifts her grip to hold him there by his throat. Time seems to slow as she raises a small red button right in front of him, just out of his reach.

He lets out a strangled scream, struggling violently against her grip, but she doesn't budge.

"Please," he chokes out. "*Please.* Take me instead. Do whatever you want. Just let Riya live."

The girl hesitates at his words, her smile faltering, but it's not enough.

I'm not going to make it in time.

She sets her shoulders, seeming to steel herself. "Unfortunately, Riya Collins is a liability."

Just before I reach her, she presses the button.

"No!" TJ screams, struggling against her. "*No!*"

The word tears from his throat in a desperate cry, his face twisted in utter devastation like I've never seen from him before.

I reach the girl and rip her away from TJ, but she doesn't put up a fight. Her job is done. Pounding down the hall behind me, a whole crowd of people join us—Hunter and Adrian, Savi and Kaz, Alec and Nora.

TJ, shaking, fumbles with the handle to what I assume is Riya's room. When he opens the door, a faint sound trickles into the hallway. A flat, high-pitched tone.

A flatline.

Nora shoves through the cramped hallway, past TJ, and disappears into Riya's room. TJ stumbles after her.

"She'll get you too, Collins!" the girl yells. I tighten my grip on her wrists, but she continues. "Holland will get you, too!"

Kaz takes one look at the situation before turning to me. "Go help him," he says softly. "Savi and I can take her, and guards are on their way to help."

I nod and hand the Draft kid over to Kaz. Savi gives me a sympathetic nod as they clear out, leaving Hunter, Adrian, and Alec. I don't have the time or energy to spare an explanation for any of them, so I turn and head for TJ instead.

He's on his knees, his head in his hands, on the floor of the small observation room. From the room on the other side of the glass, where Nora tends to Riya, the heart rate monitor has been silenced. I spare a glance to see Nora standing with drooping shoulders, dragging a hand down her face.

I switch my focus back to TJ, dropping to my knees beside him, before my eyes can land on Riya.

"She's—Nora confirmed—" he gets out between sobs.

Riya's gone.

I can do nothing to ease his grief, but I put my arm around him and offer what little support I can give as he kneels, broken and trembling, on the floor.

"Why?" he whispers. "Why her, and not—and not me? Why couldn't it have been *me*?"

I pull him close and he clings to me, shaking.

Chapter Thirty-Two

TJ Collins

I can't think. I can't breathe.

Riya.

The tremors that overtake me where I'm huddled on the floor make my throat feel like it's closing. Somewhere distant, I feel Rev's arm around my shoulders, but the darkness in my mind washes over me and numbs my senses.

Riya.

A strangled cry escapes me and Rev pulls me close. I don't have the strength to lift my head, but I lean in to her, desperately searching for something to cling to. Some last shred of hope. But I find nothing. Only darkness. Angry, roiling darkness.

Silence in the observation room, except for my cries. Nora has finally quieted that cursed monitor. My chest tightens at the thought and a silent sob wracks my shoulders as I bury my face against Rev's shoulder. She brings one hand up to the back of my head, settling her chin on my shoulder. "I'm so sorry," she whispers.

"It should've been me." My breath hitches. "It should've been *me*. Not her."

Someone clears his throat.

Slowly, I lift my head to see Adrian stepping forward. *Adrian.* What is he doing here? Alec and Hunter stand next to him, watching the scene before them in silence.

Adrian's attention is on me. I let my gaze drop. I can't look him in the eyes. Not now.

"I'm sorry about your sister," he says, his voice softer than I've ever heard it.

Those words, coming from *him*, are what finally break through whatever invisible wall has been holding back my rage. I let out a yell and throw myself at him. My sudden movement must take him by surprise, because as we tumble to the floor in a heap, I land on top. Max's training crosses my mind, but the red at the edges of my vision is too blinding, too consuming, for me to think consciously. Rage controls me now, not training. I ball my fists and strike, a sharp crack sounding as my knuckles connect with his face.

"You" —*crack*— "don't" —*crack*— "talk" —*crack*— "about" —*crack*— "my" —*crack*— "sister!" All I can hear are my own yells, the pounding of my fists, the crunch as one of my punches connects directly with Adrian's nose. Finally, I let myself go. *Finally*, the anger and hopelessness that have been boiling inside me since my time in the Draft sublevels take over.

My fingers close around Adrian's throat.

Hands grab my arms and the back of my sweatshirt, wrenching me away. I struggle to break their grips, but there are too many. Someone drags me backwards and up off the floor, away from Adrian, and more hands on my arms keep me from breaking free.

My vision begins to clear and more details around me filter in. *Voices.* Panicked voices. Something sticky, on my hands, on my hoodie—blood. Adrian, wheezing and dragging himself to the nearest wall, his face and the front of his shirt *soaked* with red.

"I've got him," comes Alec's voice from behind me. Then, more insistent, "I've got him!"

The hands gripping me release and Alec wraps his arms around me, pinning my arms to my sides. I struggle, but I can feel the rush of adrenaline fading.

"Rev, the other medics and patients in the infirmary are going to want to know what happened. I managed to keep them out of this hallway, but we don't want to cause a panic. Just tell them something happened and Nora is tending to it."

"But what about—"

"Go!" Alec orders. "I have TJ."

Rev looks at me, her eyes wide with...fear? Is she looking at me with *fear*? I sag in Alec's arms, the last dregs of my strength fading.

Across the small room, Adrian struggles to his feet with Hunter's help. Nora bursts in from Riya's room. "I heard shouts. Is everything—*oh*." Her eyes fall on Adrian and go wide. "Come on. I'll get you cleaned up in another one of the back rooms. We don't need people asking questions."

Adrian nods and, leaning on Hunter, makes his way to the door. Even he glances at me out of the corner of his eye, as if he's afraid I'll break from Alec's grip and come after him again. When I take in the damage, I understand why. His shirt is covered in the blood gushing from his crushed nose, and his face is already swelling where my blows hit. One eye is nearly swollen shut, and between his nose and other cuts and gashes, blood coats almost his whole face.

Red. All I can see is red.

My stomach churns as they leave the room, Adrian's broken nose leaking blood onto the tiles. *So much*. "I...I did that?" I ask, hoarse.

"Come on." Alec releases his grip on me, but keeps one arm wrapped around my shoulders to guide me toward the wall. "Sit."

Absently, I obey, sinking down against the wall. The *blood*. I've seen people bleed, but I've never *caused* anything like that. And my hands. It's all over my hands. I stare at the bright, sticky red and feel my breathing shorten, my pulse begin to race. *What did I do?*

"Easy." Alec crouches in front of me, his hands on my shoulders. "Breathe, kid."

"I—I just—" I stammer.

"Don't look at your hands. Look at me. Deep breaths."

I manage to tear my gaze away from the blood and meet Alec's eyes. *Inhale. Exhale. In. Out.*

"Good. Keep breathing. You're alright."

My mind feels foggy, stuffed with too many thoughts, overwhelmed by too many emotions. Alec stands and disappears into the other room for a moment.

What did I just do?

Riya...

I should wash my hands. I should—

Riya.

Red. Bright, sticky—

Riya.

I pull my knees to my chest and move to bury my head in my hands, but my stomach twists at the sight of the blood and, shakily, I lower my hands again. I can feel the front of my hoodie, soaked through, sticking to my chest. The thought makes me want to retch.

Alec returns with a damp cloth in hand. "You alright?" he asks softly, handing it to me. I take it in a limp grip as Alec crouches in front of me again.

I shake my head, staring blankly at the door to Riya's room.

Alec takes a deep breath, surveying the carnage of the observation room. Blood, all over the tiles. Me, trembling against the wall. The view through the window—

"What...what did I just do?" I rasp. "Did I—is he—"

"I don't know how helpful this is, but Adrian will be fine. I've seen brawls before. It looks much worse than it is." He nods toward the damp cloth I'm holding. "Clean your hands."

As my attention shifts to the blood covering the floor, Alec's words aren't as reassuring as they should be. "I would've killed him," I whisper after a stretch of silence. I wonder, with a sick twist in my stomach, if this is what Rev felt like before she became the Archer.

"I know," Alec says.

Tears sting my eyes as I look at the door to the other room. Behind that door, Riya…

"She's gone." The water in my eyes threatens to spill over again. "She's really…she's really gone, isn't she?"

It hits me, fully and completely, then. My baby sister. The one who pulled countless all-nighters to study medicine because of her passion to help people. The one who kept me going in my darkest moments after our parents' deaths. The one who cried on my shoulder, who teased me until I forgot about my problems, who stayed up late to look at the constellations with me, who never gave up on me no matter how many stupid decisions I made. The one with enough fire running in her veins to make her seem unstoppable. The one who I promised to protect.

The one who trusted me.

My baby sister.

Despite my best efforts, the sobs I've been holding back return full-force. Alec leans forward and wraps his arms around me and I fold into his embrace, shaking like I'm a kid again. The quiet strength radiating from him reminds me of my own father, when I was young and he'd hold me after a rough nightmare.

The problem is that this time, the nightmare isn't something I can wake up from.

"I promised, Alec," I choke out. "I *promised* I'd protect her. I promised."

"You tried," he says softly. "You did everything you could. You would've traded yourself for her in an instant. This is *not* your fault."

"I didn't even say goodbye," I whisper, the words burning as they leave my mouth. "Before I turned myself in to Holland. The last time I saw her before the serum. I had the chance to say goodbye. I had the chance to tell her I loved her. But I—I just left. What kind of a brother does that make me?"

"You're a good brother," Alec says, his voice gentle as his grip on me tightens. "You loved her, TJ. More than anything."

I bury my head into his shoulder, clinging to his quiet strength. Even after watching my blind rage, something that terrified even Rev, he just supports me as the overwhelming grief, pain, and anger drain away the last of my strength.

What did I *ever* do to deserve someone like Alec in my life?

Aside from the sounds of my anguish, the observation room is silent for long enough that I lose track of time. Alec stays with me for every minute of the pain.

Riya's really gone.

Sobs turn to silent tears, which eventually dry and leave me staring blankly into the distance. I've run out of tears to cry, but I haven't recovered. I'm not sure I'll ever recover, this time.

Alec and I sit side by side in silence.

"Thank you," I say quietly. "For being here. For staying here. After what I did."

"I'll always be here for you, kid. No matter what. You and Max..." He lets out a slow breath, controlled. I'm not the only one feeling the crushing emptiness inside—Alec watched Max be taken, right in front of him, not long ago. "You're like the sons I always wanted. Whatever happens, I'm here."

My eyes well with tears again, but they don't spill over. "Thank you," I manage again before the room lapses back into silence.

The rest of the day floats by in a haze. I can't stomach the idea of talking to anybody, especially anybody who saw my episode with Adrian. Thankfully, the few passersby I see on my walk back to my room aren't faces I recognize, and by the way they avoid meeting my eyes, they know I'm not in a place to talk. They know. Everybody knows.

I shut myself in my room, lock the door, and let the emptiness wash over me. Rev knocks at my door, voicing her concern, and so does Hunter, but I ignore them, retreating into the numbness inside my head. I skip dinner, losing track of the hours as they stretch on. Daniel comes by once, calling through the door to check on me.

Eventually, people stop knocking. The light filtering under my door from the hall dims. The digital clock by my bed reads something past two in the morning.

And sleep, despite my best efforts, takes me.

I wake up thrashing, shivering, covered in sweat. Screaming? Did I scream this time? Something hard beneath me. *Wood.* The floor. I fell out of the bed.

She pushed the button. I can feel something wet on my face, something that tastes like salt, and reality crashes into me again like a tidal wave. I sit there, on the freezing ground, tangled in my sweat-soaked sheets, until the dark room pressing in on me becomes too much and my chest grows tight. *Out. Out. Get out.*

I manage to disentangle myself from the sheets and drag myself to the door, then stumble into the hallway. I catch myself with my forearm on the opposite wall before I can collapse again and blink hard, trying desperately to muster the strength to walk to the stairwell.

An arm slides around my back, guiding me in the right direction. "Come on," a soft voice says.

"Rev?" I turn to see her, tears blurring my vision. "What...why are you—?"

"I knew you'd come out here. So I waited."

"All night?" I ask, hoarse, but her appearance gives me the answer before her slight nod. She looks almost as exhausted as I feel, although she's obviously trying to hide it. *She's been crying too.* And yet, she sat outside my door all night. Just so she could be here for me now.

"Come on," she repeats, gently nudging me down the hall.

I must look *horrible*. I haven't slept well in weeks, my shirt is soaked through with sweat and tears, and I haven't managed to change clothes since the infirmary—other than to strip off the hoodie that had Adrian's blood on it. And yet, Rev remains silent as we walk, her arm around me.

We make it up to the roof and, wordlessly, sit together at the edge. I pull my knees up under my chin and rest my forehead on them, my head suddenly too heavy to hold up. "You didn't have to wait," I eventually say, my voice small. Out here, with the stars stretching infinitely above me and the moonlight reflecting off the pale scars on my arm, I feel like a speck of dust. Tiny. Insignificant. Hopeless.

"I'd *never* leave you to face this alone," she says, quiet but firm. Without room for argument.

My eyes water as I look up at the stars. Before I consciously know what I'm doing, I find the Little Dipper.

That's the cheesiest thing you've ever said, Riya told me when I brought it up all those months ago, in our apartment. *And don't you* dare *start calling me that*.

What I wouldn't give for some of her fire at this moment.

Rev follows my gaze and must realize what I'm thinking, because she laces her fingers through mine and squeezes my hand.

"Why her?" I whisper. "Why kill *her*?"

But I know the answer without Rev having to say it. To get rid of the faulty prototype of the serum. And to hurt me.

I close my eyes and hit my forehead against my knees, then again, and again. *It should've been me. It should've been me. It should've—*

"No." Rev's voice cuts through my thoughts.

Did I say that out loud? "She should've killed me. It should've been—"

"TJ, *no*." Rev's grip on my hand tightens. "No. It should've been *neither* of you."

I barely stop myself from voicing my next words. *I wish it would've been me.*

I can feel the emotions brimming, threatening to overwhelm me again, so I retreat into the numbness. The emptiness. And...something new.

Rage. The same rage I felt when I went after Adrian today.

"I know this sounds hypocritical, coming from me," Rev says softly, "but this isn't the end. Don't let this be the end. Don't let it consume you." She hesitates, then her voice lowers even more. "Don't make the same mistake I did."

"I understand now, Rev." I lift my head and meet her eyes. "Everything. I understand the Archer."

"No." She shakes her head. "You're better than me."

"Did you not see what I did earlier today?!"

She stiffens.

"I saw the way everyone looked at me," I say, voice dropping. "We both know I would've killed him."

"You'd just watched Riya..." she trails off, grimacing. "You weren't in your right mind."

"I don't think I'll ever be in my right mind again. But you know what I *finally* understand?"

She watches me, her concerned eyes searching mine.

"I'm no better than the Archer, Rev." I can feel my expression harden. "The difference between us is that you're stronger than I am."

"The difference between us is that I'm more *callous* than you are." Rev draws her brow. "TJ, I ruined everything—*everything*—with the decisions I made. Don't take the road I did. You can *fight* this."

"Not anymore." I shake my head, my eyes brimming with moisture. "What I said a couple weeks ago? After Ethan? I wasn't sure what another loss would do to me. Now I know. I'm not just broken, Rev. I'm *shattered*."

"You're not—"

"Yes, I am!"

Rev pulls her hand out of mine.

I take a deep breath, closing my eyes. "I'm broken," I say under my breath. "I've been broken since Holland had me, and now...now there's no fixing it. But I know one thing."

I lock eyes with Rev, strength trickling back into my muscles with my next words.

"I'm gonna kill her," I whisper. "Even if it breaks me again, even if it destroys the final *shred* of me that's left, I'm going to kill Anyssa Holland."

Rev sits with me through the night until the sun begins to rise. To the left, the light highlights the ruins and the colorful market tents, which are starting to dwindle now that the market is moving. To the right, the chain-link fence stretches to encompass all three buildings of the compound, unpatrolled on this side. Too many guards this far from the gate would draw attention.

Eventually, Rev heads back downstairs. She invites me to go with her, but I shake my head, staring out at the sunrise. I don't have the strength to face people. Not yet.

Only a few minutes after Rev leaves, I catch movement out of the corner of my eye. A single figure, small, approaching the compound from the back. I walk to the edge of the roof closest to the back fence, squinting. I can make out dark curls, light brown skin, and when he tilts his face to look up at me, my eyes go wide.

It's Max.

I barrel down the stairs and scan my wristband to get out the main gates, then circle around to the back of the compound. Sure enough, Max is waiting for me. He breaks into a wide smile as I approach and runs to meet me, arms outstretched. As he draws close, I can make out tears of relief in his eyes. "TJ!"

He throws his arms around me, his incredible strength making me grunt. When he releases me, I step back, coughing. "You're alive!" *Finally*, one piece of good news. I nearly burst into tears all over again at the thought, but my eyes are puffy and dried out from last night.

"I escaped," he explains, breathless. His clothes—the same all-black I last saw him in—are tattered and covered in Nadzor dust, and his hair is more matted than I've ever seen it, but he's *alive.* "Holland had a temporary set-up in the northwestern ruins, and they brought me there, but I got out before we flew back to Ordinem."

I grab his shoulders, grinning. "Alec is going to be so happy to see—"

Max yelps and his hand darts to his neck as he staggers back. He pulls a tiny dart out and his eyes go wide. "TJ, run!"

Before I can take a step, a sharp pain jabs into the side of my neck. I pull out a dart identical to Max's. Both of us whirl around, looking for the source, but Max collapses before we can try to make it to the main gates on the other side of the compound. My knees go weak and I drop to the ground, fighting to stay awake.

I manage to lift my head in time to see Anyssa Holland herself. But...how? Where did she come from? Unless...

She followed Max. He never truly escaped at all.

She takes my chin, forcing me to meet her eyes as she gives a cold smile. "I've been looking forward to this," she says in a low voice.

That's the last thing I'm aware of before the sedative drags me into unconsciousness.

Chapter Thirty-Three

Hunter Lane

After getting Adrian cleaned up and walking him back to his cell, I try more than once to talk to TJ, but to no avail. I give up in the evening.

What Adrian told me before I took him to Nora plays in my head on repeat. It's true, then, that Daniel's lying about something. And that something has to do with the Draft.

It's time for me to get answers.

I find Reiko on her favorite eastward-facing bench outside. She jumps to her feet when she sees me. "Hunter! I heard something happened earlier today—is Adrian—"

"He's alright," I tell her. "A little beat-up, but Nora fixed him up."

"Nora? What was she doing in the prison wing?"

The corner of my mouth twitches into a smile. "She wasn't. Your brother was in the infirmary."

She gapes at me. "You—you went to see him. You brought him out."

I nod. "I needed to ask him some things about Daniel." *And Leah.* "Speaking of, I wanted to ask *you* something."

"What?"

"I'm...looking into some things. About Daniel. And I'd love your help."

She tilts her head. "How could *I* help you with Daniel?"

I grin. "Something tells me you're good at sneaking around. Come on."

Five minutes later, the two of us stand down the hall from Daniel's office, around the corner so that nobody notices us lurking. Thankfully, this hall isn't a busy one. Daniel doesn't like having people in his office all the time, and there's not much other reason to be down here.

It doesn't take long for Daniel to leave his office. When he does, Reiko and I wait for him to disappear down the other hallway before making our way to his door. As soon as we're sure nobody's looking, both of us slip inside.

"What are we looking for?" Reiko asks, moving to the filing cabinets along the back of the room.

I take Daniel's desk in the center. "Anything related to where he came from, whether he's lying, what he's lying about. Especially things related to the Draft."

Reiko nods and sets to work.

I take two paper clips and kneel behind Daniel's desk, testing the drawers one-by-one. The top two are unlocked, but reveal nothing aside from various office knick-knacks. The third drawer, bigger than the rest, requires my paperclips to open.

Inside, the drawer looks like a miniature filing cabinet. I pull papers out one-by-one, careful not to disturb anything too much. If Daniel knows his office has been messed with, after the past few conversations we've had, I'll be near the top of his suspect list.

Nothing in the first section, and nothing in the second. In the third, however, a yellowed notepad covered in Daniel's scratchy handwriting catches my attention. I pull it out, set it on the desk, and skim the pages for information as quickly as possible. "Find anything?" I ask Reiko.

"Not yet!"

The notepad in front of me appears to be contain notes and scheming—old, from the looks of it. Maybe as old as the Undrafted itself. It seems this is where Daniel first came up with the idea for the UND. His plan to ask the Nadzor government for funding, to recruit both people from Ordinem and from Nadzor, to train agents and to convert this little warehouse complex into the Undrafted compound. I almost close the notepad and move on, but a section of writing near the middle of the notepad catches my eye first.

They will *pay.*

I scan the rest of the page and my eyes go wide.

It's time for me to take back what's mine. Johnson, Holland—they took everything from me.

And they. Will. *Pay.*

I suck in a sharp breath. So, the Undrafted is Daniel's revenge mission against Silas Johnson and Anyssa Holland—but that's not the surprising part. *It's time for me to take back what's mine.* Take back. He wouldn't be able to take back a dead family member, or any number of different things Holland could have done to him. Holland and Johnson took something from Daniel.

I frantically flip back a few pages, searching for anything to give me insight. Scattered phrases come together to form a horrifying truth.

...have my own army...

...maintain control...

...use his soldiers against him...

...have to get the program back...

What Holland and Johnson took from Daniel...the *program*...

The Draft. Daniel led the Draft before Johnson put Holland in charge.

And Daniel is out to *get it back.*

I step back, fumbling the notepad closed. "Reiko, we need to go. We need to get out of here *now.*"

"Why? Did you find something?"

"*Now!*" I move to put the notepad back in the drawer, but when I raise my head, I freeze.

Daniel stands in the doorway. Looking straight at me and the yellow notepad on his desk.

"Well," he says, his tone cold as the door shuts behind him. "It was only a matter of time, I suppose."

"You used to run the *Draft*," I say in a low voice. "And all this you're doing with the Undrafted—it's not to stop the Draft at all, is it? It's to take your *revenge*."

"Indeed." Daniel gives a cold smile. "Unfortunately, I can't have anybody else knowing that information just yet. Luckily for you, now isn't the time for me to be dealing with an execution, either—so here's what's going to happen. You're both going to walk with me, peacefully, to the prison wing. A single word out of either of you and I *will* make an execution happen. Slowly." Daniel's wicked grin focuses on Reiko, and I can read the threat in his expression as easily as in his words.

One short walk later, Daniel scans his wristband and pushes open the door to Adrian's cell. He gestures Reiko inside first and stops me in the doorway. "Your wristband."

I scowl at him as I hand over my black UND credentials. "I can't believe I trusted you all these years. You—"

Daniel lands a punch to my jaw before I can respond. I stagger back, dropping my crutch into the cell behind me, but Daniel catches me by the front of the shirt to keep me from falling. "I'm truly sorry about this, Hunter. I always did look at you like a son, since the night I found you cowering in that closet. I turned you into a successful agent." He shakes his head. "Too successful, it seems."

I open my mouth to hurl an insult at him for *daring* to bring up the state he found me in, but Daniel's fist crunches into my jaw again before I can speak. My vision explodes.

The last thing I'm aware of as I topple backward is the cell door closing with a final *clang*.

Chapter Thirty-Four

Reverie Adams

After I leave TJ alone on the roof, I head back to my room for a change of clothes and a quick shower, and then to the mess hall for a meal. The peace only lasts until a few minutes after breakfast.

Kaz, of all people, stops me in the hallway. I open my mouth to make a sarcastic comment, but the look on his face freezes the words in my throat.

"What's wrong?" I ask instead.

"I just talked to Daniel—TJ—Holland took him." Kaz tugs me toward Daniel's office as my jaw goes slack.

Holland took TJ. "*What*? How? I just saw him!"

"We caught it on the cameras just barely too late," he explains. "Some kid came up to the gate and TJ went out to meet him. It looked like they knew each other. Then they collapsed, and Holland and some of the Draft kids took them both. We sent people out there as soon as we saw what had happened, but we were *seconds* too late."

My heart races as we enter Daniel's office. *TJ.* Holland has him, again. Is he okay?

Is he alive?

Yes. He *has* to be alive. If Holland wanted to kill him, she would've already. Anger spikes through my chest at the thought—this is the *second* time TJ's been at Holland's mercy. The second time Holland has bested us and put TJ's life in jeopardy.

He has to be alive.

I repeat the words to myself, over and over, trying to make my heart believe they're true. Holland wants him.

The missing piece. I suck in a sharp breath as the door to Daniel's office closes and all eyes inside—Daniel, Savi, and Kaz—turn to me.

"Rev?" Daniel stands behind his desk. "Kaz filled you in?"

"I know why Holland wants TJ," I breathe. "The flash drive—she's seen it, too. She knows that TJ has something to do with the missing piece to her serum."

Kaz and Savi look confused, but Daniel only nods. "I came to the same conclusion. Which is why we need to get to Ordinem as soon as possible. I've been trying to get the support of Nadzor's small military—they're not eager to use their limited resources on this when they could be protecting their own country instead—but we no longer have the luxury of time. We'll be going in on our own, and our only chance is stealth and surprise. Hence, why the three of you are here."

Savi's face pales. "We're going *back*? Again?"

"You three are the only Undrafted team to pull off a successful infiltration of the Draft headquarters. So yes, you're going back. And this time, we're going to end Holland's reign once and for all." Daniel turns his focus to me and Kaz, settling into his chair. "You two are going to have full sets of Enforcer armor—ceramic, visors, everything. That'll get you through the front doors. You'll make your way to the back staircase, where Savi will read you the code for entrance to the Draft sublevels. I have people working on getting it from Adrian as we speak. Rev, do you remember the room you found on your way out of the sublevels last time? Where you saw Leah Lane working on some kind of device?"

I nod.

"Her notes indicate that the device you saw is a transmitter, syncing a group of agents to a single handler. While wearing the device, the handler's will becomes the agent's will. Take the device off, the synced agents will freeze. We can use that." Daniel pauses for a breath. "The room you saw is what Leah calls the control center. In order for the transmitter to broadcast to such large numbers, it needs to be connected to a larger control system. That room is our target. We need to get there before Holland finishes her serum and injects the agents, and we need to destroy that control room. If we can do that, we delay her immediate plans—then we take TJ back and get rid of her access to her *missing piece*."

It's a good plan. A simple plan, but a good plan. Next to me, Kaz bobs his head in agreement, but Savi looks unsteady. "What's my job, then?"

"Your usual. Run comms remotely, monitor cameras. You won't be able to connect to the Enforcers' system—it's too risky to try sneaking you into the server room again—but you can monitor the building from the cameras outside."

Savi's shoulders sink in relief and she smiles. "I can do that."

"Good." Daniel stands, approaching the door. "We leave tomorrow, and I'll be coming with you. Rev and Kaz, once you're inside, one of you will come open the side alley door for me to join you." His tone turns dark. "I'll be finishing Holland myself."

The next day, the four of us are on a helicopter bound for Ordinem. We fly in silence, this mission weighing too heavily for small talk. Everything rides on this. TJ's life. Our chance to save the Draft kids before Holland uses TJ to finish her serum. The only consolation is that TJ doesn't know anything to help her, but that worries me more.

The last time TJ didn't know what Holland wanted, he ended up in an execution room and left with an arm covered in scars.

We'll make it out of this. He'll be okay. I drill the words into my head, over and over, as we make the trek from the hangar in Sector 9 to the same UND base we stayed in during our last mission. I take up the rear of the group and Kaz trails to walk next to me.

"I don't like this," he says under his breath. "The four of us, rushing in to take down the Draft all on our own?"

"I don't like it, either," I say, making sure Daniel is out of earshot. It takes me a moment of thinking to push past my concern about TJ and pinpoint what feels off. "Why does Daniel want to come inside with us? Deal with Holland personally?"

Kaz shrugs. "He always has something up his sleeve. He'd never do anything to jeopardize this mission, though. I'm assuming you've gathered that he has a personal vendetta against the Draft, by now?"

"Yeah. What's that about?"

"Dunno. He won't say anything past that. But you can trust that whatever his reason is, he'd *never* risk the success of this mission."

I nod, but Kaz's words do little to ease my quick pulse. I can't decide which is more terrifying: the idea that we're supposed to take down the Draft, today, by ourselves, or the fact that TJ is at Holland's mercy until we do.

Let him be okay. Please, let him be okay.

Chapter Thirty-Five

TJ Collins

A white light. A cold floor. The soft sound of crying.

I groan as consciousness returns, rolling so I'm on my back. My memory returns in a rush. Max. The darts. *Holland.*

I sit straight up with a gasp, my eyes wide. "No," I breathe, taking in the torturously bright cell around me. I've been here before. I'm back. *I'm back.* "No, no, *no—*"

"TJ?" A quiet sniffle draws my focus before I can lose myself in my mental spiral. I latch onto Max's voice like a lifeline, keeping me from drowning in the memories.

Max sits in the corner, his knees pulled up and his arms wrapped around them. He's been crying.

"I'm sorry," he whispers, shaking his head as soon as I look at him. "I'm sorry. I—I thought I got out—I didn't know they'd follow. This is my fault. I'm so sorry."

I drag myself to his side and slump against the wall next to him. "This is *not* your fault. I would've done the same thing. I'm just glad you're alive."

Max shivers, tightening his bare arms around himself. "I wish I knew why she's keeping me around. And why she's going after *you* all of a sudden."

I hesitate, asking myself the same question, but my mother's video flashes through my mind. I go stiff. "I know why." My voice comes out weak. "She thinks I have her missing piece. The missing piece to the serum."

"Why would she think something like that?"

"My mother."

Max's eyes widen as he looks up at me, shock crossing his tear-stained face. "Do you? Have the missing piece?"

I shake my head.

Max lets out a strained noise and tugs on one of his tangled curls. "She's going to kill us both," he says quietly. "She wouldn't have let me live for nothing. She's going to use me against you, and then—she'll..."

I put my arm around his shaking shoulders, although I'm trembling myself. *Back here. I'm back here. Back where the last time I didn't know what Holland wanted—*

I cut myself off there. *Max. Focus on Max.* "We'll make it out of here."

But the words sound hollow, even to me. Will the Undrafted come for us? Will they come for us *in time?*

Max curls into himself, leaning partially on me. "I don't want to die here. TJ, I—I just got out. I don't want to die here."

I don't want to die here, either. I press a shaking hand to my forehead, fighting a wave of fear that threatens to overwhelm me.

Rev will come for us. We'll make it out of here.

As the cell door swings open, though, my heart begins to race. The edges of my vision blur and my hands go numb as I press back against the wall. Two figures stand in the doorway—Anyssa Holland and a frizzy, blonde-haired woman with a clipboard and a small briefcase in hand.

I glare at Holland, my blood running hot beneath my skin—my rage shoving my fear out of the way, for the time being. "You killed my sister." My voice comes out raspy. Angry and pained, all at once.

"She was a loose end. You thought I'd let the Undrafted have the prototype of the serum on their hands?" Holland shakes her head, folding her arms over her blazer.

"She was *innocent!*" I yell, my voice cracking as I struggle to my feet. Max watches the exchange, tucked into the corner of the cell.

"Leah." Holland gestures for the woman to open the briefcase.

I rush at Holland, channeling the small bit of strength I have into my legs as I rear back for a punch. I'm going to kill her. Right here, right now. I'll—

Holland catches my fist in an iron grip, jarring my entire body to a stop. I struggle, but Holland grabs something from the now-open briefcase and my muscles go rigid.

A syringe. With a too-familiar amber liquid inside.

Holland gives a slight smile as she taps the needle against my skin, the tender spot between my jaw and neck. I grit my teeth, desperately fighting the flashes of memory. Of *agony*.

She drops my hand, but I remain completely frozen. Immobilized by the unbearable pain only a hair from my skin.

"Now," she says, her face only inches from mine. "Let's start again, shall we? You have something I want."

"I don't." My voice breaks. "I know what you think, and I don't know anything."

I don't know anything. I cringe back, waiting for the consequence I know follows those words. Waiting for the pain, the—

Holland plants her palm on my chest and shoves me. I stumble, but manage to keep my balance. *What is she doing?*

At a nod from Holland, Leah steps forward with an empty syringe in hand. "Lucky for you, Collins," Holland says, "I don't need what's in your head. I need your blood."

"My…"

Suddenly, it clicks. My mother's "vaccinations." My eyes. The fact that she manipulated my genetics—my mutation.

You are the key, TJ.

My mother never hid the missing piece, or the cure, in my head. She hid them in *me*. In my blood. In my *genetics*.

I shake my head, backing up against the wall as Leah approaches. "No. No. I'm not letting you take my blood."

"You need to hold still," Leah says quietly, setting the metal case down and reaching for my arm.

I wrench it away from her, staggering to the side. I *can't* let them have my blood. If they get the missing piece, finish the serum—

Max yelps. My gaze snaps to the corner where Holland has hauled him up by the collar. She grips his hair, tilting his head to expose his neck to the amber-filled syringe in her other hand.

"TJ, don't do it!" he yells. "Don't listen to them! Don't—"

A cry of pain silences him as Holland jabs the syringe into his neck and pushes the plunger down—barely.

"No!" I scream, but it's too late.

A shiver wracks his body and he closes his eyes as his limbs quake. Holland holds him upright as a moan of pain slips through his clenched teeth. Leah latches on to my arm again, but I kick her in the stomach and send her stumbling away.

Max comes to with a huge, shuddering breath, his eyes snapping open and flitting around wildly. Sweat beads on his forehead and he sucks in air as if he's been holding his breath for a long time. He winces as Holland's grip on his hair tightens.

"You're going to hold still," Holland says, enunciating each word as she drills me with a stony look. "Or you're going to watch Max experience exactly what you did."

"Don't, TJ!" Max calls, but I can tell it pains him to say the words this time. He won't be able to take a full syringe.

But I *can't* let Holland complete that serum. Maybe, if I can manage to incapacitate *Leah*...if I can take her next time she comes close, I may have a chance.

Leah approaches me again, wary this time, but Holland stops her, studying my expression. "Wait."

She knows, I think, balling my fists. Holland knows exactly what I'm thinking. I swallow hard as she holds my gaze for a few beats before uttering her next command. "Bring in Eliza."

The blood drains from my face and all thoughts of fighting flee at those words. Three Draft kids enter the room—two I don't recognize, and one with a braid and wide brown eyes that are agonizingly familiar.

"What are you going to do?" I ask, my voice trembling. Is she going to use Eliza to hurt me? To hurt Max?

She inclines her head toward the metal briefcase. Eliza lets out a low growl as one of the Draft kids lets go of her to bring Holland another syringe. He takes hold of Max, who's still weak from the first injection, as Holland moves in between Max and Eliza. She grips a syringe in each hand, and as Eliza's eyes flit nervously to the needle pointed at her, it hits me.

Holland is going to torture both of them if I don't cooperate.

My breath comes quick and short as I press my back against the wall, shaking my head. Holland is *enjoying* this. She could easily have brought her agents here to hold me down and been done with it, but she's playing games with me instead.

Max shrinks away as Holland brings the syringe closer, and even Eliza tenses.

I *can't* let Holland finish the serum. I'm the only thing standing between her and all those kids—all the kids she took from Nadzor, who she's planning on injecting.

But as I watch the needles draw close to Max and Eliza's necks, I tremble so violently that I have to brace myself on the wall. Leah steps toward me again, a pleading look in her eyes. "Stay still," she says, reaching for my arm.

I take a deep breath, tears springing to my eyes. I can't let her have my blood. I *can't.* There's a chance Eliza is only here to intimidate me—maybe Holland won't inject her, with her still being loyal. And Max would do anything to keep Holland from finishing her serum. He'd want me to at least *try.*

I hold still until Leah comes within arm's reach. Then, I strike. Max's training floods back to me—use my speed to my advantage. I knock the syringe from Leah's hand, sending it skittering across the tiles, before balling my fist and swinging as hard as I possibly can.

The first scream is Eliza's.

My punch lands and Leah yelps, staggering away, but my focus is already on Rev's little sister. She thrashes against the other agent's hold, another raw cry ripping from her throat as Holland pulls the half-empty syringe away. *Only half,* I think, holding on to my resolve with everything I have in me. It was only half. Only half.

Eliza screams again and I cringe. I can almost *feel* her pain.

Leah scowls at me, holding her jaw, but I can see the tears springing to her eyes as her gaze darts to Eliza. The pity as she returns her attention to me.

Eliza sags in the other agent's arms with a groan as the serum wears off. I clench my fists and Max struggles as Holland joins the Draft kid behind him, syringe raised. She meets my eyes with a cold determination. "You know I'm going to get what I want either way, TJ. It's up to you whether you put him through the same torture you endured." She touches the needle to Max's neck and he lets out a slight whimper.

I crack.

"Okay. Okay." I raise my hands, open my trembling palms. *She's going to get what she wants either way.* A tear slips down my cheek as it hits me.

I've already lost. I lost the moment Holland caught me.

I failed. I failed Riya. I failed my mother. I failed the Undrafted, the Draft kids.

The least I can do is save Max the agony.

I squeeze my eyes shut as Leah takes my arm. Draws a vial full of blood. Blood she's going to use to finish the serum. To take control of innocent kids.

And it's my fault.

"Why are you doing this?" I whisper, looking at Holland over Leah's shoulder. She still stands with her syringe at Max's neck. "Why Max? Why Eliza?"

Leah wraps my arm in gauze. When she steps back, Holland leaves Max with her agent and approaches me. I don't have the strength to fight as she tilts my chin up to face her. "You," she hisses, "have caused me so much more trouble than you're worth."

"You already broke me, Holland." My voice cracks. "You killed my sister. You have my blood. What more do you want?"

Her grip on my chin tightens and I wince, waiting for a harsh response. Instead, she lets me go and returns to Max's side, her back to me. "I want to see Maya's son *burn* for the trouble her family has caused me," she says, her voice low. She reaches up and grips Max's arm, leaning close to his ear. "And I want to see one more betrayal paid for."

Holland jams the syringe into Max's neck and pushes the plunger all the way down.

"No!" I scream as the Draft agent lets Max fall to his knees. Out of the corner of my eye, I see Eliza cringe and look away, but I'm more focused on getting to Max on my shaky legs. Holland beckons her people out of the cell.

As soon as the door closes, Max lets out a gut-wrenching shriek, curling up on his side. His entire body quakes, tears streaming down his face as cries erupt from his throat and fill the cell. I drop to my knees next to him and grab his shoulder. "I'm here. I'm sorry." I run my free hand through my hair, my eyes watering. "I'm sorry, Max. I'm sorry."

Another shriek tears from his throat as his curled-up body spasms, trembling against the tile floor. I shift to support his head under my hands, keeping him from hitting it against the floor. Watching him go through the same agony I endured is enough to make the tears in my eyes spill over as I kneel, hanging my head.

The serum starts to wear off a minute later. Max sucks in shaky gasps of air, his screams fading to heaving sobs. He struggles to his hands and knees, but his elbows give out. I remember the way the serum sapped my strength, the hours I spent lying on the cell floor, unable to move. "TJ..." he rasps, barely able to lift his head.

"I've got you." I swipe away my own tears and help Max sit up against the wall, settling next to him. "I've got you."

He sits with wide eyes and blotchy, tear-stained cheeks, leaning as much on me as on the wall. I wrap my arm around his trembling form. He seems almost catatonic, and I don't blame him. The amber serum had the same effect on me, and Max is even smaller. "I'm sorry, Max," I say softly, but I'm not only talking about the pain. I'm talking about Holland's serum. The serum that she's able to complete now, because of me. I slump, my shoulders hunched. "I tried to stop her. I'm sorry."

"It's not your fault."

The words don't come from Max.

I whip my head up, my body snapping to attention and my grip on Max tightening at the girl's voice. I'm not letting Holland so much as *touch* him, after...

My thoughts come to a standstill when I recognize the single girl left in the cell with us. Eliza.

"What are you doing here?" My voice comes out weak. Empty.

Eliza rubs the side of her neck, scowling at the door. "*That* is a spectacular question." Her eyes drift to Max, her expression softening. "Is he...going to be okay?"

"Like you care," I mutter.

She exhales slowly, sitting across from us. "We used to be friends, you know. Before he left."

"And I'm sure you wouldn't hesitate to kill him if Holland ordered you to," I bite off.

Eliza pauses. Then, she shrugs and looks to the side, avoiding a response.

I tip my head back against the wall, fighting another wave of emotion. Maybe it's not over yet. Maybe the Undrafted are on their way here right now to stop Holland before she can use my blood to complete her serum. But deep down, the significance of what just happened gnaws at me.

I broke. Again.

And now, all of the Draft kids are going to suffer for it.

"Do you know Rev?" Eliza asks quietly.

I lean my head off the wall, looking at her. She's still avoiding my gaze.

"Why?" I ask.

Eliza shrugs again, but goes silent after that.

I keep an eye on her as Max's shaking eases, his body finally beginning to relax. She steals a concerned glance at him every so often, shifting uncomfortably when she notices me watching. *She cares.*

"Max is going to be fine," I say softly. *For now,* my mind adds. Until Holland finishes her serum and injects Max and Eliza both.

Eliza seems to take the words as a peace offering, some of the tension draining from her shoulders as she gives a slight nod.

"And Rev…" I trail off. What would she want me to say?

Eliza finally meets my eyes, looking hopeful despite herself.

"Rev misses you," is what I decide on.

She tugs on her braid and whispers, "Thank you."

The cell lapses into silence for the following hours. Max falls asleep on my shoulder and Eliza, too, drifts off, but I can't slow my mind enough for me to sleep. When I do manage to doze, nightmares about Holland's plans with the serum and Max and Eliza's screams jolt me back to consciousness. I lose track of how many hours the three of us are left alone in here, although I'm sure it feels longer than it is. I'm almost convinced that Holland has forgotten about us, that she's going to leave us here to starve, when the cell door swings open again.

Eliza jumps to her feet and, cautiously, I follow suit. Max struggles up, leaning against the wall.

Holland's focus, however, is on me alone. I swallow hard. Is she finally going to pull the trigger? End the last remnant of the Collins family?

Instead, a slow smile stretches across her face. "Let's go."

"What do you want?" I ask, my eyes narrowed.

"You, TJ." The look in her eyes gives me chills. "I need you for one last thing."

Chapter Thirty-Six

Reverie Adams

Less than 36 hours after Riya's death, Kaz and I stand in the shadow of the towering Enforcer headquarters, staring up at the massive glass wall as it reflects the afternoon sun. I can't see Kaz's face past the opaque Enforcer helmet and visor, identical to the set of armor I wear, but I can imagine his expression reflects the same trepidation that fills me.

"You ready?" Savi asks over our earpieces.

"Ready as I'll ever be," Kaz answers.

I nod. "Same here. Everything good on your end?"

"All good. Just remember, I can only see the outside cameras, and I don't have access to the security system. As long as you follow my instructions, I'll be able to guide you based on the blueprints, although you both probably know the way this time. Which one of you is going to split off and let Daniel in?"

"Kaz should," I say. "I know the way to the control center. I can run ahead and scout."

"Good plan," Daniel's voice jumps in. "Whenever you two are ready."

Kaz and I share a look, nod, and walk directly for the front doors.

The Enforcer armor alone is enough to get the two of us through, and so long as we keep our heads down and our feet moving, nobody casts us a second glance. There are enough Enforcers crowding this building that two unfamiliar faces aren't unusual, and we keep our visors down anyways, just in case. My bow, folded into itself and hidden inside one of my Enforcer boots, digs into my ankle as we walk, and I can feel my quiver shifting on my back underneath the armor.

We slip through the lobby and into the hallway leading to the main part of the building, then find the door we escaped out of the first time we were here, when we rescued TJ. Savi reads the code to us, which Kaz punches into the keypad next to the door. The light switches from red to green as a lock whirs open. Daniel successfully got Adrian's access code, then.

"I guess Holland forgot to change the locks," Kaz says under his breath as we slip into the stairwell.

I shut the door behind us and follow Kaz down the stairs. "That doesn't sound like her."

"No," he agrees. "But why else would she have left the doors open? Especially knowing the Undrafted has Adrian? She had to have known there was a chance he'd give us his code."

A few possibilities spring to mind, but none of them are particularly appealing. Maybe she's *expecting* us. I shiver as we start down the stairs. If Holland is expecting us and unconcerned about it, then we're too late. Or we're walking into a trap.

Or maybe Holland was holding out hope for Adrian to return.

When we emerge into the Draft hallway, I expect to see guards, or Enforcers, or agents—but the hallway is empty.

"Are you two out on the main floor yet?" Savi asks us.

"Just got out of the stairwell," I say.

"Good. Rev, you know where to go—Kaz, you're going to take your first left and keep headed that way until you see a hallway to your right with a door at the end. That's the door you'll want to open for Daniel."

"Copy that," Kaz says, setting off in the direction she indicated.

I follow the route I remember from the first time I was here, focusing on the rhythm of my steps to keep my mind clear. Still, images of TJ plague my mind.

TJ going through Holland's merciless torture, again. TJ, floating limp in that glass tank, me being too late this time—

No. No.

Kaz's voice jolts me out of my head. "Savi, it's practically deserted down here. Has there been anything weird on the security cameras outside the Enforcer HQ in the past few hours? Or even the past day?"

"Let me check." Background noise filters through our earpieces as Savi's voice goes quiet, then returns a moment later. "Nothing unusual. Maybe some extra Enforcers leaving the building, but that would make sense because afternoon patrol groups would've been sent out around an hour ago." Savi pauses. "Actually, wait. I'm seeing something."

"What?" Kaz asks.

"In the lobby. One of these cameras can see in through the glass. It looks like just before we got here, a bunch of Enforcers came up through the door you two just entered through. They're still mingling with the rest of the Enforcers in the lobby, though."

"So *that's* why it felt so crowded up there," Kaz says under his breath. "Holland was using the patrol shift to cover up the fact that she sent a bunch of her Enforcers out of the sublevels. But *why*?"

"I don't think the Enforcers know what's actually going on with the Draft," I say, remembering one of my first conversations with Ethan after he discovered my identity. "At least, most of them don't. The ones who work directly for Holland have to know something, but I doubt Holland would've told them about the serum. I bet she sent them out to keep the serum a secret, and..."

I trail off as the pieces click together into a horrifying picture. The serum. The fact that Holland was in Nadzor to take new kids. That Holland killed Riya, her test subject. That Holland has TJ, her missing piece. And now, that she's sent the Enforcers away from the sublevels.

She's doing something with the serum—and there's only one thing left for her to do.

"Rev? What is it?" Savi asks.

"We need to hurry." I step out of my Enforcer boots, grabbing my bow and pressing the button to unfold it, and strip off the rest of the Enforcer armor. "Kaz, get out of your armor. If someone sees us in Enforcer uniforms, we're as good as dead. Holland doesn't want Enforcers down here any more than she wants us. I'd rather be armed than running around in armor without access to my quiver." Once I've gotten the armor off, I reach over my shoulder to make sure my quiver is still in fighting shape. Everything seems fine.

"Rev, you realized something," Kaz says. "What is it?"

"Remember how Holland had her agents in Nadzor to take more kids? Draft-age kids? Think, Kaz. She finished the serum. She proved that it works. What's her next step? The step she would send the Enforcers away for?"

"She's injecting them," Savi whispers.

"Exactly." I speed to a jog as Kaz inhales sharply.

"Rev," Daniel cuts in, "how close are you to the control center?" He doesn't even sound surprised. Of course not.

"Only a minute."

"Good. Kaz just opened the door. Don't do anything until the two of us join you."

"Copy." I take the final turn—the control center should be at the end of this hall.

"I *really* wish I had access to the cameras in there," Savi grumbles.

"What for?" Kaz asks, a hint of sarcasm in his tone. "Let me guess—you want to watch the handsome, talented Kaz take Holland down himself?"

"I want Kaz to stop talking about himself in third person," Savi says under her breath, but I can almost *hear* her blush.

I shake my head. "You two might be the most awkward people I've ever met, you know that?"

"You're one to talk," Kaz counters. "At least the two of *us* have never tried to kill each other."

"We haven't tried to—"

I realize my mistake as soon as the words leave my mouth. *We.* TJ and I. We?

That, and TJ and I *have* tried to kill each other. Or, at least, I've shot him and he's hidden in a stairwell to ambush me with a pocketknife.

Savi snorts a laugh over our earpieces, then stifles it. I open my mouth to defend myself, but the control room door catches my eye before I can speak.

The sounds of my earpiece seem to fade as I creep up to the door, careful not to catch the attention of anybody inside the room, but it quickly becomes evident that the room's occupants are too busy to be watching this window.

The room beyond is the same as I remember it, around the size of the common room in the living quarters at the UND. Screens displaying data I don't understand line all four walls, along with control boards, lights, wires, and everything in between. But what concerns me isn't the room itself—it's what's going on inside.

Holland stands to the right, just barely in my line of sight, with Leah Lane next to her, holding an open briefcase of syringes filled with bright blue liquid. I shiver as I take in the rest of the room.

A massive group of Draft kids, old and new alike, stand in organized rows to fill the space, with just enough space between them for Leah to easily walk through. I estimate there are at least a hundred, if not more. Leah moves from kid to kid, injecting each of them with a syringe of the blue serum before moving on. Holland follows her, watching each injection with intrigue.

Even Holland's expression fades to the back of my mind, though, when my eyes find TJ.

In the center of the room, against the back wall, TJ sits in a chair with metal clamps locking his wrists and ankles into place. A tube, filled with dark red—blood—runs from his arm to some kind of machine set up next to him. A small tank attached to the side of that machine fills with bright blue liquid. The serum.

Holland is using TJ's blood to produce the serum. And from the looks of TJ, she's already used *far* too much.

My gaze shifts to the Draft kids, seeking out a certain brown braid, round eyes, familiar face—

There. Near the edge of the room, where Leah must've passed through first. Her expression is totally blank, her posture straight and neutral. As Leah injects each agent, all emotion—trepidation, courage, determination, in most cases—drains from their eyes completely. A familiar head of curly black hair catches my eye. Max, already injected.

"We're too late," I whisper, watching the chilling scene unfold. "She's already injected so many of them."

Savi, Kaz, and Daniel fall silent. None of us know what to say, what to do next. A sinking feeling fills my stomach, forming a knot in my throat.

We've lost.

Inside the room, Holland says something to Leah, who pauses her injections and moves to a small desk on the far right. She picks up a device—a thin band, little more than a half-circle—and puts it on, the band wrapping around the back of her head. It's the same device I saw through the window the first time I was here. The injected kids adopt a relaxed posture, all of them looking at Leah. I press my ear to the door, hoping to catch a sliver of their words.

"...will attune them to whoever's wearing it," Leah says. A quick glance through the window is enough to see she's not talking to Holland, but someone out of sight. "You're not directly controlling their actions, but you're manipulating their will to match yours. If you tell them to do something, they'll do it *willingly*—and that's what makes it work."

Who is she talking to? I wonder, straining for a glimpse further to the side.

All the Draft kids stiffen up and go still, blank expressions returning to their faces. My eyes dart back to Leah, who's removed the transmitter. She hands it to Holland.

As soon as Holland puts it on, the injected kids snap to attention. A few who haven't been injected yet shift nervously on their feet, but they're all wise enough to avoid protesting. That would only make things worse.

I glance at TJ again, who looks even weaker than he did a few minutes ago. *She's not going to stop*, I think, my eyes going wide. Anyssa Holland is going to kill him this way.

I watch as one by one, Leah continues down the lines of Draft kids.

And then, somehow, things get worse.

From the far left, the section of the room I can't see through the window, a shorter man with gray hair and an uneven gait walks into view. If it weren't for his unmistakable face and the slightly lopsided walk, I would've never recognized him for the air of confidence he carries.

Silas Johnson. The President of Ordinem.

There are bigger forces at play. What Adrian told Hunter.

What all of us forgot about, in the chaos.

I watch in open-mouthed shock as Johnson crosses his arms, supervising the proceedings. This is *not* the senile, incompetent man I've known through the Ordinem news, and obviously, he's not oblivious to the truth of the Draft. In fact, watching the way Holland's demeanor shifts when he speaks, I'd venture to say Johnson holds the authority in the room in front of me, and everyone in there knows it.

Silas Johnson has been in charge all along. And he's here to watch his program reach a pinnacle.

"Guys?" I whisper into my earpiece as Kaz and Daniel come racing down the hall. "We have a problem."

Chapter Thirty-Seven

Hunter Lane

Reiko, Adrian, and I sit on the floor of Adrian's cell for over 24 hours.

I rest my crutch across my legs, my eyes straining to see in the darkness. If my timing is right, it's currently the middle of the day following Riya's death—but the three of us have taken enough turns dozing that it's difficult to tell. My eyelids drag after so many hours without a good rest. Adrian and Reiko are both asleep.

Daniel is planning to take the Draft back, probably to use it to take control of Ordinem, since it's Silas Johnson he wants revenge on. And Kaz, Rev, and the rest of them have no idea.

I need to get out of here—to warn them, to help—but banging on the door has gotten me nowhere. I can do nothing but sit in the dark and imagine all the horrible outcomes.

The deadbolt on the door whirs open and I twist to see, reaching for my crutch and readying myself to stand. The first crack of the door makes me wince at the brightness of the hallway outside, and I squint until my eyes adjust enough to make out a silhouette in the doorway. Short, stocky, and with fiery orange hair.

"Nora!" I use my crutch to struggle to my feet.

"*Hunter?*" she hisses. "What are you *doing* in here?"

"It's a long story. What are *you* doing here?"

Behind me, the scraping of chains signals Adrian's waking. Nora's eyes only dart to him for a moment before retuning to me. "I guess I should explain. Long story short, I found the cure for the serum."

"*What?*" Adrian's voice cuts in behind me and he stands, his eyes wide. "How?"

"The notes from Leah and video from Maya got me thinking, so I did some testing on TJ's blood and on the samples I had from Riya before she…" Nora takes a deep breath. "I found a genetic mutation in TJ's blood that I knew wasn't natural, but I didn't think much of it—until I saw how TJ's blood interacted with the serum in Riya's. The coding in that mutation is the key to all of it—the serum, the cure, everything. TJ's blood on its own reverses the effects of the serum, and the serum is produced by taking his blood and utilizing that mutation in combination with some other ingredients."

"So why are you *here?*" I ask, stepping toward her. "You have to tell someone! Rev, or Kaz, or—"

"They're gone, Hunter."

The blood drains from my face. "What?"

"They're in Ordinem. When TJ was taken, Daniel pushed the timeline up. They plan to use all we have left—stealth and surprise—to stop Holland from injecting the kids, if she's already completed her serum. And if she hasn't, they'll get TJ out of there before she can use him. I've been trying to reach Daniel about the cure, but he's gone radio silent. Nobody at the compound has been able to reach him, and all missions and research has come to a standstill." Nora's gaze shifts to Adrian. "I actually came here to find *you*. I don't know what I think you could've done, but it was the last idea I had. I'm glad I came. Hunter, I thought you'd left with the rest of them. Where have you *been?*"

"Daniel's not going to stop the Draft," I tell her, even as the full implications of her news sink in. Daniel is already *in* Ordinem with Rev, Kaz, and whoever else he brought. And he's using them on his revenge mission.

Nora draws her brow. "What do you mean?"

"He has his own vendetta, Nora." I run a hand through my hair, my jaw clenching. *I trusted him.* "He was supposed to be in charge of the Draft, and Holland and Johnson took it from him—I don't know the details, but he's going to Ordinem to get it back, and to take his revenge. He threw me in here when he realized I knew."

Nora blinks at me, then springs into motion, striding right past me. "We need to get the cure to Kaz and Rev. It won't be easy, but at least with that, they have a chance. Daniel will wait for the kids to be injected so that he can take control of them—it's probably why I haven't been able to reach him about the cure. He's not planning on curing the kids at all." She mutters something unintelligible as she paces, then whirls on me. "I can't *believe* I didn't see this sooner. Hunter, they left early this morning. You *have* to get TJ's blood to them."

I balk at her. "How am I supposed to do that?"

"Take one of the helicopters." Nora throws me a ring with two keys. "One of these goes to the helicopter left in the hangar. The other is for his manacles." She tips her head toward Adrian. "Figured you should have it. Oh, and there's another guy—Alec. He's coming with you."

I open my mouth to protest, but Nora cuts me off before I can. "I've been chatting with Alec since he got here, and he's trustworthy. Another person will be useful. Plus, he'll probably just sneak out with you if we try to stop him. He knows one of the Draft kids, and desperation will do crazy things to a person."

"Can he fly a helicopter?"

Nora hesitates, then shakes her head. "You'll have to figure something out. I wish I could help on that front."

A rattling of chains from behind makes me jump, tightening my grip on my crutch. I almost forgot about Adrian, back to sitting cross-legged.

"I can," he says, his voice raspy. "Fly, I mean."

Nora looks between the two of us, apparently at a loss. Eventually, she leaves it to me. "I'll send Alec down here with the vials."

With that, Nora leaves, the cell door wide open behind her. Reiko still dozes against the wall, leaving Adrian and I alone. Conflict shadows his face, but he gives me a slight nod when I meet his eyes.

He really has changed. In his expression, there's nothing to hint at the cocky arrogance I've grown so used to. He's serious.

And he's the only one of us who can fly.

I kneel, although it's more of an awkward sitting position with my injuries, and grip the key ring as we come face-to-face. Adrian slides back a little, obviously wary, and I can't blame him—but all I do is gesture for his manacles.

He hesitates, searching my face as if he suspects a trick. He offered to fly, but I doubt he expected me to take him up on it.

"You want to go stop your mother or not?" I wave for his manacles again. "Let's go."

No more than twenty minutes after Nora found me, I sit in the copilot seat of the Undrafted's second helicopter. Reiko and Alec sit in the back, and the headset over my ears muffles the chopping of the rotors overhead.

It took some time to get the helicopter off the ground, but fortunately, Adrian wasn't kidding about knowing how to fly. Once he got off the ground, the landscape quickly became nothing but brown Nadzor land and dots of colored tents. Now, after a few hours, we fly toward the black line of the fence that marks Ordinem's border.

Adrian glances at me out of the corner of his eye, then flashes his hand in a signal—a one, and then a four. I draw my brow, but switch my headset to channel fourteen. "Why are we switching channels?"

"I wanted to talk to you," Adrian's voice comes over my headset.

Without Reiko and Alec listening in.

I swallow. For once, I have no idea where this conversation is going. I let the silence stretch, waiting for him to speak first.

"You and Reiko seem to be close," he finally says, his voice strained.

"Yeah." I give him a sideways look. "Adrian, what's this about? Why are we on a separate channel?"

Adrian lets out a long breath, his eyes fixed on the horizon ahead. "What am I doing here?"

"What do you mean?"

"Why did you let me come, Hunter? I know what you think of me, and I know for certain that you don't trust me. And yet here I am, flying a helicopter with you in it."

How do I answer that? "We needed someone to fly. Even if your loyalties don't lie with us, I think you'd do it for Reiko. And..." I trail off, unsure of how to phrase my next words.

Adrian meets my eyes for a brief moment. "And?"

I watch the man, shocked at the emotion in his eyes. I've seen small flashes of it before, but for the most part, nothing but cold steel resides in Adrian's expression. This, though, is different. Whatever walls he's been keeping up seem to be crumbling now, letting a spot of hope glint in his eyes.

"Reiko believes in you, Adrian," I tell him. "That deep down, you want to stop Holland."

Adrian looks back to the horizon, his fingers clenched around the helicopter's control stick. "And you? What do you think?"

"Honestly? I'm not sure." I pause. "I want to believe you, though."

Adrian presses his lips together, looking disappointed, but not surprised. "Makes sense, after everything I've done. I can't expect you to trust me." He takes a deep breath, letting the silence stretch until I start to think he won't say anything further. Then, his voice returns. "Thank you," he says, little more than a whisper. "For giving me a chance. After what I did to you."

I wince at that.

When I don't respond, Adrian glances at me. "I know it probably doesn't mean much now, but I'm sorry. For everything. And I want you to know that whatever happens today...I'm on your side. Not Holland's."

"Completely? Or only for Reiko's sake?"

Adrian takes a few moments before answering. "Completely," he says softly. To my knowledge, that's the first time Adrian has ever admitted to having his own doubts about the Draft—and he seems as sincere as I've ever seen him.

"Good. Now you prove it." I meet Adrian's eyes and give him a slight nod, which he returns.

Now we just have to hope we're not too late.

Chapter Thirty-Eight

TJ Collins

The first ten minutes hooked up to Holland's machine are torturous.

The needle taped to my left arm feels foreign, unnatural, and sends shivers rippling across my body when I think too hard about it. Holland couldn't sedate me—it would mess with whatever enables that machine to use my blood to produce the serum—so I'm back in a metal chair. Wrists and ankles clamped. I fought, but I'm no match for two Draft kids.

I have no choice but to watch as one by one, Leah injects each row of Draft agents with a syringe full of bright blue.

I'm almost grateful when my mind starts to fuzz from the blood loss, until the flashing memories take control. A metal chair just like this. A syringe in my arm.

Pain.

I groan, slumped in Holland's chair, unable to tell how much of the swirling in my head has to do with the blood loss and how much is a result of the memories dredged up by the needle in my arm.

Rev would come for me if she could. I know that. But with every passing second, I grow increasingly certain she's too late.

I think back to the day I told her how I'd broken and revealed Eliza's name, my sleepless nights spent on the rooftops, the way she stayed up and waited for me the night after Holland's invasion because she knew I'd go out to the roof—because, despite my insistence, she knew I needed to not be alone.

She really hasn't given up on me. After everything we've been through together, after seeing my ugly, shattered, messed-up side, maybe she still hasn't given up on me. Maybe, through it all, she somehow manages to feel something for me other than pity.

Whatever she sees in me, it must be something I can't see in myself.

I only hope she's okay. That she'll survive this. That she'll get Eliza back, get to watch her sister grow up.

Here, as I watch the blood drain from my own body, my life trickling away, I'm suddenly aware of an overwhelming amount of things we've left unsaid.

She'll be okay. She has to be okay. But my heart sinks regardless.

Even if she is okay, I'll never get the chance to tell her. Even in my thoughts, my words slur. *I'll never...*

From there, I float in a haze between two nightmares. The memories and the waking. Somewhere in the distance, yells pierce the air. The sounds of a brawl. Chaos.

My eyes flutter open and widen when I realize that the yells aren't part of a dream.

I can hardly process the scene in front of me in Holland's control room. No more orderly ranks of Draft agents—instead, people scrambling and yelling. Holland in front of me, Rev and Kaz lunging for her, Leah Lane backing away from the last kid she injected—she hasn't made it all the way through the lines yet. Silas Johnson, holding a pulse rifle, yelling for Holland to get the situation under control, Daniel entering the room brandishing a pistol—

Johnson fires the pulse rifle toward Rev and Kaz.

The blast sends both of them crashing into a group of injected Draft kids, but the edge must catch Holland, because she stumbles back, her hands reaching up to protect the transmitter around her head. Most importantly, it clears the space between Daniel and Holland.

The scene seems to take place in slow motion. Rev and Kaz get to their feet, each held by at least three injected Draft kids—two of them, I realize, are Max and Eliza. Daniel ignores them all, launching himself at the dazed Holland.

She draws her pistol, but not in time. Daniel swipes the weapon from her hand and sends it skidding across the floor before using his other hand to knock the transmitter free of her head.

The injected Draft kids freeze in place, going rigid.

Daniel scrambles away from Holland, snatching the transmitter off the floor before the un-injected Draft kids can reach him, and slams it onto his own head. Immediately, the Draft kids near Holland spring to life, immobilizing her before she can reach Daniel. The rest of the injected agents turn their attention to holding back the handful of un-injected kids.

With effort, I raise my head to look around. Draft kids hold a red-faced Johnson and a wide-eyed Leah Lane near the opposite wall, and for every hostile Draft kid, there are at least three under Daniel's control to hold them back.

We...we did it. We did it.

A wide grin splits my face and I look to Rev and Kaz, but pause when I see them. The Draft kids—the *injected* Draft kids—haven't let them go.

I shift my gaze to Daniel, but his eyes are fixed on the side of the room with Leah, Holland, Johnson, and the rest of the Draft agents.

We did it. *Didn't we?*

A small group of injected Draft kids takes Leah's briefcase and opens it to reveal rows of syringes filled with bright blue liquid. My palms begin to sweat. What is Daniel doing?

Each of them takes a syringe and, with no hesitation, plunges it into the neck of an un-injected Draft kid.

I cringe and look away, at Daniel. I open my mouth to ask him what's going on, but before I can, he draws his gun and stalks closer to Johnson, Leah, and Holland. With a gesture, he commands the Draft kids to force Silas Johnson to his knees.

"I used to look up to you," Daniel says in a low voice, crouching down to his level. "You were almost my hero, Silas. Until you took *everything* from me."

I glance at Rev and Kaz, but they look as confused as I am.

"You were going to betray me," Johnson spits. "You think I was going to just *hand* the Draft to you and ignore the fact that you wanted to overthrow me? To wreck the stability I spent decades trying to build?"

Hand the Draft to you. My heart and mind race. This...the implication...

"You came here to watch your victory," Daniel growls, clicking the safety off his pistol. "To watch your work come one step closer to fruition. But now you get to watch as I have my vengeance."

My hands go numb, and not from the machine I'm hooked up to.

I knew Daniel kept secrets. Everybody knew Daniel kept secrets. But *this?*

What does this mean for the rest of us in this room? For me, Rev, and Kaz?

"I'm going to take back what's mine," Daniel says, his tone dangerous as he stands up and steps back from Johnson. He raises the pistol so it points directly at Silas Johnson's head. "And unfortunately, Silas, you're in the way."

Before Johnson can say another word, Daniel pulls the trigger.

Chapter Thirty-Nine

Reverie Adams

The gunshot echoes in the room, leaving my ears ringing and dead silence in its wake. Everyone is too stunned to do more than stand with a hanging jaw.

Johnson's corpse slumps directly into Leah, who screams and scrambles back into the Draft kids holding her. TJ, looking dazed in the chair, lets out a weak cry. All the Draft kids, including the ones holding me and Kaz, stand emotionless, their features like stone—a reflection of Daniel himself.

He just shot the Ordinem President.

"This was never about stopping the Draft, was it?" Kaz asks, sounding sick. Savi has no reaction—either that, or the control room has cut off our signal.

Daniel turns to face us, calm, as if nothing just happened.

"This was about stopping *Holland*. Stopping Johnson. Getting your *revenge!*" Kaz struggles against the Draft kids holding him. "We trusted you. We *trusted* you!"

Everything makes sense now. The feeling I've had from the start, that Daniel was hiding something. The reason he executed his plan the way he did—stealth, instead of bringing the entire UND to storm the Draft headquarters in a show of force. It also explains how Daniel got Kaz and me into the building so easily, and how he got us the Enforcer armor—Daniel must be in contact with, or at least allied with, at least some of the Enforcers. If he weren't, I'm sure the Enforcers would be rushing this room right now.

So then why are we still alive?

Nothing but static comes from my earpiece. It went silent as soon as we stepped into this room—probably all the technology in here messing with the signal. Not that Savi is in any position to help us.

Daniel moves toward us, stopping to reach around TJ's chair and flick a switch to unlock the clamps. TJ rips the needle out of his arm and stands, shakily bracing himself against the chair, but Daniel's already moved on.

"Oh, Kaz," Daniel says, stepping toward where the two of us stand on the other side of the room. "Don't blame yourself for trusting me. You've been in my care since you were a kid—you wouldn't have known better." Daniel moves closer, until the two of them are face-to-face.

Kaz's features twist in a mix of anger and pain. Betrayal. "Why?" he whispers. "Why are you doing this?"

"Because this program. Is. *Mine*." Daniel takes a step back, surveying me, Kaz, and TJ standing off to the side. "Rev, Kaz, you've been of immense help to me. None of this would've been possible without either of you. And so, I present you with a choice."

Out of the corner of my eye, I can see Kaz grinding his teeth, battling back tears.

"The two of you can stay here, try to fight, and be instantly crushed by the Draft agents in this room," Daniel says. "Or you can get out of this building, return to Savi and the base, and stay out of my way. I assure you, this is the only such offer you'll receive. If you leave and choose to come back, or you put yourself in my way, I can promise you I won't be so gracious."

He turns in a slow circle, surveying the room, and his eyes land on the corner where Leah, Holland, and Johnson—no, Johnson's *body*—are. Holland fights for a neutral expression, but this may be the first time I've seen her truly shaken. Leah, on the other hand, looks *terrified*. Her eyes dart between Daniel and

Johnson's corpse, and even from here I can see her trembling as she huddles against the Draft kids behind her.

Daniel cocks his head, studying her, before inclining his head toward me and Kaz. "Ms. Lane, you're welcome to join them. I know your true loyalties have never been with Anyssa Holland. I know she threatened your family to keep you here, and your work for me has been enough to earn you this mercy. You are free to go, if you so choose." He steps back to address everybody. "You three have five minutes to get out of this building before your immunity comes to an end. My contacts within the Enforcer group leads are working on clearing them out of this building and dispersing them throughout Sector 1 as we speak, and I can promise your safety for that time. Unfortunately, that also means you can't expect any help from the Enforcers. Choose your next steps wisely."

With that, the hands gripping my arms release, as do the hands holding Kaz and Leah. Kaz and I share a look, but we're both painfully aware of the fact that we don't have another option right now. At least if we get back to Savi and the base, we can try to make a plan. Get in contact with the rest of the Undrafted and find some way to fight Daniel.

TJ moves to follow us out, but Daniel grabs his arm. "You stay. We're not done yet."

"He's coming with us," I say, halting my step. "If you want us gone, TJ's coming with us."

"He stays." Daniel meets my eyes with a level look. "You have five minutes. TJ's life is not in danger—at least, not right now. Yours will be, if you don't leave."

TJ winces as Daniel's grip on his arm tightens. He's pale, shaky—far too similar to the first time I found him in the Draft headquarters.

"Four minutes," Daniel says. "I recommend you get going."

"Go," TJ rasps, focusing on me.

"I'm not leaving you—"

"Go!" He drills me with a pleading look. A look that has too many layers for me to decipher here. "Please, Rev."

Underneath those words, I can sense so much more. I want to *say* so much more. But our best shot at saving TJ is getting out of here alive.

I'm going to get you out of this, I mentally promise, holding his gaze. I hope my expression is enough to give him a little reassurance. I'm not sure what Daniel wants from him, but it can't be good.

Kaz, Leah, and I back out of the room, never taking our eyes off Daniel. As soon as we've cleared the threshold, one of the Draft kids shuts the door behind us, cutting off our view. We stand frozen for a few moments, staring at the door.

"What do we do?" Leah whispers.

Kaz and I both turn to look at her, but neither of us has an immediate answer. What *do* we do?

"The enemy of our enemy is our friend," Kaz eventually murmurs, voicing what we're all probably thinking.

"Listen, I'm sorry—"

"Don't." Kaz glares at her. "I'm not the one you should be apologizing to."

Leah winces, but shuts her mouth. I sense the history between these two, but now isn't the time to pry. Leah's loyalties aren't with Holland, if her acting as a spy is anything to go by—and that's enough for now. "Savi? Are you there?" I say instead, hoping my theory about the control room being the reason our signal was interrupted is true. If so, we should be able to talk without Daniel listening in.

A few beats of silence, then her voice comes over our earpieces. "I'm here. What's going on? You all went silent."

Kaz and I share a look, then he explains everything as quickly as he can. "There's no way we can take down Daniel," he finishes. "Not on our own when he has the Draft and the Enforcers under his control."

I fight the urge to look back through the window, to see if TJ's okay. Daniel's planning something. And, as always seems to happen, TJ's in the middle of it all. But Holland finished her serum—so what could he possibly want TJ for?

To keep his access to TJ's blood. Just in case. And to make sure we don't have the cure.

"We have to do *something*, Savi. We can't just let Daniel have free reign over Ordinem, we can't just leave those kids to be brainwashed, and we can't leave TJ in there to die!" I say, my grip on my bow tightening. *Three minutes.* "We all know Daniel's going to kill him as soon as he's sure he doesn't need him. He's not going to let the key to the cure run free."

Silence. I glance at Kaz and Leah, and I can tell we're all thinking the same thing.

"I think it's over, Rev," Savi whispers. "What are we supposed to do to stop an army?"

We can't. I open my mouth to say so when a blaring alarm drowns out my voice and flashing lights paint the hallway red.

"What's that for?" Kaz yells, spinning around to search for the source.

All three of us break into a run. *Two minutes.* But maybe there's something bigger than Daniel's countdown.

"Break-in above," Leah calls. "Someone—or something—broke through one of the walls."

"Savi, can you see it?" I ask, hoping she has a good enough view from the cameras on the surrounding buildings.

"I—yeah, I see it!"

"What's going on?!"

"There's a—" Savi hesitates. "This is going to sound really weird—"

"Savi!"

"There's a helicopter!"

I nearly trip over my own feet. "A helicopter? What do you mean, there's a *helicopter*?"

"I—someone crashed a helicopter into the lobby!"

"Can you see who?" Kaz asks.

"I can't...wait. Is that..." Savi trails off.

"What is it?"

"It's...it's *Hunter*. I can see through the window."

Kaz's face morphs into shock before he lets out a cackling laugh. "*Hunter* crashed a helicopter into the Enforcer headquarters?!"

I glance at Leah, curious to see her reaction. Surprised, obviously, but her gaze drops to the ground—nervous, or guilty. Ashamed?

"I'm not sure if he was the one flying, but...yeah, that's what it looks like. He brought Reiko and Adrian, and—a tall guy with glasses and curly hair?"

"Alec?" I ask in disbelief. "He brought *Alec*?"

"And we always thought *I* was the reckless one." The grin stays on Kaz's face as we turn another corner. "Maybe we're not out of this quite yet. Let's go let them in, shall we?"

Chapter Forty

Hunter Lane

I've seen plenty of fires from a distance, but I never imagined how intense the heat would be.

Somewhere in the distance, alarms blare, and the smoke in my lungs sets me coughing uncontrollably as I try to get my bearings. I groan as I raise my head. The haze practically blinds me, and I can't see Adrian in the cockpit next to me. Is he okay? Is *Reiko* okay?

The helicopter stands upright, but slightly tilted—one of the skids has broken. I wrap my shirt around my hand to insulate it against the heat, then try the door next to me. Jammed. I ram my shoulder against it, but the door doesn't budge. I nearly go to kick the door open, but the edge of my crutch—still intact in the cockpit—catches my eye. I won't be kicking down any doors today.

"Hunter!" a voice calls. From where? The ringing in my ears nearly drowns out the voice, making it impossible to tell where it comes from.

"Over here!" another voice yells. Hands appear through the smoke, reaching in through the broken windshield.

I grunt as I grab my crutch and heft it out of the helicopter, then take the hands and let them pull me to safety. As I clear the smoke, Adrian's curly blond hair comes into focus. He helps me get my footing and right my crutch. "You alright?"

A coughing fit is my only response. Reiko and Alec stand next to Adrian, looking unharmed aside from minor cuts and slashes.

A hand claps me on the shoulder from behind—not Adrian. I whirl around to find Kaz standing behind me, grinning. "Your timing couldn't have been better."

"How did you know we were coming?" I rasp.

"Savi saw you crash. We...well, we have some problems. A lot of problems."

I finally look past Kaz to see Rev, of course, and—

I freeze.

Leah.

She watches me with nervous, shifting eyes, and as I meet her gaze, she stuffs her hands in the pockets of her white coat.

Kaz follows my gaze. "I have a lot to explain, I know. But we don't have time right now." He rushes through the bare basics of what happened, just enough for me to understand what's going on, although Daniel's betrayal doesn't come as a shock to me.

"So what is *she* doing here?" I ask, glaring at Leah. The spark of hope I've held onto for the past weeks battles against the bitterness seeing her face again raises in me.

"We need her, Hunter. She's the only one who has a chance at finding the cure, and until you got here, we were all headed the same direction—out."

"She's not your only chance at a cure anymore." I slip one of the vials of TJ's blood from my inside pocket, just enough to let Kaz see it.

Kaz's eyes go wide. "Is that—Nora figured it out?!"

"It's TJ's blood. Put it into the serum and it reverses the effects, turning it into the cure."

Kaz looks about to burst with excitement as he stares at the vial. "With this...we might actually have a chance!"

"We need to get this to the Draft kids," Rev says. "Before Daniel can use them for whatever his revenge vendetta is."

"I can help." Leah's quiet voice draws all eyes.

I shake my head. "Absolutely not. *You* are not—"

"Hunter. Please." Leah looks up at me, practically begging. "Let me do *something*."

It's always *okay to hope. Especially for your own sister.* Kaz's words from weeks ago. Except now, looking at my desperate sister, they don't make me as angry as they used to.

"I have a syringe of the serum with me," she continues, taking my silence as an invitation. "We can turn that into the cure, make sure it works. Daniel's planning something, which means he won't just leave the Draft kids sitting in that control room. As soon as the room is cleared, we can get in there and turn the main store of the serum into the cure."

Rev nods and steps forward. "We need another group to go find Daniel. Even with the cure, we'll never get close enough to the Draft kids to use it if Daniel has that transmitter."

"So, we need two groups," I say, taking a deep breath. Leah *isn't* with Holland. And if Reiko, and then Adrian, taught me anything, it's that people aren't defined by their mistakes.

I can let go of my white-knuckled grip on bitterness toward Leah. *Temporarily.* For the sake of this mission.

And if we survive this...a stubborn part of me believes maybe, just *maybe*, we can work it out.

"One group to go with Leah and turn the serum into the cure, and one group to get that transmitter," Kaz agrees. "Who's with who?"

"I'll go with Leah," I say. "Reiko, Kaz, with me. Adrian, Alec, and Rev, you three have the harder job—getting that transmitter isn't going to be easy."

"We know," Rev says with a nod. "But it's our only shot. I'm willing to take that chance." Something else flashes across her expression—worry. There's something deeper behind her motivation. She likely sees this as her shot to save TJ.

I look over our ragged group as Leah takes her syringe of the serum from her pocket, adding a drop of TJ's blood and turning it a light purple-blue—the cure. She hands it to Rev.

Seven mismatched people against Daniel Bennett and the entirety of the Draft. This mission will by no means be easy. But Rev is right: this is our only chance.

"If all goes well," I say, "I'll see you when this is over. And if not..." I nod grimly to each member in turn. "At least we'll be dying together."

Chapter Forty-One

TJ Collins

As Rev, Kaz, and Leah leave the control room, I try to pull my arm out of Daniel's grip, but he doesn't budge. *At least Rev is safe*, I tell myself, but the words don't give me the reassurance I'm searching for.

"What do you want with me, Daniel?" I growl, fighting uselessly against his hold. The blood loss weakens my motions and makes my head spin, but I try regardless.

"Take it easy." Daniel releases me and I stumble back, straight into one of the Draft kids, who snatches my wrists and pins them behind me in one smooth motion. "You're not in danger," Daniel says. "I can't go getting rid of my *key* quite yet, now can I?"

"Wait," I croak as the Draft kid pulls me toward the door. "Wait!"

"Just hang tight. It'll all be over soon." Daniel smiles, an expression that nauseates me. "For now, I need you alive, and I also need you out of the way. But I have one more...*opportunity* for you."

I don't have time to process what that means before the Draft kid drags me from the room.

After a few minutes of walking and a flight of stairs, the hallways start to look familiar. Sweat makes my palms slippery and my heart races at the sight of the whitewashed walls, the tiled floors...*No. No, no, no. Not again. Not again, not here again, not again—*

Waking up in a cell with Max by my side is one thing. Being dragged down the halls I recognize, alone and weak, is entirely another. I struggle as we enter the prison wing. I can't go back here. I can't be here again. I—

The Draft kid opens one of the cells, shoves me inside, and slams the door closed.

Alone. I'm alone.

My breaths come quick and heavy as I bang both fists on the door, begging, *screaming*, for someone to let me out. Daniel has to know. He has to know how this place affects me. He has to know how being back in here is *torture*, right after I thought I'd been saved.

I'm not sure how long I stand there, yelling, but my voice grows hoarse and my fists sore from hitting the cold metal.

This is how I'm going to die. Alone, trapped in the Draft sublevels, betrayed. Daniel hasn't shot me yet, but what's he going to do when his plans are complete? Let me go? No. Not knowing that I'm the cure. He may keep me alive until he's certain I'm no longer necessary for the serum, but he's too smart to let me go.

I'm going to die tonight.

My legs give out and I sink to the floor, huddled against the wall right next to the door. I pull my knees to my chest and let my head hang, violent trembling overtaking my body.

After everything we've been through, everything we've sacrificed, everything that's happened, we failed. In fact, we might've made things *worse*. Ethan's death, for nothing. Riya's death, for *nothing*.

All that loss. All that pain. All that fighting to hold onto hope.

For *nothing*.

The loud clang of a lock disengaging rips me from my thoughts and I push myself to my feet as the cell door opens. A disheveled Anyssa Holland stumbles through the doorway, the same Draft kid who brought me here following behind her. One side of her face looks swollen—from a punch?

Before Holland has the chance to say anything, the Draft kid hefts a pulse rifle and pulls the trigger. I flatten my back against the wall as the blast sends Anyssa crashing into the cell wall behind her. Another pulse blast leaves her in a heap on the ground, and a third completely limp.

Without a word, the Draft kid leaves the room and locks the cell door again behind him.

I stare, wide-eyed, at Holland. Is she...dead? My throat tightens, making it difficult to breathe.

The hatch at the bottom of the cell door, used to slide food under for prisoners, opens. But instead of food, a black pistol comes skidding across the floor toward me. I scramble back, tripping in my haste and landing hard on the floor. My eyes dart between the pistol and Holland, but when they fall on the security camera in the corner, I realize what this is.

Daniel told me he had an *opportunity* for me. And he wants Holland dead.

He's setting me up to do it.

I crawl forward on weak knees, reaching for the gun. *Even if it destroys the final shred of me that's left, I'm going to kill Anyssa Holland.* My words to Rev, back on the rooftop.

I wrap my fingers around the grip and get to my feet, pistol in hand. Red haze obscures the edges of my vision as my eyes fall on the woman in front of me.

She groans and raises her head, struggling to push herself up.

"You killed my sister," I whisper.

Holland finally manages to sit up, slumped against the wall.

The familiar darkness bubbles up in my chest, the same roiling rage that overtook me when I nearly killed Adrian. Only this time, there's nobody around to stop the darkness from winning.

"It's almost poetic," Holland rasps, her eyes closed, "that after everything, you're the one who's going to end it all."

I click the safety off the gun. My hands tremble as I level it directly at Holland's head.

"Do it," she mumbles. "I know you're desperate to. I have nothing left, so put me out of my misery, TJ Collins."

I grit my teeth, tighten my finger around the trigger. *Do it. End it.* My hands shake so violently, I'm not sure where I'm aiming anymore.

"You brainwashed children." *Pull the trigger. Do it.* "You killed my friend, you broke me, and you killed my little sister. You killed my little sister!" I yell, my voice hoarse. *Why can't I pull the trigger?* She's the reason behind all of this. Everything that's happened has been the fault of the half-conscious woman in front of me. So *why* can't I shoot?

"Your mother tried to warn me," Holland says, letting out a slow breath. "She and Oliver both had doubts."

"Don't," I choke out, tears blurring my vision. *Shoot. Pull the trigger.* "Don't you *talk* about them."

"I suppose I always knew, deep down, that Maya was right about everything," she murmurs. "But I made my choice."

"You're sick," I whisper, biting back a sob.

"Maybe so." A *tear* slips down her cheek. "I never wanted to become this. I wanted to protect Ordinem. But here we are. I became what this world made me."

My chest grows tight, my heart hammering against my ribs. *Pull. The. Trigger.*

She looks up at me, eyes glistening with tears. I can't tell where they're from. Regret, maybe—but this isn't an apology. She's not sorry.

She just wants it to be over. The same way I do.

Holland leans her head back against the wall, letting her eyes slide shut. "Do it," she says quietly. "End this, TJ."

My knuckles turn white as my grip on the pistol tightens. Shoot. Shoot. *Shoot.*

I can't.

I let out a scream and swing my pistol toward the camera in the corner, then squeeze the trigger over and over, making my ears ring. Bullets fly into the walls and ceiling until one of them finally hits and shatters the camera. Even then, I keep firing into the ceiling until I run out of ammunition. I throw the gun away from me and fall to my knees, my head in my hands, my fingers digging into my scalp.

This one thing. I couldn't even do this *one* thing.

Instead of pouring out on Holland, the darkness inside me remains. It boils, raging inside my head and my chest, reminding me of my weakness over and over again. Taunting me.

It's over. Vengeance on Anyssa Holland was the one thing I had left to live for, and without that…without that, there's nothing. Emptiness. Space to be filled by that roiling darkness, that hatred, that rage.

Part of me wishes I'd left just one more bullet in that gun.

Behind me, the cell door bursts open. Hands grab the back of my shirt and haul me to my feet, roughly guiding me toward the door, but I'm only half-aware.

It's over.

Daniel waits in the hallway, eerily calm, as both Holland and I are dragged from the room. "Well, then." He turns to face me. "It appears Anyssa Holland will get the pleasure of living long enough to watch her world burn."

This, then, is how I'm going to die. Not only alone. Not only in the Draft sublevels. But also as a coward.

Chapter Forty-Two

TJ Collins

Daniel's eerie calmness makes me tremble as we walk, him in front of me and Holland beside me. Behind us, two Draft kids train pulse rifles on our heads.

Daniel planned for me to kill Holland, and Holland is still breathing. So why is Daniel so...unbothered?

Holland studies me out of the corner of her eye as we walk and I fight to avoid meeting her gaze. I wonder what she's thinking, after watching me snap. After watching me spare her life.

We climb back up to the first sublevel, the same floor as the room where Daniel turned on us. He takes us past this room, though, and into a room marked *Security*. As I cross the threshold, pulse rifle at the back of my head, I'm not thinking about how I can make a move to escape, or how I can knock the transmitter from Daniel's head. I can't.

I'm just waiting for it to be over.

Inside the security room, massive screens cover the wall in front of me, each displaying the feed from different cameras in and around the Enforcer headquarters and the Draft sublevels. My eyes dart back and forth, taking in the details one by horrifying one.

Inside the Enforcer headquarters, only a few straggling groups of Enforcers stay behind—I remember what Daniel said about using his contacts in their leadership to *disperse* them, for the time being. Likely so they won't be prepared to respond to Johnson's assassination and the havoc Daniel is wreaking on Sector 1 until it's too late.

Outside, smoke rises from several high-profile buildings. I don't know all of them, but I recognize a few from my time living in the area—apartments of government officials. Draft kids roam Sector 1, leaving chaos and panic in their wake.

Holland watches this screen, her mouth hanging slightly open, and Daniel offers her a slight grin. "It's basic strategy, Anyssa. Killing two birds with one stone. Eliminating your supporters and my opponents, along with letting the general population know what happens to my enemies."

Again, Holland's eyes well with tears—one of the greatest displays of emotion I've ever seen from her. Holland has friends, possibly even family. And she's watching Daniel target them one by one. That must be why Daniel didn't take her out as soon as he opened the cell door—after I failed to shoot her, he wanted her to see this. He wanted *me* to see this. I know exactly what's running through Holland's head as she watches her life burn on the screen, because it's the same thing that went through my own head as I mourned my little sister.

You should've pulled the trigger.

I pull my eyes to a different screen, unable to watch Holland's reaction. That turns out to be a mistake, because the scene unfolding on this screen is almost worse.

"Is that...?" I move closer, in disbelief. Rev, *Alec*, and...Adrian?

"Ah, yes." Daniel shakes his head as he steps up to my side, putting himself in between me and Holland. "Your friends should've known better, but they put up an admirable effort. I thought you'd like to see them one last time before I put an end to you."

On the screen, Rev, Alec, and Adrain stand surrounded by a group of six Draft kids, including Eliza. Max, his signature swords drawn, stands at their head. Besides him, all of them brandish pistols, rather than pulse rifles. Lethal.

My eyes go wide and I shake my head. "No," I say, my voice shaking. "Daniel, let them go. *Please.*" *Not again. Please, not again. Not another loss. Not Rev.*

Max says something and Rev drops her bow, then slowly removes her quiver. Adrian sets his pistol on the ground and Alec watches Max with pure horror in his eyes. Max gestures with his sword and slowly, the three of them get to their knees, their hands behind their heads.

"What do you want from me, Daniel?" I ask, my voice cracking. "What do you *want*?"

"I already have everything I need. I have you." His face splits into a slow smile. "And you've been such an incredible help. So I'm willing to offer you a final opportunity." He takes the pistol at his waist from his holster and extends it to me, grip first. "We both want Anyssa Holland dead," he says, lowering his voice. "And I still think it would be fulfilling to see the look on her face if you were the one to do it."

My eyes dart back to the screen. The circle of Draft kids around Rev, Alec, and Adrian stands still, and Rev glances around, confused. Daniel isn't attacking them yet. Maybe, if I keep his attention, I can buy them time.

I take the gun.

Maybe I can do it this time. Finish it. *For Riya.*

It should be easy. As I aim the trembling gun at Anyssa Holland, the woman who tore my whole life apart, it should be easy. And yet...

I chew my lower lip, trying to will myself to pull the trigger on the woman across the room from me. Trying to muster the strength.

And then, as Holland's hopeless eyes meet my own, it hits me.

It's not weakness holding me back. It's *humanity.*

And somewhere, deep down, everything Rev has told me these past few months finally sinks in.

You're not broken, TJ.

The strength I've been so desperate for floods in, stilling my shaking hands. But I don't pull the trigger on Holland. I swing the gun to the left, aim directly at Daniel's head, and squeeze.

Nothing but a soft *click* from the pistol. *Empty.*

He was never going to give me a loaded gun. He just wanted Holland to see me pull the trigger. Part of his plan for *revenge.*

The realization barely has time to sink in before a pulse blast from the nearest Draft kid rams into me, sending me crashing against one of the screens. The right side of my body screams with pain as I fall to the ground, shattered pieces of screen raining down on my head. *That blast was close.* Too close. I can't force my muscles to move as Daniel's boots approach my head.

Daniel takes the pistol and it slips out of my fingers easily—I can hardly raise my head, let alone hold onto a gun.

"I'm disappointed," Daniel says, shaking his head. "I really did want to see the look on Anyssa's face when you pulled the trigger. But I suppose you lack the strength to avenge your family."

I want to tell him that he's wrong. That mercy is a sign of strength. That after everything I've been through, I'm *not* broken, and that I've decided to keep fighting the darkness, instead of letting it rule me. But all I can manage is a groan as I struggle to push myself up.

Daniel steps back and turns his focus to the screen with Rev, Alec, and Adrian. *No. No, no—*

Max approaches Rev, swords drawn, and Rev looks up at him with fire in her eyes.

Not Rev. Please, not Rev. My entire body trembles. I can't watch her die.

And then she lunges.

She dodges his outstretched sword as she draws something from her pocket—a syringe. The serum? No, that wouldn't make sense—and it holds a more purple hue than the blue serum. She jabs it into his neck and pushes the plunger.

Max's eyes widen and his swords clatter to the ground. Rev steps back and Max spins in a circle, taking everything in as if for the first time. Daniel's expression morphs into shock.

"No!" Daniel screams, plunging his fist into the screen and leaving a web of cracks.

It's the cure, I realize. *They have the cure!*

I have no idea how, or when, they put it together, but the look in Max's eyes is undeniable. Rev has the cure.

Daniel's shock is so powerful that on the cracked screen, the Draft kids under his control all falter, their weapons lowering momentarily. Daniel lets out a low, guttural sound as he turns from the monitor to me.

He was already going to kill me when he was done, and now he's angry—however indirectly, it's because of me that the cure exists. It looks like he's no longer planning on waiting.

His eyes flash with a wild anger as he takes the pulse rifle from the Draft kid that first shot me. I manage to get to my hands and knees, sharp fragments digging into my palms.

The first blast comes from across the room, where Daniel currently stands, and knocks me sideways into the broken monitor. I scream as the shards pierce my shirt, slicing into my back when I slide to the ground. Daniel looms over me, pulse rifle leveled directly at my head, and twists the dial on the side to full power. I spare one last glance at the screen to my right, with Rev and Alec and Adrian. Even with Max on their side, they're outnumbered and out-gunned.

The moment I look away, I hear a yell from my left. *Holland*. I manage to shift so I can see her, although the slight motion sets my head spinning with pain.

She rushes across the room, toward Daniel. Her Draft guard fumbles to switch to his pistol—if he shot her with the pulse rifle, he'd hit Daniel—but Holland reaches Daniel before he can shoot. Daniel, his mad fury focused on me, doesn't seem to notice her. She leaps, hands outstretched, and knocks the transmitter from his head.

Daniel grunts as Holland's full force hits him, stumbling away from me and swinging his pulse rifle to aim at her. The transmitter clatters to the ground just in front of me.

"Destroy it!" Holland screams, before a loud blast of energy drowns her out. The pulse blast, still set to full power, sends her flying across the room faster than I can track. Her head cracks against the wall loud enough to make me cringe and she falls, limp, to the floor.

Daniel tries his pulse rifle on me, but growls as pulling the trigger does nothing. The full-power blast used up the rest of its energy. He tosses the weapon aside, glancing at the two Draft kids in the room—frozen, because nobody is wearing the transmitter—before roaring and lunging for me.

I muster up the last bit of my strength and snatch the transmitter from the floor just as Daniel reaches me. I grit my teeth and clench my eyes, the transmitter in my hands.

At least I get to die strong.

As Daniel reaches me, murder in his gaze, I lock eyes with him and snap the transmitter in half.

Chapter Forty-Three

Reverie Adams

*I*t *worked*. Leah's syringe of the cure *worked*.

Max's swords slip from his fingers and clatter to the tiled floor. He spins in a circle, his eyes wild. "What—how—what's going on?!"

His gaze finally falls on Eliza next to him, brandishing a pistol, and he pales as he stumbles back. I catch him and he joins our little group, trapped by a circle of Draft kids.

We knew going for the transmitter was a last-ditch effort, so it didn't come as a total surprise when we were intercepted by a group of Draft kids. At least Leah, Hunter, Kaz, and Reiko are still free, to the best of my knowledge—Max, when he was under control of the serum, removed and crushed my earpiece, so I have no way of confirming that.

The Draft kids haven't shot us yet, and as long as we're not dead, we have a chance. We just have to hold on long enough for Leah to return with more of the cure.

As Max regains his mind, breathing heavily next to me, it dawns on me that this might be time we don't have.

"You've really done it now, Rev," Adrian mutters behind me. He and Alec are still on their knees, facing outward, hands behind their heads.

I study Eliza, directly in front of me and Max. Emotionless eyes. Under Daniel's stony, emotionless control. So different even from the girl I saw last time I broke into the Draft.

Please, let Leah get here in time to save her.

I can see the tiniest twitch of her finger as she prepares to pull the trigger and I tense. This is it.

And then, all the Draft kids freeze, blank expressions washing over their faces. Max whips his head between me, Eliza, Adrian, and Alec. "Can someone please tell me what's going on?" he whispers, as it becomes clear that the kids surrounding us are neutralized.

Behind me, Adrian and Alec slowly stand up.

"I'd like to ask the same question," Alec says, trying and failing to keep a tremor from his voice. "They're...frozen?"

"The transmitter must be off," I say, taking the gun from Eliza and unloading it before tossing it as far down the hall as I can.

"Daniel wouldn't have just *taken the transmitter off*," Adrian says as he follows my lead, emptying two guns, dropping them, and kicking them away.

TJ. The empty gun I'm holding slips from my fingers. "TJ was with Daniel," I breathe. "He's the only person close to Daniel who would've done anything to fight him."

"You're saying *TJ Collins* just saved all of our lives?" Adrian raises an eyebrow, looking almost impressed.

"Daniel is going to make him pay for that," I whisper, starting down the hall. I have to get to him, before—

Footsteps pound through the hallway, preceding the figures that round the corner ahead and come barreling toward us. I immediately grab my bow from the floor and reach for an arrow, but drop my arm as soon as the figures come into view. Leah, Hunter, and Kaz.

They don't slow as they approach—they don't know the Draft kids are neutralized. "Wait!" I call, stepping out from the circle of motionless bodies. "Something happened with the transmitter. We're safe."

That gets the three of them to slow, coming to a stop right in front of me. Leah, red-faced and frizzy-haired, hands me a briefcase. *The cure.* "We have three of these," she gets out between breaths. "Over a hundred doses total. Enough for all of them."

"Good." Alec steps forward, taking some of the syringes. He says something about sending the group around the sublevels and into the city to get the cure to the rest of the Draft kids—something about what they've seen being enough to weaken their loyalty, talking them onto our side—but I can't fully process any of it.

TJ. I have to get to TJ.

"Go." Alec's voice cuts through my spiraling thoughts as he meets my eyes. "Go find Daniel, Rev. Make sure this is over."

In his expression, I can see the hidden message. *Go find TJ.* I give him a nod of gratitude before leaving Eliza with Alec and taking off at a full sprint down the hall. I don't know where TJ is right now, but I have to get to him. Before he gets himself killed.

Chapter Forty-Four

TJ Collins

Daniel rips the broken transmitter from my hands and plants his foot into my chest, sending me skidding across the floor and colliding with the shattered screen. I yelp as, once again, the broken shards pierce through my skin. My energy drained, I slump over. Breaking that transmitter took the last bit of strength I had left. Warm blood soaks through the tattered back of my shirt, seeping out of the gouges in my back.

Daniel stands in the middle of the room, staring at the broken transmitter in his hands, breathing hard. *He's gone insane*, I think, the words sluggish in my head. He's been stewing in his plot for so long that it's become a part of him—and now, having it ripped away from him is driving him mad. He looks at the two frozen Draft kids in the room, at Holland in the corner—unconscious or dead, I can't tell at first, until I see the wound on her head took from when it hit the wall. I grimace and look away.

When my eyes return to Daniel, his murderous gaze is fixed on me.

I try to move, but between the multiple pulse blasts and the searing pain from the slashes all along my back and palms, I can't manage more than sitting up a little straighter to face my fate. I look Daniel Bennett straight in the eye.

And I grin, knowing I've won.

He roars and throws himself at me, wrapping both hands around my neck and hauling me up off the floor, then slamming me back against the broken screen. I try to scream, but his hands block off my airways completely. Again and again, the sharp edges pierce my back as Daniel rams my body against the screen. I can feel some of the shards embed themselves in my skin and break off, only pushed deeper by the next blows. The pain. The *pain*.

The edges of my vision blur as I gasp for air, but find none. As unconsciousness draws close, reaching out to take me, the pain begins to fade—but just before I can pass out, Daniel tosses me to the floor. My back screams with pain as I hit the ground, embedded pieces of the screen being pushed in deeper, but precious air floods my chest as I cough.

Daniel's foot comes down hard on my chest, knocking the wind out of my lungs again, and a loud *crack* accompanies a wave of sharp pain. *Rib*. He removes his foot, allowing me to take a breath, before landing blow after blow, kick after kick. I curl up on my side, but that only opens my wounded back up to him. I can't move. I can hardly think through the pain. My vision goes hazy, and I can no longer make out the room around me, Daniel's figure above.

The blows stop. I let out a soft whimper, unable to move, hardly able to see. *Pain*. Something feels broken. All I can see is red—no, blood. One of Daniel's kicks left a gash above my eye. Blood coats my lips and the inside of my mouth, the coppery tang stinging all of my senses.

"I was going to do this quickly," Daniel says in a low voice, right next to my ear. "I was going to use a pulse rifle and be done with it. Show you some mercy in death. But now, I think it's better for me to do the job by hand."

He shoves my shoulder with his foot, rolling me onto my back, before settling his foot atop my throat. Slowly, he steps down, closing off my airway.

I shut my eyes.

I'm not broken.

Riya, I'm coming.

The pressure on my throat releases. I try for air, but I don't have the energy to manage anything more than a weak half-cough. A moment later, a heavy weight topples down across my body, sending another wave of pain washing over me. I fight to open my swollen eyes against the blood drying over them, but even that proves difficult.

"Oh, no," a girl's voice whispers. "No, no, no. Come on, TJ."

I recognize that voice, I think, my head feeling like it's been stuffed with heavy fabric. The weight on top of me slides to the left—being dragged. *Pain*. The voice. *It's…Reiko?*

With a final heave, she drags the weight off of me, then two cold fingers touch the side of my neck. I can hear Reiko counting underneath her breath before she sighs in relief.

"TJ?" Her hand gently grips my shoulder. "TJ? Can you hear me?"

I manage to get my eyes to flutter open, although I can't see well between the swelling and the blood. "Reiko?" I rasp, my voice barely audible.

"You're alive." She looks down at me through eyes welling with tears. "You're alive. I can't believe—you—the transmitter—"

I cough—a weak, rattling sound that sends a stabbing pain through my chest. Broken rib. "Barely," I get out.

"Are you—is there anything that could be fatal?"

"Don't know." I hold back another cough. "Don't—think so."

"Can you move?"

I try, but the second I tense up, everything flares with pain. "Not yet," I say through gritted teeth.

"Okay. Help should come soon." Reiko tears a swatch of fabric from the bottom of my shirt, dabbing at one of the gashes on my face. "You—you saved *everyone*, TJ."

I let my eyes close and focus on breathing. *In, out. In, out.* I try to ignore the burning in my back, the stabbing pain in my chest. I forgot how painful cracked and broken ribs can be.

Reiko sits in silence for a few moments, then whispers, "I'm sorry."

I can't form enough words to respond to that, so I stay silent.

"I'm sorry for everything," she continues. "For the part I played in everything that happened to you. For lying to you, for—"

"Reiko," I croak.

She pauses.

"I'm sorry," I say. "For—not believing you could change." I can't manage much more than that, so I can only hope she understands everything that's loaded into those words.

I crack my eyes to see Reiko smiling, those tears in her eyes finally spilling over. "Thank you."

The corners of my lips turn up—as close to a smile as I can manage.

Reiko's smile fades soon, though. "Holland—how did it happen?" she asks softly.

"She turned," I rasp, the image of Holland's head burned into my memory. "She's the one—who got me—the transmitter."

"She turned," Reiko echoes, staring at the corpse to her right. I imagine it'll take her a long time to process all of the emotions that the death of Anyssa Holland brings. Even I don't know if she truly had a change of heart at the end, or if she just wanted to stop Daniel.

I let out another weak cough as motion by the door catches my eye. I try to raise my head to see, but the pain of even that motion makes my vision swim. I lay my head back on the floor with a groan.

"TJ?"

Rev. Rev's voice.

In a moment, she's kneeling next to me. "Reiko! What happened? Is he—is he—?" Her voice cracks.

"He's alive. I got here just in time." My eyes are cracked just enough to make out Reiko's gesture over my body toward the other side of the room. *Daniel.* That was the weight that fell on me. "Daniel was about to kill him, but I knocked him out."

"You didn't shoot him?"

"I..." Reiko swallows. "I can't kill. Not anymore. Not even him."

To my surprise, Rev just nods.

I force my mouth to move. "Rev?"

"I'm here." She brushes back my hair, plastered to my forehead with blood. "I'm here. You're gonna be fine. Hang in there."

"There's nothing immediately life-threatening," Reiko says. "At least, not that we're aware of, although taking a beating like he did obviously isn't good. We need to get him to a medic—Daniel had to have a base set up for this mission, right?"

"It's an apartment not too far from here." She looks back to me, concern tainting her face. "Is it safe to carry him?"

"I...wait. I have a better idea." Reiko stands up. "I'll bring a stretcher from the infirmary. Easier for us to carry and less painful for him."

Rev nods. "Go."

I close my eyes, settling into the soft touch of her fingers brushing my forehead. *Safe.* Before Reiko returns, I've slipped into unconsciousness.

When I open my eyes, the first thing I become aware of is the searing brightness of the lights in the ceiling above me. I groan, blinking hard to try to clear my vision. Something wet touches my face—a cloth?—but jerks back as soon as my eyes open.

"He's awake!" a voice calls from just above me. Savi. She throws her arms around me, although she does her best to avoid aggravating my injuries. "You're alive!"

"Good to see you, too," I grunt.

She steps back, a wide grin on her face, slightly-bloody cloth in hand. "TJ. You stopped the Draft. *And* you're alive!"

I can't help but match her smile as I shift, trying to find a comfortable position. I'm lying on the bottom of a bunk bed in a small bunk room draped in shades of gray. A stack of pillows supports my upper back and props me up enough to have a good view of the room and the door leading to the rest of the apartment. The Undrafted's apartment base.

On the bottom bunk across from mine, a bucket and a pile of cloths—both clean and bloodstained—sit next to a roll of bandages. Other than a couple of chairs, me, and Savi, this room is empty.

"Where is everybody?" I croak. *Where is Rev?*

"Cleaning up," Savi answers as Rev enters through the room's only door. "I'm staying here to monitor things, and Rev stayed for you—she's the one who bandaged you up, and I offered to do what I could for you, to give her a break. Reiko went back to the Enforcer headquarters with Adrian to organize things there—to find the rest of the Draft kids and rally the Enforcers to stop the chaos they caused in Sector 1. The Enforcers' command structure is in shambles, but the rest of the Enforcers have been able to overpower Daniel's contacts."

"Everyone else? Alec? Max?" I ask.

"They're all combing Sector 1 for the last of the Draft kids. And then they'll join the Enforcers—quite literally putting out the fires."

Rev gives her a flat look.

Savi, however, returns it with a knowing grin. "Fine. I'll go back to watching the news and leave you two alone. Channel 8 hasn't found out about Johnson's death yet, but there's plenty of other chaos in the streets. Kaz says everybody else should be back soon, when they've reined it in a little. And we're hoping to have a plan for when the news about Johnson gets out."

With that, she retreats through the door into the main room.

I wince as I shift again, the pillows rubbing against my sliced back. Bandages wind around nearly my entire torso, although I can catch glimpses of bruised skin between them where ribs are broken or cracked. I spot my blood-soaked, tattered rag of a shirt crumpled on the table next to the bandages and cloths. The roll of bandages is nearly empty.

"You used a lot of bandages," I say, managing a small smile.

She smiles back, shaking her head. "That's the first thing you have to say after nearly being beaten to death by a psychopath?"

I shrug, then immediately regret the motion.

Concern flashes in Rev's eyes as she stands, takes a clean cloth from the pile on the other bunk, and dampens it with a nearby water bottle.

"I'm alright, Rev," I tell her. "Really. I'll be fine."

"I'd believe you more if your face wasn't still covered in blood." She raises the damp cloth. "Can I?"

I nod and gently, Rev sets to work getting the crusted blood off my face. She tries to avoid the bruises and cuts, but there are far too many for her to avoid completely. Each one smarts as the cold cloth passes over.

"Rev?" I say softly.

"What?"

"You were right."

She pauses, her cloth right next to my face. "About what?"

"When you told me I wasn't broken."

She smiles at that and resumes her work.

"That's what saved me down there, you know," I continue. "I was about to give up. And then I heard your voice in my head."

Rev turns her face away from me, but not before I catch that little twist of emotion in her expression.

"What is it?" I ask. "Something I said? I didn't mean—"

"No, not that. I just..." She swallows hard. "It's nothing. You need to rest."

I grab her hand, catching it before she can return to tending my face, and wait for her to lock eyes with me. "Rev. What's wrong?"

Her breath hitches, but I hold her gaze until she starts.

"You know I visited your old apartment." Now that they've begun, her words come out in a rush, like she's been holding them back for a long time. "I thought eventually I'd come to understand it—how you could just...*forgive* me, for something like that—but I don't. Forgiveness, maybe, I can believe, but...whatever's happening between the two of us? That night up on the rooftop, when you asked me to stay because it would help with the nightmares? Telling me that my voice in your head is what kept you going down in the sublevels?" Rev shakes her head. "I don't understand it. I have a hard enough time believing you can look at me with anything other than hatred, but with...whatever this is?" She meets my eyes, both fear and hope swirling behind hers.

"Is there any hope for the two of us, TJ?" she asks quietly. By the way she looks to the side, avoiding my gaze, I can tell she's terrified of my response. It took all of her to voice that question.

"I think I remember someone telling me there's always hope," I answer, my voice soft.

Rev looks back at me, her eyes welling with tears.

"That's a yes, by the way," I say, a smile tugging at the corners of my lips. "Just to confirm."

She punches me lightly in the shoulder, one of the only places it wouldn't cause me immense pain, and my smile spreads. I muster the strength to sit up straighter and pull her into a hug. I wince at the pain, but it's worth it.

Soon after, familiar faces trickle into the apartment, and Rev props the door to my room open so we can see. Kaz is the first to come through the door, and he immediately looks for Savi, who runs straight for him. He lifts her off the floor and spins her in a circle, both of them laughing the whole time—not their typical snickers or, in Savi's case, reserved laughter, but laughter infused with the kind of joy that only comes from having survived—and *won*—everything that transpired today.

Max and Alec enter next, and Max heads straight for me. "TJ! You're okay!" He throws his arms around my neck, giddy with joy. I grunt at the pain, but I hug him back regardless. Alec grins as he watches the two of us, and I smile back at him, remembering what he told me about seeing Max and me as sons.

After that, everything around me becomes too much for my slow-moving brain to process and my eyelids grow unnaturally heavy. Rev squeezes one of my bandaged hands. "It's alright," she says, quiet enough that only I can hear. "You can rest now. I think the painkillers Savi and I gave you should help."

I squeeze her hand back and let my eyes slide closed. And, for the first time in months, I fall asleep at peace.

Chapter Forty-Five

Reverie Adams

As soon as TJ's eyes start to droop, Alec ushers everybody except for me out of the small room and follows them out, closing the door behind him. I linger for a couple minutes, watching the soft peace wash over TJ's face. I can only imagine what it must feel like for him to finally be able to rest after the past months.

When I'm sure he's asleep, I slide my hand out of his and slip out of the bunkroom, into the living room. Savi, Kaz, Hunter, Alec, and Max are all here, quietly discussing. The Draft may be over, but our work is far from done. Ordinem is hanging on to civility by a thread, thanks to Reiko, Adrian, and the Enforcers, but it's only a matter of time before the news catches wind of President Johnson's assassination.

Back at the Enforcer headquarters, Adrian and Reiko are getting transport prepared to bring us and all the Draft kids to the UND, until we can find a more permanent solution. As soon as we finish here, we'll go meet up with everyone else.

I'll finally get to see my sister.

But first, we have to decide what to do about Johnson's death.

"We have an opportunity here," Hunter says. "To put someone better in charge of Ordinem. Someone who cares about its people, who's willing to work with Nadzor and Olympia to help us rebuild."

"What about the rest of the current government officials?" I ask. "Won't they fight a shift in power like that?"

"That's why we can't put just anybody in charge. It has to be someone who can garner their support." Hunter presses his lips together, thinking.

"Someone on our side who can muster the support of Ordinem's elites." Kaz shakes his head. "Hunter, you know how crazy that sounds? Nobody on our side has connections with the Ordinem government."

"Are you sure?" Max's quiet voice joins in. All of us turn to look at him and he shrugs. "Maybe there's something obvious I'm missing, but...why not Alec?"

"Max, this isn't the time—" Alec protests, but I cut him off.

"Actually, that's...not a bad idea. You do have some connections in the current government, right? From before the Draft?"

"I can't run a government, Rev!" Alec adjusts his glasses. "There's no way."

"You're the best option we can think of!" Max says. He looks at the rest of us, excitement in his eyes. "Alec knows enough people, and he's good with words—he could get enough support, I'm sure of it. And you've all seen him take charge before, I'm sure? He can do it."

"Call me crazy," Kaz says, "but I think the kid might be right. Hunter?"

Hunter studies Alec, and I can almost see the wheels turning in his head. "If you can get the support of the public and of the current government...that would be more than pretty much anybody else could accomplish. You'd need help, and you'd need to implement some way to split your power—one man should never have that much control."

"Of course."

Hunter takes another moment to study him, probably gauging his sincerity, then gives his nod of approval. "This is probably our best option, at least for now."

Alec surveys the room. "You're all actually on board with this?"

"Who better?" Max grins.

"You'll have help," Hunter says. "Nobody's going to force you to take this on by yourself. But we do need to get moving soon, before Ordinem's remaining government pulls something together."

Alec lets out a long breath, seeming to accept his burden. "Okay. We're doing this, then. Where do we start?"

We spend a few hours talking through details of Alec's new role—he has some old friends from the earliest days of the Draft, before he left, who agree to do what they can to get the rest of the government on board. Daniel targeted Holland's most adamant supporters, although we stopped the Draft kids before they got to all of them. Many of the government officials believed Johnson was incompetent and were just waiting for their opportunity to initiate change—not to mention the fact that they didn't hold much power in the first place. Other than Silas Johnson, most of Ordinem's government was for show. With Alec, though, that'll change.

Alec's persuasiveness, along with his plans for change that we helped him come up with, seems to be working thus far. One of his first moves is going to be to start a home for all the Draft kids who don't have families to return to—he and Max, and possibly Hunter, will take them in and help them to move back into society.

By the time we've set things in motion, the sun is rising over the horizon and the transports are ready to go. TJ wakes briefly, long enough for us to bring him to the Enforcer headquarters and get him settled on one of the helicopters, but between his exhaustion and the painkillers, he slips in and out.

I push through the packed crowd in the Enforcer lobby, searching for Eliza's face. It's strange, mingling with the Enforcers and Draft kids without fear of being attacked. Most of the Enforcers seem to be like Ethan—people who believed they were working for a good cause. Once Adrian, someone they trust, exposed Johnson's corruption and defeat, it came down to a matter of appealing to their basic humanity. Something Adrian proved surprisingly good at.

My eyes scan the room, skipping from kid to kid. A brown-haired boy, short and lanky. A frizzy-haired redhead climbing into a helicopter. A tall blonde girl, being guided toward another helicopter by an armor-clad Enforcer.

There.

Near the glass wall, Eliza stands in her black Draft jumpsuit, looking uncertain—the first time I've ever seen her with anything other than confidence. She notices me staring and tenses as she meets my eyes.

I start at someone's touch, nudging me forward. "Go," Savi says softly, giving me a gentle nod.

I swallow hard, brace myself, and walk toward my sister.

The crowd parts for me as I walk. Eliza shifts on her feet, but she doesn't look at me with the same hostility I've seen in her eyes too many times. She just looks...lost.

And I find myself *terrified*.

We stand there for a few moments, taking each other in amidst the cacophony of activity.

"I think I remember," Eliza finally says, so quiet I can barely hear her over the noise. She looks up at me with those watery brown eyes. "I met TJ. I started thinking. And I...I think I remember. A little."

I smile slightly, tears springing to my own eyes.

She recognizes me.

"You're really my sister?" Eliza asks tentatively.

I nod. "Yeah. Yeah, I'm your sister."

"And you...the Archer...all this..." Her eyes travel around the room.

"I started all this for you," I say softly, finishing her thought.

She presses her lips into a line, some of the tears in her eyes beginning to spill over. "All this for me? After—after all I did for Holland?"

"Eliza, you're my little sister. I'd move mountains for you."

She sniffles and looks up at me. "Thank you," she whispers. "For not giving up on me. And...I'd understand if you didn't want me to...you know, after everything—"

In response, I pull her into a hug. "I love you, Eliza."

She hugs me back and we hold each other tightly, tears streaming down both of our faces.

After eleven—nearly twelve—years of searching, I'm holding my little sister in my arms.

When we pull apart, Eliza looks up at me, a real smile finally stretching across her face. I grin back at her. We've missed so much time, but we have the rest of our lives to make it up. *The rest of our lives.* That phrase sounds different to me now than it used to—it means something more. Because I'm no longer living with the reality that the rest of my life could mean anywhere between two more hours and two more days.

It's over. I can build a *life*, with Eliza in it.

As soon as the helicopters are all up in the air, exhaustion takes its toll on our group. TJ falls asleep with his head on my shoulder, and I doze off every so often. Next to me, Eliza stays wide awake—I can't blame her for the nerves, though. Everything is new to her.

Over the next week, Nora takes charge of TJ's healing, and Draft kids reunite with their families. The curly redhead I saw in the Enforcer lobby is Nora's youngest sister. Max and Alec stay in Ordinem and, once we've reunited as many Draft kids as possible with their families, we send the remnant to them. And Daniel Bennett makes himself comfortable in the UND prison wing.

Once TJ is healed enough to walk, the two of us sit on the edge of the compound's roof, the same place we've sat together so many times before. In the distance, the setting sun silhouettes some of the ruins.

"You sure you should be up and walking?" I ask him, watching the way he moves so gingerly. He wears a baggy sweatshirt, hiding his bandages, but the slices all over his back have to be painful.

"Too late now, isn't it?" He gives a soft laugh, although it makes him wince. "It's just a bunch of cuts—and maybe a couple of cracked ribs—and some bruises, from when Daniel tried to strangle me—"

"TJ!"

He smiles. "I've lived through worse. And coming out here is worth it."

As the sun dips below the horizon, his gaze drifts up to the stars.

"You're looking for the Little Dipper," I say softly.

"Yeah." He lets out a long breath. "I miss her. I'll never stop missing her, I think. But...it's different now. The darkness is gone."

I wrap my arm around his shoulders, careful to avoid aggravating his injuries. He leans his head on my shoulder, still looking out at the stars.

"People can change," he says quietly. "I don't know if I really understood that, until yesterday. But I do now. There's hope for all of us. Even on the days when it's a battle."

I smile, remembering when I said those exact words to him. It won't be easy from here on out, but a new warmth fills me when I think about the future. It's that one word. *Hope.*

We stay out under the stars for longer than I can keep track of, leaning on each other, watching the constellations overhead.

Tonight, looking out toward Ordinem doesn't fill me with dread or nervous anticipation. It fills me with warmth, knowing that all of us—me, TJ, Eliza, Ordinem itself—have a future.

Tonight, for the first time in a long while, finding hope doesn't feel like fighting an uphill battle.

Tonight, together, we've won that war.

Acknowledgments

We've done it. We've finished a series! Finished a *whole* story! Obviously, Rev and TJ have a hopeful future ahead of them—their story isn't over in that sense—but our time taking the journey with them is. Part of me wants to cry if I think about it too hard. It's like leaving behind best friends, knowing you won't see them again. The other part of me is content. *Undrafted* was a very different journey than *Drafted* for me. The story was tougher in many ways. But in the difficulty, God gently guided my hand to craft this into the story He wanted me to tell. It turned out *so* different than I'd imagined or initially planned, but I think that's for the best. I think this book is exactly what it's supposed to be, and I pray that the Lord uses Rev and TJ's story to make an impact in someone's heart. *Undrafted* is a story about finding hope and strength in the midst of darkness, and I wrote it to point back to our one true hope: Christ.

First and foremost, the biggest thanks here goes to the Lord. For saving me, for enabling me to write Your stories, for giving me strength and hope daily, and for speaking through this duology to peoples' hearts. The stories of impact I've heard have brought me to tears more than once. The existence of this duology, and any difference that it makes in peoples' hearts and lives, is entirely by Your power and Yours alone.

To my parents: this book is dedicated to you for a reason. This whole author-ing thing grew into so, so much more than any of us knew we were signing up for, and I'm so thankful for parents who rode it out with me, who stuck lovingly by my side through the chaos of publishing a book and moving to college and doing life all at the same time. Your support means the *world*. I love you both so much.

To the team at Descendant Publishing: You. Are. The. Epic-est. Yes, you're so awesome that I'm inventing words. Troy, for all the brainstorming help and feedback and brainpower you've lent to *UND*. Stacy, for the most incredible graphics, for your friendship, and for the gray hairs you've named after me. Jeannie, for being an *amazing* editor and helping to bring this manuscript to its full potential (despite some rather comical typos on my part).

To the many artists who brought this project to life: Sariah Reed, for the amazing illustrations in the hardcover editions of the duology. Elicia Johnson, for the landscape illustrations on the back of the Deluxe Edition dust jackets. Sara and Sissy, for the many stunning watercolor designs. Josh at SecondVoltage, for the maps in both books. It has been a blessing working with each and every one of you!

For everyone else who's been a critical part of *Undrafted*: Avery Anderson, my critique partner, friend, alpha-reader, and everything-person for all things writing, thank you for sticking with me through this entire duology. I think you single-handedly saved Hunter's entire storyline in that Chipotle parking lot. To Erin Healy, the most amazing developmental editor: thank you for your detailed feedback to help me improve not only *Undrafted*, but also my craft as a whole. You brought this manuscript from good to great. To my beta readers, Jenni, Tania, Bryan, Jillian, Hailey, Elicia, and Dawn, who left a record-breaking 1,342 comments on a single doc: you have made *such* a difference. This book is half-unrecognizable thanks to your deep feedback. I couldn't have dreamed of a better team. Thank you so much for your time and energy, for all the reactions that made me laugh and comments that found problems I would've missed on my own, and for your friendship. To my Kickstarter backers, for making this publication possible, and to my ARC readers, for helping with this release. To my church family and community back home, for always being there to support and encourage me and my books. And to the community of authors I've been able to connect with, for all of your advice, encouragement, and support. The writing journey truly wouldn't be the amazing thing it is without each and every one of you.

And finally, to my readers. Without you, us storytellers can't do our jobs. Thank you for following Rev and TJ's stories to their ends, for investing your time and energy in them. Thank you to every single person who's reached out and shared how these stories have impacted you and how God has used them in your life. You're the reason I do what I do, and I hope you'll stick with me for the next set of stories God has laid on my heart to tell.

About the Author

Tommie is a Young Adult author and Christ-follower from Gilbert, AZ. When she's not writing stories, you can find her pursuing a major in Mechanical Engineering, singing in her choir or on a worship team, or sitting in a local coffee shop with an iced latte. Tommie seeks to honor God in writing clean fiction that centers on Biblical themes, where light always triumphs over darkness and flawed characters are transformed, and her favorite part of writing is taking thrilling journeys with her characters and bringing readers along for the ride.

Check out more at: www.authortommiemichele.com

Thanks for Reading

If you want to be one of the first to know about new releases and updates, sign up for our mailing list by visiting **www.descendantpublishing.com**. Scroll to the bottom of the page and fill out the form with your name and email.

Please leave a review for *Undrafted*. Reviews go a long way in helping the authors you love get noticed by other readers. So if you enjoyed *Undrafted* please leave leave a review on Amazon and recommend it to friends and family. YOU are our greatest asset for spreading the word about EPIC stories!

More from the Publisher

Descendants of Light Series

By: Troy Hooker

Book 1: The Watcher Key
Book 2: The Water Tower
Book 3: The Watcher Revealed

Infernal Fall

By: Bryan Timothy Mitchell

Almost Paradise

Book 2 in the Infernal Fall Series

By: Bryan Timothy Mitchell

Look for more EPIC stories at:
www.descendantpublishing.com